Praise for

DRAGON FACTORY

"Excellent . . . Expect this straight-ahead thriller to hook action-crazed readers and inspire them both to seek out the first Ledger book and eagerly anticipate the next installment." —*Booklist*

"Eager readers can look forward to one more volume in this humorous, over-the-top cross-genre trilogy."
—*Publishers Weekly*

And these other novels in the bestselling Joe Ledger series

PATIENT ZERO

"Plenty of man-to-zombie combat, a team traitor and a doomsday scenario add up to a fast and furious read."
—*Publishers Weekly*

"An enjoyable read and one that's hard to set down."
—*Fangoria*

"Heated, violent, and furious . . . as palatable as your favorite flavor of ice cream. [A] memorable book."
—Peter Straub, *New York Times* bestselling author

"*Night of the Living Dead* meets Michael Crichton."
—Joseph Finder, *New York Times* bestselling author

Jonathan Maberry

The Dragon Factory

St. Martin's Paperbacks

This is a work of fiction. All of the characters, organizations, and events portrayed in this novel are either products of the author's imagination or are used fictitiously.

THE DRAGON FACTORY

Copyright © 2010 by Jonathan Maberry.
Short story *Dog Days* copyright © 2015 by Jonathan Maberry.

All rights reserved.

For information address St. Martin's Press, 175 Fifth Avenue, New York, NY 10010.

ISBN: 978-1-250-06841-5

Printed in the United States of America

St. Martin's Press Trade Paperback edition / March 2010
St. Martin's Paperbacks edition / August 2015

St. Martin's Paperbacks are published by St. Martin's Press, 175 Fifth Avenue, New York, NY 10010.

10 9 8 7 6 5 4 3 2 1

To Randy and Fran Kirsch,
Charlie and Gina Miller,
Frank and Mary Lou Sessa,
and my blood brother, Arthur Mensch,

and, as always, to my beloved Sara Jo

Acknowledgments

A bunch of good-hearted and very bright people helped with the research and creation of this book and they all deserve thanks: my agent, Sara Crowe of Harvey Klinger, Inc.; my editor and fellow pop-culture geek, Michael Homler; everyone at St. Martin's Press; Julia Kats for Russian translation and Alois Lohn for German; the members of International Thriller Writers, the Horror Writers Association, and Mystery Writers of America for ongoing support and encouragement; Mike Witzgall, for devious info on weapons and tactics; my cronies in the Liars Club: Gregory Frost, Jon McGoran, Dennis Tafoya, Keith Strunk, Don Lafferty, Kelly Simmons, William Lashner, Merry Jones, Marie Lambra, Ed Pettit, Laura Schrock, and L. A. Banks; Michael Sicilia of Homeland Security; Tiffany Schmidt, Nancy Keim-Comley, and Rachael Lavin for editorial assistance; the Starbucks in Upper Southampton, PA, where I wrote most of this book; and Axel Alonso at Marvel Comics.

A number of world-class genetics experts provided crucial technical information for this book (any errors are entirely the fault of the author): Yanru Chen-Tsai, Ph.D., Director, Transgenic Research Facility, and

Associate Director, Stanford Cancer Center; Ioannis Dragatsis, Ph.D., Assistant Professor, Department of Physiology, University of Tennessee; Dr. Laurence Bugeon, CMMI, Division of Cell & Molecular Biology, Faculty of Natural Sciences, Imperial College London; G. Thomas Caltagirone, Ph.D., President and CEO, Aptagen, LLC; Aurora Burds Connor, Ph.D., Director, Rippel Mouse ES Cells and Transgenic Facility, and Director, Preclinical Mouse Models Facility for the David H. Koch Institute for Integrative Cancer Research at MIT.

Prologue

Otto Wirths was the second-worst mass murderer in the history of the world. Compared to him, Hitler, Stalin, Attila the Hun, and even Alexander the Great were amateurs, poseurs who could not hold a candle to Otto and his body count.

Only one person was worse.

Cyrus Jakoby.

That wasn't his real name, and in a way he had no real name. Like Otto, Cyrus was a freak. Like Otto, Cyrus was a monster.

A week ago I'd never even heard of them. Almost no one had. A week ago they were on no watch lists, they were not sought by any world governments, their names were not muttered in hateful curses or angry prayers by a single person on planet Earth.

Yet together they had done more harm than anyone. Together they had very quietly slaughtered tens of millions.

Tens of millions.

At night, when they sat down to their dinner they did not dwell on past accomplishments. A champion athlete doesn't dwell on the preliminaries. To them it was always what was coming next. What was coming *soon*.

One week ago, seven days before I even heard of them, Otto Wirths placed a large digital clock on the wall above the elaborate workstation where he and Cyrus spent much of their waking hours. The clock was set to tick off seconds and minutes. Otto adjusted it to read: 10,080. Ten thousand and eighty minutes.

One hundred and sixty-eight hours.

Seven days.

One week.

After he pressed the start button, Otto and Cyrus clinked glasses of Perrier-Jouët, which—at over six thousand dollars a bottle—was the world's most expensive champagne.

They sipped the bubbles and smiled and watched the first sixty seconds tick away, and then the next sixty.

The Extinction Clock had begun.

(2)
Now

I crouched in the dark. I was bleeding and something inside was broken. Maybe something inside my head, too.

The door was barred. I had three bullets left. Three bullets and a knife.

The pounding on the door was like thunder. I knew the door wouldn't hold.

They would get in.

Somewhere the Extinction Clock was ticking down. If I was still in this room when it hit zero, more people would die than perished during the Black Death and all of the pandemics put together.

I thought I could stop them.

I had to stop them. It was down to me or no one.

It wasn't my fault I came into this so late. They chased us and messed with our heads and ran us around, and by the time we knew what we were up against the clock had already nearly run its course.

We tried. Over the last week I'd left a trail of bodies behind me from Denver, to Costa Rica, to the Bahamas. Some of those bodies were human. Some . . . well, I don't know what the hell you'd call them.

The pounding was louder. The door was buckling, the crossbar bending. It was only seconds before the lock or the hinges gave out, and then they'd come howling in here. Then it would be them against me.

I was hurt. I was bleeding.

I had three bullets and a knife.

I got to my feet and faced the door, my gun in my left hand, the knife in my right.

I smiled.

Let them come.

Part One
Hunters

There is no hunting like the hunting of man,
and those who have hunted armed men long enough
and liked it, never care for anything else thereafter.

—ERNEST HEMINGWAY
"On the Blue Water," *Esquire,* April 1936

Chapter One

"Detective Ledger?" he said, and held out an ID case. "NSA."

"How do you spell that?"

Not a flicker of a smile touched the concrete slab of his face. He was as big as me, and the three goons with him were even bigger. All of them in sunglasses with American flags pinned on their chests. Why does this stuff always seem to happen to me?

"We'd like you to come with us," said the guy with the flat face.

"Why?" We were in the parking lot of Holy Redeemer Cemetery in Baltimore. I had a bunch of bright yellow daffodils in one hand and a bottle of spring water in the other. I had a pistol tucked into the back of my jeans under an Orioles away-game shirt. I never used to bring a piece to Helen's grave, but over the last few months things have changed. Life's become more complicated, and the gun was a habit 24/7. Even here.

The Goon Squad was definitely packing. Three right-handers and one lefty. I could see the faint bulges even under the tailored suits. The lefty was the biggest of the bunch, a moose with steroid shoulders and a nose that looked like it had been punched at least once from every possible angle. If things got weird, he'd be the grabby type. The guys on either side of him were pretty boys; they'd keep their distance and draw on me. Right now they were about fourteen feet out and their sports coats were unbuttoned. Smooth.

"We'd like you to come with us," Slab-face said again.

"I heard you. I asked, 'Why?'"

"Please, Detective—"

"It's Captain Ledger, actually." I put a bit of frost in it even though I kept a smile on my face.

He said nothing.

"Have a nice day," I said, and started to turn. The guy next to Slab-face—the one with the crooked nose—put his hand on my shoulder.

I stopped and looked down at his big hand and then up at his face. I didn't say a word and he didn't move his hand. There were four of them and one of me. The Nose probably thought that gave them a clean edge, and since NSA guys are pretty tough he was probably right. On the other hand, these guys tend to believe their own hype, and that can come back to bite you. I don't know how much they knew about me, but if this clown had his hand on me then they didn't know enough.

I tapped his wrist with the bunch of daffodils. "You mind?"

He removed his hand, but he stepped closer. "Don't make this complicated."

"'*Why?*'" I said, "is not a complicated question."

He gave me a millimeter of a smile. "National security."

"Bullshit. I'm *in* national security. Go through channels."

Slab-face touched the Nose's shoulder and moved him aside so he could look me in the eyes. "We were told to bring you in."

"Who signed the order?"

"Detective . . ."

"There you go again."

Slab-face took a breath through his nose. "*Captain* Ledger." He poured enough acid in it to melt through battleship armor.

"What's your name?" I asked. He hadn't held the ID up long enough for me to read it.

He paused. "Special Agent John Andrews."

"Tell you what, Andrews, this is how we're going to play it. I'm going to go over there and put flowers on the grave of my oldest and dearest friend—a woman who suffered horribly and died badly. I plan to sit with her for a while and I hope you have enough class and manners to allow me my privacy. Watch if you want to, but don't get in my face. If you're still here when I'm done, then we can take another swing at the 'why' question and I'll decide whether I go with you."

"What's this bullshit?" snapped the Nose.

Andrews just looked at me.

"That's the agenda, Andrews," I said. "Take it or leave it."

Despite his orders and his professional cool, he was a little off-balance. The very fact that he was hesitating meant that there was something hinky about this, and my guess was that he didn't know what it was—so he wasn't ready to try to strong-arm me. I was a federal agent tied to Homeland—or close enough for his purposes—and I held military rank on top of it. He couldn't be sure that a misstep here wouldn't do him some career harm. I watched his eyes as he sorted through his playbook.

"Ten minutes," he said.

I should have just nodded and gone to visit Helen's grave, but the fact that they were accosting me here of all places really pissed me off. "Tell you what," I said, stepping back but still smiling. "When it gets to ten minutes start holding your breath."

I gave him a cheery wink and used the index finger of the hand holding the bottle to point at the Nose. Then I turned and headed through the tombstones, feeling the heat of their stares on my back like laser sights.

Chapter Two

Holy Redeemer Cemetery, Baltimore, Maryland
Saturday, August 28, 8:06 A.M.
Time Remaining on the Extinction Clock: 99 hours, 54 minutes

Helen's grave was on the far side of the cemetery in one of the newer sections. The whole place was flat as a pancake, but there were enough crypts and monuments to provide nominal cover. My watchdogs could see me, but I had a little bit of freedom of movement if I kept it subtle. Out of my peripheral vision I saw the Nose and one of the other guys—a blond surfer-looking dude—circling the access road in order to flank me.

I smiled. Together the four of them may have had a shot. Separated the only advantage they were leaving themselves was observation. At the current distances I could force a two-on-one situation with either Slab-face and his backup or the Nose and the Surfer. I was comfortable with those odds.

Autopilot took me to the grave. I'd switched the flowers and water bottle to my left hand so I could stick my right in my pocket. I've become adept at surreptitious speed-dialing and used my thumbnail to tap a number and a three-digit situation status code.

It always hurt to come here, but it hurt worse to miss a week. In the two years since Helen's suicide I'd missed maybe four weekly visits. Last week was one because I was busting up a lab in Virginia where a couple of absolute fruitball scientists were trying to create a weaponized airborne strain of SARS to sell to terrorists. We had to dissuade them. I figured Helen would forgive me.

As I laid the flowers on the bright green grass on her grave my cell vibrated in my pocket.

"Excuse me, honey," I murmured, placing my palm briefly on the cold headstone, "but I have to take this."

I pulled the cell out and knelt down as if praying, so that my body hid the phone as I flipped it open. There was no name on the display, but I knew it was my boss. "I'm having an interesting morning," I said. The alert word was "interesting."

"This line is secure. Sit rep?" asked Mr. Church. I've worked for him for almost two months now and I still didn't know his real name. I've heard people refer to him as the Deacon, Colonel Eldritch, the Sexton, and a few other names, but when I'd met him he introduced himself as Mr. Church, so I used that. He was somewhere north of sixty but not where it showed. My boys had a pool going as to whether he was an ex-Delta gunslinger or a CIA spook who'd moved up to management.

"Have we pissed off anybody in Washington lately?"

"Not so far this morning," he said. "Why do you ask?"

"I'm at the cemetery. Couple of NSA stiffs have asked me to accompany them, saying it was a national security issue, but they dodged my questions when I tried to find out what the deal was."

"Do you have names?"

"Just one. John Andrews." I described him and the others. "They're not waving warrants around, but it's pretty clear this isn't a request."

"Let me make some calls. Do nothing until I call you back."

"These goons are waiting on me."

"Do you care?"

"Not much."

"Nor do I."

He hung up. I smiled at the dragonflies that were hovering over Helen's tombstone and let a few minutes pass. Inside I was churning. What the hell was *this* all about? Even though I knew I hadn't done anything bad enough to warrant this kind of thing, I still had that guilty feeling inside. It was weird, because I didn't think cops got that from other cops.

So far this made no sense. The book was closed on my last mission and I had nothing new on the griddle, and the last time I'd even had a brush with the NSA was last month, but that had been on a job that had ended satisfactorily for everyone involved. No stubbed toes or hurt feelings. So why did they want to pick me up?

My worry meter jumped a few points when I saw two government Crown Vics roll in through the gate and park on either side of my Explorer. Four more NSA agents climbed out and moved quickly to take up positions on logical exit routes. Four exits, four two-man teams. Slab-face was by the cars; the Nose and one other agent were between my car and the exit.

"Aw, crap."

My cell vibrated and I answered it.

"Listen to me," said Church. "Apparently we *have* rattled someone's cage in D.C. and the situation has some wrinkles. As you know, the President is undergoing bypass surgery, and while he's out that officially puts the VP in charge. The VP has never liked the DMS and has been very vocal about it. It looks like he's making a run at dismantling it."

"On what grounds?"

"He's somehow convinced the Attorney General that I've been blackmailing the President to give the DMS an unusual amount of power and freedom of movement."

"That's kind of true, though, isn't it?"

"It isn't as simple as that, but for legal purposes the NSA have permission to arrest and detain all DMS staff, seize all of our facilities, et cetera."

"Can he do that?"

"Yes. He's the de facto Commander in Chief. Though once the President wakes up and resumes command the VP's probably going to face some heat, but that will be in a few hours and the VP can do a lot of damage in that time. Aunt Sallie says that the NSA has landed two choppers at Floyd Bennett Field and is deploying a team. They *do* have warrants."

Aunt Sallie was Church's second in command and the Chief of Operations for the Hangar, the main DMS headquarters in Brooklyn. I'd never met her, but the rumors about her among the DMS staff were pretty wild.

Church said, "The Veep is operating in a narrow window here. We need to stall him until the President regains power. I can stall the Attorney General."

I almost laughed. "This is really about MindReader, isn't it?"

"Probably."

MindReader was a computer system that Church had either designed or commissioned—I still didn't know which—but it could bypass any security, intrude into any hard drive as long as there was some kind of link, WIFI or hardline, and get out again without leaving a footprint. As far as I knew, there was nothing else like it in the world, and I think we can all be thankful for that; and it was MindReader that kept the DMS one step ahead of a lot of terrorist networks. My friend Maj. Grace Courtland had confided her suspicions to me that it was MindReader that gave Church the clout he needed to keep the President and other government officials off his back. Freedom of movement kept the DMS efficient because it negated the red tape that had slowed Homeland down to a bureaucratic crawl.

MindReader was a very dangerous tool for a lot of reasons, and we all hoped that Church had the kind of clarity of vision and integrity of purpose to use it for only the right reasons. If the VP took control of it, we'd be cooked. Plus, Church didn't trust the MindReader system in anyone else's hands. He had almost no faith in the nobler elements of the political mind. Good call.

"Major Courtland says that three unmarked Humvees are parked outside the Warehouse," he said.

"What's the Veep's game plan?"

"I don't know. Even as Acting President I can't see

him risking force to stop us. That gives us a little elbow room."

"So why's he want me? I can't access MindReader without you personally logging me in."

"He doesn't know that. There are NSA teams zeroing four other DMS field offices and team leaders. They're going for a sweep. But whatever they're doing has to be bloodless, which is probably why Agent Andrews gave you a few minutes with Ms. Ryan."

"Maybe, but he called for backup. Two other cars just rolled in. Lots of Indians, only one cowboy."

"Can you get away?"

"Depends on how I'm allowed to go about it."

"Don't get taken, Captain, or you'll disappear into the system. It'll take six months to find you and you'll be no good to me when we do."

"Feeling the love," I said, but he ignored me.

"This is fragile," Church cautioned. "Anyone pulls a trigger and they'll use it to take the DMS apart."

"I may have to dent some of these boys."

"I can live with that." He disconnected.

As I pocketed my phone I caught movement out of the corner of my eye. My ten minutes were up. Andrews and his Goon Squad were closing in.

These guys shouldn't have come out here. Not here.

"Okay," I said to myself, "let's dance."

Chapter Three

The Deck, southwest of Gila Bend, Arizona
Saturday, August 28, 8:07 A.M.
Time Remaining on the Extinction Clock: 99 hours, 53 minutes

It's refreshing to be insane. Just as it's liberating to be aware of it.

Cyrus Jakoby had known that freedom and satisfaction for many years. It was a tool that he used every bit as much as if it were a weapon. In his view it was in no way a limitation. Not when one is aware of the shape and scope of one's personal madness, and Cyrus knew every inch and ounce of his own.

"Are you comfortable, Mr. Cyrus?"

His aide and companion of many years, Otto Wirths, was a stick figure in white livery, with mud-colored eyes and a knife scar that bisected his mouth and left nostril. Otto was an evil-looking man with a thick German accent and a body like a stick bug. He was the only one allowed to still call Cyrus by his real name—or, at least, the name that had become real to both of them.

"Quite comfortable, Otto," Cyrus murmured. "Thank you."

Cyrus settled back against a wall of decorative pillows, each with a different mythological animal embroidered in brilliantly colored thread. The newly laid luncheon tray sat astride his lap glittering with cut glass and polished silver. Cyrus never ate breakfast—he thought eggs were obscene in every form—and was never out of bed before one o'clock. The entire work, leisure, and sleep schedule here at the Deck reflected this, and it pleased Cyrus that he could shift the whole pattern of life according to his view of time.

While Cyrus adjusted himself in bed, Otto crossed the room and laid fresh flowers under a large oil painting of a rhesus monkey that they had long ago named Gretel. There was a giclée print of the painting in every room of the facility, and in every room of the Hive—their secret production factory in Costa Rica. Cyrus virtually worshiped that animal and frequently said that he owed more to it than to any single human being he had ever known. It was because of that animal that their campaign against blacks and homosexuals had yielded virtually incalculable success and a death toll that had surpassed World War II. Otto fully agreed, though he personally thought the hanging of prints was a bit excessive.

On the table below the portrait was a large Lucite box arranged under lights that presented it with the same reverence as the painting. A swarm of mayflies flitted about in the box. Tubes fed temperature-controlled air into the container. The tiny insects were the first true success that Cyrus and Otto had pioneered. That team at the Institute for Stem Cell Research in Edinburgh was still dining out on having found the so-called immortality master gene in mouse DNA, though they hadn't a clue as to how to exploit its potential. Otto and Cyrus— along with a team of colleagues who were, sadly, all dead now—had cracked that puzzle forty years ago. And they'd found it in the humble mayfly.

"What's on the schedule today?"

Otto shook out an Irish linen napkin with a deft flick and tucked it into the vee of Cyrus's buttoned pajama top. "Against your recommendation Mr. Sunderland allowed the Twins to persuade him to try and capture the MindReader computer system. Apparently they feel they've outgrown Pangaea."

"Capture it? Nonsense . . . it won't work," Cyrus said with a dismissive wave of the hand.

"Of course not."

"Sunderland should know better."

"He does know better," murmured Otto. "But he's greedy and greed makes even smart people do stupid things. I imagine, though, that he has a scapegoat in place in the event that it fails. Which it probably will. It won't land on him and it won't land on us."

"It could hurt the Twins."

Otto smiled. "You bred them to be resourceful."

"Mm. What else do we have?"

"We've successfully launched test runs in Nigeria, Zimbabwe, Benin, and Kenya; and on the domestic front, the Louisiana test should be yielding measurable results soon."

"Not too soon," Cyrus said. "We don't want the CDC involved—"

Otto tut-tutted him. "They'll be out of action long before this comes onto their radar. Not that they'd be able to do much once our Russian friends crash their system."

"Russians," Cyrus sniffed. "I don't know why you have such affection for those blockheads."

"Affection?" Otto smiled. "Not the word I'd choose, Mr. Cyrus . . . but you have to admit that they're enthusiastic."

"A little too enthusiastic, if you ask me. You used to be capable of such subtlety, Otto. Using the Red Mafia is . . . I don't know." He waved a hand. "It's cliché. And it's not 'us.' "

"It's affordable and if the assets are taken out then so what? We lose no friends. And who would ever think that we, of all people, would rely on ex-Spetsnaz thugs? No matter how heavy-handed the Russians get, no one will look in our direction. Not in time, anyway."

Cyrus made a sulky face. "I wish we had some of the Berserkers. That was the one thing I have to admit that the Twins did that was a step ahead of us."

"Maybe. My sources say that they're having some behavioral issues with the Berserkers." Otto looked at his watch. "The North Korean buyers are waiting to leave and wish to say good-bye."

Cyrus shook his head. "No, that's boring. Send one of my doubles. Send Milo; he has good manners."

Otto tidied the cutlery. "You shot Milo two weeks ago."

"Did I? Why?"

"It was a Tuesday."

"Oh yes."

Cyrus believed that Tuesday was the dullest and least useful day of the week and he tried to liven the low spot of each week with a little spice.

"Shame about Milo," Cyrus said, accepting a cup of tea. "He was good."

"That he was. But that's water under the bridge, Mr. Cyrus," murmured Otto. "We'll send Kimball."

"Are you sure I haven't killed him yet?"

"Not so far."

Cyrus shot him a look, but Otto gave his master a small wink. No smile, though.

"Maybe I should kill you next Tuesday."

"Mm, when you're done threatening me I'll go find a broom cupboard to hide in."

"What else do we have today?"

"The latest batch of New Men has been shipped to the Hive. Carteret and his lot are conditioning them. We have orders for sixty females and two hundred males. We can fill those orders with the current batch; however, if we get the heavier requests you're expecting then we'll have to up production by twenty percent."

"Do it. Speaking of the New Men—did that idiot van der Meer try to haggle on the per-unit price?"

"He tried."

"And—?"

"This isn't a buyer's market."

Cyrus nodded, pleased. He already had the money earmarked for a new research line. Something he'd been thinking about during those long hours in his sensory dep tank. He always did his best thinking in there—a place where he felt connected to the whole of the universe, a place where he could unlock every chamber in his infinite mind.

He lifted the heavy lid of the serving dish and studied the meal. Four slices of white breast meat were fanned out like playing cards in a thick cream sauce. He didn't recognize the grain of the meat, though the accompanying vegetables were from a more familiar group of exotics—fingerling potatoes, whole crowns of dwarf broccoli, and a spill of hybridized spinach-carrots. Otto took the lid from him.

"Something new?" Cyrus asked.

"Something old, actually."

"Oh?"

"Breast of dodo in a white wine cream sauce."

Cyrus applauded like a happy child. "Delightful!" He reached for a fork, then paused. "Have you tried it?"

"Of course."

"And . . . ?"

"It *doesn't* taste like chicken."

Cyrus laughed.

Otto pursed his lips. "It's a bit more gamey. A bit like bald eagle, though less chewy."

Cyrus picked up his knife and fork.

"And, not to spoil your appetite, sir," said Otto, "but I wanted to remind you that the Twins are on their way for their regular visit. Almost certainly to discuss the Berserker issue." Cyrus began to protest, but Otto held up a calming hand. "Don't worry; we've taken the usual precautions. They'll see and hear exactly what they expect to see and hear."

Cyrus cut a slice of the dodo meat and chewed it thoughtfully. Otto waited with practiced patience.

"I want them thermal-scanned during any conversation."

"We're already on that. The chair sensors in the private garden have all been checked. With the new vapor density scanners the doctor thinks we can expect a seventy to seventy-three percent confidence in the readings. If they lie, we'll probably know it."

"They're smart, those two," warned Cyrus.

"They would have to be," said Otto, then smiled. "And no, sir, that's not as obsequious as it sounds. I actually have a lot of respect for the Twins."

"As far as it goes," corrected Cyrus.

"As far as it goes," agree Otto.

"My young gods . . ." Cyrus looked into the middle distance for a long moment, a half smile playing across his lips. He blinked his eyes clear and cut a look at Otto. "What about the SAMs?"

"One Sixteen and One Forty-four are coming along nicely. They'll be getting their fourth round of psych evaluations today, and if we like the results we can process them into the Family. Ninety-five is getting high marks in surgical classes, and he seems to have a taste for it. A family trait. Most of the rest are coming along."

"Make sure they're out of sight. I don't want Hecate or Paris to see them."

Otto nodded. "As I said, they'll see only what we want them to see. The only child the Twins have seen—or ever will see—is Eighty-two, and he's still at the Hive."

Cyrus paused. "And . . . what about Eighty-two?" When Otto didn't immediately respond, Cyrus said, "I still have hopes for that one. I feel more . . . *kinship* with him than any of the others."

"I know, but you've seen his psych evals, Mr. Cyrus. You know what the doctors have been saying about him."

"What? That he can't be trusted? That he's warped? I goddamn well don't believe it," snapped Cyrus with a sudden viciousness. "The doctors are wrong in their conclusions!"

His valet crossed his arms and leaned against the footboard. "They would be the third set of doctors to come up with exactly the same set of erroneous conclusions. How likely do you think that is?"

Cyrus turned his head and glared across the room at the dozens of floral arrangements that lined one wall. His chest rose and fell and several times he began to speak, but each time he left his thoughts unspoken. This was an old argument, something he and Otto had been wrangling over for nearly three years. Cyrus's rage over the findings about Eighty-two had been towering, destructive. All six of the previous doctors had been executed. Cyrus had done it with his own hands, garroting each of them with cello strings he'd ripped from Eighty-two's instrument.

"Have them run the tests again," he said quietly, and in a tone that left no opening for discussions. "Have them run every single fucking test again."

"I've already ordered it," said Otto. "I sent a new team of specialists to the Hive and they'll run everything. As many times as it takes."

Cyrus turned to look at him and then turned away again.

"Oh, and this should make you happy," Otto said with a deft shift of gears. "That new Indian fellow, Bannerjee . . . he was able to solve the gas erosion problem with the jellyfish sensors. We'll pump a dozen of them into the Twins' jet while it's being refueled."

Cyrus smiled and turned back. He cut a piece of meat and resumed his lunch. "Give Bannerjee a bonus. No . . . hold off on that until we're sure we can track the Twins to wherever the hell they hide from me. If we can find the Dragon Factory, then Bannerjee gets double his pay as a bonus on top of his contract."

"Very generous, sir."

"And tell him that he can own the patent on whatever laminate he cooked up for the sensor, though I would appreciate fifteen percent as a tithe."

" 'Tithe'?"

"Oh, call it what you want. Kickback, whatever."

"I'm sure Dr. Bannerjee would be delighted to give you twenty percent," said Otto.

"You've become greedy in your old age, Otto."

The German bowed. "I learned at the feet of a great master of the art."

Cyrus laughed until he choked and then laughed some more once he'd coughed up the unchewed piece of broccoli. Otto turned on the TV, adjusted the channel to a split screen of *BBC World News* and CNN, with a continuous crawl at the bottom of stock prices on the technologies and biotech markets. He tidied the pillows around Cyrus, straightened the flowers in the twenty-seven vases scattered around the room, and made sure to check that the bedside pistol was unloaded. No sense taking chances.

Chapter Four

The White House
Saturday, August 28, 8:07 A.M.
Time Remaining on Extinction Clock: 99 hours, 53 minutes

"Mr. Vice President," said the aide, "all teams have reported in. Everyone's in position."

"All of them?"

"Yes, sir, and the teams assigned to solo pickups have already moved in; the main teams are at the gates of each facility. I issued the go order."

William Collins, Vice President and Acting President of the United States, nodded and sat back in his chair. He used his palms—the callused steelworker's hands so often remarked upon in his press—to vigorously rub his face until his cheeks glowed. He let out a sharp sigh and clapped his hands together. The aide flinched.

"How soon before we know anything?"

"The Agents In Charge will call in on an individual basis once they've secured their objectives. Every situation is different and I've impressed upon them the need for delicacy, the need to get this done right rather than fast."

The Vice President shot him a hard look. "Fast is pretty goddamned essential, don't you think?"

The aide was immediately conciliatory. "Of course, sir, but it has to be done right. To the letter of the law."

"Yeah, yeah . . . okay. Keep me apprised." He sat back in his chair and waited until the aide left; then the Vice President turned to the other man in the room, an old crocodile in a five-thousand-dollar suit. The man's face was fat, wrinkled, and flushed with hypertension, but his expression was calm, his eyes calculating and amused.

"Christ, this had better work, J.P.," muttered the Vice President.

Jonas Paul Sunderland, the senior senator for Texas and one of the most vocal advocates of biotech development, smiled. "It'll work, Bill. Don't get your nuts in a knot." He rattled the ice in his Scotch and took a pull. "We have good people well placed."

"I have a lot at stake here, J.P."

Sunderland gave him a bland smile. "We all do. But even if this tanks, you'll come out looking like Joe Patriot and I won't even be in the picture. This is well planned and you have the law on your side . . . which is nice. We're actually the good guys here."

"On paper," Collins said.

"Sure, on paper, but that paper is the Constitution, so calm down. If you look stressed you'll look guilty."

The Vice President shook his head. "You don't really appreciate this President, J.P. You think he's a green kid with his head up his ass, but he's a lot sharper than you think."

Sunderland did not speak the string of racial invectives that rose to his lips. He said, "You think too highly of him."

"Maybe. If I do it's because he has Church behind him. Or . . . maybe Church really is controlling him. Either way it brings Church into the picture. We're directly attacking him and the President."

J.P. Sunderland shrugged as if Church and his influence was a nonissue, though in truth he knew Church—and his potential—with greater scope and clarity than the Vice President could ever hope to possess. Sunderland finished his Scotch, hauled himself out of his chair, and waddled to the side table to pour a refill, heavy on the Scotch with a nominal spritz of soda. Then he made a fresh drink for the Vice President. The order in which these things were done was not lost on Collins.

"God, I just want this over with." The Vice President jerked the glass out of Sunderland's hand, sloshing some on his desk blotter. He scowled as he threw half of it back too fast and coughed. Sunderland looked amused as he tottered back to his chair and sank down with a sigh. Collins glared into his drink. "And I want that fucking computer."

"We all want something, Bill. You want to get your office back to the level of power it had during Cheney's time, and I want what I want."

And what I want, Sunderland thought, *is to take that computer system out of the equation.*

MindReader was the key for both of them. For Collins, acquiring it was less important than silencing it. Sunderland saw it as a short path to a veritable license to print money. His current business partners, the Jakoby Twins—those brilliant albino freaks—could use Mind-Reader to filch even the most heavily encrypted research records from every other genetics lab in the world. The Twins had sidestepped most of the normal limitations most geneticists faced—an insufficient annotation of the genome—by stealing bits and pieces of annotation from different sources. As a result they were already miles beyond anyone else, but they'd hit a wall with what their current computer—Pangaea—could steal. The Jakobys were willing to pay absurd amounts of money to possess MindReader, but as he sipped his Scotch Sunderland toyed with the idea of only leasing it to them. Why give away the cow?

That way he could also lease use of the system to their father, Cyrus Jakoby. Sunderland greatly admired the elder Jakoby and shared many of Cyrus's political, ethnic, and societal views. MindReader could push Cyrus's plans ahead by an order of magnitude. And Cyrus would pay for that advantage, no doubt about it.

His other concern was his own brother, Harold, who was close with the Jakoby Twins and often went hunting with them or their friends. Harold was never the sharpest knife in the drawer, and if MindReader was ever aimed in the direction of the Jakobys then it would find Harold—and that would lead right back to J.P. and the bills he wanted passed. Harold was really the only traceable link, even though he wasn't really a player himself. But more than one good scheme had been sunk by the presence of an idiot relative.

He shared none of this with Collins. Sunderland believed in the "need to know" philosophy, and if Collins knew, he'd either chicken out or want a huge cut.

Sunderland sipped his Scotch and watched the Vice President fret.

The things in which they both shared interest were the four biotech bills moving through Congress. At the moment there was absolutely nothing that could connect the bills with Collins's personal interests or Sunderland's private holdings. MindReader, if aimed in that direction, might change that. Any clear connection that came to light would ruin Collins, trash his political career, and make him a pariah in the business world. It was the lever Sunderland had used to convince Collins to take this action. If the bills were stopped because of some taint of insider knowledge or personal interest, then money would spill all over the place. Without approval of the bills a lot of research would have to go offshore, and that could be costly and time-consuming. Domestic licensing and approval for research led to faster patents, and that got drugs, cell lines, and procedures to market much more quickly.

Sunderland sipped his drink and hoisted a comforting and comradely smile on his face for the benefit of the Vice President.

"This had better work," the Vice President said again.

Sunderland said nothing.

They sat in their leather chairs, separated by a big desk and an ocean of personal differences, and they sipped their Scotch, and they waited for the phone to ring.

Chapter Five

The NSA guys had split into four teams, taking the corners of a big box with Helen's grave as the center point. Not imaginative, but not bad. I made sure they saw me checking them out, which in turn made them front me a bit more. They stood tall and tried to look tough as nails from where they stood. Believe me, I was impressed.

Even so, I play a pretty good hand of poker, and the game's as much about what's on your face as what's in your hand. I got up and as I walked toward Agent Andrews I let my shoulders sag a bit and deflated my chest so that I looked a good deal smaller than I was. He'd already seen me up close, but there's a lot to be said for second impressions. Along the way I took a couple of sips from the water bottle.

"Are you ready to come with us, Captain Ledger?" he asked.

"Still waiting on a 'why' or a warrant."

Andrews's face was harder and I guessed he'd been in contact with his seniors. "Sir, we're here by Executive Order on a matter of national security. We are not required to explain ourselves at this time." Andrews's partner shifted a bit to the right; I guess he wanted to show me how big his chest was.

I made a show of surprise at this pronouncement, stopping the water bottle halfway to my mouth and looking over the rim at Andrews. "You're saying that the President himself ordered this pickup?"

Andrews didn't blink. "Our orders come directly from the White House."

He was being cute, which told me that he knew about the Vice President's little maneuver. He was being very careful in how he phrased things.

"Okay," I said as I took a sip.

Andrews blinked, surprised.

I spit a mouthful of water into his eyes, then threw the bottle at the other guy—not that it would hurt him, but it made him flinch and evade. Before they could recover I was on them. I grabbed Andrews by the hair and one lapel and pivoted him around into a foot sweep that caught him on the shin. My foot acted like a fulcrum and with his mass and the force of my spin he came right off the ground like he weighed nothing. I threw him into the second agent's big flat chest and the two of them went down in a heap. I heard a huge *whoof!* and a cry of pain as the second guy fell with all of Andrews's mass atop him. Andrews was no lightweight.

I wasted no time and sprinted for the parked cars. I had my Rapid Response folding knife in my hip pocket and with a loose wrist flick the blade locked into place. I ran past Andrews's Crown Vic and did a quick jab job on one tire, and then knifed the tire of a second government sedan. But before I could run back to my Explorer, the Nose and the Surfer cut me off. Nose could run like a son of a bitch and he reached me eight strides before his backup. Dumb ass.

When he was three steps out I pocketed my knife and jagged out of my line of escape to drive right at him.

He had a lot of mass in motion; he was coming in to sack the quarterback and he'd built up such a head of steam that there was no way for him to sidestep. I jerked left and clotheslined him with a stiffened right forearm across the base of the nose. There's an urban myth that hitting the base of the nose can drive bone fragments up into the brain—even some karate instructors insist it's true, but it's not physiologically possible. However, a smashed nose, especially at high speed, can give whiplash, fill the Eustachian tubes with blood, set off fireworks in the eyes, and generally make you feel like your head's in a drum and a crazy ape's beating on it with a stick.

The Nose flipped backward like someone pulled the rug out from under him and he was out cold before he hit the deck. He'd need a lot of work on that nose of his, but he should never have put his hand on me. Not ever, and especially not here at Helen's grave. I take that shit very personally.

As he fell the Surfer closed in at a dead run and he made a grab for his gun, but I pulled mine and pointed it at him. He skidded to a stop.

"Pull it with two fingers and throw it away," I ordered. "Do it now!"

He did it. Four other agents were closing on us, the closest nearly fifty yards out. I kicked the Surfer in the nuts, then knotted my fingers in his short hair and used him as a shield while I backpedaled to my Explorer.

I spun Surfer-boy around and gave a palm shot across the chops that would put him in a neck brace for a week, and as he crumpled I popped the lock on the Explorer and dove behind the wheel.

From the time I dropped my human shield to the

moment I roared through the exit of the cemetery they had maybe six separate opportunities to take a good shot at my vehicle or me. They didn't.

I found that very interesting.

Chapter Six

The Jakoby Twins—over Arizona airspace
Saturday, August 28, 8:18 A.M.
Time Remaining on Extinction Clock: 99 hours,
42 minutes E.S.T.

Hecate Jakoby sat naked on the edge of the bed and stared out of the jet's window at the rolling mountains of clouds below. She loved the contrast of purest white and ten thousand shades of gray. It was a kind of mirror for her.

Her brother, Paris, stood in black silk boxers that were a much sharper contrast with his snow-white skin. Paris always dressed in dark colors to highlight the albino richness of his lean and muscular body. Hecate preferred softer colors; she was less comfortable with her white skin than he was, though in truth both of them were absurdly beautiful. Even the people who hated them thought so.

The woman on the bed moaned and turned over in her sleep. The drugs would wear off in an hour or so, but by then the jet would be on the ground in Arizona and the flight crew would take care of the girl. She'd be fed and paid and given all of the proper instructions. If Hecate and Paris liked the report from the staff, maybe they'd treat the girl to another round of play on the flight back. If not, the bitch would be ferried to the closest town and given enough cash for a bus ticket.

The digital recording of their sexual encounter would be burned to disk and added to the Twins' library. The library was indexed by gender, hair color, race, and number of partners. There were three—so far—disks in elegant black cases. Those were special—records of encounters in which their lovely playthings had been cremated and their ashes scattered over the ocean. Not for ceremonial purposes; it was simply an efficient disposal method.

"That was fun," murmured Paris. "She was spirited. Do you want a martini?"

"Please," said Hecate. "A double."

Paris glanced at her from the wet bar, saw that she was staring down at the sleeping woman. "What's with you? You falling in love?"

"No . . . just admiring the architecture," said Hecate distractedly. "Two onions in the martini." The girl was twenty, buxom, tan, with foamy masses of curly red hair. She had freckles and several ornate tattoos—Chinese characters and Celtic knots. She was everything Hecate was not. Although Hecate was beautifully made—tall and slender and ice pale, with snow-colored hair and eyes as dark as ripe blueberries—she wasn't a California blonde. Her own breasts were small, her nipples the color of dusty roses. The only mark on her otherwise flawless skin was a small scar in the shape of a starburst that was the same dusty rose color as her nipples. That . . . and a small tattoo on her left inner thigh of a caduceus on which two fierce dragons—not ordinary serpents—coiled around the winged herald's staff. The scales of the dragons and the symmetry of their bodies suggested a double helix.

Paris had an identical tattoo on his left upper calf and the same starburst scar on his chest. The scar was their personal mark. A bond in the flesh, as their father often called it, a sign of their greatness and a reminder of what Dad called their celestial heritage. They had been marked at birth when the doctors performing the emergency C-section on their mother had discovered twins locked chest-to-chest in an embrace, their blood-smeared cheeks pressed together. At first the doctors had feared that the twins were conjoined in some surgically challenging way, but as they were carefully lifted out of their dying mother's womb and laid in the incubator the infants rolled apart, an action that tore the fragile skin over their chests. That had been the only conjoined point, and it did them no harm except to leave a star-shaped scar on each child's chest. The star never faded.

The delivering doctor, a deeply Catholic obstetrician at the Cancún hospital where their mother had been rushed following a collapse at a Christmas party at one of the bigger resorts, saw the mark at the moment when the delivery nurse announced the official delivery time. Twelve-oh-one on Christmas morning.

"*Milagro!*" the doctor had declared, and crossed himself. A miracle.

The story made the papers worldwide. Twins, albinos with shocking blue eyes, born at the stroke of midnight as Christmas Eve became Christmas Day. The first birth of the holiday, and each child was marked with a star like the Star of Bethlehem. The story, nonsensical as it might be, was picked up by wire services around the world. The death of their mother and the coincidence of her name—Mary—fueled the story into one of beauty from tragedy. Before the Jakoby Twins were a minute old they were already legends.

Hecate touched her scar with one hand and with the fingers of the other traced the smooth and unmarked valley between the sleeping girl's breasts. *What would it be like to be ordinary?* Hecate mused. Not for the first time.

Even deep in her sleep the girl felt the touch and moaned again. Hecate bent and kissed the smooth place between the girl's breasts, paused, and then licked the skin, tasting the olio of sweat, perfume, and natural musk. Hecate wondered what her flesh would truly taste like if she could ever work up the nerve to bite. She wondered how blood would change the taste.

"Good God," said Paris as he came over with the drinks, "are you *never* satisfied?"

Hecate raised her head and smiled. Her brother never quite understood her, and that was okay. There were plenty of things about her she didn't want understood. She accepted the martini and sipped it.

"Mmm, perfect."

Paris sipped his drink, set the glass down on the deck beside the bed, and began pulling on his clothes. He put on black slacks, a charcoal shirt, and loafers without socks, his clothing choice conservative to suit the occasion. This was the second of their twice-monthly visits to their father's laboratory in Arizona. It was really a prison, but they'd sold their father a line of propaganda stating that he needed a safe haven to protect him from the mud people and the government—or at least those parts of the government that weren't sucking on the

Jakoby tit. Cyrus appeared to be convinced of the necessity for a hidden base and they'd coddled him by allowing him to design it according to his "vision." The base he created was in the shape of a dodecahedron—which Cyrus said was a crucial form in sacred geometry—and became familiarly known as the Deck. The Twins had built hundreds of security and surveillance devices into it, some of which they let Cyrus know about—they were sure he didn't know about the others.

"I wish to hell we'd built his lab somewhere closer," Paris complained. "Fucking Arizona? In August? Besides, it lacks style."

"Style?"

"C'mon," he said, "it's a secret lab with an actual mad scientist. We missed an opportunity to be cool."

"Secret lairs in hollowed-out volcanoes are so five minutes ago." Hecate sniffed. "Besides, Dad's hardly Dr. No."

"He's smarter. And eviler. Is that a word?"

"No. But it's true, Daddy certainly puts the 'mad' back in 'mad scientist.'" She and Paris laughed and clinked glasses.

"What have you heard from him lately?" asked Hecate, sipping her martini and continuing to stare at the woman she had shared with her brother for the last three hours. She could still smell the woman, still taste her, despite the vodka. The girl had tasted like summer and freedom.

"His man Otto's called me a dozen times in the last week. Hmm . . . I wonder if Otto qualifies as an evil assistant or henchman?"

"Evil assistant, definitely," decided Hecate.

"I suppose. Anyway, he said that Dad wants the new generation gene sequencer, the Swedish one that was on the cover of *Biotech Times*."

"So? Let him have it," said Hecate.

"He wants two of them, and I think he wants them just because they were on the cover."

"Who cares? Buy him a roomful."

"He already has a roomful of Four Fifty-four Life Sciences sequencers," complained Paris. "He says they're garbage and his attendants had to restrain him from having a go at them with a fire axe."

Hecate shrugged. "Why are you making an issue of this? If Alpha wants twenty new computers then let him have them. We can debit his allowance for it. God knows he's been enough of a cash cow lately to allow him some toys. What's it to you?"

Paris sneered at his sister's use of "Alpha." Dad had started calling himself that a month ago and insisted that his children only address him by that name. Their father's staff had to address him as Lord Alpha the Most High. For two years before that he'd only answered when addressed as the Orange, which was a vague reference to some alien race whose origins and nature seemed to be in some dispute among UFOlogists. Paris was grudgingly indulgent; he had a vein in his forehead that started pulsing every time he had to shape his lips around one of those names. The only one of his father's names Paris had ever liked was Merlin, which Cyrus had used for most of their teenage years.

Hecate raised one delicate eyebrow.

"Don't look at me like that," Paris snapped. "I'm not being cheap or, god help us, 'thrifty' . . . it's just that it's getting harder and harder to tell the difference between necessary requests and his go-nowhere whims. Like the swimming pool filled with mercury."

Hecate finished her martini and stood up. She was exactly as tall as Paris—six feet on the dot—and had legs that been commented upon everywhere from *Vogue* to *Maxim*. The most common phrase in the magazines was "legs like alabaster." Crap like that, which Hecate had found flattering when she was in her teens but now found trite. Her silver-white pubic hair was shaved to a tiny vee, and when she raised her leg to step into her panties the cabin lights sparkled on the golden rings in her labia. Her nipple rings were platinum. For her twenty-seventh birthday she was considering having her eyebrows pierced, though she was absolutely certain it would give Dad a coronary. As far as he knew, the Twins were completely without marks except for the starburst scars. He told them over and over again that purity was important, though none of his explanations as to *why* it was important made any rational sense. Something about keeping the channel open for the celestial god force that was supposed to flow through them.

She pulled on a short pale green skirt and a white satin blouse that caught stray flickers of light when she moved. She sat down, snugged back into the deep cushions in one corner of the Lear, legs crossed, dangling a sandal from her big toe.

The reference to the mercury pool was fair enough; it had been absurdly expensive—$5.35 per hundred grams—and yet startlingly beautiful. Ten thousand gallons of swirling liquid metal. The purchase of it through various companies they owned had caused a brief stock market run on the metal, and there was still speculation in some of the science trade journals that someone somewhere was developing something new that would wow the world.

Hecate said, "By the time he'd gotten tired of the metal consciousness experiment the market price had gone up twenty-six cents an ounce. We made a killing."

"That's hardly the point," Paris said irritably. "It's part of a pattern of deterioration and excess that's making it harder and harder to separate his crazy bullshit from actual research."

"Which is why we pay Chang, Bannerjee, and Hopewell to validate his work."

"The Three Stooges? They're idiots."

Hecate gave her brother a tolerant smile and a mild shake of the head. "They're not and you know it. They're the best of the best."

Paris made a rude noise and threw back the last of his drink. "With Otto always at Dad's side our three idiots can never get close. I think we need to invite him down to the Dragon Factory for a few days."

"Are you nuts? He's been trying to find out where it is for years now. No way we can *bring* him there!"

"It's not like we'd send him a plane ticket, Paris. We'd go get him and control what he sees and knows. We could block out the windows on the jet, maybe slip him something so he'd sleep through the trip—something so that he wouldn't know *where* the Dragon Factory was. But I really think some tropical air would do him good, and we'd have a chance to get some actual quality time with him. And maybe see if we can figure out if he's totally bonkers or just half-crazy. We could show him the Berserkers and the stuff we have in development for the work camps. He'd—"

There was a soft *bing!* sound, indicating that their

plane was beginning its descent. A moment later Paris's cell phone rang. He paced the length of the cabin, mostly listening, grunting now and then. He said, "Shit!" and disconnected. His face was flushed red.

"What's wrong?" asked Hecate. "Who was that?"

"Sunderland," Paris said. "They're having problems getting the computer system. Apparently they're meeting more resistance than anticipated."

"He has the entire NSA!"

"I know; I know."

Hecate bit her lip and looked out of the window for a long moment. "We need that system. Pangaea's not good enough for the next phase. We need MindReader."

As brilliant as the Twins were, they could not take full responsibility for much of their transgenic work. Most of it was stolen. Pangaea, a computer system given to them by Alpha, was an advanced intruder model, and with it they had been able to infiltrate the mainframes of many of the world's top genetics research labs and clone the databases. This gave them a bank of knowledge broader than anyone else's, and broader by a couple orders of magnitude. However, Pangaea was not a new system and some of the modern firewalls were starting to give them trouble. The only computer system capable of slipping through those firewalls was MindReader, and it could more easily decrypt the data.

They'd already tried putting a mole in the DMS to try to steal a MindReader unit or obtain specs on it. They acted on a tip that there were some security holes in the organization, but they hit only brick walls and wasted over a million dollars that they would never see again. Using the Vice President had been Sunderland's grand scheme, and he'd already banked a lot of Jakoby cash just to set it in motion. If the plan failed, there was no chance in hell of getting a refund from the fat blowhard. That, they both agreed, was one of the downsides of being criminals. Unless you could pull a trigger on someone there was just no accountability, and Sunderland was not someone they could dispose of.

"Well, there's still the Denver thing," Paris said after a long silence. "The way Dad reacted when we told him about it . . . there must be something amazing down there. Maybe even the schematics for MindReader."

"More likely it's early genetics research," cautioned Hecate. "Could be a complete waste of time for us."

"Maybe," Paris said diffidently. One of the many goals of Sunderland's gambit with the Vice President was to keep the DMS too busy to notice anything happening in Denver. The discovery of a trove of old records belonging to one of Alpha's oldest colleagues was huge. The Twins had long suspected that Alpha had ties to groups who had pioneered genetic research, and the existence of a legendary trove of data based on covert mass human testing had long been the Holy Grail of black market genetics. No one knew exactly what was in it, but since the 1970s more than a dozen people had been murdered during the search for it. Alpha had mentioned it several times and had slyly gotten the Twins to look for it, but when they said that they thought they had a solid lead on it in a records storage facility near Denver, Alpha had tried to play it down as a whim that had passed. The Twins hadn't believed him. There had been a moment of naked hunger in Alpha's eyes that had electrified them.

The Twins were using this trip to visit Alpha as a

way of distracting him and the Sunderland gambit as a way of distracting the DMS. If everything went according to plan, then Paris and Hecate would have the contents of those records by the time they returned to the Dragon Factory.

"You're right. When it comes right down to it," Hecate said with a smile, "it's not like we don't have a Plan B. Or a Plan C."

"Or Plan D," he said brightly.

She held up her glass and he reached over to clink.

Paris took her glass and refilled it.

"Why does Dad need the new sequencers?" asked Hecate.

"He wouldn't say, of course. He never does unless he can stage a big reveal. God, he treats this like a fucking game show sometimes. When I pushed for an explanation he just rattled off some mumbo jumbo that wasn't even real science. He refuses to tell me anything specific unless you're there. He wants both halves of the Arcturian Collective to bear witness."

" 'The Arcturian Collective'? Is that our new name?"

Paris nodded and sipped his vodka.

"Well," Hecate said, "it's better than the Star Children. That one sounded like a late-seventies glam rock band. I keep hoping he'll settle on Ziggy Stardust and the Spiders from Mars."

Despite his sour mood, Paris grinned. "How about the Space Oddities?"

"Now that," Hecate said, "would be too close to truth in advertising."

They both burst out laughing. The girl moaned and turned over in her sleep. Hecate got tired of looking at her and pulled a sheet over her, a sneer touching the corners of Hecate's mouth. How could she have thought those big cow breasts were attractive?

Paris made fresh drinks and handed one to her.

"You don't think he suspects," Hecate asked softly, "do you?"

"Suspects what we're doing or what we have planned for him?"

"Either. Both."

Paris shrugged. "With him it's hard to know," he admitted. "Dad thinks he's still in charge. But really— does it matter? By the time he could find out for sure it'll be too late for him to do anything about it."

Their jet dropped its flaps and began a long, slow descent toward the desert.

Chapter Seven

The Akpro-Missérété Commune, Ouémé, the Republic of Benin, Eleven days ago

Dr. Panjay stepped out of the tent and pulled off her mask to reveal a face that was deeply troubled and deeply afraid. She peeled off her Latex gloves and her hands were shaking so badly she missed the biowaste bin on the first try. She heard the tent flap rustle and turned to see her colleague Dr. Smithwick come out into the dusty afternoon sunlight. Despite his sunburn, Smithwick was white as a ghost. He stood next to Panjay and removed his blood-smeared gloves and threw them, his mask and apron into the biowaste bin.

"You see why I asked you to come here? To see for yourself?" Panjay looked up into his face. "Thomas . . . what are we going to do?"

He shook his head. "I . . . don't know. Aside from sending samples and our notes . . . I don't know what we *can* do. This is beyond me, Rina."

"Thanks for coming," she said. "But . . . perhaps I should have prepared you better."

Smithwick looked back at the big tent. With the flap closed he could not see the rows upon rows of cots, each one occupied by a farmer from the Ouémé River basin. Sixty-two people.

"Is this every case?" he asked.

She bit her lip and shook her head. "No. These are the healthiest cases."

"I . . . don't understand. . . ."

"Since I came here three weeks ago we've had three hundred people present with symptoms. Most of them have hemoglobin levels in the range of six to eight grams per deciliter with a high reticulocyte count. Some have demonstrated features of hyposplenism Howell-Jolly bodies."

"You tested them all?"

"Yes . . . and five hundred other people chosen at random from the same towns or farms. Every single one of them showed signs of sickles hemoglobin. I tested their Hb S in sodium dithionite, and in every case the Hb had a turbid appearance."

"Christ!"

"Not everyone has active symptoms, but when symptoms present we're seeing a wide range of them. We've seen ischemia resulting in avascular necrosis; there have been cases of priapism and infarction of the penis in males of all ages; bacterial bone infections . . . the list is endless. Every symptom in the book. Even symptoms typically common in different strains are showing up in the same patients, including strokes due to vascular narrowing of blood vessels. There have been nineteen cases of cerebral infarction in children and widespread cerebral hemorrhaging in adults. And we've had increased occurrences of *Streptococcus pneumoniae* and *Haemophilus influenzae* in any patient who had undergone surgery. And not just splenectomies—I mean *any* surgery."

"What are the primary causes of death?"

"Renal failure," she said. "Across the board."

Her words hit Smithwick like a series of punches. He staggered back and had to grab a slender tree for support.

"All of them?"

"Every one. Every person."

"That's not possible." He licked his lips. "Do you have a map? Can you show me where the cases were reported?"

She nodded. "I knew you'd want to see it, so I have it already prepared."

Rina Panjay led the way through the nearly deserted village. The only sound they heard was that of quiet weeping from people huddled around fresh graves in the cemetery and a single high keening moan of loss echoing from a child's bedroom where a desolated mother sat clutching a doll to her chest as she rocked back and forth. Panjay's eyes were red from all the tears she had wept for this village over the last few weeks. She felt used, destroyed, totally helpless.

They entered the small World Health Organization blockhouse that normally served as the hospital for this rural corner of Ouémé. There were no patients in the hospital now—everyone had been moved to the big tent that had been erected in the middle of a field far from town and well away from the water supply.

There was a large map of the district that was littered with hundreds of colored pins tacked to the wall. The rest of that wall and some of the next was covered floor to ceiling with printouts of digital photographs of the victims. These, too, were color coded by pins. Victims without active symptoms had white pins. Victims with active symptoms had red pins. The dead were marked with black pins. Panjay pointed to a spot on the map. "This is where the first case was reported. The next was here, the next here." She tapped the pins as she spoke and Smithwick's face, already ashen, went paler still.

"No . . . ," he said.

Panjay lowered her hand. The pins on the map said all that was necessary. The pattern was clear. A first-year medical student could understand the implications, though to a seasoned WHO epidemiologist like Thomas Smithwick it was so clear that it screamed at him.

"This is impossible, Rina," he said. "What you're describing *can't* be sickle-cell. You must have made a mistake. The samples must have been contaminated."

She gave a weary shake of her head. "No. I had the results checked at three different labs. That's why I called you. I don't know what to do . . . this isn't something I'm trained for."

It was true, Rina Sanjay was an excellent young doctor, fresh from her internship at UCLA Medical Center and a brief stint as an ER doctor in Philadelphia's Northeastern Hospital. She could do anything from deliver a baby, to diagnose HIV, to perform minor surgeries for wound repair. But all of the tests said the same thing: sickle-cell anemia. A genetic disorder.

Smithwick on the other hand had spent twenty-six years with the World Health Organization. He had been in the trenches in the fight against the spread of HIV throughout Africa. He'd worked on two of the most recent Ebola outbreaks in Uganda and the Democratic Republic of Congo. In any other circumstance he was the wrong specialist to call in for something like this.

"What you're describing is impossible," he insisted. "Sickle-cell is not a communicable disease. It's strictly genetic. But this . . . this . . ." He waved his hands at the map. "This map suggests the spread of a communicable disease."

Rina Panjay said nothing.

"It's impossible," Smithwick said again. "Genetic diseases are not communicable."

"Could it have mutated?"

"So fast? And to this degree of virulence?" He shook his head. "No . . . there's just no way that could happen. Not in ten thousand generations of mutation."

"Then *how* could it happen?" she asked.

The air between them crackled with tension as Smithwick fought against the words that were forming on his tongue. The answer was as simple as it was preposterous. As simple as it was grotesque.

Smithwick said, "It's theoretically possible to *do* it. Deliberately. In a lab. Gene therapy and some host, perhaps a virus . . . but there would be no point. Gene therapy has a purpose, a goal. This doesn't. This is . . ." He fished for a word.

"Evil?" she suggested.

He was a long time answering, then nodded. "If this is something someone has done . . . then it could only have been created for one purpose. To do harm. To intentionally do harm."

Dr. Panjay looked at the map and then her eyes moved across the hundreds of color photographs pinned to the wall. Many of the pictures were of people she knew. Over fifty were from this village. Everyone in the village she had tested had come up positive for this new strain of sickle-cell. Every single person.

"We have to inform WHO," Panjay said. "We have to warn them—"

"No," Smithwick interrupted. "We have to warn everyone."

He stared at the pins.

"Everyone," he repeated softly, but in his heart he was terrified that they were already too late. Far too late.

Chapter Eight

Baltimore, Maryland
Saturday, August 28, 8:25 A.M.
Time Remaining on the Extinction Clock: 99 hours, 35 minutes

Things are seldom what they seem. After leaving the cemetery I drove eight blocks, doing double backs and sudden turns and all of the other stunts that cops learn from crooks about losing a tail. Nothing. Nobody was tailing me. I was sure of that.

"Ah, shit," I said aloud, and immediately pulled off the street into a parking lot of a big strip mall. Couple of things to remember about the NSA: they weren't stupid, not on their worst days . . . and they weren't clumsy.

I got out of the car, locked it, and ran like a son of a bitch.

They weren't tailing me because they didn't need to. I hadn't seen one or heard one, but I'd bet my complete collection of Muddy Waters on vinyl that one of Slab-face's boys had put a tracer on my car. Either they were tracking me in the hopes that I'd lead them somewhere sensitive to the DMS or they were herding me toward an ambush point. I didn't wait around to find out. I ran.

They were already closing in on me. Two blocks from where I dumped the Explorer I rounded a corner and there was a black car cruising the street, heading in the direction I'd just come from. As it passed I flicked a glance at it and looked right into the surprised face of Agent John Andrews. Slab-face.

Shit.

I only saw him for a second, but it was long enough for his scowl of frustration to blossom into a big smile like a happy bloodhound. He was yelling at the driver as I jagged left and raced down an alley. I heard shouts behind me and Andrews and his buddy were pelting after me with alarming speed.

Okay, I thought, *if you want me bad enough then see if you can keep up.*

I poured it on, leaping over garbage, ducking through a rent in a chain-link fence, vaulting a green Dumpster, and spider-climbing up a fire escape. I'm moderately big, but I can run like a cheetah on speed when I'm motivated.

Andrews, for all his size, was even faster than me.

He was less than ten yards behind me as I tore down a garbage-strewn alleyway toward a dead end. If he hadn't wasted breath yelling at me he might have grabbed me before I could make it to the end of the alley. Mistake. I leaped as high as I could and grabbed the chain-link fence three-quarters of the way up and scrambled up and over like a nervous squirrel. I swung over the top pole and did an ugly somersault, spilling the change and car keys out of my pocket, and landed in a crouch, fell sideways, and used the momentum to get back to my feet. It wasn't pretty, but I was up and running.

I didn't look back. I heard Andrews slam into the fence, but his dress shoes weren't made for climbing and he fell. I heard him land, and his curses followed me all the way down the alley.

Andrews yelled at me to stop, but he still hadn't pulled his piece. Curiouser and curiouser. I didn't want to know how he'd vent his frustrations if he ever got me cuffed to a D ring in a quiet interrogation room, so I ran and ran and ran.

The rest of the alley was clear and I poured on the juice, but just as I was about to make a break for daylight a second Crown Vic screeched to a stop in front of me, tires smoking, its bulk entirely blocking the alley. Two agents started opening their doors, but I didn't stop. I threw myself into the air, hit the hood of the car, and slid on one ass cheek across the hood. As I landed, the agent on the passenger side made a grab for me, but I spun into him, head-butted him, and then threw him onto the hood as the other agent tried to slide across like I'd done. The two agents hit hard and slid off the front of the car into the street.

I hated messing these guys up, but Mr. Church's words were banging around inside my head. *Don't get taken, Captain, or you'll disappear into the system.*

Call it an incentive program.

A third agent came out of nowhere, jumped over his pals, and pounded after me. Slab-face and the other agent were too far back now, so I let the driver catch up to me two blocks away. I cut diagonally across a basket-ball court, scattering black teenagers out of my way as I went. They yelled at us the way kids will and then I gave them something to yell about. As I reached the foul line of the far court I angled for the thin metal pole that supported the rusted hoop from which only tattered threads of a net remained. I leaped at the upright, grabbed it with both hands just as the driver caught up, and I flagpoled around it like a vertical version of a spin on a high bar. My sneakers slammed into the driver's chest and knocked him flying into a row of overflowing trash cans. It wasn't a dangerous fall for a fit adult, but it was loud and messy. As I ran, I heard the kids behind me cheering. At least someone appreciated me.

I knew that I'd been lucky, and that was okay. I'd go light a candle in church next chance I had. Right now I had to run the luck as far as it would go.

I wished I had the time to cut one of these goons out of the pack, drag him into an abandoned room, and see if I could convince him that confession was good for the soul. But I doubted any of the agents would know more than Church could find out, and besides, the pos-sible reward wasn't worth the risk.

So I cut left into a low-rise apartment building, ran down hallways and out the back door, vaulted a couple of backyard fences, nearly got my ass bitten off by a startled bull terrier, made my way to another set of alleys, and zigzagged my way through West Baltimore. I was a white guy running through a rough black neighborhood, but I looked crazy and I looked like a cop, and those were two things nobody of any color wants to mess with.

After another two blocks I slowed to a walk and paid a teenager fifty bucks for his Orioles cap. Sweat ran down my body and pooled in my shoes; my shirt clung to me, outlining the shape of the pistol clipped to the back of my belt. I could feel the eyes of everyone on the street on me, but I knew that no one was going to drop a dime on someone running from the cops—even if he looked like a cop himself. I went into a convenience store and bought an oversized souvenir Baltimore T-shirt. I squatted in the street and rubbed it against the macadam until it was filthy and torn, then pulled it on over my Orioles shirt. With the hat sitting askew and a baggy shirt that looked like it hadn't been washed since Clinton was in office, I looked like a homeless person. Every time I turned a corner I dropped a little more into that role, lowering my head, changing my walk into a meandering shuffle, twitching and mumbling to myself in a variety of languages. Eventually anyone who saw me would have sworn I was a junkie looking to score. Somewhere along the way I picked up two actual junkies, and the three of us moved in a haphazard line deeper into West Baltimore until there was no trail at all for the NSA to follow.

Half an hour later I stole a car and drove out of town.

Chapter Nine

The Deck
Saturday, August 28, 8:35 A.M.
Time Remaining on Extinction Clock: 99 hours,
25 minutes E.S.T.

Otto and Cyrus strolled through the hallways of the Deck, smiling and nodding at the workers and technicians. Except for three scientists in the laboratory—all

Indian—every face was white and every lineage could be traced back to Aryan origins. In some cases, because the worker was particularly valuable, allowances were made for indistinct bloodlines. In the end, as both men knew, it didn't matter, because no one here, not the workers or lab staff, not the SAMs, and not even Otto and Cyrus themselves, was part of the future. They were the shoulders on which the next evolutionary level of mankind would stand. Otto and Cyrus were content and delighted with that; the others simply did not know.

"How are things going in Wilmington?" asked Cyrus as they stopped at a viewing stand built to look down on the zoo. There were forty separate cages, and the screams and calls of animals filled the air. The rich scent of earth and animal dung and musk clung to the water vapor in the humid biosphere. The zoo was a hundred yards below the Arizona desert, but it felt like a tropical rain forest.

"The Russians were able to get the information from the man Gilpin—the computer nerd who used to work for the Twins. He was able to confirm the content of the Haeckel records."

"Is Gilpin alive?"

"I doubt it. The Russian team commander downloaded the information to us just a few minutes ago. However, Gilpin was able to confirm that the Haeckel records are at a storage facility called Deep Iron, near Denver."

Cyrus looked pleased. "Who do we have in the area?"

"In Denver? No one, but I sent a team."

"More Russians?"

Otto shrugged. "Better them than our own."

They watched the animals. A juvenile mammoth was

trumpeting and banging its massive shoulders against the sides of its cage. The air above them was filled with a flock of passenger pigeons. Cyrus leaned his forearms on the pipe rail and watched as handlers used winches and slings to carefully off-load a sedated dire wolf from an electric cart. The female had received in vitro fertilization but had miscarried twice already. The embryologist—one of the Indians—thought they'd solved the problem. A gene that was coding for the wrong hormone sequence.

"She's beautiful, isn't she?"

Otto grunted. He had almost no interest in reclamation genetics. To him it was an expensive hobby that drained time and manpower from more important work, but for Cyrus it was a lifelong passion. To reclaim the past and then improve it so that what went forward was stronger and more evolved.

"This is how God must feel," murmured Cyrus. It was something he said at least three or four times a week. Otto said nothing.

In the adjoining cage a saber-toothed cat sat and watched the handlers with icy patience. Even from here the cat reminded Cyrus of his daughter, Hecate. The same eyes, the same arctic patience.

He glanced at his watch, which was not set to real time but synchronized with the Extinction Clock. As the numbers ticked down, second by second, Cyrus felt a great happiness settle over him.

Chapter Ten

I was scared. I admit it.

I'd been in worse physical danger before. Hell, I'd been in worse physical danger two days ago, so it wasn't that. But as I drove I started getting a serious case of the shakes because the NSA—the actual National Security frigging Agency—was trying to arrest me. If they hadn't had just cause beforehand, they certainly did now, and I was beginning to regret how I had played it.

Sure, Church had warned me not to get taken. Message received and understood; but I know that I did more collateral damage to those guys simply because they braced me at Helen's grave. If they'd come at me in the parking lot of my apartment building they might have gotten off with a couple of bruises. But I was pretty sure that at least two of them were in the hospital and a couple of others would be carrying around bruises that would be daily reminders of Joe Ledger, world's oldest adolescent.

I took a bunch of random turns, double- and triple-checking that I had no tail.

My best friend, Rudy Sanchez—who's also my shrink and used to be Helen's shrink right up until she killed herself—has been working with me for years to control some of my less mature urges. He calls them unrefined primal responses to negative stimulation. I think he gets wood when he can toss out phrases like that.

My boss may think I'm hot shit and even the guys on

Echo Team might think I'm cool and together, but Rudy knows the score. I've got enough baggage to start a luggage store, and I have a whole bunch of buttons that I don't like pushed.

Disrespecting Helen—even through ignorance of her existence—did not play well with me. If they'd pushed harder I would like to believe that I wouldn't have gone apeshit on them. There are a lot of things I'd like to believe in.

I was gripping the steering wheel too hard. The more I thought about it, the more anger rose up to replace the fear. I didn't want either emotion screwing with my head. It was already a junk pile.

I dug out my cell and tried to call Rudy, but I got no answer.

"Shit," I snarled, and tossed the phone down on the seat.

And kept driving fast, heading nowhere.

Chapter Eleven

Hebron, Louisiana
Saturday, August 28, 8:55 A.M.
Time Remaining on Extinction Clock: 99 hours, 5 minutes

Rabbi Scheiner was an old man, but he had bright green eyes and a face well used to smiling. However, as he walked beside his nephew, Dr. David Meyer, the rabbi's mouth was pulled into a tight line and his eyes were dark with concern.

"How sure are you about this, David?" the rabbi asked, pitching his voice low enough so that the nurses and patients in the ward could not overhear.

David Meyer shook the sheaf of papers in his hand. "We ran every test we could, and the lab in Baton Rouge confirmed our findings."

"It's unfortunate, David . . . but it *does* happen. You know more than I do that there's no cure for this, and that the best we can do is screen young people and counsel them before marriage. Warn them of the risks."

"That's the point, Rabbi," insisted Meyer. "We did those screens. We have a very high concentration of Ashkenazi Jews here, most of them from families that fled the Rhine as things were going bad in the late nineteen thirties. Virtually everyone in Hebron, Tefka, and Muellersville has been screened—we still get grants from Israel to run the polymerase chain reaction techniques, and they're very accurate. We know the carriers, and we have counseled them. If these occurrences were within the group of known carriers, then I wouldn't have called you."

"Then I don't understand. *Haaretz* reported that the disease was virtually eradicated. You yourself told me that there had been no babies born to Jewish families here in America with the disease since 2003."

Meyer took the rabbi by the arm and led him into a small alcove.

"I know; I know," said Meyer. His face was bright with stress, and sweat beaded his forehead. "However, in the last month clinics throughout the area have been reporting many cases of patients presenting with classic symptoms: slurred speech, difficulty swallowing, unsteadiness of gait, spasticity, sharp and sudden cognitive declines, and a variety of psychiatric illnesses that include psychosis typical of schizophrenia. Individually any one or two of those symptoms in an adult would not suggest LOTS, but when five or six symptoms present in virtually every patient . . . then what else could I think? I sent nurses out to take samples for genetic testing and we ran our own enzyme assay tests, but they're not as precise at genetic testing as PCR tests, so I had the samples shipped to a lab in Baton Rouge." He shook the sheaf of papers. "These are the results."

Rabbi Scheiner reluctantly took the papers from Meyer and quickly read through them. In the comment notes he read: "Late Onset Tay-Sachs (LOTS) disease is a rare form of the disorder, typically occurring in patients in their twenties and early thirties. This disease is frequently misdiagnosed and usually nonfatal."

He looked up.

"So you have several patients who have become sick?"

Meyer shook his head slowly. "Rabbi . . . I've had eleven patients here in Hebron, and there were nine in Tefka and six in Muellersville."

The rabbi caught the phrasing. "You say you 'had' eleven patients. . . ."

Meyer gave him a bleak stare. "Three have already died. Two more are . . . well, they have lapsed into comas. The others are getting sicker almost as I watch. The muscles needed to swallow become atrophic and paralyzed. We've intubated them, and I've even trached a few, but the paralysis spreads so fast. I don't know how to treat any of them."

"There's no cure. . . ." The rabbi said it as a statement. "God help us."

"Researchers have been looking into gene therapy and other treatments, but even if we had a genetic option in hand, these people don't have the time for it."

"These are all children?"

Meyer shook his head. "No, and that's what scares me the most. Infantile and Juvenile TSD are both fatal, but not LOTS. And yet every one of these patients is over twenty. Some are in their forties and fifties. It doesn't make sense."

"Could . . . could the disease have mutated?"

"It apparently has," said Meyer, "but *how*? It was nearly eradicated. We'd beaten it. We've never had a single case here in Hebron, or in the other towns, and most of the people here are second- and even third-generation American born. We haven't married strictly within the communities of Ashkenazi Jews, which means statistics should be on our side."

Rabbi Scheiner put his hand on the young doctor's arm. "Be strong, David. Tell me . . . what will you do?"

"I'll have to report this. Now that I have the results from the genetic tests I can reach out to the major university hospitals."

"What about the disease people?" asked the rabbi. "What about the Centers for Disease Control up in Atlanta? You went to them with the botulism problem a few years ago—"

"No," said Meyer, "this is a genetic mutation, not a pathogen. It's not contagious in any way that could cause an epidemic."

Rabbi Scheiner's eyes were intense, probing. "Are you sure?"

"Of course," said Meyer. "It's an inherited disorder. You can't just catch it."

The rabbi nodded and turned to look out of the alcove at the patients in the ward. "Are you sure?" he asked again.

Chapter Twelve

After I drove around for twenty minutes I switched on my scramble and tried to make some calls. Church's line rang through to voice mail. His voice message was: "Speak!" I was tempted to bark, but instead I left a simple request for callback.

Next I called Grace, but she got on the line long enough to tell me that she got outside to "take a butcher's at a bunch of dodgy blokes with federal badges who have me totally hacked off, so I'd better sort them out." The more pissed off Grace gets, the more British she becomes. There are times I can't understand one word in three, and English is my mother tongue.

Finally I got Rudy Sanchez on the phone. A few years ago my dad—who was Baltimore's police commissioner until a couple of months ago—got Rudy a job as a police therapist, and Rudy's association with me got him hornswaggled into the DMS. It's a bit of a sordid soap opera. Rudy still did a couple of days with BPD, and today he'd be at his office near the Aquarium. He was very low profile, so maybe he'd be off the NSA sweep.

"Joe!" he answered, and from his tone of voice I knew that he was already aware of what was going on. "Thank God!"

"You heard?"

"Of course I heard!" he snapped, and said something about the Vice President in back-alley Spanish that was too fast for me to catch anything except vague references to fornication with livestock. When he finally slowed to a crawl, he asked, "*Dios mio*, Cowboy—are you all right?"

"I'm wearing filthy clothes, I've been hanging out with junkies and I'm driving a stolen car that I'm pretty sure someone peed in—"

"Okay, okay, I get it . . . you're having a bad day. I hear there's a lot of it going around."

"I wouldn't know, Rude; I'm the spy who can't come in from the cold."

"Mm. I guess I'm on the run, too. Sort of," he said. "Mr. Church told me to go hide somewhere, so I'm sitting in St. Ann's. They're painting the place, so it's just me and a bunch of workmen putting up scaffolding."

"Listen," I said. "I called for a couple of reasons. First, to tell you to watch your ass. You're still officially a consultant psychiatrist for the Baltimore Police. If you get nabbed, play that card. Have them call my dad."

My father was making a run for Mayor of Baltimore and the pundits were calling it a slam dunk for him. He had friends on both sides of the badge.

"I have him on speed dial," Rudy assured me. "What's the other thing?"

"Two other things. The NSA guys came for me at the cemetery."

"Ouch," he said. "How are you?"

"I vented a bit by beating on them some."

"But it's still with you?"

"Yeah, and that's the other thing. And Helen's a part of that, too. In a way. Today started off weird even before I woke up."

"How so?"

"I know this ain't the time for this, but it's weighing

on me and I've got to kill time until I hear from Church—"

"Don't apologize. Just tell me."

"Okay . . . tomorrow is the anniversary of Helen's suicide."

"Oh, *dios mio*," he said with real pain in his voice. With everything that had happened over the last two months he had forgotten. "Joe . . . I . . ."

"I dreamed about it last night, man. I dreamed about her sister Colleen calling me, saying that Helen hadn't answered the phone in days. I dreamed about going over there. Every single detail, Rudy, from picking up my car keys on the table by the door to the feel of the wood splintering when I kicked in Helen's door. I remembered the smell in the hallway, and how bad it got when I broke in. I remember her face . . . bloated and gassy. I can even remember the bottle of drain cleaner she drank from. The way the label was torn and stained."

"Joe, I—"

"But here's the really shitty part, Rude . . . the worst part."

He was silent, waiting.

"In my dream, when I walked over to her body, knowing that she was dead and had been dead for days . . . when I stood over her and then dropped to my knees and pulled her into my arms . . ." I paused and for a moment I didn't know if I was going to be able to finish this.

"Take your time, Joe . . . ," he said gently. "It'll hurt less once it's out."

"I . . . don't think so. Not this time."

"Why, Joe? Tell me what happened when you held Helen in your arms."

"You see, that's just the thing. . . . I picked her body up and held it, just the way I did back when it happened. And her head kind of flopped over sideways just like it did. But . . . aw, fuck me, man . . . it wasn't Helen I was holding."

"Tell me. . . ."

"It was Grace."

Rudy was silent, waiting for the rest, but there was no more. That's where the dream had ended.

"I woke up in a cold sweat and I never went back to sleep. Stayed up all night watching Court TV and reruns of the Dog Whisperer. Anything to keep from going back to sleep."

"Joe, this isn't all about strength. It's obvious you have feelings for Grace, and both of you are in a highly dangerous line of work."

"Shit, I knew you wouldn't get it," I snapped, then immediately regretted it. "Sorry, Rude . . . belay that. What I meant to say is that I knew I couldn't explain it the right way."

"Then tell me what the right way is, Cowboy."

"I. . . ." My voice trailed off as I drove aimlessly through the streets. "I . . . know that having, um, 'affection' for Grace is ill advised. Got it, got that filed away. But there was something about this that felt weird and dirty and wrong. Wrong in a guilty kind of way."

"What do you mean?"

"Like . . . I failed her. The way I failed Helen."

"Joe, we've been over this a thousand times. You were not responsible for Helen's life. You were not her protector. She had been rehabilitated back into a lifestyle where all of her doctors agreed she was capable of taking care of herself. You visited as often as you could, more than anyone else. More than her own family."

"But I took the job with the Homeland task force and that kept me away for days and even weeks at a time. Don't try to tell me that I wasn't aware of how that job would impact my regular visits to Helen."

"Which still doesn't make it your fault. You don't rule the planet, Joe. And even if you lived with her, if she wanted to end her life—as she clearly did—she'd find a moment when you were asleep or in the shower and she would do what she ultimately did. You can't save someone who doesn't want to be saved."

I didn't feel like going down that road with him again, so I switched tack. "So why did I see Grace in the dream last night? Are you saying that I feel responsible for her?"

"I hope not."

"It's not like we're in love," I protested.

Rudy said nothing, and then his phone clicked. "It's Mr. Church calling me, Joe. I'd better take this."

"Okay."

"But Joe . . . ?"

"Yeah."

"We need to come back to this."

"Sure, Rude . . . when the dust settles."

And it starts snowing on the Amazon, I thought.

I closed my phone and drove, aware that I was driving myself a little crazy.

Chapter Thirteen

It was a routine pickup, a classic no-shots-fired thing where the after-action report would be short and boring. Only it wasn't.

First Sgt. Bradley Sims—Top to everyone who knew him, and second in command of Joe Ledger's Echo Team—was on point at the door knock. Like his two fellow agents he was dressed in a nondescript navy blue government-issue suit, white shirt, and red tie. Flag pin on his lapel, a wire, and sunglasses. The motel hallway was badly lighted, so he removed his shades and dropped them into his coat pocket. He might have been NSA, FBI, or an agent of any of the DOJ's domestic law enforcement agencies, maybe a middle-grade agent in charge of a low-risk field mission. He dressed for the part. He had FBI credentials in his pocket, though he'd never so much as set foot in Quantico. He also had badges for the ATF and DEA in the car.

The Department of Military Sciences did not operate under the umbrella of the Department of Justice, nor did it fall into the growing network of agencies under the Homeland charter. The DMS was a solo act, answerable to the President of the United States. They didn't have their own badges. They weren't cops. The credentials Top Sims carried, however, were completely authentic.

He knocked on the door. "FBI!" he announced in the leather-throated roar of a lifelong sergeant. "Please open the door."

Out of habit he stepped to one side so that the reinforced frame rather than the door was between him and whoever might be inside. Cops did that; so did soldiers. Top had been a soldier since he enlisted on his eighteenth birthday, and that was twenty-two years ago and change.

Both of the agents flanking him were bigger and younger than Top. They looked like a pair of giants. To his left was Big Bob Faraday, a former ATF field man who stood six-five and had massive biceps that strained the fabric of the off-the-rack blazer. To Top's right was Bunny—born with the unfortunate name of Harvey Rabbit—who had joined the DMS after eight years as a sergeant in Force Recon. Bunny was two inches taller than Faraday and though he was also heavily muscled, his build was more appropriate to volleyball, which until recently he'd played at the Pan American Games level. His service in Iraq had kept him out of the Olympics, but he didn't hold a grudge.

There was no answer at the door.

"Maybe he ain't home," suggested Bunny.

"It's Saturday morning," said Big Bob. "Guy's got no job, no friends. He's here or he's at Starbucks."

"Maybe I'll just knock louder," said Top.

He did. No answer.

"Let's kick it," Top decided.

"I got it," said Big Bob, moving past Top to front the door. Big Bob had thighs like bridge supports and could bury the whole rack on the Nautilus leg press. Twice now he'd kicked doors completely off their hinges. He wanted a hat trick.

Top shrugged and stepped aside. "Entertain yourself."

Top and Bunny drew their weapons and quietly racked the slides. The man they were there to arrest, Burt Gilpin, was a middle-aged computer geek who had figured a way to hack into the mainframes of several major universities that were involved in medical, viral, and genetic research. He'd constructed elaborate Web sites with phantom pages and rerouted e-mail drops so he could advertise the stolen data and accept bids from interested parties. Gilpin knew his computers and he understood security, but MindReader was designed to spot certain kinds of patterns related to key topics. Genetics and virology were major red flags and it zeroed him in a nanosecond, and Church had taken a personal interest because the method Gilpin used to hack the systems bore some similarities to MindReader. Nobody else was supposed to have that technology, and Church wanted to have a long talk with Gilpin.

Top drew the pickup detail and tagged the first two members of Echo Team to report that morning to go with him. Gilpin had no police record apart from parking tickets; he had never served in the military, never belonged to a gun club or registered a firearm, and didn't even go to a gym. Sending Top, Bunny, and Big Bob was overkill, but it was also an excuse to get out of the shop for the day.

"Kick it," said Top.

Big Bob raised his leg and cocked his foot, but just as he was about to kick, Bunny saw a shadow move past the peephole on the motel door.

"Wait!" he started to say, and then the door seemed to explode as heavy-caliber bullets ripped through wood and plaster and slammed into Big Bob Faraday.

The big man screamed as two bullets tore into his leg;

one smashed his shin and the other struck the underside of his kneecap and then ripped a tunnel through the meat of his thigh, tearing muscle and tendon and missing his femoral artery by three one-hundredths of an inch. Three additional rounds struck him high in the abdomen. The Kevlar vest is designed to flatten bullets and stop them from penetrating the body. The foot-pounds of impact still hits like a hammer, but the wearer can live with broken ribs.

Kevlar is not designed to stop steel-core Teflon-coated rounds. Street thugs and gangbangers call them cop killers for a reason.

The bullets chopped through Big Bob Faraday like he'd been bare chested. The combined impact slammed him backward with such force that he hit the door of the motel room opposite and tore it out of the frame so that he fell halfway into the room.

All of this happened in a second.

In the next second Top and Bunny threw themselves down and out of the line of fire as bullets continued to rip the doorjamb apart. Hundreds of rounds tore chunks of cement and pieces of lath out of the walls and filled the air above them with a hurricane of jagged splinters. They both knew, even as they were diving for cover, that Big Bob was down. Down and maybe dead.

Top flattened on the floor and reached his arm out to point his gun into the room. He opened fire, knowing he had little chance of hitting anything, but return fire can disrupt an attack and he needed to buy time.

A voice yelled, "*Perekroi dver!*" And though Top didn't understand the words, he could recognize the language. Russian. It made no sense.

He unloaded his full magazine and there was a sudden shrill scream from inside. He'd gotten a lucky hit.

"Bozhe moi!"

Top saw that Bunny had squirmed around and was ready to imitate his blind shooting trick. Their eyes met and Bunny mouthed the word *Russians?* Top nodded and there was no more to be said. His receiver locked back, and as he withdrew his hand Bunny reached around the shattered jamb, his hand angled up, and began firing. The return fire was fierce and when Top whipped his hand back his skin was a cactus plant of tiny splinters that covered him from knuckles to wrist.

As Top dropped his mag and slapped in another, Bunny cut a lightning-fast quick-look through an apple-sized hole in the wall. He immediately moved away from the spot as bullets reamed the hole. The afterimage of what he'd seen was burned into his brain. He hand-signaled to Top. Four men in a firing line. One injured. What Bunny couldn't convey was that a fifth man was duct-taped naked to a chair, his limbs streaked with blood. Gilpin.

Top signaled to Bunny to go high and left while he went low and right. He finger-counted down from three and then they spun into different quadrants of the ruined doorway and opened fire. Neither hit anything with his first shot, and they hadn't expected to; the first round was fired to cover them as they came into position and to give them a fragment of a second to locate their targets. Four men in a small room. Very little in the way of cover. They both saw what they needed. Their next shots punched into the four Russians, hitting legs and groins and torsos and heads, the bullet impacts dancing them backward so that they looked like a film of people walking played in reverse. The heavy automatic weapons of the Russians filled the air with bullets, but Bunny's and Top's bullets spoiled all aim and accuracy. It was a perfect counterattack and it turned the apartment into a shooting gallery.

The slide locked back on Bunny's gun and Top spaced out his last two shots to give Bunny some cover and time to reload. Then Top dropped his mag and slapped in his last one.

But it wasn't necessary. The gunfire from inside had died.

Bunny and Top got to their feet and spun around the smoking edges of the shattered wall and entered the room hard and fast, guns up and out. Nothing moved except the pall of smoke eddying around them like a graveyard mist.

Bunny kicked open the bathroom door. "Clear!"

"Clear!" Top yelled as he checked all points of the small main room. He kicked the weapons away from the slack and bloody hands of the Russians. "Secure this and call it in," he ordered as he pivoted and ran back out into the hallway to check on Big Bob.

Bunny called a man-down report to the DMS command center, who in turn notified local police and EMTs. He checked Gilpin, but the little computer hacker was as dead as the Russians, his body covered with the marks of savage torture, his throat cut.

"Damn," Bunny said, and then joined Top in the hall.

Top had used a switchblade to cut away Faraday's jacket shirt and the straps of his Kevlar vest. Bunny tore the shirt into pieces and they used it to pack the three entry wounds in Big Bob's chest and the three much larger exit wounds in his back. Top used Faraday's tie as a tourniquet to staunch the bleeding in his ruined leg.

Big Bob was unconscious, his eyes half-closed and his lips beginning to go pale with the massive blood loss and the onset of shock. Both agents peeled off their own jackets and used them as a makeshift blanket. In the distance they could already hear the wail of sirens.

"Christ, this is bad," Bunny said as he cradled Big Bob's head in his lap.

Top was a lifelong expert in karate and knew a great deal about anatomy. He studied the placement of the wounds and shook his head. "I think the rounds clipped his liver and one kidney. There must be lung damage, but it's not sucking."

"Is that bad?"

"It's not good. Lung could be filled with blood already."

The sirens were louder now, outside. He heard people yelling and then the pounding of feet as EMTs and uniformed cops ran down the hall toward them. The EMTs pushed past them and began their own wound care, but they listened to Top's professional assessments.

"We'll take over from here, sir," they said, and the agents backed off.

The cops circled them and Bunny flashed his credentials. Somebody at the DMS must have made the right call, because the police deferred to them, even to the point of staying outside the crime scene. The DMS operator had assured Top that Jerry Spencer, the head of the DMS's high-tech forensics division, would be on the next thing smoking.

Top stood in the doorway and looked at the carnage.

"This don't make sense," Bunny said, looking over

Top's shoulder. "I mean, am I crazy or were these clowns speaking Russian?"

"Sounded like it to me. Or close enough."

"Russian Mafia?" Bunny ventured.

"Shit if I know, Farmboy. But these guys were pros of some kind. Ex-police or ex–Russian military. They knew how to ambush a door knock."

On the floor by the overturned table was a device that looked like a PDA. Someone, presumably one of the Russians, had attached it to Gilpin's hard drive with narrow cables.

"Looks like they were downloading his shit," said Bunny. He nudged the device. The PDA and the hard drive had been smashed to junk by gunfire.

"No way to know if they were downloading the data to take it or forwarding it on. Maybe they tortured him to get his passwords."

"All this for a computer hacker?"

"I think we just stepped in somebody else's shit."

Bunny grunted. "It's our shit now. Big Bob makes it or not, I'm going to want a piece of somebody's ass for this. Whoever ordered this."

"Hooah," murmured Top. "The captain's going to take this amiss."

"We'd better call him."

"He's at the cemetery this morning."

"He'll want to know about this," Bunny said, but before he could punch in a number Top's phone rang.

Top looked at the code. "Uh-oh," he said. "It's the big man." He flipped open his phone. "Sir."

Mr. Church said, "Operations just informed me that there's been an incident, that one of ours is down. Give me a sit rep."

Top told him everything. "EMTs don't like what they're seeing. Big Bob's in the ambulance now. We were just about to call Captain Ledger."

"Scratch that, First Sergeant. We have a more pressing problem."

"Sir?"

Church told him about the NSA. "It's possible you men are off their radar because you've been operating with Bureau credentials, but now that this has happened the bloodhounds will be running."

"What do you want us to do?"

"As soon as Captain Ledger surfaces we'll find you some air transport and the three of you will head west. We've lost track of the Denver team and that incident may be separate from this—and it may be a lot more important," Church said. "I want you two to vanish. Get off the radar and stay off until you make contact with Major Courtland, Captain Ledger, or myself. Don't get taken. You may use any methods short of lethal force." He read off a string of possible locations and made Top read them back. "Go to each one in order. Wait ten minutes. If Captain Ledger does not come, proceed to the next one until you rendezvous. He'll have further instructions."

"Yes, sir." Top paused. "But what about Big Bob? We were going to go to the hospital once Jerry Spencer gets here."

"Agent Spencer will neither need nor want your help, First Sergeant; and as for Sergeant Faraday . . . he'll be protected. I have some friends in Wilmington who will watchdog him. I want you and Sergeant Rabbit to get mobile and get gone most riki-tik."

He hung up.

Bunny, who had leaned close to eavesdrop, stepped back and looked at Top. "What the fuck is going on here?"

"I don't know, Farmboy, but the man said to get our asses into the wind, so let's boogie."

Bunny lingered for one moment longer, first looking at the bodies sprawled in the motel room and then turning to gaze at the smears of blood where Big Bob had gone down.

"Son of a bitch must pay," Bunny said.

Top nodded. "Hooah."

Then they were gone.

Chapter Fourteen

Cotonou, Benin
Six days ago

Dr. Arjeta Hlasek sat back in her chair, her pointed chin resting on the tips of steepled fingers. Her expression was a patchwork of doubt, concern, and alarm. The two doctors who sat on the other side of her desk looked road worn and deeply stressed, their eyes hollow with exhaustion. Both of them sat straight in their chairs, their hands fidgeting on the stacks of test results and lab reports they each had on their laps.

"I . . . don't know what to say," began Dr. Hlasek. "This is disturbing to say the least, but what you're describing . . . Well, I don't know."

The younger of her visitors, Dr. Rina Panjay, leaned forward, her voice low and urgent. "Dr. Hlasek . . . we've done the tests. We've had blind verification from two separate labs, and they verify what our own tests show."

"She's right, Arjeta," agreed Thomas Smithwick. "And I can understand your hesitation. I didn't believe it, either, when Rina first told me. I ran every kind of test I could think of—most of them several times. The lab work doesn't even vary; it's not like there's a margin for error here."

"But," Dr. Hlasek said, half-smiling, "a genetic disease that has mysteriously mutated into a water-borne pathogen? There's no precedent for something like this."

Smithwick paused, then said, "There wouldn't be . . . not outside of a biological warfare facility."

"You think that's what you've found? A new bio-weapon that somehow escaped quarantine and has gotten into the water supply in Ouémé? That's a lot to swallow, Thomas. Who would do such a thing? More-over, who would fund research of that kind? It's absurd; it's fantasy."

"Haven't you been listening? We have over three hundred infected people right now," snapped Dr. Panjay, and then suddenly regretted her tone of voice. Dr. Arjeta Hlasek was the Regional Director for the World Health Organization and a major political force in the United Nations. She was one of Switzerland's most celebrated doctors and had three times been part of teams nomi-nated for the Nobel Prize. Hlasek was not, however, a patient or tolerant person, and she wilted Panjay with a blast from her ice blue eyes.

Dr. Panjay dropped her eyes and stammered a quick apology.

"Arjeta," said Smithwick in a mollifying tone, "my young friend here is exhausted. She's been in the thick of this, caring for dozens of patients at her clinic and doing fieldwork to collect samples and helping to bury the dead. She's running on fumes right now."

"I appreciate the diligence and dedication," said Dr. Hlasek with asperity. "Still . . . I find this rather a lot to swallow. Our organization is built on veracity. We've had bad calls in the past that have weakened public trust, and weakened financial support."

Smithwick shook his head, his own patience beginning to erode. "This isn't like the cock-up with the Ebola scare last year. This is a real crisis backed by irrefutable evidence." He took his entire stack of notes and thumped them down on Hlasek's desk. "This is immediate and it requires immediate action."

The Swiss doctor blew out her cheeks and studied the papers and then the two doctors.

"Understand me, Thomas . . . and Dr. Panjay," she began in a measured tone. "I *will* act. But this needs to be handled with the greatest of care. What you've just put on my desk is a time bomb. If you're right about this—and I warn you now that I will have another laboratory verify these test results—then we will act, but this could blow up out of control very easily. Between political and religious tensions and the shoddiness of the public health and education systems, we are going to have to plan how to release this information."

"But people are dying!" urged Panjay.

"Yes, they are," agreed Hlasek, "and more are going to die before we verify the results and map out a protocol for handling this. However, if we don't move with the greatest care then many, many more will die in the ensuing panic. Thomas, you've seen this happen; you tell her."

Smithwick nodded and patted Panjay's hand. "She's

right. A panic breaks down the lines of communication that are, quite literally, the lifelines for the people. You'll not only have masses of people fleeing blindly, which would make effective treatment impossible, you'll also see warlords and criminals raiding our supplies for treatments, food, pure water . . . no, Dr. Hlasek is quite correct. This needs to be handled correctly or we'll have thrown gasoline onto this fire you've discovered."

Panjay turned away to hide the tears that jeweled her eyes. Her mind was filled with the faces of all of the people in the village where she ran her clinic. Half were already dead, the rest sick. She understood what Hlasek and Smithwick were saying, could accept the reality of it, but just as certainly she knew that it was a death sentence for everyone in the village. Maybe for everyone in the region.

She could feel the eyes of the other doctors on her, and though it cost her to do it, she nodded her acceptance.

"Very good," said Hlasek. "I'll make the necessary calls to get things in motion. We need to make sure that everyone else who knows about this is brought into our confidence. It's important that everyone be made to understand the vital importance of keeping this quiet until we're ready to move. Who else have you told?"

"Just the people in the village," Panjay said thickly. "And my two nurses. They're at the clinic."

"I don't mean to be indelicate," said Hlasek, "but what race are they? This disease affects sub-Saharan blacks, as you know. We'll need to rely on those persons who are not likely to become infected; otherwise we'll lose our workforce. Our ground troops, so to speak."

Panjay cleared her throat. "Both of my nurses are African. Black African. One from Angola, the other from Ghana. We've taken every prophylactic measure—"

"I'm sure that will be fine. I'll call them myself at the clinic. And we'll get a truckload of supplies out this afternoon."

She stood up. "Dr. Panjay, Dr. Smithwick, you probably think I'm a heartless monster, but please let me assure you that I appreciate the seriousness of this, and I respect the work you've put in here. I also want to thank you for bringing this directly to me. We will work together to do whatever is necessary to get in front of this dreadful matter." She extended her hand and they all shook. Hlasek remained standing as Smithwick and Panjay left.

When they were gone, Hlasek sank back into her chair and stared at the stack of lab reports for a long minute. Then she picked up her phone and punched a long international number.

"Otto?" she said when the call was answered. "We have a problem."

"Tell me."

She told him everything that Panjay and Smithwick had told her. The man on the other end of the call, Otto Wirths, listened patiently and then sighed.

"That was careless, Arjeta. We shouldn't be at this point for three days." He made a clucking sound of disapproval. "You're sure that only four people know about this? The two doctors and the nurses?"

"Yes. They came to me first."

"How long before anyone else is likely to make the same kind of report?"

"I don't know . . . it's still confined to the Akpro-

Missérété Commune. I can quarantine it quietly. Say, two weeks. Three at the outside."

"We only need a week," he said, "but we need the full week. Find out what hotel the doctors are staying in."

"I don't want any of this to land on me, Otto. Headlines won't help."

Otto laughed. "An electrical fire in a cheap hotel in Cotonou will barely make headlines even *in* Cotonou. And as for the nurses . . . something will be arranged."

"Do whatever you have to do, but keep me out of it."

Otto chuckled again and disconnected.

Dr. Hlasek hung up the phone and stared at the stack of reports. Then she stood up, straightened her skirt, picked up the reports on the sickle-cell outbreak, and carried them over to the paper shredder.

Chapter Fifteen

Druid Hill Park, Baltimore, Maryland
Saturday, August 28, 10:13 A.M.
Time Remaining on Extinction Clock: 97 hours, 47 minutes

I drove randomly for another hour, then pulled in behind a Cineplex and swapped license plates with another car. I stopped in a McDonald's to wash up as best I could, and then I closed myself in a toilet stall, leaned against the wall, and tried to sort this out. The reality of what was happening caught up to me again, and shock outran adrenaline. My hands were shaking and I forced myself to go still and quiet, taking long, deep breaths until the panic eased its stranglehold on my nerves.

I was on the run from the NSA, and there was a real possibility that the whole DMS could get torn down. If that happened I was screwed. I'd already passed up the opportunity to start at the FBI academy. My old job with Baltimore PD was probably still there if it came to that, but a bad report in my jacket wouldn't do much for my career.

The main thing, though, was that since I've been running Echo Team for the DMS I've seen a much bigger picture of the world and how it works—and of the major wackos who were trying to burn it down. The DMS was doing good work here; I knew that for a fact. Hell, even *I* was doing good work here. Having this organization destroyed would do a lot more harm than just screwing up my career path. How could the Vice President not see the value of the Department of Military Sciences? Hell, we'd saved his wife's life less than two months ago.

I guess my problem was that I found it hard to buy that the Vice President was doing this because he believed Church was blackmailing the President. That didn't feel right. Maybe I'm getting cynical in my old age, but it seemed to me that there had to be some kind of hidden agenda.

Of course, there was about one chance in a zillion that I'd ever find out what it was. Maybe Church would, if he wasn't in jail. I tried calling him but got no answer. Swell.

The smell of the bathroom brought me back to the moment and I washed my hands again and left the grungy little room. Outside I bought a sack of burgers and a Coke, then got back in the car and drove to Druid Hill Park in northwestern Baltimore. I parked the car and walked into the park, wolfing down the burgers to put some protein in my system. After wandering around to make sure that I had nobody dogging me, I sat cross-legged on one of the tables inside Parkie's Lakeside Pavilion and pulled my cell.

This time Church answered on the second ring. He never says "hello." He simply listens. You called him, so it's on you to take the conversational ball and run with it.

"I'm having a moderately trying morning, boss," I said.

"Where are you?"

I told him. "What's the status on my team?"

"I'll tell you, Captain, but in the event that anyone is within visual range of you I want you to keep everything off your face. This isn't good news."

He told me about Big Bob Faraday. There was no one else in the Pavilion, but I kept it off my face. I also made sure to keep it out of my voice, too, but inside there was an acid burn working its way from my gut to my brain.

"These were Russians?" I asked, and from the tone of my voice you might have thought I was asking about last season's baseball scores. "Care to explain how my team gets ambushed by Russian shooters in Wilmington?"

"We're short on answers today. We're running their prints through NCIC and Interpol. Too soon for returns, but I suspect we'll get something."

"Since when does the NSA hire out hits to the Russians?"

"They don't, and as of now we have no evidence of a connection between Wilmington and the NSA other than the bad luck of this happening on the same day as the Veep's run at the DMS."

"You don't think they're related?"

"I said that we have no evidence of that. And, let's face it, that isn't a likely scenario." He paused. "Actually, a lot of unusual things have happened in the last twenty-four hours, Captain. Some old colleagues of mine have died under unusual circumstances over the last few weeks, and I just got word that a close friend of mine was killed in Stuttgart yesterday."

"Sorry to hear that. Is that related to this NSA stuff?"

"Again, we have no evidence of it, but my tolerance for coincidence is burning away pretty quickly."

"I hear you." I sighed. "Is Big Bob going to make it?"

"Too soon to tell. He's at a good hospital and getting top-quality care, but he had a collapsed lung and damage to his liver, his right kidney, and his spleen. He'll probably lose the spleen and, unless he's very lucky, part or all of one kidney."

"When this NSA bullshit blows over I'm going to run this down," I said.

"I have no doubt. Use whatever resources you need. Carte blanche."

"Thanks."

"Losing men is hard, Captain. It never gets easier."

"No, it fucking well doesn't . . . and it pisses me off that I can't be there with my guys because of this bullshit." I only had three active operatives in Echo Team. There were six others almost ready to join, but they were in Scotland doing some field training with a crack team from Barrier, the U.K.'s most covert special ops unit. With Big Bob down that left Top and Bunny. It made me feel like they were suddenly vulnerable.

"For what it's worth, you're not the only one on the VP's most hated list. There are two NSA agents in the hospital in Brooklyn. They attempted to forcibly arrest

Aunt Sallie, but that didn't go as they expected. Some convalescent leave and a few months of physical therapy and they'll be fine."

"Ouch."

Church said, "There's more, and this probably does have something to do with Wilmington. We've lost touch with the Jigsaw Team out in Denver."

"The whole team?"

"Yes. The Hub itself went into lockdown, but Jigsaw was on a mission and went radio silent about thirty minutes before the NSA started trying to kick doors."

The Hub was the Denver DMS facility. I'd worked only one three-day operation with Jigsaw and they were very tough hombres. Their leader, Hack Peterson, was ex–Delta Force and he looked like he ate pit bulls for breakfast.

"Do you see the NSA taking the whole team into custody, 'cause I don't."

"Captain Peterson may have gotten a sniff and gone dark," said Church. "But I have a bad feeling about it. I'd like you to head out there."

"When?"

"Now. I'll have someone pick you up at the park. You'll recognize the driver. Be at the exit closest to I-Eighty-three, say twenty minutes."

"Um . . . hate to break this to you, but this might not be the best time for travel. The U.S. government seems to want my head on a pole."

"Cry me a river," said Church. "I need you in Denver. I have private transport waiting in several secure locations." He read them off to me and gave me a rendezvous timetable. "Get to one of those and head west. First Sergeant Sims and Sergeant Rabbit already arrived at the first location. I was going to have them wait for you, but just in case you're taken I've sent them on ahead. They'll meet you at the other end."

Son of a bitch moved fast.

"Normally I'd wait on this and let the Los Angeles office deal with it, but they're in lockdown and you're the only senior officer on the streets. Besides," he said, "the Denver thing looks like it's going to break big."

"Meaning . . . ?"

"Meaning that it's starting to look like a DMS project. There's a high probability it's tied to the deaths of my colleagues overseas, and to some old cases that were supposed to have been closed a long time ago. Now it seems that we were wrong. Once you're airborne you'll teleconference with Dr. Hu, who will send you a feed of a video we received from an anonymous source."

"A video of what?"

"I'd prefer you watch and form your own opinions, but . . . it's compelling."

"Can you vague that up a little for me?" I said.

He ignored me. "Contact me when you've watched it. This is a bad day, Captain, and tensions are running high. I need you to be cool. Tell your people the same thing. This other matter, the Denver job . . . if it turns out to be what I think it is, then it's big."

"Bigger than the Vice President launching a witch hunt?"

"Potentially," he said.

"Swell. Okay, I'll go see what I can do . . . but one last thing about the Vice President: if anyone else at the DMS gets hurt because of this—politically, legally, or otherwise—then I'm going to want to do some damage."

"Are you talking about revenge, Captain?"

"And what if I am?" I snapped.

There was a sound. It might have been a short laugh. "I just wanted to make sure we were on the same page."

With that he disconnected.

Chapter Sixteen

Baltimore, Maryland
Saturday, August 28, 10:15 A.M.
Time Remaining on Extinction Clock: 97 hours, 45 minutes

Mr. Church closed his phone and laid it on the desk in front of him. He was a big man, broad shouldered, blocky, strong. There were gray streaks in his dark hair and old scars on his face, but rather than serving to reveal his age they stood as marks of use; their presence toughened him in ways the people who knew him could recognize but not define.

For over a minute he sat with his big hands resting on either side of the phone, which sat just off-center of the green desk blotter. He might have been a statue for all the animation he betrayed. His eyes were only shadows behind the lenses of his tinted glasses.

To his left was a glass of water, no ice. Beside it was a plate of vanilla wafers. After he'd sat for two full minutes, Mr. Church selected a cookie and bit off a piece, munching it thoughtfully. He brushed a crumb from his red tie.

Then he swiveled in his chair and reached for his office phone. He punched a code to engage the scrambler and then entered a special number. It was answered on the fourth ring.

"Brierly," said a crisp male voice.

"Linden," said Church, "I know you're busy, but I want you to listen very closely. This is a Brushfire Command Protocol."

"Ah," said Brierly, "it's you. I was hoping you lost my number."

"Sorry to disappoint. Please verify that you're on active scramble so we may proceed."

Brierly made a sound that might have been a curse, but he verified the scramble. Linden was the Regional Director of the Secret Service and was directly responsible for overseeing the safety of the President while the Commander in Chief was in Walter Reed for his heart surgery. One slip and Brierly would be working out of a field office in the Dakotas. A successful job, on the other hand, could be the last résumé item needed for the step up as overall Director of the Secret Service, which would make Brierly the youngest man to hold that office. The hot money—and the heavy pressure—was on him during the current crisis.

"Here is the Brushfire code," said Church, and recited a number-letter string that identified him and his authority to make this call.

Brierly read back the code, moving one digit and adding another.

Church repeated the code and made his own two-point change.

"Verified," said Brierly. "Brushfire Protocol is active."

"I agree," said Church.

"You just activated a Presidential Alert, my friend. We'd better have missiles inbound or Martians on the White House lawn. You *do* know what's happening today?" Even with the mild audio distortion of the scrambler, Brierly's sarcasm was clear as a bell.

Church said ten words: "The Vice President is trying to take down the DMS."

"What?"

Church explained.

"Jesus H. Christ, Esquire," Brierly growled, "the President will fry him for this. I mean *fry* him. Even if he has the Attorney General in his corner, Collins can't possibly believe that he's going to make a case against you."

"He seems to think so."

"This is weird. I know him pretty well, and this is not like him. For one thing, he doesn't have the *balls* for this."

"Then he grew a set this morning. For now let's assume he wouldn't attempt this kind of play if he didn't have some interesting cards in his hand. What they are and how he'll ultimately play them is still to be seen."

"I'm starting to get a bad feeling about why you called me."

"Listen to me, Linden. If the VP gets MindReader he also gets everything stored *in* MindReader. Take a moment and think that through."

Brierly didn't need a moment. "Christ!"

"Yes."

"Can't you take it offline? Dump the hard drive and wipe it with an EMP?"

"Sure, and we'd lose active tactical analysis on forty-six terrorist-related database searches, including the two assassination plots your office sent to us. If MindReader goes blind, then so does the Secret Service, a good chunk of the DEA, CIA, FBI, and ATF, and Homeland will essentially have its head in a bag. We lose our data sharing with MI6 and Barrier, not to mention certain agencies in Germany, Italy, and France. We'd be playing Texas hold 'em with blank cards."

"Jesus, Mary, and Joseph, Church . . . you should have shared this system with everyone from the start."

"Really? You'd personally like to see everyone from the VP on down have total access to your records? You'd want to grant everyone in every agency the ability to read all secrets and access all files without leaving a footprint? You'd want all of the President's personal business made public?"

"I—"

"Two words, Linden: 'Houston Marriott.' "

Brierly hissed, "Don't even joke."

"I'm not joking, and I'm not threatening. With the President out of power, MindReader and the DMS are vulnerable. I'll hold the line, but I don't think either of us want to see what happens if this turns into a shoving match between the NSA and my boys."

"They have you outnumbered and outgunned, Church."

"You've met Major Courtland and Captain Ledger, I believe. You've seen them in action. Where would you place your heavy bets?"

"This isn't the O.K. Corral."

"It shouldn't be," Church agreed, "but the VP is making a hard play. He's well organized, too, and using a lot of field resources. None of this went through e-mails or active command software packages, so he must have set it all up via cell phone or word of mouth. He knows enough about MindReader to do an end run around it for this operation."

"You sound calm about it," Brierly said.

Church bit a cookie, said nothing.

"You're describing a coup."

"No, this isn't directed against the President, and the VP will probably yield power in the proper way and at the proper time. But ultimately this could bring down the presidency. Maybe the VP knows that, maybe he doesn't . . . but the effect will be the same. So, indirectly this is an attack against the President."

"No kidding."

"This is time critical for another reason," Church said. "We've just started picking up the threads of something that could be a significant threat. That's Threat with a capital *T*. We're probably already coming into this late—that's the nature of these things—but with all of my people dodging the NSA or gone to ground we could fall completely behind the curve. I need the Vice President to call off the dogs so we can get back to work."

Brierly sighed. "What do you want me to do?"

"What do your loyalties suggest you do?"

"Switching jobs sounds good right now. I hear they're hiring at Best Buy."

Church crunched his cookie, drank some water, waited.

"It's not like I can strong-arm a doctor and force him to revive the President. He's in recovery now, but there are protocols."

"Yes, and Brushfire is one of them."

"I'm going to lose my job over this."

"Not if the President takes control before we lose MindReader."

Brierly was a long time thinking it through. Church had time for a second cookie.

"Okay," Brierly said, "but when the Commander in Chief is back on the checkerboard I'm going to dump all the blame on you."

"Not a problem."

"And what if we fail? What if the Veep gets control of your records?"

"That might require alternatives you cannot hear from me. Not even unofficially."

Brierly cursed.

"Linden," said Church quietly, "this is not a fight of my choosing, and I don't know why the VP is risking so much here, but we cannot let MindReader be taken. It's your job to make sure I don't need to get creative while trying to keep it."

" 'Creative' doesn't sound like a very nice option."

"It isn't," said Church. "So let's both do what we need to do to keep that option off the table. I'll do what I can for as long as I can, but I'd like to hear a clear weather report from you soon."

"Okay. I'll find the chief of surgery and see if I can appeal to his patriotism."

"You know my number," Church said, and disconnected.

He set the phone down on his desk blotter. He laid his hands on either side of it and sat quietly in the stillness of his office.

Chapter Seventeen

"They're landing," Otto said as he set down the phone.

He and Cyrus stood in the command center of the Deck. All around them hundreds of technicians were busy at computer workstations. A second tier of workstations was built onto a metal veranda that circled the central area. The *clackity-clack* of all those fingers on all those keys was music to Cyrus's ears.

Below the command center, visible through clear glass panels in the floor, were two isolated cold rooms. The left-hand one was crowded with fifty networked 454 Life Sciences sequencers. Technicians in white self-contained smart suits worked among the computers, constantly checking their functions and monitoring every minute change. The right-hand room looked like a brewery in which vast tanks worked around the clock to grow viruses.

The tank directly below Cyrus's feet was dedicated to mass-producing a weaponized version of the human papillomavirus that had been genetically altered to target Hispanics. Sure, there was crossover to some white population because racial purity was—sadly, as far as Cyrus and Otto were concerned—more myth than truth, but the rate of cervical cancer for female Hispanics was 85 percent and the crossover to Caucasians only 6 percent. The synthetic growth medium they were currently using allowed for a 400 percent increase in growth time.

The tanks had been running so long now that Otto estimated that they would have enough to use it to launch the second phase of the Extinction Wave in sixteen weeks rather than the previously anticipated thirty months. Cyrus only wished that they'd settled on this new method last year so that it would have been ready with the rest of the first phase.

Thinking about it made Cyrus want to scream, to run and shout with joy.

"We should close up," advised Otto.

"I know; I know." Cyrus waved his hand peevishly. "It's just that I hate to do it."

"We can't let the Twins see—"

Cyrus silenced him with a look.

"They probably won't even come in here." However, Cyrus knew that Otto was quite right. Taking chances was never good at the best of times, but with the Extinction Wave so close—so wonderfully, delightfully close— nothing could be left to chance. And neither of them trusted the Twins.

"I wish we could bring them in," said Cyrus.

Otto turned away so Cyrus wouldn't see him roll his eyes. This was an argument that had started before the Twins had hit puberty, and he and Cyrus had come at it from every possible angle too many times to count.

"Everything in their psych profiles suggests that they would oppose the Wave."

"I know."

"Their ideologies are too—"

"*I know.*"

Otto pursed his lips.

"Mr. Cyrus, their plane is touching down as we speak."

Cyrus sighed. "Very well, damn it." He flapped his hand and turned away.

He walked slowly away, hands clasped behind his back, head bowed thoughtfully. At the door he paused and turned to watch as steel panels slid slowly into place to hide the rooms below. Heavy hydraulics kicked in and Cyrus glanced up as shutters rolled into place to hide nearly 80 percent of the technicians. A faux wall rose up to cover a half-mile-long corridor that connected the Deck to the viral storage facility buried under the hot Arizona sands. The whole process took less than three minutes, and when it was completed the room looked small, almost quaint. High-tech to be sure, but on a scale suited only for research rather than mass production. Cyrus sighed again. It depressed him to have to hide this from his own children. Just as it depressed him that his children were such serious disappointments.

"I'll be in the garden," he said to Otto. "Bring them to me there."

Otto bowed and watched him go.

Chapter Eighteen

The Deck
Saturday, August 28, 10:22 A.M.
Time Remaining on Extinction Clock: 97 hours,
38 minutes E.S.T.

Paris's cell rang as their plane was rolling to a stop on the tarmac.

"Yes?" he answered in a musical voice.

"It's me," said J. P. Sunderland.

"And—"

"It's a wash. We hit all of the DMS bases likely to have a MindReader substation, but without an Executive Order to shoot, the best we could manage was a standoff. Actually, kiddo," Sunderland said, "we have several agents in the hospital and ears are up in local and regional law coast to coast. The Vice President is probably going to get his ass dragged before a subcommittee for this."

"So," Paris said with ice, "basically you fucked it up."

"Basically, yes."

"You could at least sound contrite."

"Blow me, snowball," said Sunderland. There was no heat in his voice; there never was. He was too practiced a game player to let any bad hand of cards, or even a bad run of cards, fracture his cool. "This was a fifty-fifty at best and we all knew that going in. You and your sister called this play. I was against it from the start, as you well know. It's a waste of resources that could have been better used further down the road."

"We need that system. Without MindReader the money train's going to slow to a halt, J.P."

"I'll practice singing the blues later. Right now it looks like the NSA will be stalled long enough for the power to shift back to the President. And, like I said, we may lose the Vice President over this."

"What a pity," drawled Paris. "That would bring the free world to its knees."

"Okay, fair enough, who cares if he sinks? Point is, the NSA ploy would have had more pop to it if we'd used it when the big man was dead."

"Who?"

"Who do you think?"

Paris laughed. "What are you saying? That you plan

to have Church whacked?" He liked saying the word "whacked."

"Me? Hell no . . . but there's a rumor in the wind that there's a contract out on him. Church and a few other troublemakers. If I didn't know your dad was on a leash I'd say it was his kind of play. Doesn't really matter, though. With any luck whoever has the contract will close it out before all the dust from today's cluster fuck settles down. Otherwise Church might start looking around to see what's in the wind, which is exactly what none of us wanted."

Hecate had been leaning close to Paris in order to hear the conversation. Their eyes met and they shared a "he has a point" look.

"So now what?" Paris asked.

"Now we let the NSA thing play out. It'll still take a while for the President to take back the reins, so we've still effectively hobbled the DMS for the rest of today. Maybe into tomorrow, but that's starting to look like wishful thinking. After that we let the Vice President play the rest of his cards. Throw some scapegoats to the congressional wolves, yada yada . . . and then go to the next phase."

Paris looked at Hecate, who nodded.

"Okay, J.P. You have any other ideas for how to get hold of MindReader?"

"A few," Sunderland said. "But nothing we can try until after Church is out of the mix."

"Shit."

Sunderland chuckled. It was the deep, throaty, hungry laugh of a bear who had a salmon gasping on the riverbank.

"Now," he said, "let's talk about Denver."

Chapter Nineteen

I was waiting by the exit for my ride when my phone rang. I looked at the screen. Grace. Normally that would make me smile, but I had a flash of panic wondering if something bad had happened to her.

"Hello?"

"Joe . . . ," she said, sounding on edge.

"Hey," I said. "Eggs?" A coded query about scramblers.

"Of course, you sodding twit."

"Nice language. You kiss the Prime Minister with that mouth?"

She told me to sod off, but she said it with a laugh. I breathed a sigh of relief.

Grace Courtland, an agent for the British government and now head of the Baltimore Regional Office of the DMS, was one-third my local boss, one-third a comrade in arms who had stood with me in several of the weirdest and most terrible battles since I'd started working for the G, and one-third my girlfriend—and if anyone has ever had a more interesting, complex, and smoking-hot girlfriend, I never heard about it. The relationship was not a public thing; we were trying to keep it off the public record, though we were both realistic enough to accept that we were working with about a hundred class-A trained observers, so our little clandestine fling was probably old news in the pipeline.

"I'm glad to hear your voice," I said.

"Glad to hear you, too," she said. "I had images of you in the back of an NSA car with a sodding black bag over your head."

"It's not for a lack of them trying. I hope you're not calling with more bad news. I'm going to stop answering my phone."

"Yes. I heard about your man Faraday," she said. "Bloody awful, Joe. I'm so sorry."

I knew she meant it. Grace had lost a lot of people in the years she'd been one of Church's field commanders.

"Thanks."

Grace was on semi-permanent loan to the DMS from Barrier, a group in the U.K. that was a model for rapid-response science-based threat groups like ours. Church had asked for her personally, and he usually got what he wanted.

"I have some updated info for you, though," she said. "Jerry Spencer is at the crime scene now. Some of Mr. Church's friends in Wilmington were able to float false credentials for him. He's at Gilpin's apartment and will call in as soon as the smoke clears."

"That's something." I felt a flicker of relief. Jerry Spencer was a former D.C. cop who'd put in twenty-plus as a homicide dick before acting as DCPD's contribution to the same Homeland Security task force I'd worked. He could work a crime scene like no one else I ever met, and there had been some talk about the FBI recruiting him away to teach at Quantico once Jerry finished his twenty-five with D.C., but the DMS got to him first and now he runs our crime lab.

"Grace, it's nice to know that the DMS hasn't been forced to completely close up shop today. I guess you already know about Denver?"

"Yes. I tried to get the go-ahead to take Alpha Team out there, but we're buttoned up too tightly here. Church tells me that Top and Bunny are on their way out there and that you'll be joining them."

"Did he tell you about the friends of his who have been killed?"

"He mentioned it, but he hasn't gone into details yet. He also said something about a video I'm supposed to watch when I get a moment. No idea what's on it, but Church seemed pretty upset."

I smiled at the thought. "Church? Upset? How can you tell?"

"His tie was ever so slightly askew. With him that's a sign of the apocalypse. He's the only bloke I know who would probably show up to his own autopsy in a freshly pressed suit and talk the doctor through the postmortem."

"No joke. But, listen, do you have any idea what's brewing? Church is being even more cryptic than usual."

"He's that way when he's caught off-guard. He plays it close until he knows the shape of it and then he drops it all on us. If he's stalling us that means he's digging for information himself." She paused. "I suspect, my dear, that your cynical mind is traveling on the same routes as mine."

"Yep. We've had stuff come at us this way before. A bit here, a fragment there, and suddenly we're ass deep in it. I hate this part of the job, Grace. I feel like someone's lit a fuse and all we can see is a little smoke."

"Too bloody right. Whatever this is, it's tied to something stored at a facility in Denver, Russians are involved, and it has something to do with computer theft. Plus I got a faint whiff of the Cold War from something Church said. When he was telling me about the colleagues that had been killed he mentioned they were mostly from the U.K. and Germany, and that they worked together on projects in the early eighties."

"Germany and Russia, the U.K. and America. You're right, Cold War's a good call," I said. "I can't wait to see this video. But more than that, I want to get into this game. I know it's not the right way to look at it, but going to Denver feels like running away from this thing."

"I know. And I feel like I'm locked in a cage." She let out a breath. "So . . . how are you holding up, mate?"

"Oh, just peachy, babe."

" 'Babe'?"

"Sorry. *Major* Babe."

"Bloody Yanks," she complained.

The realities of the moment couldn't support jovial banter and it collapsed around us.

"It's funny," I said, "but there are always guys you think have some kind of Kevlar painted on them, guys that are never the ones to take a hit, and Big Bob had that in spades." After my initial DMS mission had cut Echo Team in half, Big Bob had been the first new guy we signed on. Big Bob was affable, diligent, and though he could storm hell with the best of them, he had a gentle heart. My mind suddenly twitched when I realized that I'd already begun to categorize his virtues the way you do when someone dies. "He's a fighter," I said lamely.

"That he is."

I saw a car approach and the driver flicked his lights on and off.

"My ride's here. Got to go."

"Me, too. I've got a bunch of NSA lads outside who

have their knickers in a knot. I'd better go see if I can sort them out."

"Take care of yourself, babe."

"That's *Major* Babe."

"Yes, it is," I said.

"Be careful, Joe," she said, but before I could reply she'd hung up. It may have been her thick London accent, it may have been the distortion of the scrambled phone, or it may have been my own screwy emotions . . . but it almost sounded like she said, "Be careful, love." I thought about it. Nah . . . she'd never let herself get into that kind of emotional quagmire. Not with a colleague.

Would she?

I closed the phone and closed my eyes for a moment, indulging in a memory of the last time I saw Grace. Yesterday morning as she left my bed. Tall and tan and fit, with extraordinary legs, lush curves, and eyes that could make me melt or instantly charge me with electricity. I'd never met anyone like her, and I counted my blessings every day that I had found her at all. It was a crying shame that we'd met as fellow officers in the ongoing war against terror, a war that had no end in sight. Wars are great breeding grounds for enduring love, but warriors should never allow themselves to fall in love. It made the risks that much worse.

I opened my eyes and watched the car approach, forcibly shifting my mind back to the crisis du jour.

Chapter Twenty

Maj. Grace Courtland was slender, very pretty, and thoroughly pissed off. The only thing keeping her from leaping at the NSA Agent in Charge was a double row of electrified fence and her last shreds of self-control.

The AIC was a big blond-haired jock type with mirrored sunglasses and a wire behind his ear. Five other agents were spread out behind him like a Spartan phalanx, and the street in front of the Department of Military Sciences' Baltimore Regional Tactical Field Office—the Warehouse for short—was jammed with government vehicles of every make and model.

Major Courtland had only two guards with her: McGoran and Tafoya, a pair of hard-eyed former MPs who had been headhunted by the DMS. The guards wore khakis and three-button Polo shirts in the August heat. Both of them held M4s at port arms. Neither was smiling.

The AIC was shouting at Grace. "I have a federal warrant to search and seize this building and all its contents, and an arrest warrant for Major Grace Courtland, Dr. William Hu, Captain Joseph Ledger, and Mr. Church—no first name given."

"Wipe your ass with it," said Grace.

"This base is federal property, Major, and this is a duly served warrant."

Grace folded her arms across her chest. "By Executive

Order G15/DMS Directive Seventy-one I am denying you access to this secure facility."

The AIC growled and shook his warrant at her. "*This* Executive Order officially rescinds any previous directive and places this entire facility under the authority of the National Security Agency. I am ordering you to shut down the power to this fence, open the gates, and surrender to my team."

Grace leaned as close to the fence as she dared, aware of the dull musical hum of ten thousand volts flooding through the chain links. She crooked a finger at the AIC and he bent forward, apparently thinking she wanted to speak in confidence.

Instead she pointed at the document he held in front of his chest like a shield. "Notice anything?" she asked with a smile.

Even looking at it from his side, the AIC could see the glow of a red pinpoint of hot light. The light held on the center of the paper, and its filtered glow brushed the AIC's shirt, just to the left of his tie.

"Now look at your men," Grace murmured.

Moving very cautiously, the AIC turned his head first to the left and then to the right and saw half a dozen red laser sights dancing in tight clusters on each agent's chest.

The AIC looked up at the windows of the Warehouse. The sashes were up and the rooms in darkness. He saw no gun barrels, but he was experienced enough to recognize the threat. Snipers don't stick gun barrels out a window; they sit back in the shadows where their guns and scopes won't reflect sunlight and there in the quiet darkness they pick their kill shots. However, even from that distance he could see the flicker of red laser lights in virtually every window. His face went pale beneath his volleyball tan.

"Are you out of your goddamned mind, Major?"

"I'm barking mad," she agreed.

"Harm any of us and you'll be committing treason. We have legal authority to—"

She cut him off. "You force this play and we'll all regret how this turns out."

Five more red lights appeared on the AIC's chest.

"I—," he started to say, but he was truly at a loss.

"Here's how we're going to play this," Grace said, her cat green eyes flashing. "You and your Huns are going to stop trying to storm the castle. Go sit in your cars. Feel free to make any calls you want. Leave or stay, but until both of our bosses get this sorted out you are going to stop waving paper in my face and stop making threats. You don't lose face that way. But hear me on this and make no mistake: You are not getting inside this compound. Not on my watch."

"You're going to regret this, Major."

"I regret a lot of things. Now kindly piss off."

She stepped back from the fence. The laser lights followed the NSA agents back to their cars, and over the next hour the lights caressed the windows of each parked vehicle. When more NSA cars pulled up to reinforce the siege, more laser sights reached out to remind everyone of who held the tactical high ground. Above them the sun slowly burned away the minutes of the day.

Chapter Twenty-One

J. P. Sunderland closed his phone and sighed, then cut a covert glance at Vice President Bill Collins, who was sitting at his desk with his head in his hands.

Sunderland cleared his throat. "That was Mike Denniger, my man inside the Secret Service."

That made the Vice President jerk his head up. "Did anything happen to the President?"

"That hopeful look on your face doesn't speak well of the depth of your compassion," Sunderland drawled. When Collins's only response was a glare, he said, "Denniger said that there's been a lot of quiet conversations between Linden Brierly and the doctors. He wasn't privy to the conversations, but he got the impression the doctors were arguing with Brierly. My guess is that someone got to Brierly to try and hurry up the process of waking up the President."

"That's got to be Church."

"Not through official channels."

"He doesn't *use* official channels."

"No, I guess he doesn't."

They sat in silence as seconds fell from the clock in handfuls. Finally Collins said, "So, what's our move? Wait until the President is awake and pissed off and then throw him the scapegoat, or should we play it like we figured out that we were duped and go to the Attorney General first? Lay out the story for him, keep him on our side."

Sunderland considered. Despite the calm expression

on his face, he was sweating heavily. He absently patted his pocket to make sure the bottle of nitro tablets was there.

"There's still a chance—an outside chance of course—that we'll still nab MindReader before the President is awake and in power," said Sunderland. "Even if Brierly bullies the docs into doing something, we probably still have six, seven hours. So . . . let's use the time."

"To do what? Cross our fingers?"

"Might help."

Collins almost laughed. "Christ."

"Denniger will give me a heads-up if things start happening at Walter Reed. If it looks like this is totally played out, then you can call the AG. It's the best way, Bill. If you move too soon you look weak, if you let the President slap you down you look criminal, but if you save the day in the eleventh hour you're a goddamn hero."

"And if we snag MindReader in the meantime?"

"Then you'll very quietly become the richest Vice President in history." Sunderland mopped his smiling face. "Either way, you can't lose."

"Christ, don't say that," Collins snapped. ". . . You'll jinx me."

Chapter Twenty-Two

Druid Hill Park, Baltimore, Maryland
Saturday, August 28, 10:41 A.M.
Time Remaining on the Extinction Clock: 97 hours, 27 minutes

The car pulled to the curb and I bent down to peer through the passenger window at the man behind the wheel.

Dr. Rudy Sanchez grinned nervously at me. "Hey, sailor, new in town?"

"Hilarious," I said as I climbed in.

Rudy is shorter and rounder than me and usually drives a roomy Cadillac DTS, but now I was crammed into a twenty-year-old Geo Prizm with no legroom.

"What the hell's this?"

"Mr. Church told me to be nondescript, so I borrowed it from my secretary, Kittie. I told her I had an emergency and that my car was in the shop. I gave her cab fare home."

The car was a patchwork of dusty gold and primer gray. The interior smelled of cigarettes. A pine-tree-shaped deodorizer hung in total defeat from the rearview mirror.

"Jeez, Rude, you gotta pay that gal better. My grandmother wouldn't drive this."

"Your grandmother's dead."

"And she still wouldn't drive anything this crappy."

"It's a good car, and it's nondescript as ordered. Besides, being a prima donna isn't becoming to a fugitive."

"Shut up and drive," I grumbled.

He said something inappropriate in gutter Spanish as he went up the ramp to I-83. Rudy seemed to know where he was going. For the first few minutes he said nothing, but even with the air-conditioning at full blast he was still perspiring.

"How'd you get roped into playing chauffeur?"

"I wasn't at the Warehouse when all this started happening. El Jefe called and said to come and pick you up."

"How much do you know?"

"Enough to scare me half to death." A minute later he said, "I hate politicians."

There was nothing to argue with, so we kept driving.

Later he said, "I can't believe I'm aiding and abetting someone wanted by the National Security Agency. I can't believe that someone is my best friend. And I can't believe that the Vice President of the United States of America would trump up charges just to further his own political aims." Half a mile later he added, "No, I can believe that . . . I just hate that it's true."

"Not happy about it myself. Of course, the charges aren't entirely groundless, Rude."

Rudy breathed in and out through his nose. "I hate that, too. I mean . . . we both believe that Church is a good guy, maybe even *the* good guy. If there is anyone with the strength of will and the solidity of moral compass to not misuse something like MindReader, then it's him. I'm not sure I'd be able to resist the temptation. That said, how screwed up is our world that it takes blackmailing the President and members of Congress to allow us to do our jobs, considering that our jobs involve stopping terrorists of the most extreme kind? Tell me, Joe, how does that sound like a sane world?"

"You're the shrink, brother; you tell me."

"If I could figure out the logic behind the way the political mind thinks, I'd write a bestseller and spend the next two years on the talk show circuit."

"Beats driving fugitives around in a hooptie."

"Most things do. So . . . how are you, Cowboy?"

"Not happy about the way things are spinning. And worried about Big Bob."

"Can we call the hospital to check on him?"

"We shouldn't. He's registered under a false name so the NSA can't find him. Church is fielding the info about him. He'll update us."

Rudy's knuckles were white where he gripped the wheel and every few blocks he cut a look my way.

Before he could ask, I said, "Yes."

"Yes what?"

"Yes, I'm feeling it. Big Bob. The NSA. I'm feeling it."

"It's okay to show it, to let it out."

I nodded. "In the right place and at the right time."

"Which isn't now?"

"No."

"Even with me?"

"Rude," I said, "you're my best friend and you're my shrink, so you get a lot of leeway most folks don't get. You can ask me anything, and probably eventually I'll tell you everything. But not right now."

"You've had a lot of stress today, Cowboy. Are you the best person to make that call?"

I nodded. "When the soldier comes home from the war the shrinks call all the shots. They poke and prod and ask and ponder to separate the soldier from the stress of combat, to free him from the thunder of the battlefield."

"Ah," he said, his eyebrows arching, "but we're still *on* the battlefield."

"Yep."

"You believe that we're in the middle of something."

"Yep."

"Something bigger than the NSA? This Russian thing, whatever it is."

"Whatever it is, yes," I said.

"So. Now's not the time to debrief."

"Right."

He nodded. Rudy is the best of companions. He knows when to stop harping on a point, and he knows how to give space, even in the cramped confines of a compact car. We drove the rest of the way in silence.

We took the first exit off the JFX and headed west and north on a number of seemingly random roads, but then twenty minutes later Rudy pulled onto a rural road and drove a crooked mile to an upscale small private airfield. He made a bunch of turns until finally pulling to a stop fifty feet from a sleek late-model Learjet.

The stairs were down and the pilot sat on the top step reading *Forbes* and sipping Starbucks out of a paper cup. As we parked he folded the magazine and came down the steps to meet us.

"Captain Ledger?" he said, offering his hand. "Marty Hanler."

I smiled. "Marty Hanler . . . the writer?"

"Yep."

Rudy whistled. Hanler's espionage thrillers always hit the number one spot on the bestseller lists. Four of them had been made into movies. Matt Damon was in the last one and I had the DVD at home.

"You going with us?" I asked.

"Be more efficient that way," he said. "I'm flying this bird."

Rudy blinked.

Hanler was amused by our reactions. "A buddy of mine called me and said you needed a lift."

"A 'buddy'?" I asked.

"Yeah. Your boss, the Deacon."

"He's . . . your 'buddy'?"

Hanler was in his mid-sixties, with receding gray hair

and a deep-water tan. Bright blue eyes and great teeth. He winked. "I didn't always write books, fellas."

"Ah," I said. His handshake had been rock hard and he had that *look* that I've seen in other old pros. The "been there, done that, buried them" sort of look.

"Come on," he said. "The Deacon asked me to fly you to Denver."

"Good luck, Joe," Rudy said, and I turned in surprise.

"Wait . . . you're not coming with me?"

He shook his head. "Church wants me local so that I can help the staff deal with everything that's going on."

"And who's going to help *you* with this crap?"

"My good friend Jose Cuervo."

"Ah," I said. We shook hands. "In the meantime, stay low and stay loose."

"And you watch your back, Cowboy."

"Always do."

Hanler said, "When you fellas are done spooning maybe we can get this bird in the air."

I shot him the bird and he grinned. Three minutes later we were in the air heading west to Denver.

Chapter Twenty-Three

MacNeil-Gunderson Water-Bottling Plant, Asheville, North Carolina
Two weeks ago

Hester Nichols was a nervous woman. For twenty years she had overseen production of bottled water at the big plant in the mountains near Asheville. She was there when MacNeil bought the plant from the bankrupt soda company that had owned it since the fifties, and she was there when the Gunderson Group bought a half interest in it during the spring-water boom of the nineties. When she was promoted from line supervisor to production manager she had suffered through three FDA inspections, two audits, and a transport union strike. Each of those were stressful, but they were also part of the job, and she weathered the storms one after the other.

Now she was actually scared.

It wasn't just the unsmiling faces of the quality control advisors from Gunderson who hovered over employees at every step of the bottling process. It wasn't even the fear that the IRS would somehow discover the new offshore account that Otto Wirths had set up for her.

What worried Hester was that she didn't know what was in the water.

Otto told her that it was safe. But he had a weird little smile on his scarred face, and that smile haunted Hester, day and night.

She stood on the metal catwalk, fingers curled tightly around the pipe rail, and looked down at the production floor.

MacNeil-Gunderson owned three plants. Two in North Carolina and one in Vermont. This one was the largest—a massive facility that had the second-highest bottled water output in the South—and Hester oversaw the bottling and shipping of twelve hundred bottles per minute. Twenty-four hours a day, seven days a week. It was just a drop in the bucket of the 170 billion liters of water the industry bottled worldwide, but it was a high-profit business.

Her plant did not bother with spring water but went for the more lucrative purified-water market. Hester had overseen the installation of top-of-the-line reverse osmosis water purification systems and the equipment for enhancing taste and controlling odor through activated carbon. The water was sterilized by ozone and then run through remineralization equipment before flowing like liquid gold into plastic bottles. The plant was fully automated, with only a skeleton crew of mechanics and quality-control technicians on hand. It was much easier to slip things past a small crew, and in the current economy few employees risked making any kind of fuss. Except for shipping, MacNeil-Gunderson was a nonunion shop, and that helped, too.

Before Otto had walked up to her in the parking lot of a Quick Chek four months ago, Hester's main concern was playing spin doctor for press questions about the source of the water. A Charlotte newspaper had broken the story that purified bottling plants used water from any source, including tap water, seawater, brackish water, river water, polluted well water, and even wastewater streams. The paper emphasized that and glossed over the fact that purification was the key. And the water was actually pure. Or at least as pure as the FDA required.

Until Otto Wirths.

Wirths had offered Hester an absurd amount of money. The kind of money that made her knees weak, that actually took her breath away. More money than Hester could make in twenty years as a manager. Wirths showed her credentials that proved that he was CEO of the Gunderson Group. He could have fired her, but he never even threatened that. Instead he offered her money, and that was enough to buy her cooperation. And maybe her soul. Hester wasn't sure. He only wanted two things from her: to allow him to provide the quality-control specialists for the plant and to make sure she paid no attention to whatever additives they chose to add to the water.

"It won't affect the taste or smell," Wirths had said; then he gave her a sly wink. "But . . . don't drink it, my dear."

When Hester had hesitated, Otto Wirth added another zero to the money he offered. Hester nearly collapsed.

She wrestled with her conscience for nearly a full minute.

That was at the beginning of May and now it was near the end of August. Seven hundred and twenty thousand bottles an hour. One million, seven hundred and twenty thousand, eight hundred bottles a day. For four months.

What was in the bottles? The question nagged at her every day, and every day the money in that offshore account seemed smaller; every day she wondered if she had sold her soul for too small an amount.

Her fingers were so tight on the pipe rail that her knuckles were white. She stared down at the production floor as the thunder of the machinery beat at her like fists.

What was in those bottles?

Dear God, she thought, *what is in that water?*

Chapter Twenty-Four

N'Tabo stopped on the twelfth circuit and lighted a cigarette. He smoked one for every dozen turns around the compound, rewarding himself for four kilometers with an American Marlboro. He liked the menthol ones. The moon was a dagger slash of white against the infinite black of the sky. He could only see a few stars; the lights on the perimeter fence washed the rest away. N'Tabo was okay with that. He wasn't much of a star gazer.

He took a deep drag on the Marlboro, enjoying the menthol burn in his throat, the icy tingle deep in his lungs. His wife said he smoked too much. He thought her ass was too flat. Everyone had problems.

The rifle on his shoulder was heavy—an ancient AK-47 that his boss had given him ten years ago. It kicked like a cow and the strap had worn a permanent callus over his shoulder from shoulder blade to nipple. No amount of padding or aloe seemed to keep it from rubbing a groove in him. He believed he'd wear that mark until he died. Of course he figured he'd be dead by the time he was thirty anyway. The boss's crew—the deputy warlords, as they called themselves—would probably shoot him just because they were bored, or because he was pissing against the wrong tree, or because he was just *there*. They were like that. Three of N'Tabo's friends had been killed like that in the last six years. For fun or for some infraction of a nonexistent rule. It made N'Tabo wish that the Americans would come back. At least his father and two of his uncles had died in a real battle, back in Mogadishu. Allah rewarded death in battle. How would He reward death by boredom?

The cigarette was almost down to the filter and N'Tabo sighed. Just below the surface of his conscious thought he wished that something—*anything*—would happen just to relieve the tedium. The thought had almost risen to the point of becoming words on his tongue when he heard the sound.

N'Tabo froze with his hand midway to taking the cigarette from between his lips. Had he heard it or was his mind using the ordinary sounds of the jungle to play tricks on him? It wouldn't be the first time.

He tried to replay the sound in his mind. It had been a grunt. Low, soft, the kind someone might make if they bumped into something in the dark.

N'Tabo spit out the cigarette and as he turned he swung the gun up, his hands finding the familiar grips without thought, his ears straining into the darkness.

But there was only silence. By reflex he tuned out the ordinary sounds of the dense forest and the desert that surrounded it. The sound had come from the west, toward the arm of the jungle that separated the compound from the town beyond. N'Tabo waited, not daring to call out a challenge. Raising a false alarm would earn him a chain whipping at the very least. Two men had been whipped last week. One had died, and the other's back was an infected ruin of torn flesh over broken bones.

So N'Tabo stood there with his gun pointed at a black wall of nothing, and waited.

Ten seconds. Twenty.

A minute crawled by. The only sound was the tinny

sound of a Moroccan radio station from inside the compound and the ripple of laughter from the deputy warlords who were playing poker in the blockhouse where they bunked.

From the forest . . . nothing.

N'Tabo licked his lips. He blinked sweat from his eyes.

He waited there for another whole minute, and then gradually, one stiff muscle at a time, he relaxed. It was nothing.

Then a voice said, "Over here."

It was low, guttural, a twisted growl of a voice. And it came from *behind him.*

N'Tabo did not understand the words. He spoke four languages—Somali, Bravanese, Arabic, and English—but the voice had spoken in Afrikaans, a language he'd never heard.

Not that it mattered. He jumped and spun, and as he landed three things happened all at once. He *saw* the person who had spoken—a strange, hulking figure silhouetted against the stark glare of the compound lights. N'Tabo opened his mouth to shout a warning. And the figure behind him whipped a huge hand toward him and closed it around his throat. All three things happened in a microsecond.

N'Tabo tried to shout, but the hand was too strong—insanely strong—and not so much as a hiss escaped the crushing stricture. He tried to fire his weapon, but the gun was ripped out of his grip with such savage force that N'Tabo's hand was folded backward against the wrist and a half-dozen small bones snapped, the ends scything through the cartilage and tendons. The pain was massive, but N'Tabo had no voice with which to scream at the white-hot agony in his arm. Within the cage of iron fingers his throat began to collapse and he could hear his own neck bones grind. The trapped air in his lungs was a burning fireball.

N'Tabo swung his other hand at the figure holding him; he used every last scrap of strength he possessed and he felt his fist blows slam into shoulders and arm and face. His attacker did not even flinch. It was like beating a statue, and N'Tabo's knuckles cracked on the hard knot of the attacker's cheekbone.

A different and far more impenetrable darkness began to engulf N'Tabo, blossoming like black poppies in his eyes. The last thing he saw before the darkness took him was a line of brutish figures swarming out of the shadows and leaping up absurdly high, grabbing the top of the corrugated metal compound fence twelve feet above the hard-packed sand. One by one the figures hauled themselves up and over the wall.

Blood roared in N'Tabo's ears, but he heard two distinct sounds.

The first was the mingled chatter of gunfire and the high-pitched shrieks of men in terrible pain.

Then he heard his own vertebrae collapse with a crunch like a sack dropped onto loose gravel. N'Tabo clearly heard the sound of his own death, and then he was gone.

Chapter Twenty-Five

I had the Lear to myself and sank into a large leather swivel chair next to a self-service wet bar that saw a fair amount of action during that flight. I'm pretty sure black coffee laced with Kentucky bourbon is neither tactically sound nor medically smart in light of what I'd been through and what might lie before me, but damn if I didn't give a shit. It felt good going down, and since I didn't want it to be lonely I had another. I also wolfed down six packets of salted peanuts. I've never understood why they can't put a decent serving in a single bag.

After we were at cruising altitude Hanler put it on autopilot and came back to show me how to use the videoconferencing setup; then he retired to the cabin, cranked up an old Bob Seger and the Silver Bullets CD. Either he didn't want to participate or his current involvement with Church didn't extend to DMS secrets.

I clicked on the remote and immediately the screen popped on with a real-time webcam of the video lab at the Warehouse. I had ten seconds of an empty room and then Dr. Hu came and sat down. He was wearing jeans and a Punisher T-shirt under a white lab coat that probably hadn't been washed since last winter. Instead of his name he had "Mad Scientist" embroidered over the pocket. Hu was a Chinese American über-geek who ran the DMS science division; he was a few thousand neurons beyond brilliant, but he was also an insensitive ass-hole. If the building was on fire and it came down to a choice of saving him or my favorite pair of socks, he'd be toast. He hated me just as much, so we had a balanced relationship.

"Captain," he said.

"Doctor," I replied.

All warmth. Like a Hallmark special.

He said, "Has Mr. Church told you anything about the video?"

"Just that it came from an anonymous source and that it's tied to whatever's brewing."

"It's because of the video that Hack Peterson rolled Jigsaw Team," Hu said. "We received that video two days ago. We ran the faces of each of the people in the video through our recognition software and got some hits. Mr. Church will conference in with us to discuss those with you. Bottom line is that one of the faces is that of a man known to have been associated with a major subversive organization back in the Cold War days. Don't ask me for details, because Lord Vader hasn't deemed it necessary to share those with me yet."

Cold War, I mused. Grace was right.

"You know," I said, "Church could be eavesdropping on this call."

I said it just to be mean and Hu looked momentarily unnerved, but he shook his head. More to himself than to me. "Point is, Church initiated a MindReader search on the man and found that almost everything about him has been erased from government databases. MindReader couldn't reclaim the data but was able to spot the footprints."

" 'Footprints'?"

"Sure . . . think of them as scars from where data was forcibly erased from hard drives. It's like forensics . . . every contact leaves a trace."

"Except for MindReader."

"Well . . . okay, except for MindReader. I think one of the things bugging the boss is that it would take a system a lot *like* MindReader to expunge this much information. Mind you, MindReader wouldn't have left a mark, so we're not looking at someone using our own system . . . but this is weirdly close."

"Not sure I like the sound of that."

"No one does. Anyway, we used MindReader to do extensive pattern and connection searches and located relatives of Gunner Haeckel, the man from the video. Stuff this other system, good as it was, missed. We accessed court records from family estates and pending litigation. His only living relative was an uncle who died in 1978."

"And . . . ?"

"And everything the uncle had is stored at a place called Deep Iron, which is a private high-security storage facility a mile under Chatfield State Park in the foothills of the Rockies, southwest of Denver. Mr. Church sent Peterson and his team to the facility at dawn this morning. He never reported in."

"What kinds of records are stored there?"

"We don't know. The Deep Iron system only lists them as 'records.' Could be a collection of old forty-fives for all we know. All sorts of things are stored at Deep Iron. People store yachts, film companies store old movie reels, you name it. And about a million tons of paper and old microfilm records."

"And we don't know how it relates to the video?"

"No, so Church is looking for you to get us some answers. Your boy Top Sims is already in Colorado."

"Call Top 'boy' again, son, and you're likely to end the day as a girl."

He blinked. "It wasn't a racial slur," he said defensively. "It's street talk. You know . . . Echo Team are your boys and all."

"Doc, you were never cool in school and you're not cool now. Stop trying."

He pretended to adjust the nosepiece of his glasses, but he did it with his middle finger. You could feel the love just rolling back and forth between us.

"Video," I prompted. "Do I ever get to see it?"

Instead of answering me, he cleared his throat and tried to look serious. "What do you know of cryptozoology?"

"Crypto-what?" I asked.

"Cryptozoology," he repeated, saying it slower this time. "Depending on who you ask, it's either a minor branch of biology or a pseudoscience. In either case, it's concerned with the search for cryptids—animals that do not belong to any known biological or fossil record."

"You lost me."

Hu smiled thinly. "It's simple. Cryptids are animals that are believed by *some* to exist . . . but which usually don't."

"What? Like the Loch Ness Monster?"

Hu gave me a "wow, the caveman had a real thought" sort of look but nodded. "And Bigfoot, the Jersey Devil, El Chupacabra, and a bunch of others."

"Please don't tell me that I busted my ass to dodge the NSA just to go on a Bigfoot hunt. I'm just starting to not entirely dislike you, Doc; don't make me have to kill you."

His smile would have wrinkled a lemon.

"No," he said with exaggerated patience, "we're not searching for Bigfoot. However, there have been instances of presumed mythological creatures being found. Until a few years ago the giant squid was considered a myth. And two hundred years ago the first people to report an egg-laying mammal with webbed feet, a duck's bill, and a poisonous sting were branded as liars, but we now know the platypus exists."

"Platypuses are poisonous?" I asked.

"Male *platypi* are," he said, correcting me with a sneer. "Some of these animals may be UMAs, or Unidentified Mysterious Animals, that, due to lack of physical evidence, spoor or DNA, resist scientific classification in the known biology. Others are relicts—that's with a *t*—surviving examples of species believed to be extinct or so close to extinction that living examples are rarely found."

"Wow, this is fascinating, Doc," I said. "By the way, did anyone mention that the Vice President of the United frigging States of America wants us all arrested?"

Hu peered at me for a moment. "Exciting," he said. "Another more exotic example is the coelacanth, a large fish believed to have become completely extinct over sixty million years ago, and yet one was netted in December of 1938 by the crew of a South African trawler. Since then living populations of them have been sighted and caught in the waters around Indonesia and South Africa."

I grunted. "Sure, I've seen them in the Smithsonian."

"Generally cryptozoologists search for the more sensational megafauna cases—like Bigfoot—rather than new species of beetles or flies. And before you ask, 'megafauna' means 'large animals.' In biology it's used to describe any animal weighing more than forty kilograms. And we occasionally find relicts or UMAs that do exist."

"Okay, I get that this is like porn for you science geeks, but if there's some reason I have to sit through it then for Christ's sake get to it."

"I wanted you to have this in mind before I played the video."

"Church said he wanted me to watch it without preconceptions so I could form my own opinions."

From Hu's look it was clear that he didn't think me capable of anything as complex as an "opinion." He tapped a few keys. "This video was blind e-mailed to us. Someone logged on from an Internet café in São Paolo, created a Yahoo account, sent this, and then abandoned the account. We hacked Yahoo, but all of the info used to create the account was phony. All we have is the file."

"Sent to whom?"

"To an old e-mail account owned by Mr. Church. Don't ask about the account, because he didn't tell me. All he said is that it's one he never uses anymore but which he occasionally checks as a matter of routine." Hu rubbed his hands together in a way I'd only ever seen mad scientists do in bad movies. "Now . . . watch! I can guarantee you that this is going to blow you away."

He wasn't wrong.

Chapter Twenty-Six

"We have a virus," said Judah Levin. He couldn't help smiling.

It was an old joke in the CDC's IT department, and it always got a laugh, or at least a groan.

His boss, Colleen McVie, looked up from the papers on her desk. She wore her glasses halfway down her nose and measured out half a smile.

"Unless it's urgent," she said, "go practice your standup on someone else. I'm ass deep with the payroll, or don't you want to get paid?"

"Being paid is nice, but we actually do have a virus, Colleen. A couple of the secretaries have been complaining about it. It's a bounce-back program that came at us through—"

"So . . . deal with it," she interrupted. "We get fifty viruses a week."

"Okay," he said, and left her office.

He went back to the main office, where several secretaries were standing around the coffeemaker. Judah had told them to log off and they seemed to take that as a sign to do no work at all. He shrugged—it wasn't his problem, and Colleen would be buried with her payroll for the rest of the day.

The virus hadn't been overtly destructive, but it had been new and oddly configured enough to catch his attention, especially since it arrived as a bounce-back response to the CDC's daily alert e-mail bulletin.

Judah sat at one of the workstations, opened his laptop on a wheeled side table, and logged onto both computers. Everything loaded normally all the way to the password screen. He used one of IT's secure passwords that would open the system but reroute it to his laptop. Again the screens loaded normally. He ran several different spyware scans and came up with nothing.

He frowned. That was weird, because he had definitely seen the virus warning message pop-up. He tapped a few keys and did a different kind of search.

Nothing.

Very weird.

He logged into the office e-mail account and looked for the e-mail that had likely carried the virus. It was gone.

Without saying a word he got up and went to the adjoining desk and logged on. Same result—no trace of the e-mail, no trace of a virus. He repeated this four more times, but there was no trace of either the e-mail or the virus anywhere in the system.

Judah picked up the secretary's phone and punched the number for Tom Ito, his assistant. When Ito answered, Judah said, "Did you do a system search on an e-mail virus this morning?"

"No, why—you need me to run one?"

Judah explained the situation.

"Got me, Jude. Do we have a problem?"

Judah thought about it. "Nah. Skip it. If it's not there, then it's not there. Nothing to worry about."

He hung up and walked over to the secretaries. "Look, the system seems to be clear, but if you get anything else call me right away."

Chapter Twenty-Seven

Cyrus Jakoby received his children in a garden that was so beautifully designed that visitors could easily believe that they were out in the fresh air rather than half a mile under the heat-baked Arizona desert. Cyrus remained seated in a tropical cane rattan chair with a high fan back. He was cool and composed in tropical whites. The Twins bowed to him. They had never hugged their father and only rarely shook hands. Bowing had always been the custom among them. They bowed from the waist in the Chinese fashion, and Cyrus inclined his head like an Emperor and waved them to seats.

Their chairs were of the same style as his, though not as big, and from past experience Hecate knew that their chairs were built with slight and carefully planned imperfections. The seats were too deep, so that they had to either perch on the end or sit back and have the sharp edge of the seat cut into the tender flesh above the back of their knees. The legs were ever so slightly uneven, so that they sat off-angled in a way that cramps and aches would gradually form in the lower back and obliques. The chairs were also positioned lower on a slope whose incline was hidden by copious decorative shrubbery and a forced-perspective distraction mosaic made from multicolored tiles. The overall effect was of a lack of comfort and an imbalance that made one feel inferior to the person sitting higher and in obvious comfort in the big chair. And although the design of Cyrus's chair was island rustic, he rode it like a throne.

Hecate had long ago found the most comfortable position, half-turned, with her knees together and feet braced to keep her from sliding to the wrong side of the chair. She approved of the chairs and long ago had stopped wondering why she didn't share her insights with her brother.

"It's good to see you, Father," said Paris, uncomfortably crossing his legs and then uncrossing them.

Cyrus studied the hummingbirds flitting from one exotic flower to another.

"It's good to see you, *Alpha,*" corrected Hecate.

Cyrus looked at them as if seeing them for the first time. "And how are my young gods today?"

"Well, Alpha," said Hecate. "And you're looking especially fit."

Paris hid a sneer behind a cough and Cyrus affected not to notice.

Cyrus said, "I'm self-renewing, as you know."

"Of course," Hecate said, though she had no idea what that meant. She made herself look pleased and knowing.

"Before we discuss whatever it is that's putting such troubled looks on your faces," Cyrus said smoothly, "please let me have an update on the shipping."

Hecate shrugged. "The entire distribution network is in place. We have three cargo ships of bottled water and bottled sparkling water en route to Africa and six shiploads already in the warehouse in Accra in Ghana, four in Calabar in Nigeria, and two each in Libreville, Gabon; Lomé, Togo; and Tangier. Two of our Brazilian ships will make stops in Callao, Peru, and Guayaquil, Ecuador. The shipments to Chile and Panama will go out next. And we can handle the domestic shipments to New York, Louisiana, and Mississippi by water or rail."

For a moment Cyrus's eyes seemed to lose focus and his skin flushed as if the news touched him on an almost erotic level. It was a reaction Hecate had noted before, but she let no expression show on her face.

Paris laughed and it broke the spell. "It's kind of ironic that one of the world's great criminal enterprises is largely financed by the sale of *purified* water."

"Yes," Cyrus said with a wolf's smile. "Life is full of delightful ironies. But don't forget that illegitimate business cannot succeed without legitimate business. Even those greaseballs in the Mafia understand that."

They all chuckled over that, but Hecate's laugh was as false and measured as her father's and she knew it. She just did not know why Cyrus thought it was funny. She'd had toxicology screens done on random samples of every shipment of water, and as far as she could tell there was nothing in there but purified water and enough trace minerals to make the health club set think they were actually getting something for the money they spent on glorified tap water. Maybe it was time to run an entirely different set of tests on the water.

"Father," began Paris, and then corrected himself with an irritable grunt, " 'Alpha' . . . we're moving into Phase Three of the South African account. We've run the Berserkers through three field tests with variable results, the most recent of which was last night in Somalia. What we'd like is—"

" 'Variable'?" Cyrus interrupted.

"That's really why we're here, Alpha," explained

Hecate. "Our clients have some concerns about certain behavioral anomalies. Concerns that, unfortunately, are borne out by the test results."

"What kind of anomalies?"

Hecate looked at Paris, who gave her a "well, you started this" wave of his hand. She took a breath and plunged ahead. "In the second and third field tests we've documented aggression increases in levels beyond what the computer models predicted. In short, the test subjects have become too violent."

"Of course they're violent," snapped Cyrus. "They're killers. They're supposed to be violent. What kind of idiocy is this?"

At the sound of his raised voice two animals stalked quietly out of foliage behind his chair. Hecate and Paris did almost comic double takes on them because at first glance they appeared to be large dogs, Danes or American mastiffs, but immediately that idea was torn to shreds as the animals stepped from shadows into sunlight. The animal to Cyrus's left was the bigger of the two, a female with heavy shoulders between which a hideous head lolled. He stared at Hecate with the hateful slitted yellow eyes of a hunting lion. He hissed silently at the Twins and pawed at the ground with retractable claws that left furrows in the tile. The second animal, smaller but thicker in the shoulders, circled the entire clearing at a slow and silent pace.

Hecate and Paris were frozen to their chairs. Paris's eyes tried to follow the stalking creature; Hecate couldn't take her eyes off of the big animal. There was a gas dart pistol in her pocket, but she knew she had no chance at all of drawing it if that thing moved. He crouched there, his tension etching the taut lines of each muscle.

Paris was always the better actor and he reassembled his composure first. He recrossed his legs and cocked one eyebrow as if appraising a pet poodle.

"Cute," he drawled. "What do you call them?"

"Otto calls them tiger-hounds."

"That's boring."

"It won't be the catalog name," snapped Cyrus, and just as quickly his voice softened. "We're working on something catchier. The big one is Isis; her mate is Osiris."

Moving very casually, Paris reached under his shirt and withdrew his dart gun. It was made from a high-density polymer blend and had a gas-injection clip that could fire .32 pumpkin balls filled with glass flachettes. He laid it on his thigh, his finger straight along the outside of the trigger guard. He said nothing.

Cyrus smiled and then made a clicking noise with his tongue. Osiris stopped prowling and came over to sit on Cyrus's right. Isis stopped hissing, but her eyes never left Hecate's. The animals sat straight, their bodies as motionless as stone statues carved into the legs of a throne. Every once in a while one of them would blink very slowly, the action serving to remind the Twins of their reality and potential.

"Hmmm, trainable," murmured Paris, nodding approval. "Will they bond with multiple handlers?"

"Within limits," said Cyrus, "but push comes to shove they'll protect whoever feeds them first. They bond very quickly with the initial human handler but can be taught to tolerate others." He reached down and stroked the head of the bigger of the two animals. "I make it a point to be the first person with whom each of my animals bonds."

"They're . . . beautiful." She could feel the gaze of the animals like a physical touch.

"They're ugly as ghouls," Cyrus snorted. "However, I didn't design them for their beauty. Pretty can be frightening," he observed, "but not in a guard dog."

"Are they dogs?" Paris asked.

Cyrus shrugged. "Technically they're about sixty percent canine. The rest is a mix of useful genetic lines. They're very much made to order as the perfect free-roaming guard animals. Nothing comes close."

Hecate stared, lips parted, at Isis, and the big creature stared back at her and into her with an intensity that was palpable and a personality that was *familiar*. Hecate said nothing, but when she blinked the animal blinked.

Paris wasn't paying attention to his sister. He was hiding a smile provoked by Cyrus's claims that these creatures were perfect. Paris personally disagreed with that assessment, but that wasn't a topic he wanted to discuss with his father. Back home, at the lab Paris and Hecate called the Dragon Factory, he had his own guard dogs, and he thought how interesting it would be to pit his *Stingers* against these tiger-hounds. The Stingers were a breakthrough in deliberate chimeric genetics. The Twins had managed to create animals with mammal and insect genes, a feat of morphogenetics that had kicked open a lot of doors for them. It was one of the benefits of being able to combine research from so many different sources, thanks to Pangaea. A pit fight between his Stingers and the tiger-hounds would be a huge moneymaker. He'd already made some side money with steroid and gene therapy on standard fighting dogs. This would be a more select market, but the more exclusive the commodity the higher the price.

"We could move twenty mated pairs of these things by close of business," he said. "One photo and some bare-bones specs in an e-mail and you could name your price."

Cyrus shook his head. "I'll sell pair-bonded brothers, but you can't have any of the bitches."

"That'll drop the price."

"It sustains the market," Hecate corrected him, earning a nod from their father. "We want to sell fish, not teach our customers how to catch fish."

Paris shrugged. This was one of the areas on which his father and sister always agreed. For his part, Paris preferred constantly bringing a series of new products to market rather than establishing ongoing markets. "Well, at least let me take orders on the males."

"Talk to Otto," Cyrus said, and dismissed the topic with a wave of his hand. "Now, what about the Berserkers?"

Hecate smoothed her skirt. "For reasons we can't quite chart, the transgenic process has had several unexpected side effects. On the plus side, physical strength is about ten percent above expectations, but intelligence seems to be diminishing. They're not idiots, but they seem to rely too much on instinct and too little on higher reasoning. But it's their aggression level that has our clients concerned. If their aggression continues to escalate with each mission, then there is a very real concern that their behavior will deteriorate beyond a point of practical command control. That will shorten their duration of usefulness in the field."

Cyrus opened his mouth to reply, but Paris jumped in. "We understand that planned obsolescence is part of any sensible manufacturing system, but this is way too fast. We're expected to turn over comprehensive reports for six field tests, and just based on the preliminary reports we've shared with our clients the aggression factor has caused concern. We could bullshit our way through a three or four percent increase in violent behavior, throw in some mumbo jumbo about the natural variables of transgenics and so on, but we're talking about a fifteen-point-seven increase in aggression between test one and test three."

Cyrus pursed his lips. "Ah," he said, "I see your point. That's higher than our worst-case computer models."

"By almost eight percent," said Hecate. "With a comparable drop in higher reasoning. We can't fudge the math on that kind of behavioral shift."

"Is this just in the GMOs?"

Genetically modified organisms were the easiest to bring to market, but anomalous behavior and other gene-clash problems tended to come at them out of the blue. The much more stable genetically engineered organisms were ideal, but they had to be grown from embryos and raised to full maturity. For the Berserkers that was a fifteen- to twenty-year span. The Twins had chosen the faster route of making modifications through the introduction of viral vectors carrying exogenous pieces of DNA. It was quicker, but the likelihood of unexpected mutations was much higher.

"Of course," she said, "but we don't have GEOs mature enough for field-testing."

Cyrus leaned back in his seat, chin on his breast, and pondered the problem. Hecate and Paris waited while Cyrus thought it through.

"I doubt you'll see these problems in the genetically engineered animals. Different blueprint, different results. But in the modified animals . . . it's difficult to control random gene incompatibility. Even if you suppress a gene, it doesn't remove it and unwanted traits can emerge."

The Twins waited. They knew this, but interrupting Cyrus was not a path toward obtaining his cooperation. Cyrus chewed on it for a while, his eyes narrowed and focused inward.

"What steps have you taken?" he asked.

"Nothing yet," Hecate said. "The Somalia test was just last night completed and our people are still crunching the numbers."

Paris nodded. "We've been playing with some ideas, though. A time-release dopamine dampener that would kick in just as the mission started. By the time the Berserkers were in full attack we're hoping to cause a down-spike in the dopamine to start a cool-off."

Cyrus made a face. "That's a Band-Aid, not a cure. Besides, none of the dopamine dampeners we could use are reliable. Nothing has been field tested on anything remotely like a Berserker. Plus there's adrenaline rush and other factors. You'd burn through six months of chemistry trying to get the dose right, and then another six working out how to make the dose appropriate to each individual Berserker." He shook his head. "Nice theory, but impractical. Medication isn't your answer."

Paris made a disgusted face. "We know, Alpha . . . that's why we're here. We have fifty ideas, but none of them are practical in the time we have left. We have contracts with hard delivery dates. We burned through our swing time early this year when we had unexpected effects of cognitive dissonance. The buyers want their products now."

"*Fuck the buyers!*" snapped Cyrus. Both of the tiger-hounds stiffened at his sides. "And fuck your salespeople if they can't figure out how to put positive spin on this."

"Our people can—"

"Your people are idiots, Paris!" When Cyrus was angry his carefully acquired American accent slipped and the more staccato German accent emerged. "Otto could sell that product for single use and get nearly the money you two are getting for extended use and ownership." The Twins flinched and Paris looked away. "What's your current guarantee?"

"Eighteen to twenty-four months at ninety percent operational efficiency," Hecate said quietly.

Cyrus stared for a moment, then smiled. "You gave a two-year window on a transgenic soldier? I'm crazy, my young gods, but I think you two are crazier by an order of magnitude."

Despite their best efforts, the Twins flushed with shame.

In a small voice Paris said, "We needed a buyer who could finance—"

"Don't!" growled Cyrus. "Don't embarrass yourselves with an excuse. You're supposed to be above that sort of thing and you should at least *try* and act the part."

Isis let out a low growl that was eloquent in its meaning, but this time it was directed only at Paris. Hecate noted the shift.

Cyrus steepled his fingers. "When you made that deal you were cash poor. Is that still the case?"

"Well," Hecate said, ". . . no. The hunting business alone has brought in over two hundred million and the—"

"Then, as I said, fuck the customers. You *tell* them what the product will and will not do. Don't discuss it with them. *Tell* them."

"Yes, Alpha," said Paris.

"Yes, Alpha," said Hecate.

Cyrus gave them a broad fatherly smile. "Now, my young gods, let's see what we can do to solve all your problems."

Chapter Twenty-Eight

Over Denver airspace
Saturday, August 28, 10:55 A.M.
Time Remaining on Extinction Clock: 97 hours, 5 minutes E.S.T.

I leaned forward in my chair and watched as Hu pressed the play button and the forest came alive on the video screen.

"The sound cuts in and out—mostly out."

"Can you clean it up? Run it through some filters or something?"

"This is the enhanced version," Hu said. "From the angle and the image jump we figure it to be a cheap lapel camera. No lavaliere mike to extend the pickup. The rustle of clothes and the breathing of the cameraman kill most of the sound anyway."

The camera image changed as the person with the lapel camera began to move forward through intensely dense tropical foliage. Occasionally we'd get snatches of sound, mostly of the cameraman's labored breathing or the whisk of big leaves as they brushed across his chest. We heard a few muffled snatches of conversation. Not enough to make out words, but enough to get a sense that there were several people with the cameraman. After a minute or two of this the image changed as several people passed by the cameraman to lead the way through the jungle. I counted five white men, all of them in their forties or early fifties. All of them fit but not hard. Except the man leading the pack, a stern-faced guy who looked like he was carved from granite. The rest looked like they had muscles courtesy of LA Fitness. Good dentists, expensive tans. Everyone carried expensive hunting rifles, top-of-the-line, with all sorts of doodads. The stern guy's rifle was of the same quality, but all he had on it was a good scope. His gun looked worn but immaculate.

"Big-game hunters," I observed.

Hu just smiled.

The group of men burst through the wall of foliage into a wider trail that paid out into a broad clearing that had a barren slash-and-burn quality to it. The blackened stumps of vegetation barely reached to the ankles of the men's boots.

There was a few minutes of them walking, and then they stopped to drink from canteens. The sound was off for most of this, though I caught snatches of a few words. "Africa," a couple of racial invectives, and then what sounded like "Extinction Wave," but they were both joking and I lost both ends of that sentence as the sound cut out.

"This sure as hell isn't Denver," I said. "Looks like the Brazilian rain forest. Clear-cut land for cattle farming, probably owned by a fast-food chain."

"McMoo," agreed Hu. "We identified two of the bird species in the video." He froze the picture and touched the screen. "That parrot there is an *Amazona aestiva*—or

Blue-fronted Amazon—which is definitely indigenous to Brazil."

He restarted the video and we watched as the men fanned out in a line facing a point far across the clearing and off-camera.

"Right over there!" one of them said, and it took me a half second to process that he'd said, "*Gleich da drüben!*" The others shouted and then the sound cut out again.

"That's German," Hu said.

"I know. But one of the other guys—the one with the Australian bush hat—rattled off something in Afrikaans . . . though it sounds like he has an accent under the South African. Might also be a German."

The five men and our unseen cameraman were still focused on the spot way off across the field. Suddenly one of them pointed.

"There it is!" he said in English. A British accent. "We found it!"

"*Gelukwensing!*" cried the South African. *Congratulations.*

They all gaped, staring in stupid shock at whatever they saw. A couple of them actually had their mouths hanging open.

"Guns!" the Brit hissed, and everyone raised their weapons.

"Not yet, not yet!" growled the South African in thickly accented English. "Wait until they flush it this way."

"Good God A'mighty," drawled one of the men in a thick Cajun accent. "Will you look at *that*!"

"*Hou jy daarvan, meneer?*" murmured the South African, then said it in English: "Do you like it, gentlemen?"

"It's beautiful," murmured the fifth man. His accent was pure West Texas.

Our unseen cameraman stepped farther into the clearing and turned toward the far end of the field. The sound cut off and on several times, giving us just enough so we could hear the racket of drums and sticks beating on metal pots as a line of brown-skinned men in threadbare old jeans and shorts emerged from the row of trees in the distance to drive a single animal into the center of the clearing. At first the animal was just a shapeless white blur, indistinct against the greens and grays of the tree line, but with each second it moved closer to the camera and the group of hunters.

For a minute I thought it was a horse.

Then my heart caught in my throat.

"What the fu—?"

The hunters pointed their guns.

"No . . . ," I murmured.

The sound cut out again so it all played out in a grotesque silence as four barrels jerked and red flame leaped toward the center of the field. The animal wheeled to run, but on its first step it stumbled and went down to its front knees. It was snow-white and beautiful, but suddenly red poppies seemed to blossom on its flanks. The guns fired again and the sound came back on long enough for us to hear the flat echo of the reports and the high-pitched scream of the animal as it went down.

Then all of the men were running and the cameraman was running with them, the image bouncing sickeningly. The group slowed to a trot and then a walk and came to a stop in a half circle around the fallen, bleeding animal. Its chest heaved with the labor of staying alive and it rolled one terrified eye at them.

"I hit it first!" said the man from Louisiana.

The sound faded to a crackle, which was some relief, because we could not hear the animal's final, desperate scream as the American stepped up, chest puffed out and face flushed with excitement. He put a foot on the animal's shoulder, drew a pistol, and took aim at the animal's head. But the South African touched his arm to correct the placement of the pistol's laser sight and then the gun bucked once in dreadful silence. Blood geysered up and the animal's body convulsed once; then it settled down into the terminal stillness that cannot be mistaken for anything but what it is.

"God damn it," I said.

The clip ended with the South African squatting down, a big hunting knife in his hands as he began to field-dress the animal. The screen went dark and I sat for a long minute in stunned silence.

"Now that's something you don't see every day," Hu said as the video feed of him filled the screen once more. He looked at me and what he saw on my face wiped the smile from his.

"What is this? Some kind of sick game?" I demanded. "That animal—"

"We studied this file a hundred times," interrupted Hu. "If this is makeup effects, then it's the best I've ever seen."

"But it's impossible," I said. "It can't be real."

"It looked pretty real to me," Hu said.

"But it *can't* be. That animal . . . It was a . . . a . . ."

Hu nodded.

"It was a unicorn," he said, and the smile crept back onto his face.

Interlude

He had a mind like an insect. Cold, efficient, uncluttered by personal attachment, unpolluted by emotion. It made him a superb killer.

If there had been even a spark of humanity in him, he might have been famous, or even infamous, but he never once sought glory and he viewed the desire for personal recognition as a foolish mistake. An amateur's risk.

Conrad Veder never made mistakes, foolish or otherwise.

He accepted assignments based entirely on gain, and even that was measured. He was not a greedy man. Greed creates vulnerability, a rudder by which he could be steered. Veder could not be steered. To him the acquisition of money meant that he could afford certain physical comforts and that he would have the capital necessary for the kind of investments that would allow him to retire at a young enough age to genuinely enjoy retirement. He'd once seen a Florida bumper sticker that read: "Retirement is wasted on the old," and he couldn't agree more. He was forty-six and his various portfolios and holdings—maintained under a dozen aliases— could already be cashed out to yield 11 million euros. It was a comfortable amount, but it needed more cushion to buffer against the uncertainties of the world's fluctuating currencies.

At his current rate of 1 million per hit and a reliable employment of two to three hits per year, he figured that he could retire at fifty with enough in the bank to generate a nice interest-income cash flow. Properly managed, that money would grow faster than he would spend it and see him into his nineties, no matter how much of a beating the dollar took on the global market. Besides, he had a man working on currency exchanges and the switch to Canadian dollars in late 2007 had already yielded a nice windfall.

This current job would be Veder's third this year and it was only the middle of May. There might even be a fourth and fifth contract before Christmas, which would give him his second $6 million year in a row. It was a nice way to end his thirtieth year as a paid killer.

Veder's first murder had been a five-hundred-dollar hit he'd taken while he was still in tenth grade. He hadn't felt a single flicker of emotion when he murdered the wife of his social studies teacher. It had been quick; it had been clean. And Veder had been paid. He remembered it now for mental records-keeping purposes only. Veder never formed an emotional attachment to his targets. That was also a fool's game and it crossed the line from professional to psychotic, and Veder was calmly certain that he was as sane as the next man. Kings and presidents and generals were often far more emotionally involved in the deaths they ordered, even with the legal mandates their positions provided. Veder was a problem solver, no different in his calculating mind than the operators in Delta Force or Mossad or any of the other clandestine groups of paid killers. He needed as little proof of guilt or justification of the kill order as they did. The only real differences were that they had backup and that Veder seldom used or required any, and he got paid a lot more.

The closest he ever came to idealism was a brief stint with a cadre of shooters working for a group of international businessmen who were working toward one of those grand causes, one of those "betterment of the species" things, but though Veder was content to take their money and listen to the occasional geopolitical or ethnic tirade, he was never a convert to their cause. He had agreed to join a team of four elite assassins—sadly labeled with the ludicrous nickname of the Brotherhood of the Scythe—and had done some quality work there. When their program had collapsed he was sorry to see the steady stream of income end, but in truth he really enjoyed the freedom and simplicity of the life of a solitary operator. Fewer complications, no tirades.

Now he sat in a cantina in the shadow of Chihuahua City's city hall, which sat like a Gothic cathedral on the Plaza de Armas. He was drinking lukewarm mineral water and waiting for his contact to arrive. The man was late—a passive-aggressive maneuver he often used—but Veder didn't care. He never let things like that provoke him. He sipped his water, nibbled a corn tamale, and let his insect mind process the data of everything that touched his senses.

He had spent much of the morning strolling along the short blocks to the north side of Plaza Hidalgo to view political murals by Aarón Piña Mora on the walls of the government palace. Veder had a passing interest in art. Enough to like looking at it but not enough to invest money in it. But it passed the time, and as he sat waiting for his contact he reconstructed the faces of the Mora murals in his mind. It was a useful exercise: remembering the shapes of ears, the cut of cheekbones, the fullness of lips, the angle of noses. If any of the men from those murals, Benito Juárez, Simón Bolívar, or Miguel Hidalgo, had still been alive Veder would have been able to pick them out of a crowd at twilight.

When his contact, a sweaty Portuguese man named DaCosta, finally showed, Veder didn't complain, didn't comment. He waited until DaCosta sat down and ordered a beer. When the beer arrived and the waiter had gone, DaCosta opened the conversation.

"You had a pleasant trip?"

Veder said nothing.

From experience he knew that DaCosta would jabber on for several minutes, complaining about the heat or the inconvenience of travel, bragging about golf scores or women, expounding on the peso and the dollar. Veder let him ramble. To engage him on even the smallest point would invite a conversational tangent that would drag this out even further. When DaCosta finally wound down, the fat little man shifted from chatty tourist to businessman. He looked around to make sure there was no one in easy listening distance of their table and then reached into an inner pocket of his white tropical suit to produce an envelope from which he removed several four-by-six-inch color prints. He placed them one by one on the table as if he was casting a fortune. There were seven faces. Five men, two women, each of them middle-aged or older.

He recognized three of the seven faces, though Veder glanced at them without showing any interest and looked at DaCosta, cold, waiting.

"The job is all of them," said DaCosta.

"One location or separate?"

DaCosta licked his lips. "At least five locations, though there may be one chance of getting at four of them in the same room at the same time. A funeral always draws a crowd, yes?"

Veder sipped his water. "Seven targets mean seven paychecks."

"You agreed to do this job."

"No, I agreed to meet you and hear about the job."

"You *always* do the job. . . ."

"Only when I agree to it," Veder said calmly. "I haven't agreed to this yet."

"It's not too big for you, is it?" DaCosta was grinning as he said it.

Veder said nothing.

DaCosta drank some of his beer. Veder waited him out, certain that DaCosta was authorized to pay full price for all seven hits but equally sure that the man was trying to work out some way to skim the fee.

"Who are the targets?" Veder asked, trying to move this along while making sure not to betray his interest.

DaCosta went through them one at a time, giving him the names and a brief history. He laid the photos out like a hand of seven-card stud.

"That's only six," Veder said. He nodded toward the last picture in the row and made sure that his voice betrayed nothing of what he felt. "Who's that one?"

"Ah," said DaCosta as he raised his eyebrows and lowered his voice, "that's a much more challenging target."

"Challenges can be expensive."

DaCosta made a face, clearly sorry that he'd used that phrasing.

"What's this man's name?" Veder said, looking at the picture. The man had a stern face with hard lines and an uncompromising stare. Veder had an excellent memory and he knew this face from a long time ago. He'd seen it once, only briefly, in the crosshairs of his scope; but there had been too many people in the crowd and his shot was not guaranteed, so he hadn't taken it. It was one of only three kills he had been unable to complete, all during the same series of assignments. Then things had changed and that assignment came to an abrupt and bloody end, his employers dead or scattered.

DaCosta hesitated. "That's where it gets complicated." He winced at having to use that word. "This man is a big shot in a new government agency put together by the Americans. Like Homeland, but smaller, more aggressive. This man is the head of it and his group has a history of interfering with my client's projects. His death will stop any further involvement . . . or at least slow it down to a manageable pace."

"His name," Veder prompted.

"He has a dozen names depending on who you ask. When my client first met him he was known by the code name 'Priest.' "

"Does he have a real name?"

DaCosta shrugged. "I don't know for sure, but lately he's been calling himself 'Mr. Church.' "

Veder studied the picture. Yes, this was a face he knew. His employers had feared this man above all others. Veder thought it interesting that Fate or chance had cycled this target—and the two others whom he recognized—back into view after all these years. It felt very clean, very tidy.

"Seven kills, seven fees," he said flatly, his tone carrying a terminal finality to it that even DaCosta was sensible of.

"Sure, sure," DaCosta said with just a hint of reluctance. "No problem."

Veder looked at the photos for a while, particularly the American with the many names, and finally picked them up.

"No problem," he agreed.

Part Two
Killers

There is no flag large enough to cover the shame of killing innocent people.

—HOWARD ZINN

Chapter Twenty-Nine

"A fucking *unicorn*?" I said. "What kind of bullshit is this?"

"It's not bullshit," said Hu. "At least Mr. Church is taking this very seriously. He—," but his words were cut off by the theme music for Darth Vader. Hu looked at his cell phone. "Speak of the devil."

"That's your ring tone?" I asked.

"Just for Mr. Church," explained Hu as he flipped open the phone. "Yes? . . . Sure. Okay, I'm keying you in now."

The image split to include Mr. Church seated in his office. "This conference call is scrambled so everyone can talk openly," he said.

"What's with this video crap—?" I began, but he held up a finger.

"First things first. You'll be happy to know that Sergeant Faraday's condition has been upgraded to critical but stable. He has lost his spleen, but the doctors are optimistic about the rest."

"Thank God . . . that's the first good news today."

"Unfortunately it's all of the good news I have to share," Church said. "The NSA is still trying to storm the gates and the President has not yet revived sufficiently to take back control of the office. So, we're all still fugitives."

"Peachy. Have any of our guys been taken?"

"Unknown. Ninety-three percent of the staff are accounted for. The remaining seven percent includes a few agents who have likely gone to ground. And *all* of Jigsaw Team."

"Shit." I chewed on that for a moment. There was no way the NSA had bagged Hack Peterson's entire team.

"What's your opinion of the hunt video?" Church asked.

"It's horseshit," I said. "They can do anything with CGI."

Hu shook his head vigorously. "It's not computer animation. We had three guys here from Industrial Light and Magic—you know, George Lucas's special effects guys?—and they—"

"How the hell'd you get *them*?" I interrupted.

Church said, "I have a friend in the industry."

I suppressed a smile. Church always seemed to have a friend in "the industry," no matter which industry was in question.

"Can you get the Ark of the Covenant?" I asked dryly.

"The real one or the one from the movies?" Church asked with a straight face.

"Point is," Hu said, taking back the conversation, "these ILM guys watched the video on every kind of monitor and through all sorts of filters and meters. We even did the algebra on the shadows on its mane hair based on movement and angle of the sun. Bottom line, it was real."

I snorted. "Then it was a horse with a strap-on."

"That's an unfortunate image," said Church.

"You know what I mean."

"Again," interjected Hu, "we studied the video and that horn doesn't wobble. There's no evidence that the animal was wearing a headdress or a strap. The horn appears to be approximately eighteen inches long and relatively slender at the base. That creates a lot of leverage that would definitely cause a wobble if it was just held in place by straps. The creature tossed its head and then fell over, and the horn didn't move in any way consistent with it being anchored to the skull by artificial means."

"Then I got nothing," I said. "I must have been out the day we covered mythical beasts at the police academy."

Church took a Nilla wafer and bit off a section.

"We can rule out natural mutation," ventured Hu. "The horn was perfectly placed in the center of the forehead and there are no other apparent signs of deformation, which you'd probably get if this was a freak of some kind."

"What about surgical alteration?" I asked.

"Possible," said Hu, "but unlikely, 'cause you'd also be talking about a lot of cosmetic work to hide the surgery and we don't see any signs of that. Even good cosmetic work leaves some kind of mark. Let's leave it on the table, though, because it's the most reasonable suggestion. I mean, unless this animal is a surviving example of a species that until now was only believed to be part of mythology."

I said, "I thought the unicorn myth grew out of early reports of travelers seeing a rhinoceros for the first time."

"Probably did," Hu admitted. "And from sightings of narwhales, which are cetaceans that have a single tooth that looks almost exactly like the horn on the animal in the video. Back in the eighteen-hundreds people would sell narwhale horns claiming that they were taken from unicorns."

"Any other suggestions?" asked Church. His face was hard to read, but my guess was that he wasn't buying the cryptid theory any more than I was.

"There's always genetics," suggested Hu. He saw my expression and added, "No, I'm not talking about reclaiming the DNA of an extinct species; no *Jurassic Park* stuff. I'm talking about radical genetic engineering. Transgenics—the transfer of genes from one species to another."

"Okay," I said slowly, "but what the hell would you mate a horse with to get a unicorn, because I don't see horses and narwhales doing the dirty boogie."

Even Church smiled at that.

"Not crossbreeding," Hu said. "That's too problematic and it's also becoming old-fashioned. Transgenics is genetic manipulation during the embryonic phase. Someone may have taken genes from either a rhinoceros or a narwhale and introduced it to the DNA of a horse to produce what we saw on that tape."

"Can we *do* that?" I asked.

"If we set the Wayback Machine to last month I'd say no. But hey . . ." He clicked the remote, and the picture of the dead animal popped onto the screen. "Check it out. Transgenic science is growing exponentially. They have goats that can produce spider silk in their milk.

They were given genes from the orb weaver spider. There's a whole farm of them in Canada."

"Jesus . . . that's disturbing," I said.

Hu seemed excited by it and was warming to his topic. "Actually, there are two really good ways of doing this. Either you transform embryonic stem cells growing in tissue culture with the desired DNA, or you inject the desired gene into the pronucleus of a fertilized animal egg. We've been doing it for a long time with mouse eggs. Very easy to work with."

"I'll bet you were an extremely creepy child," I murmured. Hu shot me a malicious look. "Okay, okay . . . so we got someone out there making weirdo animals. Hooray for insanity. Why would someone send us this video and why do we give a shit? Seems like we have bigger fish to fry."

Church said, "Before I get to that, speculate for me. If such an animal existed, or was created, who would want to hunt it? And why?"

"A hunt for something genuinely unique? That's easy."

"How so?"

"When I was in college I had a roommate whose father was a big-game hunter," I said. "You know the type—a businessman by day whose hunter-gatherer gene isn't as recessive as it should be. Point is, he paid for information on cats, and if there was a report of a particularly large one he and his friends would book a flight to some part of the U.S. or Mexico, or to some remote spot in a jungle somewhere. They went all over the world. Each man in his group would bring a small-caliber rifle with only three bullets. It was a challenge. The small caliber and the short ammunition increased the risk, especially against a big animal. When I went with my roommate to his dad's house for Christmas there were five cat heads on the wall . . . all from enormous cats. Record-sized cats. His dream was to eventually go to Asia, but then tiger hunting became illegal." I paused. "In our senior year his dad went away to a 'conference,' supposedly in Japan. He was gone for a couple of weeks. Five months after he returned a 'friend' gifted him with a mounted tiger head. My roommate told me about it. I never asked him if his father had somehow managed to find a way to hunt a tiger. My roommate was pissed because he didn't believe—any more than I did—that his dad would have hung someone else's trophy."

Church nodded. "I take your point."

Hu frowned. "I don't. Are you saying that someone's genetically designing unicorns just for trophy hunters?"

"Why not?" I said. "If this footage is as real as you say it is, then I think we were watching a private hunt. A public hunt would be all over the Net and in every paper. And considering how much my friend's dad paid to hunt his large trophy cats . . . I can only imagine how much someone would pay to hunt a truly unique animal."

"Yes," Church said slowly. "The superrich would pay through the nose. Millions. Excellent assessment, Captain, and that ties in neatly with the men in that video. We ran facial recognition and voice pattern software on each of them and we think we've ID'd three of the five so far. One of them is Harold S. Sunderland, brother of Senator J. P. Sunderland of Texas. Harold is basically a rich layabout who lives off of family money. His brother, J.P., is the brains, and he's one of the strongest proponents of biotech legislation. He's pushing for earmarks for genetic research for agriculture. MindReader hasn't found a direct financial connection between Sunderland and biotech profits, but in light of this video I'll be very surprised if we don't dig some up."

"Again . . . so what?"

"J. P. Sunderland is a very close friend of Vice President William Collins."

"Yikes," I said. "That puts a weird topspin on this."

"It does and we're still sorting out how Sunderland's interest in advanced genetics ties to the Vice President's crusade against the DMS."

"It might be a coincidence," said Hu, but we both ignored him.

"Who's the other guy in the video?"

"Ah," said Church, "that's the real issue. The man leading the hunt . . . what did you notice about him?"

I shrugged. "He's a German guy trying to fake a South African accent. Or maybe a German who has been living in South Africa long enough for the accents to overlap. Who is he?"

"If he's who he appears to be—and the recognition software came back with a high probability—then he's the reason this video is more than a scientific curiosity, and it moves us into some very dangerous territory. We believe his name is Gunnar Haeckel. You won't have heard of him, but once upon a time he belonged to a group of assassins known as the Brotherhood of the Scythe. Despite the rather melodramatic name, these were very heavy hitters. Also very isolated—the four members never met each other so they wouldn't be able to identify one another if captured. Each of the assassins had a code name: Haeckel was North; the others were East, West, and South. These codes do not appear to relate to their homelands and may have no significance at all except to hide their actual names. They operated for a few years during the latter part of the Cold War. We know for certain that three of the Brotherhood were terminated."

"But Haeckel got away?" I asked.

"No. Gunnar Haeckel is supposed to be dead."

"Please don't tell me he's a zombie," I said.

Church ignored that. "Haeckel and the Brotherhood were players in some bad business that was concluded during the last years of the Cold War. They were the muscle for a group with an equally cryptic name—the Cabal—which was made up of expatriated Germans, many of whom were Nazis who had escaped the post-war trials. Haeckel was the son of a Nazi scientist, and though he was born after the war he was a ruthless killer with a lot of notches on his gun. Until now we believed that he was permanently taken off the board."

" 'Taken off the board'?" Hu asked.

"Killed," I said. To Church, "How good's your intel on the hit on Haeckel?"

His eyes glittered behind his tinted lenses. "Personal knowledge."

That hung in the air and we all looked at it for what it was.

"There are three possibilities," I said. "Four, if Haeckel has an identical twin."

"He doesn't."

"A son?"

"His only known child was a girl who died at age two in a car accident in which Haeckel's wife died. Haeckel was a suspect in the deaths. The man in the video looks to be about fifty. If Haeckel is alive, then he would be fifty-one next April. Has to be the same man."

"Okay, then either the recognition software is wrong, but from what you've told me that's unlikely, so that means the hit wasn't as successful as you thought it was. You say you have personal knowledge . . . could you be wrong?"

"I have a copy of his autopsy report. It includes detailed photos of the entire postmortem. As soon as the NSA is off our backs I'll forward a diplomatic request to South Africa for an exhumation of Haeckel's grave. Ditto on a request for any tissue samples that might still be stored in the hospital in Cape Town where the autopsy was performed." Church sat back in his chair. "I can't account for why he appears to be alive and well in this video. At least one of the men in the hunting party was carrying a late-model weapon, so we know this isn't old footage. Until we know more we're going to go on the assumption that somehow Haeckel survived. Our real concern is what he represented. The Cabal posed a very grave threat to humanity. The list of crimes attributed to them is considerable, though most of their atrocities were perpetrated at three or even four removes by using terrorist organizations funded by layers of dummy companies."

"What were they after?"

"Ethnic cleansing for a start, and their fingerprints are all over some of the most violent racial conflicts of the last half of the twentieth century. They had vast resources and privately funded insurgents, rebels, coups . . . they even sent covert ops teams in to deliberately pollute water sources throughout Africa and Israel. They're suspected of having helped the spread of diseases that target third world cultures. There were several cases where they funded both sides of a genocidal conflict because it served their goals to rack up bodies of anyone who was not 'pure.'"

"So . . . we're talking the Nazi extermination ideal here. Kill the Jews, Gypsies, blacks . . . anyone who wasn't a blond-haired, blue eyed son of Odin."

Church nodded. "The death of Adolf Hitler hardly put an end to genocide. It just became more politically useful to world governments to keep it off the public radar, to call it something else. To blame terrorists and splinter groups." Church's voice was uncharacteristically bitter. Couldn't blame him a bit. "But understand me, Captain, this long ago ceased to be part of German culture or even the Aryan ideal. Germany stands with us in the war on ethnic genocide. No . . . these men and women are a shadow nation unto themselves. They no longer want to remake a nation; they want to remake the world."

"And Haeckel was a button man for these assholes?"

"Was. Possibly still is." Church adjusted his glasses and his tone shifted back to neutral.

"And I think I get why that video has you so jacked. If that animal is the product of some kind of newfangled genetic design, and if Haeckel's working for whoever made it, and if they are these same assholes—this Cabal—then that means that they've ducked your punch, been working in secret for a lot of years, and are screwing around with cutting-edge genetics."

"Yes," Church said slowly.

Dr. Hu smiled at me. "I told you that video would blow you away."

"Yeah, glad you're happy about it, Doc."

"Hey," he said, pushing up his sleeve to show his light brown skin, "I'm on the hit list, too. But you have to admire the scope of it. The imagination of it."

"No, I fucking well don't," I said.

Church said, "When you get back to the Warehouse I'll give you a more complete account of the Cabal and the efforts to dismantle it. In the meantime it's important to know that we have only two links to Gunnar Haeckel, and Haeckel is our only link to the Cabal—if it indeed still exists. The first connection is this video, though we still don't know who sent it, or why. The second is whatever is stored at Deep Iron. It might be nothing, but considering that Jigsaw went off the grid while running this same mission, I think it's safe to say that there will be a connection."

"You make anything out of the other stuff . . . the comment about the 'Extinction Wave'?"

"No, but we'll do a MindReader search on it. Hard to search for something without more to put in the search argument. Otherwise I'd Google it."

"*Did* you Google it?"

He ignored the question.

There was a soft *bing!* and I heard Hanler's voice: "Buckle up, Captain. We're making our descent."

"Mission objectives?" I asked Church.

"Your first priority is to locate and secure whatever the Haeckel family stored there. Secondary mission is to locate Jigsaw Team."

From the bitter lines on his face I could tell that he didn't like the order of priorities any more than I did.

Church said, "We're operating without support here. I'd prefer to have you met by SWAT, HRT, and the National Guard, but those are calls I can't make under the present circumstances. You have Sims and Rabbit. I was able to get a technical support vehicle out to them, which means you'll have weapons and body armor but no advanced equipment. And we have no other boots on the ground."

"Three of us on a mission in which a dozen operators went missing? Swell."

"It's asking a lot of you, but believe me when I tell you that this is of the first importance. There may be opposition that we don't know about."

"If we have a new enemy, boss . . . they may have some opposition *they* don't know about."

Church gave me a long, considering look.

"Good hunting, Captain," he said.

Chapter Thirty

Sandown Park Racecourse—Surrey, England
Nine weeks ago

Clive Monroe looked nothing at all like what he was, but he looked exactly like what he had been. He wore a gray city suit with a chalk stripe, polished brogans, and a bowler hat. His clothes at least looked the part of an investment banker down from London to have a flutter on an afternoon of jump races at Sandown. He even had an umbrella in the car and a precisely trimmed mustache. He could have been on a poster for British business.

A casual passerby might have made that mistake, but everyone who caught Clive Monroe's eye changed their opinion. His eyes were dark brown and utterly cold. Not emotionless, but rather filled with a calculating and deliberate cold. Ruthless eyes. When he smiled, the humor never reached those eyes, and they were never idle or inattentive. When Clive Monroe took your measure you knew that he could value you to the last penny. Not just in the expected business sense, but in every sense. You believed that he knew enough about you that he could predict what you'd do, what you'd say.

It was a fair enough assessment.

Clive Monroe had been an investment banker for twenty years, and his eyes and his assessing coldness made him a formidable opponent, whether over the details of a portfolio of holdings or over a round of golf.

Twenty-one years ago he had been a different man in a different job, and in the years before that his ability to assess a situation or a person had kept him alive when others around him fell.

Monroe walked past the oddsmakers in Tattersalls, heading for the stairs to the reserved boxes where he was expected for drinks between the third and fourth race. Monroe never placed bets on the races, though he amused himself by reading through the form books, reading the history of each horse and weighing their breeding against the weather conditions and the orientation of the field, the number of jumps, the angle of the incline run to the winning post. If he was a betting man, he would have made money on two out of three of the races run so far that day. When he spent a whole day at the track he would mentally calculate his theoretical wagers and winnings. Last year he would have been up thirty thousand pounds, even taking into account a horse he would have backed in the Two Thousand Guineas who'd fallen on the third fence and taken down two of the other favored runners.

He climbed the steps to the row of glass-enclosed boxes where he was greeted by Lord Mowbry and three conservative members of Parliament who were well known for their love of horses. Mowbry himself was seldom away from the jump-racing world and conducted nearly all of his business between races.

They shook hands and a white-liveried waiter brought Clive his usual: gin and tonic with extra tonic. Even though Clive took pills for the malaria he got in the fetid swamps of West Africa, he still favored the quinine-rich tonic. Old habits.

They toasted and settled into leather chairs.

"So," said Lord Mowbry as soon as the waiter was gone, "have you considered our offer?" His tone was brusque.

Clive sipped his drink, shrugged.

"Is it the money?" asked Sheffield, the most senior of the MPs.

"No, the money's fine. Very generous."

"Then why the hesitation, dammit?" Mowbry demanded. He'd been the head of a wealthy family and owner of so many companies that he'd long ago lost his deferential air. Clive understood that and never took offense.

"I'm comfortable where I am," Clive said. "I've been at Enfield and Martyn for a long time. I can retire in two years with my full pension and spend my sunset years going to the races."

"You could make more money with us," insisted Sheffield.

"If it was just about the money, Cyril, I'd be down there having a flutter on Blue Boots in the fourth."

"That's another thing," said one of the other MPs.

"You come to the races, but you never bet. Where's the fun in that?"

"Everyone finds amusement in their own way."

"And that's beside the damn point," snapped Lord Mowbry. "He's already said that money wasn't his motive." Mowbry glared at Clive with piercing blue eyes over a hooked nose and a stern patrician mouth. "We need you in this venture, Monroe. You know the way these people think. No one pulls the wool over your eyes. That's why we sought you out for this. This whole scheme hinges on having a man with actual experience in this sort of thing."

It amused Clive that neither Mowbry nor the others would actually put a name to what it was they were planning. Clive appreciated the circumspection while at the same time mentally labeling these moneyed and powerful men as amateurs. It was one thing to make fortunes in trading currencies as Sheffield had or in genetic animal husbandry as the other two, Bakersfield and Dunwoody, had, or in agriculture, as had Mowbry's family for the last five hundred years, but the men were stepping out into very different territory here. Their scheme, at its simplest, was to purchase bulk genetic research from bankrupt companies of the former Soviet Union. Millions of man-hours of research was lying inert in various public and private businesses throughout Russia, Tajikistan, and Latvia. Much of it was badly out of date, having been abandoned in the financial crash following the dissolution of the Soviet state, but Mowbry and his overseas partners knew that whole sections of this material could boost existing research for their client companies. The key was to acquire the data and use modern networked computers to separate unexplored or underexplored areas of research from the chaff of commonly known information. Soviet scientists were often radical in their research, bypassing or ignoring international prohibitions on certain aspects of human and animal research.

The idea had been Mowbry's initially after he'd acquired a set of old hard drives in which he found unexpectedly useful data on transgenic salmon that led his small company to ultimately produce a salmon that was an average of 8 percent larger than the usual salmon. That 8 percent weight jump put millions into his pocket. Mowbry discreetly purchased other defunct research materials, most of which were wastes of time and money, but two years ago he found research on growth hormones for cattle that was unlike anything in development anywhere. His cattle farms in South and Central America had become gold mines.

The problem was that the cat was out of the bag. Other buyers had started vying for the same research, and Russia itself was trying to claim ownership over much of it. The materials had to be gotten sooner rather than later, before a bidding war made the whole thing cost prohibitive. They'd gotten an extra window of a couple of years when the U.S. economy imploded in the fall of 2008, but now that biotech was universally viewed as one of the safest growth industries, a feeding frenzy was starting.

The real problem was that a lot of the best materials were only available on the black market or through brokers who were ex–Soviet military. Greedy, heartless, and ruthless men who did not follow the normal rules of business. Not even the accepted rules of under-the-table international business. What Mowbry and his colleagues needed was a man who spoke the same language, someone who had once swum in these shark-infested waters. Someone who was himself a shark. Someone like Clive Monroe.

"You say that money isn't your motive," said Mowbry quietly. "Let's put that to the test, Monroe. We talked and we're willing to provide an extra half-million pounds. Call it a signing bonus."

Clive steepled his fingers and rested his chin on his fingertips.

A half million on top of the 3 million they were already offering. Though he didn't let it show on his face, the figure made Clive's pulse jump. When he'd left MI6 twenty years ago he'd left behind the spy game and the dirty intrigues that went with it. And yet he still maintained his network of contacts. Just in case. Until now he had thought he would need the contacts in case his country ever needed him again, but as the years passed he realized that the old Cold Warriors belonged to a different age of the world. Now his network was worth more to men like these and he was no longer a hero of the state but a commodity no different from the things Mowbry and his colleagues bought and sold every day. Even so . . . three and a half million pounds. Untaxable, deposited offshore.

"If I were to agree," he said slowly, watching the predatory gleam in the eyes of each of the men, "then my name appears on no records. We don't sign papers; I don't sit on any boards; I'm not listed as an advisor. Essentially I'm a ghost. At most I'm a friend who meets some gentlemen once in a while at the races."

"Not a problem," said Sheffield.

"Second condition. The half-million *bonus* is

matched by a similar fee at the other end. If I can get the bulk research packages from Chechnya and Vilnius—"

"And Kazakhstan," added one of the other MPs.

Clive nodded. "Those three. If I get all three, then I get the second bonus."

The partners exchanged looks, but Mowbry looked hard at Clive. "Very well."

"Last condition," Clive said.

"You want a lot," Sheffield muttered.

"You ask a lot. This last part is not negotiable. I do this for you and then I'm out."

None of the other men looked happy about that. Mowbry frowned and shook his head. "Can we agree that once this is over we can *discuss* other projects? You can decide on a case-by-case basis."

Clive smiled. "My prices would very likely go up in that eventuality."

"We're not Arabs haggling over a rug, Monroe. We know what you're worth, and if another batch of research comes up that we must have, then we'll make you an appropriate offer."

Clive Monroe thought about it for a full three minutes. Mowbry and the others held their tongues, each of them afraid to say anything to break the spell of the moment.

"Very well," Clive said, and he stood up. The others stood as well and they all shook hands, clapping Clive on the back, congratulating one another.

"Time for champagne," declared Mowbry. He plucked a chilled bottle of Bollinger from an ice bucket and held it up for inspection. "I knew you'd agree, Monroe. I knew I could count on you."

Suddenly the champagne bottle exploded, showering them all with wine and bubbles and tiny splinters of glass. There was no bang, no hiss of troubled gasses from the bottle. It just disintegrated and showered the room, leaving Lord Mowbry holding the neck in which the cork was still firmly seated.

"Bloody hell!" cried Sheffield, pawing at his clothes and stepping back as if trying to back away from the mess on his suit.

Mowbry looked shocked and embarrassed. "Good lord," he said, aghast, "the bottle must have been shaken or—"

He stopped speaking and stared at Clive, who was similarly spattered with champagne but who had a peculiar smile on his face, as if he'd just remembered something wryly amusing. His eyes has lost their calculating coldness and stared at the other men without focus.

"My dear fellow," Mowbry began, tentatively reaching for Clive, afraid that the exploding bottle had cut him. "Your chest . . ."

Clive looked down. His tie hung askew and his coat unbuttoned. The crisp white of his shirt was dark with moisture, but not with the pale stains of wine. From the center of his chest a red flower bloomed, spreading petals of crimson that vanished under the folds of his jacket.

"I—"

His knees abruptly buckled and he dropped to the floor with a heavy thud of bone on carpet.

Sheffield looked from Clive to the broken bottle and then, driven by some premonition of horror, turned to the big picture window. There was a single hole punched through the reinforced glass with dozens of crooked cracks spreading out in a spiderweb pattern.

The second shot exploded the entire pane of glass and this time the bullet—unheard and unseen—punched a hole above Clive's left eyebrow and blew out the back of his head. Bone and brain splashed the back wall of the box. The crashing of the thick glass and the terrified shouts of the four men muffled the sound of Clive Monroe's body crumpling backward onto the carpet. The sound of the gunshot report drifted lazily toward them from far away.

Three hundred and twenty yards away, deep inside a stand of trees by the far turn, Conrad Veder dropped the rifle on the ground. It was one he had purchased for the job and sighted in for this hit. He stripped off the long rubber sleeve protectors and removed the plastic welding mask. He had never touched those items with his bare flesh, and all traces of gunpowder residue would be burned into them. He dropped them into a shallow ditch he'd prepared, emptied a whole can of lighter fluid over them, and dropped in a wooden Lucifer match. Fire bloomed at once. Veder pulled off the rubber surgical gloves and dropped them into the blaze.

He moved quickly through the trees, retrieving the fawn coat and trilby hat he'd hung on branches, and pulled them on. A pair of Wellingtons stood by the edge of the copse and he stepped into them. The shoes he wore were size 10 trainers of the most common and inexpensive generic brand. Probably half the people on the racecourse would be wearing the same brand. With his feet inside the boots and the coat and hat he looked like what he was: a racecourse official. One of the nameless, faceless men hired by the day to stand at various points along the racecourse to watch for falls or other problems. Veder had worked at the racetrack for three weeks. He moved out of the trees and crossed the track and then cut through another wooded area, coming out on the far side of the stands. Then he joined the crowd that moved and yelled in confusion as word of the murder spread through the rumor mill. He eventually ducked out of the crowd, found a bathroom, removed his coat, hat, and boots, and left them in a stall. From under the plastic trash bag in the bathroom dustbin he removed a small parcel that contained new shoes, a blue windbreaker printed with the name of the local football team, wire-framed glasses, and a pair of spectator binoculars. He flushed his mustache down the loo.

When he rejoined the crowd he was one of hundreds who looked and dressed and acted like startled spectators at an afternoon's event that had become suddenly more interesting.

It was the second kill since he'd accepted the seven-target job from DaCosta. The first had been simpler—the poisoning of a man in a wheelchair whose once brilliant mind was lost in the unlit labyrinth of early-onset Alzheimer's. Two down, five to go.

Chapter Thirty-One

The Deck
Saturday, August 28, 2:06 P.M.
Time Remaining on the Extinction Clock: 93 hours, 54 minutes E.S.T.

"The Twins are still in the staff room," said Otto. "They're interviewing Bannerjee and their other *spies*. Before you ask, yes . . . Bannerjee and the others have been briefed. They should be wrapping up in a couple of hours. You could stay in the tank a bit longer if you'd like."

"No," said Cyrus as he climbed out of the sensory deprivation tank. "I'm done." He cut a sharp look at Otto. "What's wrong?"

"We lost another one," said Otto as he held out a bathrobe.

Water sluiced down Cyrus Jakoby's legs to form a salty puddle on the floor. He turned and held his arms backward so Otto could slide the robe on.

"Another what?"

"Researcher. Daniel Horst."

"Virology?"

"Epideminiology."

"How?"

"He broke his bathroom mirror and cut his wrists," said Otto. "He bled out in his tub."

Cyrus scowled as he padded barefoot to the workstation in the corner. He called up the staff directory, found Daniel Horst, and entered a password to access the man's most recent psychological evaluations. Cyrus read through and his frown deepened.

"It's all in there," said Otto mildly. "In the after-session notes. Both Hastings and Stenner remarked on Horst's increased levels of stress, frequent headaches, nervousness, lack of direct eye contact. Plenty of signs of depression and diminished self-esteem. He was also a late-night regular at the staff bar every night. Classic stuff."

"We missed it," said Cyrus.

"We didn't see it," corrected Otto. "We've been otherwise occupied."

"It's my fault. I'm weeks behind in reading the staff evaluations."

"Neither of us saw it for the same reason. We need to delegate more, Mr. Cyrus. We're spreading ourselves too thin. If we try to do everything, then we'll get sloppy." He paused. "We need to process more of the SAMs into the Family. We need to put them to work."

"I wish Eighty-two . . ." Cyrus let it hang.

"He's not ready."

"The others are?"

"Some are. Enough to take some pressure off of us."

Cyrus shrugged. "Horst's death could be trouble."

"No. The cleaning woman who found him reported directly to the security shift supervisor, and he contacted me. I quarantined the cleaner. She'll be on the next flight to the Hive. The security supervisor is one of the Haeckels, so there's no problem with him keeping his mouth shut."

"Good, good," Cyrus said distractedly. "Do we have a cover story for Horst being missing?"

"He was needed at the Hive. A rumor can be started that he got a juicy promotion and went to the Hive to head up a new division. A component of the rumor will be that his apparent stress was him sweating whether he'd get the promotion or not. It's worked before and the rumor does some good for morale and overall team efficiency."

Cyrus nodded. Staff sent to the Hive were never allowed to return to the Deck. Except for a special few—Otto and Cyrus, the SAMs, several of the Haeckels, and one or two key scientists—no one else was allowed to travel between the two facilities. No one outside that circle even knew where the other facility was.

Disinformation was frequently seeded into the rumor mill. There was even an abiding belief that there was a Laboratory A somewhere in Mexico and a new facility set to open in Australia, though neither was true. It was useful to sustain the belief when it became necessary for staff members to disappear.

This latest suicide was troubling. Suicides among the virology and epidemiology staff were very high. Drug addiction and alcoholism were even higher, though the recent increases in random urine and blood testing had decreased the risk of technicians staggering into a clean room while high. That had been a lesson they'd learned the hard way.

"What was Horst working on?"

"Tay-Sachs."

"Why the stress? Surely you vetted him for—"

"We did. He's not a Jew; he never had any significant Jewish friends, never dated a Jewish woman. His distrust of Jews was marked in his initial evaluations and recruitment interviews. He even scored in the high sevens for resentment against Jews for jobs and grants in his field."

"Then why was he depressed?"

"Why do most of the suicide cases go soft on us? It's always the same thing. Conscience. No matter what we do to prevent it, they reach a point where their vision and trust in the New Order is overmatched by fear."

"Fear of what?" Cyrus snapped.

"Damnation, probably. In one form or another."

"Bullshit. We screen for atheism in every single member of the science staff."

"Most atheists are closet agnostics or disappointed believers."

"So?"

"As you point out in so many of your staff speeches, Mr. Cyrus, we're at war. The saying that there are no atheists in foxholes is more often true than not. Even if the belief is momentary and conditional."

"So . . . you're saying that this is *my* fault?"

"Not at all, Mr. Cyrus. I'm saying that this is evidence of the kind of inherent weakness that the Extinction Wave will wash away."

Cyrus cinched the robe more tightly around his waist and walked to the window. The view was that of the production tanks and the white-suited technicians who milled around them.

"We should have tried harder to find the gene that controlled the conscience," said Otto.

"What I don't understand—and *I* should understand, Otto—is why and how this happens when we systematically and exhaustively treated every person on the science team to deactivate VMAT2."

VMAT2—Vesicular Monoamine Transporter 2—was a membrane protein that transports monoamines like dopamine, norepinephrine, serotonin, and histamine from cellular cytosol into synaptic vesicles. Geneticist Gene Hamer had pioneered the belief that the gene was more active in persons who held strong religious beliefs and less so in those who held little or no beliefs. Cyrus accepted this as likely and subscribed to several similar neurotheological views. He had spent years exploring the links between N, N-Dimethyltryptamine levels in the pineal gland and spiritual beliefs.

"None of the team should be capable of religious beliefs of any kind," Cyrus said gruffly.

"We've had this discussion before, Mr. Cyrus. You told me that you did not totally accept the 'God gene' theory."

"That's not what I said, dammit," Cyrus barked. He leaned close and shouted at Otto. "I said that I don't believe it accounts for all faith. It doesn't account for true faith. False faith may be controlled by genetics. Faith in ideals and deities that are clearly unrelated to the divine path of racial development. No one with a pure genetic line, no one who believes in the right and only way, requires a gene for faith. That's a fundamental truth to faith itself. It's the so-called mystery of faith that those Catholic swine have been beating themselves up over for two thousand years."

Otto wiped Cyrus's spittle from his shirtfront.

"As you say."

Cyrus leaned back, his eyes still hot and his face flushed.

"The gene therapy must be flawed."

"Of course, sir," said Otto neutrally. "That must be it."

"We'll run the sequence again. We'll do a new round of gene therapy."

"Naturally."

"I don't want any more inconvenient attacks of conscience."

"God forbid," said Otto with a smile. He left before Cyrus began throwing things.

Chapter Thirty-Two

Private airfield near Denver, Colorado
Saturday, August 28, 2:29 P.M.
Time Remaining on the Extinction Clock: 93 hours,
31 minutes E.S.T.

Top and Bunny met me as I got off the jet. They were dressed in black BDUs and wearing shoulder rigs but had no other obvious weapons. Neither of them looked very happy. There was a lot of that going around.

Hanler shook hands all around but stayed with his plane as we headed to a small hangar at the edge of the field. There was a Mister Softee truck parked inside; however, the man who leaned against the rear corner didn't look like he sold ice-cream cones for a living. He looked like the actor Ving Rhames, except for the artificial leg and the shrapnel scars on his face.

"Cap'n," said Top, "this is Gunnery Sergeant Brick Anderson, head of field support for the Denver office."

Brick fit his name and he had a handshake that could crush half-inch pipe.

"Good to meet you, Cap," said Brick. "I've heard stories."

"You look like you could tell a few stories of your own, Gunny," I said. "How'd you slip the NSA?" I asked.

"They heard I was a cripple. Only sent two guys to pick me up." He shrugged. "Didn't go like they planned."

Bunny murmured, "Not handicapped—handi-*capable*."

"What's the plan?" I asked.

Brick shrugged. "Big Man back home said to give you whatever on the ground support I can manage. Deep

Iron's a half hour from here. I pretended to be a potential customer and asked if I could come out sometime this week. Asked what their hours are. They're open now. Head of sales is on the grounds. Name's Daniel Sloane. Here's his info." Brick handed me a slip of paper with contact numbers. Then he handed me a slim file folder. "This is basic stuff I pulled off their Web site. Specs and such."

"Good job." I flipped open the folder, took a quick glance, and closed it. "I'll read it on the way. How are we set for equipment? I have a handgun and two magazines. Can you load me up?"

The big man grinned as he led us to the back of the truck and opened the door. The whole thing was a rolling arsenal. I saw just about every kind of firearm known to modern combat, from five-shot wheelguns to RPGs.

"My-oh-my-oh-my," Top said, breaking out into a big grin. "I'm so happy I could cry."

"It's like Christmas, isn't it?" said Bunny.

A few minutes later we were cruising down an industrial side road that curved toward the snowcapped Rockies. Along the way we read and discussed the facility. Deep Iron was tucked away in the foothills of the Rockies southwest of Denver, built into a vast series of limestone caverns that honeycombed the region. Records were stored in various natural "floors" of the cavern system, and the highest security materials—meaning the stuff people were willing to pay the highest fees to squirrel away—were in the lowest levels, nearly a mile underground. I punched in the secure number for the DMS Warehouse back in Baltimore and asked to speak to the head of the computer division—Bug.

He was born as Jerome Taylor but he'd been a computer geek so long even his family called him Bug. His understanding of anything with circuits and microchips bordered on the empathic.

"Hey, Cap," he said brightly, as if none of what was happening was any more real to him than the events in a video game. "What's the haps?"

"Bug, listen—Top, Bunny, and I are in Denver at a place called Deep Iron and—"

"Oh, sure. Big storage facility. They filmed a couple of sci-fi movies there back in—"

"That's great," I said, cutting him off before he could tell me details of everything from the source material of the films down to the Best Boy's shoe size. He really was a geek's geek and could probably give Hu a run for his money. "See if you can hack their computer system."

He snorted. "Don't insult me."

I laughed. "What I need are floor plans for the whole place. And I need an exact location for anything related to Haeckel. Dr. Hu has the basic info, but I want you to go deeper and download everything to my PDA."

"How soon?"

"An hour ago."

"Give me ten minutes."

It took nine.

When he called back he said, "Okay, you have the floor plans and a searchable database of all clients. There's only one Haeckel in their directory. First name Heinrich. It's an oversized bin, thirty by forty feet, located on J-level."

I pulled up the schematic on my PDA and cursed silently. J-level was all the way at the bottom, a mile straight down.

"What can you get me about what's stored there?"

"Minute," he said, and I could hear him tapping keys. "Okay, the main hard drive says 'records,' but there's a separate database for inspections and that specifies the contents as file boxes times three hundred fifty-one. The bin has two doors—both locked by the estate attorneys. Contents are listed as mixed paper records. One box is listed as MF. My guess is that's microfiche or micro-film."

"Any idea what they're records of?"

"Nope. It says the boxes were sealed by Haeckel prior to his death and there was a provision in his will that they not be opened except by a proven family member. No living family is listed, though. His estate provides for storage and oversight of the whole thing by a law firm. An inspection of the seals is required every year. Looks like it's an attorney who checks the seals. Several attorneys over the years, all from the same firm. Birkhauser and Bernhardt of Denver. The seals are also witnessed by a representative of Deep Iron. Looks like it's still there because they haven't found an heir. I'll hack the law firm and see if they have any-thing."

I thanked him and brought Top and Bunny up to speed.

"No heir," mused Top, "except for Gunnar Haeckel, who is apparently back from the dead and hunting unicorns in South America. Funny old world."

Bunny grinned. "I wouldn't give this job up for any-thing."

"We're here," said Brick.

Chapter Thirty-Three

"Hey, Jude," said Tom Ito, "remember that virus you were asking about before? The one that was there and then up and vanished?"

"Sure, what about it?"

"It's back. Log onto the e-mail screens."

Judah swiveled in his chair and began hammering keys on his laptop. The set of screens used by the secretaries for handling e-mail, newsletters, and alerts popped us as cascading windows.

Ito leaned over his shoulder. "Look for auto-response e-mails. See, there's eight of them. The virus is in there."

Judah quarantined the e-mails and ran virus detection software. A pop-up screen flashed a warning. Judah loaded an isolation program and used it to open one of the infected e-mails. The software allowed them to view the content and its code with a heavy firewall to prevent data spillover into the main system.

The e-mail content said that the outgoing CDC Alert e-mail was undeliverable because the recipient e-mail box was full. That happened a lot. However, the software detected a Trojan horse—a form of malware that appeared to perform a desirable function in the target operating system but which actually served other agendas, ranging from collecting information such as credit card numbers and keystrokes to outright damage to the computer. A lot of "free" software and goodies on the Internet, including many screen savers, casino betting

sites, porn, and offers for coupon printouts uploaded
Trojan horses to users. On the business and government
level they were common.

"Trojan?" asked Ito.

"Looks like. Can't block the sender, though, because it's really using replies to our own mailing list
to send it."

"Maybe someone hijacked some of our subscribers
and is using their addresses."

"Probably." Judah frowned. "Okay, we're going to
have to identify the bounce-back e-mails and then block
those subscribers. Send a message to everyone."

Ito headed back to his cubicle to work on it while
Judah uploaded info on the virus to US-CERT—the
United States Computer Emergency Readiness Team,
part of Homeland Security. The CDC was a government
organization, and though this was very low-level stuff,
it was technically a cyberattack. Someone over at CERT
would take any warnings of a new virus and add it to
the database. If a trend was found an alert would be sent,
and very often CERT would provide updates to various
operating systems that would protect against further in-
cidents. It was routine and Judah had sent a hundred
similar e-mails over the last few years.

That should have done it.

It didn't.

There were no additional e-mail bounce-backs that
day. None the next. Had Judah been able to match the
current e-mail with the ones that had appeared—and
then vanished—from the computers earlier he would
have seen that the bounce-back e-mail addresses were
not the same. Nor was the content, nor the Trojan horse.
The senders of the e-mails were cautious.

When similar e-mail problems occurred at offices of the National Institutes of Health in Bethesda, Maryland, the main office and many regional offices of the World Health Organization, the Coordinating Center for Health Information and Service, the Agency for Toxic Substances and Disease Registry, the Coordinating Center for Infectious Diseases, and the Coordinating Office for Terrorism Preparedness and Emergency Response and a dozen other health crisis management organizations, there were no alarms rung. Each group received a completely different kind of e-mail from all the others. There was no actual damage done, and other than minor irritation there was no real reaction. Viruses and spam e-mails are too common.

The real threats had not yet been sent.

The Extinction Clock still had ninety-three hours and twenty-nine minutes to go.

Chapter Thirty-Four

Deep Iron Storage Facility, Colorado
Saturday, August 28, 3:11 P.M.
Time Remaining on the Extinction Clock: 92 hours,
49 minutes E.S.T.

Deep Iron looks like a water treatment plant. From outside the gate all we could see were a few medium-sized buildings and miles of electrified security fence. According to the info Bug had sent me, the surface buildings were mostly used for equipment storage and garages. The main building had a few offices, but mostly it's a big box around a set of six industrial elevators, two of which were big enough to fit a dozen SUVs. The real

Deep Iron is way underground. The upper tiers of storage start one hundred yards down and the rest are far below that.

Brick drove us to the front gate. There was no guard. We exchanged a look and Bunny opened the door and stepped out. He checked the guard shack and leaned close to the fence for a moment and then came back, a frown etched into his face.

"Guard shack is empty, no sign of struggle. The fences are electrified but the juice is off," he said.

Top pointed to my PDA. "Stuff Bug sent says Deep Iron has its own power plant."

I took out my cell and dialed the contact number for Daniel Sloane, the sales manager, but it rang through to voice mail. I called the main office number, same thing. "Okay, we're playing this like we're on enemy territory. Lock and load. Bunny, open the gate."

Bunny pulled the gate open and then jumped onto the back step-bumper of the truck as we rolled into the compound. Brick did a fast circuit inside the fence. There were eleven cars parked in the employee lot. None of them was a DMS vehicle. We paused at the rear guard shack, but it was also empty. I told Brick to head to the main office and we parked outside, the vehicle angled to keep its reinforced corner toward the building's windows. We were already kitted out with Kevlar and we used the truck's steel door to shield us as we stuffed extra magazines into pockets and clipped night vision onto our steel pots. None of us said it aloud, but we were all thinking about Jigsaw Team. A dozen of them had come out here this morning, and now they were missing. Were they in hiding? Was there still that chance? Or were they truly MIA?

Now three of us were going down into an unfamiliar vast cavern system that may have swallowed all of Jigsaw. No backup except Brick, and he had one leg. We couldn't even call the State Police or the National Guard.

I caught the looks Top and Bunny were shooting back and forth and made sure my own eyes were poker neutral as I began stuffing flash bangs into a bag.

I glanced at Brick. "Don't take offense at this, Gunny, but are you able to provide cover fire if we need it?"

He grinned. "Don't need two legs to pull a trigger, Captain. Little Softee here," he patted the side of the truck, "has a few James Bond tricks built in to her."

Brick clambered into the back of the truck, folded down a small seat by the wall closest to the building, and fiddled with some equipment on rails. There was a hydraulic hiss and a metal case on the floor opened to allow a six-barreled, air-cooled minigun to rise and lock into place. Brick reached across it and slid open a metal vent on the side of the truck, then turned back to us, beaming.

"The whole floor has rails on it so the gun can be maneuvered to either side and down to cover the rear. I have grenade launchers fore and aft, and the truck body is half-inch steel with a ceramic liner. I've got enough rounds to start a war, and probably enough to end it."

"Fuck me," said Top.

"Hey, boss," said Bunny, "can we send him in and wait here?"

Brick chuckled. "Five years ago, kid, I'd have taken you up on that."

"Outstanding," I said. "Okay, Gunny, if the power's off in there we may not be able to use landlines, and once we're down deep we'll lose cell and sat phone communication. I don't even know how to estimate how much time this is going to take, but if Church can get the NSA to back off then I'd very much appreciate you calling in every U.S. agent with a gun and send them down after us."

"You got a bad feeling about this, Captain?" he asked.

"Don't you?"

"Shit . . . I've had an itch between my shoulder blades since I got up this morning."

"Keep one eye on the sky, too," said Top. "We didn't see any vehicles that don't belong here. These jokers may have come by chopper."

"I got me some SAMs if I need 'em," Brick said. I really wished he had two good legs.

I said, "If you send anyone down after us, give 'em today's recognition code."

The day code was "bluebird" for challenge and "canary" for response. Anyone in DMS tactical who logged in after 2:00 A.M. would know it. Anyone we met down there who didn't know it was likely to have a worse day than we were having.

We synched our watches and checked our gear. I gave them the nod.

Even with all the unknown waiting for us, it felt good to stop running and start hunting.

Bunny took point and he ran low and fast from the corner of the truck to the corner of the building while we covered him. Except for the whisper of his gum-rubber soles on the asphalt of the parking lot there was no sound. There was no wind at all, and the sun was behind us. Bunny hit the wall and crouched to cover Top as he ran in, and they covered front and back as I joined them. We couldn't see Brick, but knowing that the cold black eye of the minigun was following us was a great comfort. Brick had the look of the kind of soldier who generally hit what he aimed at, and I doubt anyone ever caught him napping.

The door to the office stood ajar and we crouched down on either side and fed a fiber-optic camera in for a snoop. Nothing. Bunny checked for trip wires and booby traps and found nothing. We moved inside.

According to the intel Bug had provided there were four guards on each shift, two two-man teams made up of ex-military or ex-police. We found them right away, and right away we knew we'd just stepped into something bizarre and unbearably ugly.

The four guards had been killed, and there was a fifth man in a business suit. Sloane, the sales manager. Each had been shot repeatedly, but their bodies were in an indescribable condition. Legs and arms were broken and jerked out of their sockets, the victims' heads were smashed, their faces brutally disfigured.

I couldn't stop and stare; there was too much to do. We rushed deeper into the building and worked as a three-man team to clear each room, taking it in turns to be the one to open a door and step inside while the others provided high and low cross-fire cover. There were six rooms in the building. Mostly offices and a bathroom. Nothing else, and no one else.

We returned to the guardroom.

"Holy mother of God," whispered Bunny.

Top and I moved into the room and checked the bodies. "Multiple gunshots, Cap'n," he said. "Heavy-caliber hits."

"How long?"

"These guys aren't even cold. Maybe two hours, not more."

I tapped his arm and pointed to the blood spatter on the floor and walls. There are three major categories for blood spatter: passive, projected, and transfer. In the first case the bloodstains are caused by gravity with blood dripping from wounds. Projected stains come from blood under pressure—say from a torn artery—or rapid movement, as with someone shaking blood off their fingers. Then there are transfer spatters where something covered in blood comes into contact with a surface. Footprints, fingerprints, that sort of thing.

We were seeing a little of everything, but it didn't look right. There were spatter marks on the walls, but they didn't have the tight grouping you see with arterial sprays. These were random, erratic.

Top watched me and then went through the process himself, calculating the amount and distribution of blood. Then he looked down at the broken bodies.

"This is some voodoo shit right here."

"Talk to me."

He kept his voice low. "Those patterns only make sense if someone *shook* blood off these boys. Like whipping water off a towel. Or threw these boys around. But . . . that's wrong, ain't it?"

I didn't want to answer. "Top . . . look at the pools of blood under the bodies. Corpses don't bleed unless there's a wound under the body, in which case gravity will pull the blood down to the lowest point and then out through a wound. Not all of the blood, just whatever's in that part of the body. You with me?"

He was right with me. "I think someone messed with these boys after they were dead."

"Uh-huh."

"Tore 'em up, threw 'em around."

"Wait—what are you saying?" asked Bunny, who had come up behind us.

Top shook his head. "I don't know . . . this looks like rage. Someone went apeshit here. Whoever did it was a strong motherfucker. I couldn't do it. I doubt Farmboy here could."

Bunny squatted down and picked up several shell casings. "Well, well, well . . . check this out."

He showed us a steel-cased 7.62×39mm FMJ shell casing.

Top looked at it and then at me. "That's a Russian short, Cap'n. Same thing we saw in Wilmington."

Bunny turned to look at the bodies and then back to the casing. "Now, how the hell's this stuff connected to Wilmington? And how the hell are the Russians involved?"

I was just reaching for my commlink when a *bing-bing* in my ear signaled a call from DMS command. It was Grace.

"This is a secure line, Joe. I have a situational update."

"So do I, but let's make it fast. We're in the woods with the bears."

"We've ID'd two of the four Russians who ambushed Echo Team in Wilmington. They're ex-Spetsnaz."

"Okay," I said, "I'll see your dead Spetsnaz and raise you a full hit team." I told her about the shell casing and the dead guards. I described the blood spatter and the postmortem mutilations.

"Bloody hell."

"What the hell are we into here, Grace?"

"I . . . don't know."

"Is there any whiff of official Russian involvement? Could this be something political?" Spetsnaz was a catchall label for Russian Special Forces and included operatives of the Federal Security Service, the Internal Troops of the Russian Ministry of Internal Affairs, and units controlled by the GRU—their military intelligence service. After the USSR crumbled and the Russian economy collapsed, a lot of these soldiers were either discharged or they went AWOL. The Russia Mafia employed a lot of them worldwide, but they've also been recruited by private security companies for dirty work everywhere mercs were useful. Which is a lot of places in these times.

"I don't think so, and in our current position we can't call the State Department and ask. Mr. Church thinks the team in Wilmington were mercenaries. These may be part of one large team . . . but we have no idea who they'd be working for," she said. "Any sign of Hack or Jigsaw?"

"No, but we're still topside. We're heading down now. We could use some backup."

"I've none to give. We're locked up tighter than a nun's chastity." She paused, then said, "Joe, if you wanted to abort the mission I'd back you."

I did, but I wasn't going to. She probably knew that.

"Jigsaw," was all I had to say.

"Look, Joe . . . at the moment I care bugger all about protocol. If you run into anyone down there who isn't DMS . . ." She let the rest hang.

"Roger that, Major." I almost called her "Major Babe" but luckily my presence of mind hadn't totally fled.

I clicked off and told the others about the Spetsnaz connection. I saw the information register, but it didn't take the heart out of either of them. Even so, Bunny looked rattled by the condition of the corpses. His eyes kept straying to them and then darting away, then straying back. I knew what was going through his head. He understood killing, but the rest . . . that wasn't soldiering. It had a primitive viciousness about it that was inhuman.

"Cap'n," said Top from across the room. "Looks like the power's still on in here. The elevator lights are green."

"Phones?"

He pulled one off the wall, shook his head.

"We're going to be out of communication real fast," said Bunny. "Without a hard line we'd be better off shouting."

I tapped my commlink for a patch to Brick, filled him in, and told him to establish a command link with Major Courtland.

"If the elevator's working I can come in—," he started to say, but I cut him off.

"Truly appreciated, Gunny, but we need to move fast. No offense."

"None taken."

"And make sure no one else comes in here who doesn't belong to the club."

"I guarantee it."

We took one elevator, but we sent all six of them down at the same time. We stopped two of them—ours and one other—at the next to last level, and as soon as the doors opened and we cleared the area around us we bent low and listened to the sounds coming up from the elevator shafts. We heard the other cars stop, heard the doors open.

The limestone caverns were huge and dark and smelled of mold and bad dreams. There were long rows of fluorescent fixtures overhead, but the power to the lights was off. The elevators must have been on a different circuit or had their own power supply. It made sense that the intruders would leave the elevators on—it was a mile-long climb back into the sunlight if they had to take the stairs.

We crouched and waited, using night vision to look for movement, but there was nothing. No ambush gunfire. No explosives.

It didn't mean that there weren't Russian shooters lying in wait—it just meant that they weren't shooting randomly at anything that moved. That could be good or bad. I pointed to the stairwell door, and after checking it for trip wires we entered the stairwell and looked down.

All of the battery-operated emergency lights had been smashed, and the stairwell was a bottomless black hole.

The night-vision devices used by the DMS are about six cuts above anything on the commerical market and a generation newer than most special ops teams had. A lot of the standard NVDs used passive systems that amplified existing environmental ambient lighting; ours had an option for an active system that emmitted an infrared light source to provide sufficient illumination in situations of zero ambient light. The downside was that the infrared from an active system could be spotted by someone else wearing night vision. It's a risk that also had rewards if the other guys weren't using something as sophisticated, and that wasn't likely. The only other option was flashlights, and that screwed with your natural night vision and was a sniper's paradise. The other useful feature of our NVDs was the new panoramic lens that gave us a ninety-five-degree field of clear vision and a thermal-imaging component. If there was something alive down here, we'd see it in total darkness and we'd see it better than a hunting owl. With night vision everything is a ghostly green, but we were all comfortable with it and we all automatically made the mental shifts necessary to function with top-level efficiency.

Even so, when I looked down the stairwell all I saw were flights of stairs at right angles that descended beyond the effective range of the NVP optics.

We went down slow and careful, expecting traps.

We found the first trip wire thirty-seven steps down. In my goggles it was a slender spider's web of glowing green. Whoever placed it was smart, setting it close into the back of the riser so that it wouldn't trigger as someone stepped down on the ball of his foot but would catch the fall or rise of the heel. Smart.

I showed it to Bunny, who nodded his appreciation, but Top shook his head dismissively. He was more seasoned than Bunny. The trap was smart, but it was too soon to be smart. The best way would have been to rig an obvious trip wire and then the more subtle one. Set and then exploit the expectations of the person you're trying to trap.

We moved forward slowly and found one more trip wire. Same as before. Like the first, it was attached to a Claymore and set back near the riser. Bunny disabled them both. If backup came, we'd like them to arrive in one piece.

A few times we encountered something smeared on the banister, but with the night vision it looked like oil. It smelled of copper, though. Blood.

"Maybe a guard clipped one of those Russian boys," Top suggested in a whisper, but I didn't think so. The smears were on the outside of the railings that surrounded a central drop all the way to the floor. You might get smears like that if something was thrown down the shaft and hit rails on the way down.

At the bottom of the stairwell we solved that mystery. A man in unmarked black BDUs lay twisted into a ragdoll heap at the bottom of the stairwell. It was clear he had been thrown over the rails and had struck several times on the way down to the concrete floor. His body was torn to pieces. I looked up through the vacant hole around which the stairwell curled for over a mile. It was a long, long fall. I wondered if the man had been alive during any of that horrible plummet.

Top knelt by the man. He checked first for booby traps, and when he found none he went through the man's pockets. No ID, no personal effects. All he had on him were gun belts and equipment bags. Some hand grenades and lots of spare magazines. The ammunition was 7.62x39mm FMJ. Russian.

Top weighed a magazine thoughtfully in one hand and looked up at me. "Jigsaw?" he suggested.

"I don't know," I said, but in truth I didn't like the feel of this.

Bunny was by the door to J-level, checking it for traps. "We're clear here," he reported.

I pulled up the floor plan on my PDA and we studied it. Right outside the stairwell door was a wide corridor with elevators on one side and the first of the storage units on the other. The schematic couldn't show us anything more than a blueprint, so we had no way of knowing what kind of actual cover might be out there.

"Scope," I said, and Bunny fished a fiber-optic scope from his pack and fed it under the door. The scope fed images to a palm-sized screen that folded down from his chest pack. He had it set for night vision, but that couldn't show thermals. Bunny turned the scope in all directions. We saw a row of electric golf carts and stacks of file cartons. Thousands of them standing in rows that trailed off far beyond the visible range of the optics. Nothing moved.

Using hand signals, I indicated that we would open the door and give cross-fire cover as we exited. I'd use the shelter of the stairwell landing to provide cover while they ran out and went left and right. They nodded and Bunny stuffed the scope back into his pack. I finger counted down to zero, and then we went through into the cavern.

Gunfire shattered the silence around us and suddenly we were in one hell-storm of an ambush.

Chapter Thirty-Five

The Warehouse, Baltimore, Maryland
Saturday, August 28, 3:13 P.M.
Time Remaining on the Extinction Clock: 92 hours, 47 minutes

"How is the President?" asked Mr. Church.

"Unhappy, unwell, and unwilling to deal with this crap," barked Linden Brierly.

"Tell him that he has my sympathies, but I need to speak with him."

"I can probably set up a call later this—"

"Linden . . . I need to speak with him now."

Silence washed like a cold tide back and forth between their phones.

"You're killing me, Church," said Brierly. "The doctors here already want me lynched, and if I ask the First Lady to let him take a call she will have my nuts for lunch."

"Tell her that this concerns Joe Ledger," said Church.

Brierly was quiet. Two months ago Joe Ledger and Echo Team had saved the First Lady and half of Congress from terrorists who wanted to release a deadly plague. The First Lady had seen Ledger in action, had seen his heroism and his absolute viciousness. It had changed her as a person, and Brierly had not yet put his finger on whether that change was good or bad. He'd been part of that fight, and it had been a step up for him.

But this was asking a lot.

"I'll see what she says," Brierly warned, "but don't expect much."

Mr. Church sat in his office and waited. He did nothing else. He didn't even eat a cookie, though he eyed the plate of vanilla wafers with interest. The wall clock ticked and the boats in the harbor sloshed noisily through the choppy water.

"Mr. Church?" The First Lady's voice was soft, but it was like silk wrapped around a knife blade.

"Good afternoon—"

"Is Joe Ledger in trouble?"

Right to the point. Church admired that. "Yes, ma'am." In a few short sentences he explained what was going on. He even told her about Joe's mission to Deep Iron.

Church was a good judge of character who was seldom let down by his expectations.

The First Lady said, "And you want my husband, who has just come out of surgery, to not only take back the reins of office but take on the stress of a major political upheaval in his own administration?"

"Yes," said Church. She would have fried him for an attempt to sugarcoat things.

"Will this help Joe?"

"Because of the NSA, Joe has had to go into an exceedingly dangerous situation without proper backup and no hope at all of rescue if things go wrong. That should never have happened."

"Can you tell me what this mission is about? Not the incidentals but the big picture?"

"I could," he said, "but you're not cleared for it."

"Mr. Church," she said quietly, "I'm speaking to you on a secure line and I will have the final say as to whether my husband takes back his office. Not the Vice President, not the doctors here at Walter Reed, not the AG or the Speaker of the House. Believe me when I tell you that you need to convince me of the importance of this or this conversation is going to end right here and now."

"You do that well," he said.

"What?"

"Play the big cards."

"My God . . . is that a compliment from Mr. Church?"

"It is. Call it respect from one pro to another."

"So you'll tell me?"

"Yes," he said. "I think I'd damn well better."

Chapter Thirty-Six

"Go! Go! Go!" I yelled, and laid down a stream of fire with my M4. Top dropped low and dove behind a parked golf cart, rolled, and came up into a shooter's crouch. Bunny made a dive for cover behind a stack of boxes, but I saw his body pitch and twist in midair as he was hit by at least one round. He dropped out of sight.

I saw muzzle flashes from four points. A pair of shooters hidden behind the towers of boxes and two more on opposite sides of the row of golf carts. The stairwell was wider than the door, so I had a narrow concrete wall to stand behind, but every time I tried to lean out and fire, bullets slammed into the wall inches from my head. If it hadn't been for the night-vision goggles the flying stone splinters would have blinded me and torn half my face off.

"Eyes!" Top yelled as he hurled a flash bang like a breaking ball. I closed my eyes and heard the dry *bang!* Then I dropped to one knee, leaned out, and looked for a target. I saw a dark figure staggering away from the point of explosion, and I gave him two three-round bursts. He spun away from me, hit a wall, and collapsed backward. To my left I saw Top edging along a wall of boxes toward the shooter on my far left. I laid down some cover fire and ducked back as the shooter returned fire, but then Top wheeled around the edge and put two in the guy's throat.

I was running before the man had even dropped and I went fast and bent over along the row of carts knowing that the shooter on my right would be aiming in the direction of Top's muzzle flashes. Suddenly there was movement in front of me and in a microsecond I realized that the shooter was running down the row of carts in my direction, but he had his head craned sideways as he tried to get an angle on Top.

The shooter never saw it coming. I closed to zero distance and put my barrel under his chin and blew his helmet off his head.

The last Russian must have seen me, because he opened up right away and I had to dive into a belly slide as bullets tore chunks out of the concrete floor behind me.

There was movement to my right and I saw Bunny, alive and crouched low, crabbing sideways toward me. When he caught my eye he pointed to a spot where a wall of stacked boxes stood between him and the remaining shooter. I nodded and he moved forward. The gunman kept me pinned down, but the carts were good cover. I had no idea where Top was, but I guessed he was closing on the shooter's position from the far side.

When Bunny was in position I tapped the commlink and whispered, "Top, we got a runner on third. Wait for the pitch."

There were two short bursts of static in my earbud as Top broke squelch twice for affirmative.

I said, "Throw him out at the plate. Let's hear some chatter from the dugout."

Top and I opened up and the cavern echoed with thunder as Bunny spun around the wall and ran across five yards of open space to come up at the shooter from behind. When he was ten feet out he put two bursts into the man, and the impact slammed him into the wall. He slid down onto his knees like a supplicant and then fell backward in a limp sprawl.

"Clear!" he yelled.

"Clear!" echoed Top.

"Hold there!" I yelled.

I didn't trust the situation and I hugged the shadows as I skirted the open spaces to close on Bunny's position. Top was there a step behind me and we secured the spot. Top took up a shooting position behind a short stack of boxes.

"You hit?" I asked Bunny. He grinned and folded back a torn flap of his camo shirt to show a long furrow that had been plowed along the side of his armor vest.

"Hooray for glancing blows," he said.

"Hooah," I agreed.

I bent and examined the dead man. No ID, no nothing, but his face was almost classical Slavic and weapons and gear were Russian. Same with the other three.

"When I woke up this morning," Top said, "I didn't expect to be at war with Mother Russia."

"If the opportunity presents itself," I said, "give me someone with a pulse so I can ask some questions."

They nodded.

Before us was a sea of boxes. File boxes and crates of every description, stacked in neat rows that trailed away into the distance. Hundreds of thousands of boxes, millions of tons of paper records. There were hundreds of chambers in the natural limestone caverns, and thousands of rooms and vaults. Miles of cement walkways. I accessed the floor plan on my PDA and we studied it and made some decisions.

"Okay," I said quietly. "We don't know how many more of them there are, but we know these guys are smart and they've had time to get creative. We go slow and we look for booby traps. No assumptions, no undue risks."

"Hooah," they responded.

We moved out, making no sound at all as we moved through an eternity of darkness. We found a few traps—mostly shape charges and rigged grenades—but they were crudely set. The way soldiers will do when they don't have time to do it right. We disabled each trap and kept moving, the three of us spread out in case we missed one.

Then we almost walked into a cross fire they'd set up in a big vault stacked to the rafters with file boxes from Denver law firms. But Top stopped us before we stepped in it.

"What?" I whispered to him. "You see something?"

"No, Cap'n," he murmured, "but if I was going to rig a shooting gallery it would be in there. How 'bout we get bright and noisy, see if we can flush some rabbits from the tall grass."

I nodded and we tossed in a pair of our flash bangs. As soon as the starburst brightness faded, we rushed the room. There was a sniper on top of a stack of crates, but even as we rushed in he was rolling off onto the floor, hands clamped to his ears. He fell twenty feet and landed badly.

Top got to him first, kicked the rifle out of his hands, and was bending to restrain him when he slowed and gave it up. When I reached him I could see why. The sniper had landed headfirst, taking the full impact on the side of the head. His neck must have snapped like a twig.

"Balls," I said.

We kept going. We could only move forward at a snail's pace. We'd found a few more traps, but we were trail-wise now, inside their heads, and we spotted the next few before anyone else got hurt. We were one mile down and going deeper, creeping along miles of slanting corridors, breathing air that had never felt sunshine or smelled rain. This would be a dreary place to die, and I had a flicker of superstitious dread about my ghost getting lost down here in the endless dark.

There were phones mounted on walls, but the cords were cut and the boxes smashed. We moved on, passing through rooms where law firms kept records of cases from thirty years ago, where film studios kept tens of thousands of reels of film and people kept furs and art and who knows what else. We passed through rooms crowded with classic cars and fifty of those terra-cotta soldiers they'd dug up in China.

We found two more security guards and half a dozen record clerks. All tied, all executed. Thirteen innocent people murdered . . . for *what*?

"God damn," swore Top, "I really want to catch up to these sons of bitches."

"What the hell are they looking for?" asked Bunny. "They're taking an incredible risk, and they're taking a lot of frigging time. They have to know they're not getting out of here."

I said nothing.

"So, this is . . . what?" Bunny continued. "A suicide mission to get old records? In what world does that make sense?"

"Maybe they expected to get in and out faster than they did," Top suggested. "Maybe they lost their window."

"Must be something pretty damned important down here," Bunny said, "for them to still be at it knowing that we're on their ass."

"We don't know how many of them there are," Top said. "They might have twenty guys down here, in which case they can make a pretty good run at getting past us. They might also be waiting on backup. There were no vehicles outside, so if they plan to get out they must have a ride coming. Could be extra guns in that."

It was a sobering thought, and none of us were getting cocky just because we'd managed to fight past their first couple of traps.

We pushed on. I used the schematic to plan our route, and that took us through a series of smaller chambers with more modern equipment that looked like it was part of the facility's records management system.

"Clear!" called Top Sims as he and Bunny checked the room ahead of us.

"Two minutes' rest," I said. I tapped the PDA. "We're half a klick from the target." The tiny display screen showed a zigzag trail leading to the Haeckel bin. It crooked through twenty-three turns and a dozen doorways. It was an ambusher's wet dream.

Top asked, "We getting anything from Brick?"

I shook my head. "We got about a billion tons of rock and steel between us and a signal."

We moved out once more, and now we were down to it. Nerves were on hair triggers, and if my virgin aunt had stepped out from behind those crates with a puppy in one hand and a baby in the other my guys would have capped her.

Those Spetsnaz nimrods had fired first, no questions asked. It seemed only right to extend the same courtesy, but the Russians had no new surprises for us. We did find one spot where there were expended shell casings—all Russian—and a lot of blood but no bodies. No drag marks, either, so the wounded must have walked out or been carried.

I used the interteam communication channel on my commlink to try to raise someone on Jigsaw. Got nothing but white noise. I took another look at the PDA. "Two lefts and then fifty feet straight in," I murmured.

At the first left we paused while Top quick-looked around the corner. He had started to say, "Clear," when the whole world exploded in a firestorm of automatic gunfire.

"Down!" I yelled, and everyone got low and went wide, gun barrels swinging around to find targets, but there were no muzzle flashes. The rock walls amped up the sound of the chattering guns, but we hadn't stepped into anything. At least not at the moment.

"It's not in the next room, Cap'n. This is from around the second corner," Top said as he slithered like a snake back from his observation post and wriggled behind a stack of wooden crates.

"Hey . . . Jigsaw's come to the party!" Bunny yelled; then he frowned and cupped a hand to his ear. "No . . . no, wait, all I hear are AKs."

Top nodded, crouched down next to me. "Farmboy's right. That's a one-sided gunfight."

"Unless," Bunny began, and then bit down on what he was going to say.

So I said it.

"Unless it's an execution."

Jigsaw. Christ, don't let it be so.

"Saddle up!" I bellowed, but as we clustered by the door to make our run something changed. The gunfire had been hot and heavy for nearly half a minute, with dips in the din as magazines fired dry and were replaced, but during one freak gap in the noise just as I was reaching for the doorknob there was a new sound.

It was a roar.

Nothing else describes it. The sound was deep and rough and charged with incredible power. It slammed into the walls and bounced through the shadows and came howling through the crack in the door.

It sounded like an animal. A really big and really pissed-off animal.

"What the hell was *that*?" Top yelled.

"I don't know and I don't want to find out," said Bunny.

"I do," I said, and opened the door.

The hallway was empty and I could hear another roar and more shouts coming from down the hall. I crept along, keeping close to the wall and low, barrel ready to pop a cap in anyone who stepped out of the next chamber. I knew Top and Bunny were behind me, but they moved as silently as I did.

We stopped outside of Haeckel's bin. The metal door was still closed, but there were dozens of jagged bullet holes in it, all of them chest high.

Top leaned his head toward me. "We going in, Cap'n?"

Just then the gunfire started up again. We dropped down and got wide. None of the rounds had penetrated the block-stone walls of the bin.

I cupped my hands around my mouth and waited for a lull.

"*Jigsaw!*" I yelled as loud as I could.

The gunfire flattened out for a moment and then there was a second roar. Not a response to my call. Not a human voice. Definitely an animal of great size and immense power.

"*JIGSAW!*" I yelled again. "*ECHO! ECHO! ECHO!*"

Then a man's voice cried out in response. It said, "Help!"

But he said it in Russian. *Pomogite!*

Not Jigsaw.

I yelled back using Hack Peterson's combat code name: "Big Dog! Big Dog . . . this is Cowboy!"

The voice cried out, "*Nyet! Nyet! Bozhe moi!*"

No! No! Oh, my God!

Then, "*Perekroi dveri!*"

Block the doors!

There was another roar, this one slightly different in pitch, not as deep but just as feral, and a new flurry of gunfire.

Top looked at me for orders. I leaned close to the bullet-pocked door and tried it in Russian. I called for Hack. I called a general question asking what was going on.

No one answered my question. There were more roars, more gunshots, more men yelling in hysterical Russian. "*On moyrtv!*"

He's dead! I heard that twice. And then a single voice crying, "*Othodi!*"

Fall back! Over and over again.

"Are we joining this party?" Top asked, but I shook my head.

The flurry of gunfire thinned.

"Fewer guns in play," Bunny observed. "Still no return fire that I can make out unless everyone's using AKs."

The last gun cleared its mag and then we heard something that froze the hearts in our chests. Another throat-ripping scream tore through the darkness, but this one was definitely a human voice: high and filled with pain and choked with a dreadful wetness. It rose to a piercing shriek and then suddenly cut off, leaving behind a terminal silence.

Then nothing.

I pushed the door open and crept out, low to the cold concrete floor, my .45 pointed at the bend in the hall, finger ready to slip inside the trigger guard. A moment later there was another scream, but this wasn't the cry of a man in pain—no, this was an ear-rending howl of bloody animal triumph. Even after the thunder of gunfire it was impossibly loud; the echo of it slammed off the walls and assaulted our ears like fists.

The silence that followed was harsh and filled with dreadful promise. We stared at the bend in the corridor, and then one by one my team looked to me for direction.

"We're going in," I said. "I'm on point. I want two rounds in anything that isn't DMS."

"Hooah," they whispered.

I reached for the door handle and gave it a quick turn. There was no gunfire. I took my last flash bang and lobbed it inside. We covered our ears for the big bang, but a split second later we were going through that door in a fast line, ready to finish this fight.

We stopped in our tracks.

What I saw hit me like a punch to the brain, but I had enough presence of mind to keep my mouth shut and my weapon ready. Behind me I heard a small gasp escape Bunny's throat. Top came up behind us. Everyone stopped and we all stood there staring at the Spetsnaz team.

"*Mother of God,*" Top whispered.

The room wasn't big. Maybe forty by fifty, stacked to the ceiling with file boxes. A few of the old punch-card computers draped in plastic sheeting stood against one wall. There was a desk, a chair, and a sorting table. The floor was littered with hundreds of shell casings. Smoke hung like green ghosts in the air, and on the floor, strewn around like refuse, were the Russians.

All of them, the entire Spetsnaz hit team. Eight of them.

Dead.

And not just dead . . . they'd been torn to pieces. Their guns still smoked; hands were still curled around the stocks, fingers hooked through trigger guards. Arms and legs and heads were scattered like islands in a sea of blood.

Bunny moved up beside me. "God . . . what the hell *happened* here?"

I sensed more than saw the stack of boxes to my left begin to shift and then I was moving, shoving Bunny and Top backward as a ton of boxed paper canted over and fell. Bunny tried to pivot and run, but the bloody shell casings rolled under his feet and he went into a wet slide. His flailing left hand clubbed Top right across the face.

A second stack of boxes began to fall and I leaped

aside, swinging my gun around to aim at the shadows behind them, ready to kill.

"Cap'n!" I heard Top yell. "On your—"

But that was all I heard as something came out of the shadows behind the stack to my right and slammed into me. The blow was so fast and so shockingly hard that for a moment I had the unreal thought that I'd been hit by a car. I could feel my body leave the ground as I hurtled ten feet through the air and slammed into another stack of file boxes. I tucked my chin into my shoulder to buffer the impact, but I struck so hard that the whole tower of boxes canted and fell, knocking me to the floor and then slamming into the adjoining tower. Suddenly the whole room seemed to be collapsing around me as columns of dusty boxes toppled. I heard a barrage of shots, but there was no coordinated counterattack as everyone scrambled to avoid being crushed by the tons of paper.

There was a sound—a roar like a bull gorilla—and I turned to try to see what the hell was in the room with us, but I was half-buried beneath hundreds of pounds of paper, my night-vision goggles knocked askew so that one eye saw green and the other saw blackness. I had the vague sense of something moving toward me very fast and I tried to bring up my pistol, but it was slapped out of my hand so hard and fast that I thought my wrist was broken. I never saw the hand that disarmed me.

I saw the guy—he was a brute with a barrel chest and huge shoulders. I caught a glimpse of a black metal helmet and fatigues, and then he came at me, head down like a boxer, and fired off a punch that was a green blur.

I got just enough of my shoulder up to protect my head, but his massive fist crunched into my helmet and tore it off my head. I heard the straps pop. My vision went from green to black as I lost the night vision, but there was light from some other source—one of the Russians' flashlights on the floor. Bad light, but enough to allow me to fight.

I dropped and rolled sideways and came up into a crouch with my Rapid Release folding knife. I wasn't going to go down without a fight, not like the Russians, and unless this guy was very damn good I was going to take him with me. The blade snapped open as the big son of a bitch closed in. He was wearing night black BDUs and a balaclava that hid his face. All I could see were his eyes, which were small and sunk into gristly pits, and his wide slash of a mouth. His lips curled back from jagged yellow teeth and he opened his mouth to bellow at me as he lunged forward.

A thousand bits of information flashed through my head in the second before we collided. He was bigger and stronger than me. And unless he was a silverback gorilla he was wearing thick layers of body armor. Something that could stop armor-piercing rounds. There's a lot of experimental stuff out there, and some of it even diffuses the foot-pounds of bullet impact. He had a handgun strapped to his hip; I had a knife in my hands. There were yells and gunfire all around me.

The bruiser made a grab for me, and he was fast. Really damn fast.

I'm faster.

I twisted to one side and his fingernails raked across my chest armor. I didn't try to grapple. I'm good at it, but I'm not stupid. And though I know a knife can often cut through Kevlar, I wasn't in the mood to find out whether the stuff he wore could turn a blade.

So as I twisted I rammed the blade into his mouth.

I drove my fist almost all the way into his maw, the blade ripping deep into the soft muscle of his tongue and soft palate until it struck bone. I twisted my wrist and tore the blade free, and that tore a scream of white-hot agony from him that was the loudest sound I've ever heard from a human mouth. It was like the animal roar we'd heard earlier, but now it was filled with searing pain. His body began thrashing wildly, all control lost. His huge fists swung out in all directions. I evaded the first but caught the second on my shoulder and suddenly I was flying into another stack of boxes.

I crumpled to the floor, and before I could scramble out of the way a full stack of boxes crashed down on me.

Chapter Thirty-Seven

The Deck
Saturday, August 28, 3:22 P.M.
Time Remaining on the Extinction Clock: 92 hours;
38 minutes E.S.T.

The Twins walked arm in arm toward their plane. It was an old affectation—a European habit they'd picked up that also allowed them enough physical closeness to have a confidential conversation.

"Slow down," Hecate said, tugging gently on her brother's arm. "He's watching. Probably Otto, too."

"They're always watching," murmured Paris. "God!

I can't wait to get out of this place. He gives me the creeps."

"Who? Dad or Otto?"

"Either," Paris muttered. "Both. A couple of pit vipers, the two of them."

"Mm. Useful pit vipers," she said, and tapped her purse, in which she carried several CD-ROMs of data Cyrus had downloaded for them. Material that would either solve the rage problems with the Berserkers or at very least dial it down.

They reached the jet. Two of their own guards flanked the stairs and straightened as the Jakobys drew close.

"Anything to report, Marcus?" Hecate asked quietly.

"Nothing much, ma'am. The jet's been refueled and no one has been aboard."

Paris snorted. "Did anyone try?"

"Yes, sir," said Marcus. "Mr. Otto asked to go aboard to leave you both some flowers. I told him that we were under orders to allow no visitors."

"The flowers?"

"He took them with him."

Paris shot Hecate a knowing look. "Probably a tracking device hidden in the bouquet."

Marcus said, "I can promise you, ma'am, that no one and nothing got aboard this plane."

"Good job, Marcus," Paris said.

Hecate cast a quick, doubtful look at the plane; then she turned and ran lightly up the stairs. Paris threw a wicked glance back at the Deck and hoped his father or Otto was watching. He mouthed the words: *Kiss my ass.* Smiling, he climbed aboard.

A few minutes later the jet was rolling fast down the runway.

* * *

Otto wirths stood looking out of the observation window in the Deck's communications center. Now that the Twins had left, the techs had pushed buttons that sent a big wall sliding backward in sections to reveal the other two-thirds of the room, in which there were many more workstations for communication and scanning. The deck panels slid away to reveal the glass floor below which the computer cold room and the virus production tanks hummed with terrible potential. As he had told Mr. Cyrus, the Twins saw only what he wanted them to see.

"They're airborne, sir," said a tech at a nearby console.

Otto looked down at the screen. "Wait until they're at twenty thousand feet," he said softly. "And then turn on the jellyfish sensors."

"Yes, sir."

When the Twins' jet had been refueled the fuel had included dozens of tiny sensors no bigger than a drop of water. They floated in the gasoline and transmitted a signal via several wiry tendrils. The sensors used collaborative nannite technology—singly their signal strength was faint, but a dozen of them could broadcast a strong, clear signal for miles.

"What's the status on the pursuit craft?"

"Birds one, two, and four are at thirty-five thousand feet. Bird three is coasting along the deck at one thousand feet. All remote stations are on alert and the infiltration teams are on deck. Everything's ready to go, sir."

Otto smiled.

"Good," he said as he watched the blip on the radar climb into the sky and begin a slow turn toward the southeast.

Chapter Thirty-Eight

Dr. Hans Koertig banged through the swinging doors of the field surgical suite, tore off his mask and gloves, and threw them into the trash. For two minutes he stood in the center of the scrub room, his eyes bright with fury, his fists balled into knots. He didn't turn or look when the doors opened and Frieda Jaeger came in and quietly began stripping off her stained scrubs.

"I'm sorry, Hans," she said softly, but he said nothing. Cartilage bunched at the corners of his jaws. "You did your best, but these things happen—"

Her words died on her tongue as he suddenly wheeled on her. "Did my best? Is that what you think, Frieda? That I did my best?"

He took a step toward her and she backed up.

"What I did in there was *superb* work. Superb." Spit flew from his mouth as he shouted. "I've done reconstructive surgeries on two hundred noma patients in the four years I've been in Nigeria. Two hundred. I have never once—*not once*—lost a patient on the table." He pointed at the doors. "That boy in there is the sixth child to die under my knife in eight days. Don't you dare tell me that these things happen!"

"Perhaps you're just overworked—" But as soon as she said it Frieda Jaeger knew that it was the wrong thing to say. Koertig's eyes blazed with dangerous fury and for a moment she thought he was going to hit her, but instead he wrenched himself away, stalked to the sink, and began scrubbing his hands as if he wanted to wash the reality of it from his skin.

"I don't lose patients, Frieda," he said over his shoulder. "You can call me an arrogant ass, but the facts are the facts. I don't lose patients. Not here, not in Kenya, not back home in Munich. God damn I *don't* lose patients. Not children with noma. This isn't the nineteen fifties, for Christ's sake. This isn't an aid station treating gangrene with a first-aid kit and a prayer. This is an AWD-Foundation surgical unit. No one on the continent has a better record than us for saving children."

"I know, Hans," she said weakly, "but the children are dying. It's not just you. We've lost thirty in six weeks."

Koertig wheeled on her. He looked stricken. "Thirty? What are you saying?"

Noma was a terrible disease, a severe form of infectious gangrene of the mouth or cheek that affected malnourished children throughout Africa, parts of Asia, and sections of Central America. Nearly all of the patients were between two and six years old and the disease literally ate away at the flesh of their cheeks and mouths, leaving them horribly disfigured and vulnerable to secondary infections. Since the mid-nineties the AWD-Stiftung Kinderhilfe, Dutch Noma Foundation, and Facing Africa has sent medical teams to Nigeria and other afflicted places. The teams, like this one in Sokoto, had done miraculous work in combating the disease and improving living conditions for the people. Plastic surgeons from Interplast had volunteered to do hundreds of reconstructive surgeries for children so they could return to normal lives. So they could *live*.

The disease was no longer universally fatal unless left untreated . . . but treatments existed, preventive medicines were being distributed, and food supplies were coming in from humanitarian organizations around the world.

And now this. Children dying from a disease that should no longer be able to kill them.

"How are so many dying?" he demanded.

"We . . . don't know."

"Have you done tests, for God's sake?"

"We have. It's noma . . . but the disease has become more aggressive."

"Are you talking mutation?"

She shook her head, then nodded. "I'm not sure what to call it."

Frieda Jaeger was a pediatric nurse in her fourth month in Nigeria. She was clearly out of her depth.

"Who is handling the tests?" snapped Koertig.

She gave him the name of the lab. The doctor finished scrubbing and then hurried out to make some calls. Noma was an old disease. It was vicious but stable, predictable.

Terror gripped his heart as he ran to his trailer and the satellite phone he used for emergencies.

God help these children if it had mutated.

God help the children everywhere.

Chapter Thirty-Nine

I kicked my way out from under the boxes and rolled over into a crouch, pulling my Beretta.

Top Sims knelt nearby, his M4 in his hands. He had a shallow cut across the bridge of his nose and one eye was puffed shut.

"Clear!" he yelled.

"Clear!" I heard Bunny growl, and to my right I saw him crawling out from another mountain of toppled boxes.

"Where are the hostiles?" I demanded.

Bunny switched on a minilantern and pointed to the rear door, which stood ajar. He kicked it shut. There was no interior lock.

"We giving chase?"

"No. Barricade the door."

We worked fast and stacked boxes in front of both doors. Top was watching me as we worked.

"What?" I asked.

"Looked like that last box hit you in the head. You need me to go through all that 'do you know who you are and who's the President of the United States?' crap, Cap'n?"

"I know who I am, and for the record the Vice President's a total dick," I said.

Top grinned. "You'll live."

Bunny sat down on the floor and began applying

butterfly stitches to a long, shallow slash on his thigh. "Well," he said, "this was fun. Don't know about you fellas, but I'm getting tired of being ambushed by people who shouldn't even be mad at me. I mean . . . what the hell was that all about? Did we just have a firefight with the Hulk and the Thing?"

"Something like that." I looked at the bloody remains of the Russian team.

Top said, "Any idea what the hell we just stepped into, Cap'n?"

"I'm starting to," I said but didn't elaborate. "It seems pretty clear that there were at least two teams down here searching for the same stuff."

"Three teams," said Top, "if Jigsaw's down here somewhere."

I didn't comment on that. If Jigsaw was in Deep Iron and hadn't come to investigate the gunfire, then it meant that they weren't able to. Top read my face and didn't pursue it. Bunny was watching us both and he cursed under his breath.

The flashlights did a good job of lighting the room. The firefight with the Russians had taken place in one corner, over by the door through which we'd come. That part of the room was a charnel house of mangled bodies. I'd seen a lot of death and I'd caused a lot of death, but there was something about this that was jabbing wires into my brain. I wanted to turn away, but I knew that would be the wrong choice. Denial is always a bear trap—you'll forget about it and step in it later.

Top pulled the magazine from his M4, saw that he was down to three rounds, and replaced it with a full one. "Cap'n, either I'm getting too old for this shit or we nearly got our asses handed to us by just two guys.

They were winning, too, until you shanked one in the mouth."

"No joke," said Bunny. "One of those guys knocked my rifle out of my hands—and not to blow my own horn, but that's not so easy to do. So I laid into him, hit him four times. Two uppercuts, a hook to the ribs, and an overhand right. I might as well have been brushing lint off his lapels." Bunny had twenty-two-inch biceps and could bench 460. When he laid a combination into a pair of boxing mitts, whoever was holding them went numb to the wrists. Bunny's blue eyes looked deeply spooked. "Son of a bitch didn't even grunt. It's not doing a lot for my self-esteem."

"He's right, Cap'n," Top agreed. "I put a full mag into both of those assholes and it barely even knocked them back. Sure as hell didn't knock them down. I think we're seeing a new kind of body armor, something that absorbs impact like nothing I ever seen. It was only when I went for a head shot that he turned tail and ducked behind the boxes. But . . . until then I was slowing him down, but I wasn't hurting him."

"Nobody's got body armor that good," Bunny said.

"I may have clipped one of them in the leg—the one you didn't stab—because he was limping when he went out the door. He should have been Swiss cheese, though. And, considering how strong these guys were, maybe we're looking at an exoskeleton. They've been working on that stuff for—"

Bunny cut him off, "No way. He was hard, Top, but that was flesh and bone I was punching."

"Rubber cushions with air baffles and metal struts can feel like muscle and bone," Top suggested. "What with all the confusion—"

"Doesn't matter," I said. "They had something extra, so we're lucky we were able to turn the tables on them. We may not have dropped them, but we didn't get our heads torn off, so let's put it in the 'win' column."

"Glass half-full," said Bunny, nodding. "I'm okay with that."

They stood on either side of me and looked at the bodies. I turned and assessed the room. The blood was contained to that one corner. There were blood spatters everywhere, but most of the floor was clear.

"Okay," I said slowly, "here's what we need to do. We have to check the bodies for ID. Probably won't find much, but we have to look."

"Balls," murmured Bunny.

"Then I want to move the remains to that section of wall." I pointed to a ten-foot stretch where there were no boxes.

"Why touch 'em at all, Cap'n?" asked Top.

"Because we have work to do and we don't want to have to trip over anything. You feel me?"

He nodded.

I squatted down and began searching the dead Russians. It was grisly work, and though Bunny and Top joined me, none of us were happy about it. Bunny paused and pulled a tube of peppermint ChapStick from his pocket, rubbed some under his nose, and handed it around. We each dabbed our lips. Peppermint kills the sense of smell pretty quickly, and between blood and other bodily substances the room was getting ripe.

As expected, the search yielded nothing. No ID. Nothing.

Without saying a word we began moving the bodies

over to the wall. I knew that Top had done this kind of
thing before in Iraq—pulling bodies out of the rubble
after suicide bombers. Bunny and I had our own separate experiences. I'd been part of the contingency of Baltimore cops who worked Ground Zero after the planes
hit the towers. It was always bad, always beyond the
capability of the rational mind to associate this with
deliberate human action. I know, that's a funny thought
coming from a guy like me—someone who's killed
people with guns, knives, grenades, garrotes, and bare
hands—but there is a difference between combat killing and this. I wasn't even sure what to call it. "Murder" is too vague a word, and "mutilation" seems oddly
clinical. This was . . . what? The two brutes we chased
out of here had done this to the Russians here and to the
staff upstairs. They had enjoyed it. Maybe that was the
key. Even when the death of an opponent—say a terrorist holding a gun to a sixth grader's head—had given
me a bit of momentary satisfaction, I'd never enjoyed it.
Never gotten a visceral or erotic delight from the death
of another person . . . and I believed that's what I was
seeing here.

As this was going through my head, Top muttered
three words that said it all.

"This is evil."

Bunny and I looked at him and then each other. None
of us spoke as we worked, but we knew that Top had
put his finger on it. This *was* evil.

When we were done we washed our hands from our
canteens and used the lids from some of the file boxes
to cover the corpses as best we could.

I turned and surveyed the rest of the room. Half the

boxes had fallen to the floor. So far it looked like all that was stored here was paper.

"Top, Bunny . . . the guys we chased off, did they take anything with them? Boxes, computer records? Anything?"

"Not that I saw, unless it was small enough to fit into a pocket," said Top. "We staying or going, Cap'n?"

"We're staying for the moment. If those guys with the body armor are out there I don't want them dogging us all the way back to the elevators, and there's not enough of us to guarantee a safe run back."

"I'm good with that, Cap'n," said Top. "Don't know about you fellas, but I've never been roared at by enemy combatants. Can't seem to get that noise out of my mind."

Bunny nodded. "Yeah, that's hitting ten on my freak-o-meter, too."

"All the more reason to stay put," I said. "We're secure in here. Besides, if they didn't take anything, then that means that it's still here." I went over to the wall so I could see the room better and assess its layout. "We still have our primary mission objective, so we need to go through these records. We have at least two players—the Russians and the other team—who think this stuff is worth killing a lot of people over. Let's find out why."

It was clear from the expressions on Bunny's and Top's faces that they didn't like it any more than I did.

"If those guys are on their way out of here then they're going to run into Brick," Bunny said. "It'd be just him against them."

Top snorted. "Him in an armored vehicle with a minigun. Body armor be damned."

Bunny grinned, but it was mostly faked. "Yeah, I guess."

"Either way, it's beyond our control," I said. "We'll leave that up to the gods of war. In the meantime let's get to it. We've been behind the curve on this thing all along. Let's see if we can figure out what the hell's going on."

So we set to work . . . but as we worked we each listened to the big silence outside of the storage unit. Listening for the sound of elevators, for the shout of familiar official voices, for the sound of footsteps running with that precise speed that you only hear with SWAT or special ops teams. We heard nothing.

We were alone down here, and as long as the NSA was still chasing the DMS, there was no chance of the cavalry coming.

We tried not to think about that; we tried to focus on the task at hand.

We tried.

Chapter Forty

Bulawayo, Republic of Zimbabwe
Five Days Ago

Gabriel Mugabe sipped tea as he watched the forklift drivers move back and forth to shift pallet after pallet of bottled water from the train depot to the warehouse. He was pleased with the quantity. An American had given him a very tidy kickback to make sure that customs cleared the delivery quickly.

"Why so quickly?" he'd asked.

"We've invested a lot of money in advertising," said

the American. "Our advertisements go live on September 1, and we want the product available right to the moment."

"But you said you're *giving* the water away. What does the timing matter?"

"Impulse buying is one of the few things that still survives in this economy. Give a little and they'll buy more."

Mugabe thought that the American was being stupid. Giving away sixty tons of bottled water was like flushing good money down the toilet. But the American insisted that worldwide one-day buzz was worth many millions at the launch of a product. Mugabe neither knew nor cared if that was true. All that mattered to Mugabe was the fat envelope of money the American discreetly gave him. Mixed currencies—American dollars and South African rand—none of the Zimbabwean dollars that were worth less than toilet paper. Very nice.

They'd shaken hands on the deal. Mugabe wasted very little of the money on bribes to the custom officials. Mugabe's name was enough to inspire cooperation. What little he spent was to grease the wheels in the port of Beira in Mozambique. The cargo ship unloaded there and the water was sent by train to the depot in Bulawayo and from the train yard to warehouses owned by men who feared the Mugabe family.

Gabriel Mugabe was the nephew of the President of Zimbabwe, who had been accused by organizations around the world, from Amnesty International to the African Union, for human rights violations. Gabriel privately agreed, but in his view the issue of human rights was an attempt by the weak to undermine the strong. He believed that strength came with rights that superseded anything the weak had to say. History, he felt, supported this view, and Mugabe could cite historical precedent going back to the Old Testament and up to the hypocritical U.S. so-called War on Terror.

Though Gabriel Mugabe was not the flesh-eating lion that his uncle was, he was rightly feared here in Bulawayo. The water arrived safely and most of the cash the American had given him was still in his personal safe at home.

He sipped his tea, which had been fresh brewed with water from the pallet Mugabe had appropriated for his personal use.

"Free water," he said with a sneer. "Fucking Americans."

Chapter Forty-One

The House of Screams, Isla Dos Diablos
The Morning of Friday, August 27

The boy's name was Eighty-two. Or SAM. It depended on who was speaking to him. Otto always called him by the number; when Alpha was in a good mood he sometimes called the boy SAM. The boy seldom thought of himself as anything other than "me." He didn't believe the number or the name was truly his. He suspected he had a real name, but if he was right it was one he would never be allowed to use—and would never want to use.

He crouched on the sloping terra-cotta roof in the shadows cast by the fronds of a pair of towering palms. Eighty-two was small and well practiced in the art of being invisible. Most people here at the Hive were not allowed to talk to him, and those who were mostly ignored him. The people who paid attention to him terrified him, and so the boy avoided them. He lived among them, seeing scores of people every day, but he sometimes went a week without so much as a meaningless exchange of commentary on the weather. In the span from November 10 of last year until March 2 of this year he did not have a single conversation. Even the doctors who tested him seldom spoke to him. They grabbed him, poked him, pierced him with needles, took samples, made him lie down under scanners— all without directly addressing him. They knew he knew what was expected of him and mostly they pointed to where they wanted him to sit, stand, or lie down.

It hurt him for a long time, being alone, but recently he'd come to prefer it. It was better than engaging in conversation about what was going on here at the Hive. And it was better than when Otto's men dragged him along on one of their hunts. Eighty-two went on those because he had to, because Alpha expected it and Otto demanded it, but so far he had not shot at any of the animals. In another year, when he was bigger, he knew that he would be expected to participate in the hunt rather than tag along with the videographer.

Nobody—not even the videographer—knew that Eighty-two had taken his own camera, a little button camera he'd stolen from the previous videographer's gear.

The hunters had gone to São Paolo for a single day of celebration, and Eighty-two had slipped away from the pool area for forty minutes and found a cybercafé half a block from the hotel. Sending the e-mail with the video had been the single bravest thing he'd ever done, and those forty minutes were the most frightening of his life. He was not able to wait around to see if there was a response. He wished and prayed that there was, that the Americans were on their way.

Now he was back at the Hive. Back at the House of Screams, Eighty-two's name for it, though he suspected many of the New Men thought of it in that way, too. After all, it was their screams that filled the corridors of the building day after day and night after night.

The boy wore only a pair of swim trunks. His skin was pale. He was not allowed to tan, and if he allowed himself to get a sunburn Alpha would have Otto beat him. Otto's beatings lasted a long, long time. Eighty-two suspected that Otto enjoyed them and was sad when Alpha told him to stop. Otto's lips were always wet with spit when he was done giving a beating, and his eyes burned bright as candles.

Down in the compound three of the New Men were working to dig postholes for a chicken pen. The boy watched them, fascinated. The New Men had thick features and coarse red hair, and when no one was around they chattered back and forth in surprisingly high-pitched voices. The boy recognized two of the New Men. One of them was the oldest of the community still living here on the island, maybe twenty-five, though his hair had already started to go gray and the skin on his face was creased with lines. He looked sixty or seventy. The young man working beside him was not much older than the boy, but the New Man was top-heavy with muscles and looked at least thirty. The third member of the party was a woman. Like the others she was dressed in lightweight cotton trousers and a tank top, but she was sweating as she dug and the shirt was pasted to her breasts so that the boy could easily see the dark outlines of her nipples.

Eighty-two felt a stirring in his loins and looked away, embarrassed that he was spying on her. And ashamed that it was affecting him.

The female's shovel hit a stone in the dirt and she bent quickly and used her fingers to dig it out of the ground. Without thinking she threw it over her shoulder and picked up her shovel.

Suddenly there was a harsh shout from across the compound and the boy turned to see one of the guards—a huge man with a blond crew cut and a gun belt slung low on his hips—come striding toward the work party.

"What do you think you're playing at, you ugly slut?" he shouted in an Australian accent that was sometimes hard for the boy to follow.

The three New Men froze in place, terror blooming instantly on their faces. They looked frightened and confused, unsure which rule they had broken but knowing that they had done something. They reacted to their conditioning and dropped to their knees, heads bowed, as the Australian approached. He towered over them, and the boy saw three more guards come down from the veranda and spread out in a loose line behind the blond man. They were all grinning.

The Australian nudged the rock with his booted toe.

"What's this shit?" he demanded. The New Men did not move except to tremble with fear. It made the Australian grin broader. He raised his voice. "I said . . . what's this shit?"

No answer. Even from his perch on the roof Eighty-two could see the female begin to cry, saw the first silver tears break from her brown eyes and roll down over her lumpy cheeks.

"You!" called the Australian. "Yeah, I'm talking to

you, you ugly ape-faced bitch. Look at me when I'm talking to you."

The female slowly raised her eyes toward the man; her companions kept their heads firmly down, though their muscles were rigid with the terror that washed through them in icy waves.

"Who told you to make a mess of the whole damned yard? Look at this squalor." He nudged the stone again. It was the size of an egg. "You get your ass over here and pick up this mess. *Now!*"

The female bowed several times and then scuttled forward, keeping low to the ground, so frightened of giving further offense that she scuttled forward on all fours. But as she drew close to the guard she slowed and stopped almost out of reach before extending one tentative hand toward the stone.

The guard looked down at her and the boy could see the moment when the Australian became aware of the thin cotton shirt clinging to the female's heavy breasts. The look on the man's face changed, shifting from vicious anger to something else, something that was beyond the boy's understanding. The boy knew that the man might rape the woman—he had witnessed enough abuse to understand the forms it could take. Rape, sodomy, beatings, even murder. However, no matter how many times the boy saw these acts, or saw the aftereffects of them, he could not understand it. Even in his own personal darkness, even deep in the strangeness of his own damaged dreams, he had no connection to that kind of hunger. Eighty-two leaned forward, his muscles tensing, wondering for the hundredth time what would happen if he shouted at the men while they did this. Would they stop because of who he was? Or would interference merely result in another of Otto's beatings? Indecision trapped Eighty-two on his perch as, below, the female picked up the rock.

She bobbed and bowed and mumbled apologies in her high-pitched nasal voice.

The Australian kicked her in the stomach.

A single sharp kick that drove the toe of his steel-tipped boot into the softness of her upper abdomen and slammed all the air from the female's lungs. She could not even scream. Her body convulsed into a ball of knotted, trembling, gasping agony as the guards laughed and the other New Men knelt nearby and wept.

The guards made jokes about it and turned away, heading back to the veranda, back to their beer and dominoes, leaving the female in the center of the yard, the stone still clutched in her fist.

A minute dragged by as the boy watched. He sniffed back a tear and then froze as the two male New Men suddenly turned and looked up. Eighty-two remained stock-still. Had they heard him? Could they see him?

Even the female slowly raised her head and looked in his direction.

The guards were laughing and talking about football. They hadn't heard anything. The boy's eyes burned with tears, and he slowly lifted a hand to his eyes to wipe them clear.

Down in the garden the oldest of the New Men stared upward with a furrowed brow. Then he lifted a hand and mimicked the action. Or had he simply wiped away his own tears, the action merely a coincidence?

Then the second New Man did the same.

Eighty-two held his breath and did not move.

Finally the oldest of the New Men turned back toward the female. He cast a cautious glance at the guards and then slowly crept toward the female, gathered her in his arms, helped her to her feet, and walked with her back to their companion. Both of the New Men hugged her and kissed her, but always one watched the men while the others embraced. From time to time they all cut quick glances up to the shadows on the porch roof. Then they went back to work.

The boy watched the female's hand, hoping that she would covertly pocket the stone. He would have taken it to use later if an opportunity presented itself. To use on Carteret while he slept. It was something Eighty-two wanted to do, had thought long and hard about doing, though he had not yet done it. But the female apparently did not have that thought or was afraid of being caught, because she dropped the stone onto the pile of dirt they'd dug from the hole and picked up her shovel.

After five minutes, the boy edged back along the porch roof and climbed into his bedroom window. Eighty-two sat on the edge of his bed and thought about what to do.

Chapter Forty-Two

Deep Iron Storage Facility
Saturday, August 28, 4:06 P.M.
Time Remaining on the Extinction Clock: 91 hours,
54 minutes E.S.T.

Debris is a puzzle if you look at it the right way. You can retro-engineer it. You look at a roomful of junk and you pay attention to what's lying on what, because that will eventually tell you what fell first. When I was working homicide for Baltimore PD I had one of those classic cases where there's a dead body amid a bunch of broken plates and scattered books. A novice would think that the victim came home and interrupted a robbery in progress and that the place either was already trashed or was trashed during a struggle. But the carpet under the body was completely clean, no litter, which established that the murder happened first. Sure, we considered the fact that the place could have been trashed afterward, but when we looked at what lay under what it became clear that someone had walked around the room smashing things. It had been done in a circular pattern—deliberate and systematic. That's when we started looking at the wife, who had reported finding her husband dead. The debris pattern, plus the angle of the blunt-force blow that had killed him, gave us a pretty solid circumstantial case. After that it was a matter of breaking down her alibi and grilling her in a series of interviews.

This part of the mission was cop work, so I switched mental gears to let that part of me do his job. I may not be Jerry Spencer, but I can work a crime scene.

There were dozens of overturned boxes. We knew from the firefight when some of them were knocked over. Most of the boxes were sealed with two-inch-wide clear tape. The tape had burst on about a third of the boxes, and some of the boxes and papers had landed in pools of blood. We started in the driest corner.

So I had to do some horseback math: if a stack of ten boxes fell at such and such an angle, encountering an obstacle—and for the sake of argument let's call that obstacle the back of my head—then they'd hit the floor with x amount of force and scatter their contents in such and such a fashion. Calculating the way the papers slid out of the boxes was similar to the way blood spatter experts estimate flying blood.

And that thought made me aware of the torn bodies hidden under the box lids and I had to squash down the horror that wanted to make me either scream or throw up.

The boxes were also chewed up pretty well by gunfire. The Russians had emptied a couple of magazines each into the room. The cinder-block walls were pocked with holes and heavy-caliber bullets had plowed through the contents of the boxes. Luckily paper is a great bullet stop, so the damage wasn't as bad as it could have been. Grenades would have made this job impossible.

Each of the boxes was made from corrugated cardboard. Most were a dark brown with a faux walnut print and a little metal sleeve on the front in which an indexing file card could be placed. There was a code on the file cards that was apparently something used internally by Deep Iron.

It was Top who figured out the code on the file cards. He held out the card—HH/1/3/6-8/051779—and said, "Okay, the second *H* is probably our boy Heinrich Haeckel. Now, this box came from that corner over there. This other box here was two rows up. It has a card with 'III' on it. Roman numerals for the rows. Follow me?"

"Right with you," I said, pleased.

"Six-dash-eight's next. Sixth box in a stack of eight. See? And the other number's got to be a date. These boxes have been here for a long time, so it ain't a stretch to see that as oh-five, seventeen, seventy-nine. With this code we can restack every box in the right place without doing Sherlock Holmes stuff."

"You just earned your pay for the month, Top," I said. "And a pretty damn good bottle of Scotch."

"Make it Irish and we're square."

"Let me guess," Bunny said. "You like 'Black Bush'?"

Top gave him a sniper's squint. "Don't make me hurt you, Farmboy. I know forty-three separate ways to make sure you can't ever have kids."

Bunny held up his hands. "We're cool."

We went back to work and now the only thing that slowed us down was deciding which papers went into which box.

"What is this stuff?" Bunny asked, reaching to pick up a clipped sheaf of papers.

"Careful," I cautioned. "We need everything to go back in the right box."

"Okay," he said, "but . . . what *is* this stuff?" He tapped the top page and I bent over him to look. The page was covered with columns of numbers whose value made no sense. At the top of each column was a number-letter identifier that also made no sense. I lifted the first page, then the second. More of the same. The pages were old, the entries all done by hand.

"Accounting?" Bunny asked.

"I don't know."

"Got something!" called Top. He was going through the boxes stacked by the door. "This one's not paper. Looks like microfiche."

He handed me several sheets of film, and when I held them up to the light I could see dozens of tiny pages smaller than postage stamps. Without a reader I couldn't tell if they were the same as the pages we had here or were something else. We searched around and found only eight sheets of film, scattered as if dropped.

"If those are microfiche copies of this stuff," Bunny said, "then it sure as hell doesn't add up to all of this crap. I'm thinking the Hulk and his buddy took the rest of them."

"Yeah, dammit," I said, and reached for another box of paper.

We worked together to repack and restack the boxes that had fallen during our part of the fight. All of the boxes that had fallen on me were filled with the same kind of handwritten notes. Then Bunny found a page with annotations in a box he was carefully repacking.

"Take a look, boss," he said and I squatted down next to him.

At the top of one of the columns someone had used a pencil to write: *Zwangs/Trauma*.

"Is that German? What's that mean?" he asked.

I nodded and took my notebook out of my pocket to copy down the ID code on the front of the file box. Something began niggling at the back of my brain, but it was too timid to step into the light. We kept working.

Outside the room there was only silence. No cavalry with trumpets blowing.

"What the hell are these?" Top asked as he held up a stack of index cards. Each one had notes written in some kind of medical code and in the upper left corner was a fingerprint. Top peered at the prints. "This ain't ink, Cap'n. I think it's old, dried blood."

"Don't smudge any of them," I cautioned. "We don't know what the hell we have here."

A few minutes later Bunny said, "Hey, boss. I got another one with words on it. And . . . a couple of names."

Top and I picked our way through the mess to see what he had. He passed me an old-fashioned wooden clipboard, marking its place on the floor with his canteen. The numbers here were written in a different hand, and on the lower right of each page were the initials "JM." The words "Zwangs/Trauma" were scribbled on the upper left of the page, and over each column was either a single word or a few: "Geschwindigkeit," "Winkel," "Druck in Pfund pro Quadratzoll."

Speed. Angle. Pounds of pressure per square inch.

Then vertically along the left side of the page:

"Kette," "Schläger," "Pferde-Peitsche," "Faust," "Barfuss," "Gestiefelt."

I swallowed a throat that was as dry as dust.

Chain. Club. Horsewhip. Fist. Bare foot. Booted foot.

"Oh my God," I whispered, and the others stared at me. They peered over my shoulder at the page. I translated for them and saw the meaning register on their faces.

"Fuck me," said Top, and he looked older than his forty years.

"If this is what I think it is, then we're into some sick shit here." Bunny said, "Who would collect this kind of information?"

I didn't answer as I rifled through the rest of the papers and then handed the clipboard back to him. "Let's repack this box. Check everything. I want to see any scrap of paper with words, especially handwritten notations."

They set to work, but there was nothing else in that box.

The next box, on the other hand . . . well, that changed everything.

I was sitting on the floor putting the pages in some kind of order when I found a single handwritten note tucked inside a file folder. It was in German, which was no problem for me. As I read it my mind began spinning with shock and nausea:

Heinrich,
The third phase was completed this morning and we have sufficient material to initiate the next part of our research. I will present the test results to Herr Wirths on Thursday next. I hope you will be able to join us.

I must confess that I am as excited as a schoolboy with what we are accomplishing here . . . and with what we are going to accomplish. We are doing God's work here, my friend. Thank you for your compliments on the work I have been doing with twins. Your notes and suggestions on that have been of inestimable value, as are your observations on zoonosis and the noma work.

Please let me know if you can join me for the presentation. Your observations would be of tremendous value to the audience, and to me personally.

The letter was dated 22 February 1942. It was addressed to Heinrich Haeckel. I sat there and stared at the envelope to which it was clipped. Haeckel's address had been in Berlin. The sender's address was in a town called Birkenau in Poland. My blood froze in my veins.

Birkenau.

Good God Almighty.

Birkenau was the small Polish town where the Nazis built Auschwitz.

The man who sent the letter was Josef Mengele.

Chapter Forty-Three

The House of Screams, Isla Dos Diablos
The Evening of Friday, August 27

All afternoon and into the evening Eighty-two thought about what had happened down in the garden. Not simply the guard kicking the female—that sort of thing happened fifty times a day here in the Hive—but the way the three New Men had looked at him. If they had even seen him . . . and he was sure they had. Or sensed him. Or something.

They had heard him sniff back tears. When he had brushed those tears out of his eyes they had mimicked the motion. Why? What did it mean? Did it even *have* a meaning, or were they acting on their imitative impulses? Eighty-two had overheard Otto saying that it was hardwired into them, that they were natural mimics. Like apes, only smarter, more controlled. It had been an intentional design goal. That was how Otto had phrased it when discussing it with one of the doctors.

But had it been only that?

What if it had been something else? Eighty-two hoped so. If the New Men were capable of independent thought and action, then maybe once the Americans got here the New Men could be shown how to break out of their conditioning.

If the Americans got here. It was already two days

since he had sent the hunt video. He ached to sneak into the communications room and check the e-mail account he set up. Would the techs realize it? Would they—or more important *could* they—somehow determine that it was him? If so, what would Alpha do? Worse, what would Alpha let Otto do?

The more the boy thought about it, the more frightened and desperate he became . . . and the more he wanted to do something else to try to reach out to the man known as Deacon.

The August sun set slowly over the island and Eighty-two sat on the floor, in the corner between his bed and the dresser, staring at the TV without watching it. He was required to watch six hours a day, every day. Nothing of his choosing, of course. Otto made the schedule and programmed his DVD player. This week it was all war films. Eighty-two didn't mind those as much as the sex stuff he had to watch. He didn't completely understand why, though, because there was a lot of violence in both kinds of videos. There was violence in almost everything Otto scheduled for him. Even the videos of surgeries looked violent. The blood . . . the screaming of the patients strapped to the tables. Even with the sound down it was ugly.

And it was no good closing his eyes or lying about having watched it. Otto always asked Eighty-two questions about what he saw, questions that he could only answer if he watched. Eighty-two had learned fast not to get caught in a lie.

The sun was down now, but he didn't turn on the lamp. He heard noises and walked to the window and peered out into the night, listening to the sounds that filled the air almost every night. Shouts. Cries of ecstasy, cries of pain, sometimes overlapping in ways that turned his stomach. Screams from the labs and the bunkhouses where the New Men lived.

He thought about the stone that the female had been kicked for throwing. It burned him that she hadn't picked it up and taken it with her. It seemed to Eighty-two that it was the smartest thing to do. Keep it. Maybe . . . use it.

But she had tossed it in with the dirt being dug from the hole, unwilling or unable to find a better use for it.

The wrongness of that refused to leave his mind. It burned in his thoughts like a drop of frying grease that had spattered on his skin. Why hadn't she thought to take the stone for which she had been beaten? What was it about the New Men that kept them from fighting back? There were hundreds of them on the island and only sixty guards and eighty-three technicians. The New Men were very strong, and though they screamed when beaten it was clear to Eighty-two—who knew something about hurt and harm—that they could endure a great deal of pain. They would cringe, cry out, weep, even collapse to the ground when being beaten, but within minutes they were able to return to hard labor. Eighty-two did not yet know if they faked some of their pain, amplifying their screams because that's what was expected of them, because screams satisfied the guards and satisfaction was part of why the New Men existed. It was an idea Eighty-two had been playing with for weeks, and it was what made the incident of the stone so crucial to his understanding.

In his dreams—sleeping and waking—the New Men rose up all at once and tore the guards to pieces. Like the animal men in the H. G. Wells book *The Island of*

Dr. Moreau, Eighty-two's dreamworld ideal of the New Men saw them finally throwing off the abuse and torment and slaughtering the evil humans. Eighty-two longed to see the House of Screams echo with the same kind of cries of furious justice that had shook the walls of Wells's House of Pain.

And Eighty-two would have believed it to be more of a possibility if the female had just taken the damn stone.

The evening burned on and Eighty-two found that he could not endure another night of doing nothing.

He left his room and crawled along the sloping tiled roof to the end, waited for the security camera to pan away. Eighty-Two had long ago memorized every tick and flicker of the compound's cameras. When you're that bored you find ways of filling the time. Once the camera turned away he would have ninety-eight seconds to reach the rain gutter on the far side of this wing. He made it easily, paused again as another camera moved through its cycle. One move at a time, always counting, always patient, Eighty-two made his way from his bedroom window to the spot where he'd perched earlier today. The garden below was draped in purple shadows.

Eighty-two jumped from the corner of the roof to the closer of the two big palms, caught the trunk in a familiar place, and then shimmied down with practiced ease. At the base he stopped, waited for the ground camera to sweep past, and then he sprinted along the edge of the new chicken coop to the flower bed on the far side. The rich black dirt from the postholes had been spread out atop the flower bed. Eighty-two bent low and let his night vision strengthen until he could make out every detail. He ran his fingers over the dirt, sifting it back and forth, up and down, until he found the lump. His nimble fingers plucked the egg-sized stone from the soil and he weighed it in his palm. It was a piece of black volcanic rock, smooth as glass.

Eighty-two rolled it between his palms as he crouched there, and his eyes drifted toward the porch where the guards had been playing dominoes. The big Australian's name was Carteret. Eighty-two could imagine him drowsing in his hammock, stupid with too much beer, a porno movie playing on the TV, a cigarette burning out between his slack lips. The image was as clear as if Eighty-two was actually looking at the man. Carteret.

Another part of Eighty-two's brain replayed the image of the female lying in a knot of convulsed agony. And the laughter of the guards as Carteret walked away from her as if she was less than nothing.

The stone was a comfortable weight in Eighty-two's hand.

He looked up into the sky—a great, vast, diamond-littered forever above the trees—and he wondered why the man named Deacon had not come. Did the e-mail ever reach him? Was he coming at all? Would anyone come?

Eighty-two closed his fist around the stone, feeling its ancient solidity and hardness.

He wondered if he could risk reaching out one more time.

If that didn't work . . . then what would he do?

There was a high-pitched female scream from the House of Pain. Was it the same female? Had thoughts of her festered in Carteret's mind all day, the way the thought of the stone had burned in Eighty-two's?

The boy stared with narrowed eyes at the laboratory

complex. The House of Screams. Above him the speakers in the palm trees began to wail. The dog handlers were getting ready to release the dogs for the night.

Time to go.

He smoothed the dirt to hide the spot where he'd removed the stone, waited for the ground camera to move, and then went from stillness into action. He ran across the garden, scaled the palm tree effortlessly, and leaped onto the roof. The stone was in his pocket.

Chapter Forty-Four

The White House
Saturday, August 28, 4:10 P.M.
Time Remaining on the Extinction Clock: 91 hours, 50 minutes

The Vice President of the United States sat behind his desk, but he felt like he was under a spotlight in the back of a police squad room. Three people stood in front of his desk. Two men and a woman. They'd declined seats or coffee. None of them were smiling. Bill Collins looked from face to face and knew that he had no friends in the room.

The Speaker of the House, Alan Henderson, ran the show. As second in the line of succession, it was his job, if it was anyone's. He wore an expensive suit with a faint pin stripe and a bow tie that was forty years out of style. Even during the gravest of national emergencies, the Speaker usually wore a smile of mild amusement that was emblematic of his well-known "this, too, shall pass" point of view. Now his face was as lugubrious as a mortician.

"Well, Bill, I'd say you screwed the pooch on this

one. Screwed the pooch and then ran the damn thing over with a steamroller. I just came from seeing the President. You gosh-darn near gave him the heart attack his doctors were trying to sidestep with the bypass."

The Secretary of State cleared her throat. "I find it alarming that you didn't consult with me before launching this operation."

"Are you finished?" Collins asked coldly. "First things first, Alan. When I issued those orders I was the Acting President of the United States, so let's be quite clear about chain of command here. Whereas I appreciate your loyalty and service to the country, I don't appreciate your taking that tone of voice with me."

That shut them all up.

"Second, before I acted I consulted with the Attorney General. Nathan . . . ?"

Nathan Smitrovich, the Attorney General, nodded, though he clearly looked uncertain as to how this was going to play out. "That's right, Alan. He called me and we talked it over. I . . . um, advised him to bring a few other people into the loop, but he said that there was an issue of trust."

"Trust?" Alan Henderson suddenly looked anything but mild and homespun. "What the hell . . . who the hell do you think you—"

"Calm down, Alan," said Collins. "No one is leveling any accusations. At least not at you. Or at anyone in this room. But you have to understand my position. I received confidential information from a source who is positioned well enough to have insider knowledge. The information not only outlined an ongoing campaign of blackmail against the President but included hints that many other members of Congress might be under similar control. I couldn't risk making this an open issue. If anyone else was involved, then the blackmail material Mr. Church has might have been made public, and that could have brought down this administration. At the very least it would have crippled it." He sat back and looked at them, his face calm and open. "You tell me how you would have acted? Tell me how you would have done things differently?"

The Secretary of State, Anne Hartcourt, folded her arms and cocked her head. She didn't look convinced. "I could buy the confidential informant bit, Bill, and if I stretch my credulity I could accept your rationalization for not including any of us. But are you going to sit there and tell me that this entire operation was cooked up, planned, and set into motion only after the President went under sedation?"

Collins laughed. "Of course not. This information was brought to me a few days ago. After it was announced that the President was to undergo surgery. My informant said that it was the only opportunity he felt would allow for me to make a swift and decisive countermove."

"Who is this informant?" asked Henderson.

Collins flicked a glance at the AG. "I told Nathan that I wanted to withhold the name of the informant pending the resolution of the situation. And the situation has *not* been resolved. Yes, the President is back in power, but this does not remove the threat."

"If the threat is even real."

"I believe it to be real."

"Why?" asked Anne Hartcourt. "Why are you so convinced?"

Collins hesitated. "Because . . . the informant had

information that could have come from only two sources: the President himself or someone who had somehow gathered very private information about the President."

"What was that information?" asked the Attorney General. "You wouldn't tell me earlier, but I damn well want to know now."

"Not a chance, Nathan. I'm leaving for Walter Reed in five minutes. I'll discuss this directly with the President. If he chooses to allow anyone else to participate in that conversation then it'll have to be his choice. I will not break the confidence of the President. Not to you and not under any circumstances, even if you drag me before a subcomittee."

When the others said nothing, he added, "I argued against forming the DMS from the beginning. I warned that it could become a threat, something we would never be able to control."

Alan Henderson sighed. "I agreed with you about that, too, Bill, but we were overruled. And I do not believe that Mr. Church blackmailed everyone who voted against us. There are some who think that the DMS is doing a valuable, even *crucial* job. Right now the Secretary of Defense and the Secretary of Homeland both want your head on a platter, and they don't even *like* Church. But they understand the value of the DMS. Maybe your short-term memory is slipping, Bill, but DMS agents saved your wife's life two months ago. They saved my life, too. And Anne here, and the First Lady. They've prevented terrorists from bringing nukes and weaponized pathogens into this country. They've stopped six separate assassination attempts on the President's life. They prevented the kidnapping of the President's daughters. And they closed down forty-three separate terrorist cells that were operating inside the United States."

"I didn't say they didn't do some good," Collins said. "I said that they were going beyond their orders and now pose a threat to this administration."

"If your informant is correct," said Hartcourt.

"Yes. And once I speak with the President I will cooperate in every way possible to verify this information."

"Maybe it's just me," muttered Henderson, "but this has a bit of the stink of WMDs on it."

Collins ignored that. "MindReader may be a useful tool in the War on Terror, but it's also highly dangerous. That computer system can intrude anywhere, learn everything. Even Church isn't authorized to know *everything*. You don't think I looked into this? Asked around? People have been quietly complaining about Church for years, hinting that he's used his computer to find things out about people and then used that information as a lever to always get his way. They're blackmailing the President; they're forcing him to give the DMS more and more power!"

Alan Henderson looked at the others for a moment. The Secretary of State folded her arms and said nothing; the Attorney General shrugged.

"Okay, Bill," Henderson said, "but you'd better be right about this or this is going to come back and bite you on the ass."

"If I thought I was wrong, Alan, I would never have done this."

He looked at his watch.

"I have to get going. My car will be downstairs in two minutes."

* * *

Once Vice President Collins was in his car and had the soundproof window between him and the driver shut, he took out his cell and called JP. Sunderland.

"How'd it go?" asked Sunderland.

"I feel like I've been worked over by prizefighters."

"Did they buy it?"

"So far, but they're not exactly on our team. Since we didn't actually come up with MindReader and can't prove that Church has anything on the President, we're going to have to switch to Plan B and do it mighty damn fast. I'm on my way to Walter Reed now to meet with the President. He's going to want to tear me a new one, so it would be useful if his people got a call about our scapegoat. I don't want this coming through me, you understand?"

"Sure. Don't worry, Bill . . . I've got it all in hand."

They disconnected and the Vice President sank back against the cushions and watched the gray buildings of Washington roll past. He looked calm and collected, but inside he was screaming.

Chapter Forty-Five

Deep Iron Storage Facility
Saturday, August 28, 4:22 P.M.
Time Remaining on the Extinction Clock: 91 hours, 38 minutes

The satellite phone buzzed and Gunnery Sgt. Brick Anderson reached for it without taking his eyes off of the front door of the main building at Deep Iron. He identified himself and received today's command code. When he verified it a voice said, "Hold for Mr. Church."

A moment later Church said, "Give me a sit rep, Gunny."

"Nothing new at this end. Captain Ledger and his team have been in the hole for seventy-one minutes and I've been sweating bullets for seventy of those minutes."

"Any activity?"

"Nothing from them, and nothing from anyone else."

Church was silent for a moment. "Very well. Listen to me, Gunny; the situation has changed. The President is awake and back in charge, though he's still in the hospital. The Vice President has been ordered to tell the NSA to stand down."

"Well, halle-freaking-lujah. And about goddamn time, too, sir. Company would be appreciated."

"Agreed. I've notified the Hub and backup is rolling. You'll have technical support in thirty minutes from your own office, and I've just gotten word that the Colorado State Police SWAT units are airborne and inbound to your twenty. ETA thirty-five minutes."

"Orders, sir?"

"Sit tight until the backup arrives. SWAT has been informed that this is a National Security matter and that you are in charge until Captain Peterson or Ledger is located. If neither has turned up by the time SWAT arrives I want you to enter Deep Iron, assess the situation, and if there is no immediate threat I want you to locate our people." Church paused. "I know you're no longer on active mission status, Gunny, but I need one of my people down there to lead the search. Are you up to this?"

"Sir, I lost my leg," Brick said, "not my trigger finger."

"Good man. Keep me updated."

Church disconnected the call.

Brick set the sat phone down, looked at his watch,

and then leaned back into position, staring down the length of the minigun at the front door. He was relieved that the NSA problem was over, at least for now, but the bad feeling he'd had all day was still there. Stronger than ever.

On the far side of the building two misshapen figures crawled out of an air vent and moved away, keeping low. One limped heavily from a bullet wound in his left thigh; the other staggered along behind him, hands clamped to the ruin of his mouth. They both trailed dark blood as they went. They paused at the edge of the roof and surveyed the foothills on the far side of the facility. No one and nothing moved except withered grass in the late August breeze.

One of the figures opened a Velcro pouch on his hip and withdrew two syrettes. He handed one to his companion and they both injected a cocktail of morphine and adrenaline into their arms. Almost immediately the pain diminished to manageable levels.

The one with the injured leg pulled a sat phone from a belt holster, turned it on, checked his watch, and then punched in that hour's frequency. The call was answered by a woman with a sensual feline voice.

"Mission accomplished." The injured soldier's voice was a complete contrast to the woman's. It was deep and guttural, his words badly formed, as if his mouth and tongue were ill suited to the task.

"Status?" asked the woman.

"We're both injured but able to move. Request extraction at the drop point."

"How soon?"

"Ten minutes."

"Very well." The woman disconnected.

The man returned the sat phone to his holster, pocketed the used syrettes, and exchanged a nod with his companion. They clambered over the wall, moving as quickly as their injuries would allow, ran across the back parking lot, scaled the chain-link fence, and headed into the foothills, making maximum use of natural cover. Within minutes they were gone.

Chapter Forty-Six

Deep Iron Storage Facility
Saturday, August 28, 5:21 P.M.
Time Remaining on the Extinction Clock: 90 hours, 39 minutes

The lights came on and a few moments later we heard the heavy hydraulics of the elevators. A couple of minutes later we heard voices. Muffled and distant. We checked our weapons and took up firing positions behind the stacked file boxes.

Then I heard Gunnery Sgt. Brick Anderson's bull voice bellowing, "Bluebird!"

The cavalry had arrived.

"About damn time, too," said Bunny.

He and Top began moving boxes away from the door. They opened it carefully and Top cupped his hands around his mouth and yelled into the echoing cavern.

"Canary!"

We heard shouting, the whirring of machines, and the sounds of men running. Brick called the challenge again and Top verified it and then opened the door as Brick rolled to a stop in a golf cart with a BAR laid across the windowless dashboard. He was surrounded by a dozen men in full SWAT rig, weapons at port arms, eyes looking at us and then past us at the dead Russians on the floor by the wall. The box covers did little to hide the raw reality of what lay beneath.

"You boys been busy," Brick said with a grim smile.

But I shook my head. "That's not our work, Gunny."

"Captain Peterson?" Gunny asked, his smile beginning to dim.

I shook my head. "We've seen no sign of Jigsaw."

I told Brick and the SWAT team leader an abbreviated version of what had happened, omitting what we'd found in the boxes. Brick looked stricken. The SWAT commander relayed to his men that there were at least two heavily armed hostiles in the facility. I was okay with a "shoot on sight" approach, but that was my nerves talking. My common sense told me to get prisoners we could interrogate. Answers would be nice.

The team dispersed for an active search, but I didn't think they were going to find much.

I pulled some of the file boxes and loaded them onto Brick's golf cart.

"Post a couple of men on this door," I said, indicating the Haeckel bin. "Nobody gets in there, nothing gets touched, unless I give the word."

Brick searched my face, but I wasn't showing anything. Or I thought I wasn't, because he saw something in my expression that darkened his. He nodded and relayed the orders to the SWAT team.

A few minutes later a technical support team from the DMS's Denver office showed up and with them were another dozen armed soldiers from the Hub. More help was inbound from the State Police, including a full bird colonel from the National Guard and two hundred men. It sounded like a lot, but the limestone caverns were vast. The Hub communications officer told me that Jerry Spencer was airborne and heading our way, so I amended my orders to that effect. Let Jerry play with the mess.

I processed all of this, but my mind was elsewhere. That letter wouldn't let me go. In any other circumstance it would be an historical oddity, the kind of thing a scholar could build a book around. And maybe that was all it was, but I didn't think so. There were already way too many coincidences today, and I wasn't buying any of them. When someone sends two armed teams to retrieve something at all costs, then that material is more than grist for a History Channel special.

Given that, the implications were staggering, and as I stood to one side and watched Brick, the Hub team, and SWAT do their jobs, I tried to make everything fit into some kind of shape. My inner cop took over and began sorting through the separate elements of the day.

Russian hit teams here and in Wilmington. The Wilmington hit had been on a guy selling pilfered medical research. *Exactly what was that research?* I wondered. Church knew and I would find out. A second Russian team here in Denver looking for old records that turn out to be—big surprise—more medical research . . . but medical research conducted by Nazi doctors in Auschwitz? Boxes and boxes of them. Statistics and results. *Zwangs/Trauma.* That had been written on one page. It was German for "forced trauma." The notations indicated that the results were categorized according to speed, angle, and PSI classified by chains, clubs, horsewhips, fists, bare feet, and booted feet. Extensive, thorough, and exhaustive documentation of the effects of deliberate physical abuse. Even as cynical as I've become, it was hard for me to grasp the scope and degree of personal corruption required to undertake such a program. That it went on for years was unspeakable.

So, if these records were real, then how the hell did Heinrich Haeckel smuggle them out of Germany after the war? This stuff should not exist, and certainly not in private storage here in the states. Yet here it was, and men were willing to kill one another to recover it, just as men were willing to torture and kill Burt Gilpin in Wilmington and shoot down my own men.

Why?

When Top and Bunny described the Wilmington incident to me they mentioned that the Russians had been downloading information from Gilpin's hard drive. Could Gilpin, during his adventures in hacking, have somehow stumbled upon some reference to Haeckel and traced that to estate records that led the Russians to Deep Iron? Very likely. The timing certainly fit, at least as far as the Russians went.

Church had said that a Cold War–era group called the Cabal had been interested in this sort of thing, but he was convinced that the Cabal had been torn down. Was he wrong? Or had someone else picked up where the Cabal had left off? Someone who hired either the Russians or the two big bruisers to find something that was stored among these records. That seemed likely, though it still didn't answer the question of who sent the other team.

My reverie was interrupted by Top Sims, who handed me a sat phone. "The geeks from the Hub ran a series of relays down the stairwell. Mr. Church is on the line."

I nodded and clicked on the phone.

"You heard about the NSA?" he asked. He didn't wait for an answer. "Bring me up to speed."

I did and there was a long silence at the other end. I could hear the relays clicking as Church processed it.

"I have a bunch of questions," I began, but he cut me off.

"I'll have a C-130 at the airport in forty minutes. I want every scrap of paper from Haeckel's unit on that plane and heading my way asap. I want you on that plane, too."

"What the hell's going on?" I demanded.

"Remember when I told you that there was a worst-case scenario attached to the man in the video?"

"Yeah."

"This is it."

He disconnected.

I handed back the sat phone. *Okay,* I thought, Church needed time to process things. So did I, and I was starting to see the shape of this thing. In a weird and thoroughly frightening way it was starting to take form, kind of like a monster coming slowly out of the mist. It would take a few hours for the C-130 to get us to Baltimore. Plenty of time to think this through.

The thing is . . . I wasn't sure if I wanted to be right or wrong about my suspicions. If I was wrong, then we didn't even have this thing by the tail and we were just as much in the dark now as we were before we came to Deep Iron.

On the other hand, if I was right . . . dear God in Heaven.

Chapter Forty-Seven

Walter Reed Army Medical Center, Washington, D.C.
Saturday, August 28, 5:23 P.M.
Time Remaining on the Extinction Clock: 90 hours, 37 minutes

The President of the United States lay amid a network of tubes and monitoring cables. He was a tall, slightly built man who looked frail at the best of times, but in a hospital gown and with the aftereffects of surgery he should have looked much frailer. Instead rage made him look strong and dangerous. His dark eyes seemed to radiate real heat.

William Collins stood at the foot of the bed—he had not been offered a seat—and endured that glare. It was nearly a full minute since he had completed his full explanation of his actions. Behind the bed a heartbeat monitor was beeping with alarming speed, but when a doctor poked his head in the President snarled at him to get out. The only person allowed to remain within earshot was Linden Brierly, Regional Director of the Secret Service.

When the President spoke, however, his voice was remarkably controlled. "That's your story, Bill?" he asked. "You're comfortable with that?"

"Sir," said Collins, "that's the truth. I acted in the best interests of the American—"

"Skip the bullshit, Bill. Be straight or we're done here."

"I told you the truth. My actions were based on information received that I felt was compelling and believable. I informed the Attorney General about it before I took a single action, and we agreed that it was the best and safest legal course."

"You honestly believe that Church has a leash on me?"

"Based on the information I received, yes. How many ways would you like me to phrase it? Look . . . you can ask me to step down and I will. You can put me in front of Congress and I'll do it without ever taking the Fifth. I'm willing to jump through any hoops you want, Mr. President, but my answer is going to be the same thing every time. The information my source brought me was compelling. It still *is* compelling."

"Are you willing to tell me what that information is?"

"I'm reluctant to do so with Linden here."

"I can step out," offered Brierly, but the President shook his head.

"If there are any skeletons in my closet, Bill," said the President, "then Linden already knows about them. I also think it's important that there be a witness to this conversation."

Collins looked from one to the other, clearly uncertain.

"Mr. President . . . are you sure there is nothing too confidential for—"

"Nothing," insisted the President.

Collins blew out a breath. "Very well. My source told me that Mr. Church has evidence that you used government assets and personnel to squash a link between companies for which your wife served as legal counsel to misappropriation of funds during the first round of financial bailouts."

The President stared at him. Brierly's face was a stone.

"If that were to be made public," Collins continued, "it would destroy your credibility as President, seriously undermine the economic recovery of this country, which could cause an even worse market crash than we had in 2008 and early 2009, and very likely result in impeachment. It would effectively kill your presidency and reverse any good that you've done."

"I see."

"What would you expect me to do? I saw a chance to get you out from under the control of a blackmailer and at the same time protect you and this country from a catastrophe. You want to fry me for that, then do it. I won't even make this public if you put me on trial or before a hearing. What I also won't do, Mr. President, is apologize for my actions."

The President nodded slowly. "Does the name Stephen Preston mean anything to you?"

Collins stiffened.

"I see it does. He's your source, isn't he?"

Collins said nothing.

"Bill, a few minutes before you arrived I received a call from the Attorney General. For the last eighteen months Stephen Preston has been the deputy information analyst for Homeland. His clearance is above Top Secret. He's respected and well placed, and if anyone would be in a position to discover a scandal of the kind you've described it would be him. Likewise if anyone was able to crack MindReader and the DMS and learn of an ongoing campaign of blackmail it would be him. Agreed?"

Collins said nothing.

"So, if someone like Stephen Preston came to you with information of this kind it's understandable, perhaps even imperative, that you would give serious credence to him. I can see that; Linden can see that. The Attorney General must have seen that, because he backed your play in this matter."

Collins said nothing.

"Forty minutes ago a security guard found Stephen Preston at his desk, dead of a self-inflicted gunshot wound to the head."

"What?"

"He had a note on his desk. While not exactly a suicide note, it was nonetheless a very long and rambling letter about the corruption of the American system and the need for it to be wiped away so that it can be replaced by a system created by God and dedicated to His will. That sort of thing. Six pages of it. Superficially the handwriting appears to be his, but the FBI will run their tests. The entire office is now a crime scene, and I've asked the Attorney General to work with the Bureau to make sure that the forensics are done without bias and with no stone unturned."

"Good . . . *God*. . . ." Collins looked stricken and Brierly pulled up a chair for him. The Vice President sat down with a thump. "I . . . I . . . don't understand. He had records; he had proof. . . ."

"Bill, there are probably very few people better suited to fabricate that exact kind of proof. Our biggest concern now is to determine if Preston acted alone or if this is part of some larger conspiracy. I am debating going public with this once we have the facts so that there is absolutely no stink of cover-up."

"I . . . don't know what to say. Mr. President, I—"

The President smiled for the first time. "Bill, I don't like what you did. People were hurt, trust was broken, and tensions now exist between the NSA and DMS—two crucial groups that *need* to be able to trust one another and work together without reservation. And I'll be straight with you . . . I'm going to look very closely at you. You're going to be vetted all over again and if I find anything—*anything*—out of place I'm going to drop you into a hole and bury you with it."

Collins shook his head. "I believed—"

"I know. I'm trusting you, Bill, but I have to be sure."

"But Church . . ."

"Bill, if Mr. Church was really the enemy here he would destroy you. Don't think I'm exaggerating." He snapped his fingers, a sound that was as loud as a dry branch breaking. "Just like that."

"He . . . MindReader . . ."

"Does Church know things about me, Bill? Things that I would prefer not be made public? Sure he does. Has he tried to use them as leverage? No. Not once. I won't speculate on what happened during the previous administration. If Church had secrets then, and if he ever tried to use them, then I don't know about it." The President's eyes were intense, his smile gone. "Does Church and his damned computer have too much power? Probably, and if I ever—*ever*—get a whiff that he has abused that power, lost control of it, or used it in ways that do not serve the mutually agreed best interests of this country I won't bother with the NSA—I'll send the National Guard against him and every one of his facilities."

Collins sagged back in his chair.

"But I know the man. I know him very well, and I truly believe, Bill, that Church and his group are one of the strongest and most correctly used weapons in our arsenal. I've seldom met anyone in whom I place as much personal trust as I place in Mr. Church."

"You don't even know his real name!"

The President's smile returned.

"Yes," he said, "I do."

Twenty minutes later Vice President Bill Collins was in the back of his limousine, the soundproof window in place.

"How'd it go?" asked Sunderland on the other end of the line.

"He goddamn near tore my balls off."

"What happened?"

"He bought it. Hook, line, and sinker."

Sunderland's exhale was so long that it sounded like a hot air balloon deflating.

"J.P.," said Collins, "I don't want to know how you stage-managed the suicide. We're never going to discuss this topic again."

"We don't need to. You're out of it."

"I'm out of it," Collins agreed. "Now you have to watch your own ass."

Sunderland made a rude noise.

"I wish we'd never tried this, J.P."

"Little late to cry over it now . . . and we might still spin something useful out of it."

"You might. . . . I'm out of it."

Before Sunderland could reply, Collins closed his phone. He folded his arms tightly against his chest and crossed his legs and wondered if he had just jabbed a tiger with a stick. In his mind Sunderland was not the tiger. Nor was the President.

The tiger was Church.

Chapter Forty-Eight

The Deck
Saturday, August 28, 9:46 P.M.
Time Remaining on the Extinction Clock: 86 hours, 14 minutes E.S.T.

"We've located the facility," said Otto as he tucked the Irish linen under Cyrus's chin.

"Where?"

"In the Bahamas, those arrogant brats. They bought an island. Dogfish Cay. Thirty-eight acres, volcanic but with a solid bedrock base. Very lush, with several buildings and a lagoon that looks like it might have been dredged to take small cargo ships. My guess is that most of the facility is built down into the bedrock."

"My young gods," Cyrus said with a smile. "They learned well."

Otto grunted and arranged the platter on his lap tray. "It gives them easy access to the states, they can hide small shipments among the tourists and pleasure craft, but they're outside of U.S. waters."

"Which is why we couldn't find them. I was sure they would build in one of the Carolinas. They bought property there under half a dozen names." He paused and picked up his knife and fork. "Mmm, now that I see the whole picture I can see where the land purchases were misdirection. Good for them."

"What do you want to do now?"

"Now I'll eat. What is it? Not more dodo—?"

"No, it's Alsatian. Grilled with onions and peppers."

"Do I like dog, Otto?"

"You requested it specially."

"Whatever could I have been thinking?" he said as he cut a piece of meat, speared a plump slice of green pepper, and ate it. He chewed thoughtfully. "Mm. This is a bit of a disappointment."

"What do you want to do about the Dragon Factory?"

Cyrus cut another piece of meat and stabbed it with his fork, then waggled it at Otto. "Infiltrate it, of course. Send two teams in a look-and-follow pattern. The New York boys will do for the first-in. What's the weather like on Dogfish Cay?"

"Eighty-six degrees with light and variable winds out of the southwest. Cloud cover coming in over the next few hours."

"Are the teams ready?"

"They were in the chase planes."

"Then go tonight."

"Very good."

"And Otto . . . ?"

"Sir?"

"Have them kill either Hecate or Paris. One or the other, but *not* both."

Otto stared at him in surprise. "Are we having one of our episodes, Mr. Cyrus?"

Cyrus smiled. "No, we're not, and don't be a smart-ass. God! Look at you—you're white as a ghost."

"Kill one of the Twins . . . ?"

"Sentimentality creeping in on you in your dotage, Otto?"

"Hardly. I just don't understand why you want one of your children murdered. What does it do for us?"

"If we do it right, Otto, if we make it look like a government hit—which is easy enough considering where we get our equipment—then it will drive the remaining Twin closer to me. A family brought together in shared grief. Us against the world, that sort of thing. Instead of stealing the secrets of the Dragon Factory he—or, more likely, *she*—will beg us to take them." His eyes glittered like black glass. "And then our real work can finally begin."

Chapter Forty-Nine

Private airfield, Denver, Colorado
Saturday, August 28, 10:59 P.M.
Time Remaining on the Extinction Clock: 85 hours,
1 minute E.S.T.

Jerry Spencer reached the airfield just as we were loading the last of the Haeckel records onto the C-130. I waved him over and we shook hands.

"What the hell's going on today, Joe?" he asked in his usual gruff voice. "You look like you just got kicked in the nuts. What is it?"

I told him about the ugly secrets we found down there in the dark.

He paled. "First Russians and now frigging Nazis? Are you shitting me?"

"Wish I was. Look, we had to mess up the crime scene—Church wants those records back in Baltimore—

but try to find me something to go on. We're starting to make headway, but we could still use a few more answers. One of the Hub boys will run you out to Deep Iron. Go down there, man . . . do your magic."

Jerry took a pipe out of his pocket and tapped the stem on his thumbnail. He gave up smoking a couple of years ago, but he carried the pipe so he could fidget with something. It beat biting his nails.

"You didn't find any trace of Jigsaw Team?" he asked.

"Nothing. Maybe you will. . . ."

From the look on his face I was sorry I said it. At this point there was a good chance that anything he found would be bad news.

"I'll do what I can, Joe," he said. "Call you when I have something."

He headed off, head down, his cold pipe tight between his teeth.

I headed across the tarmac to the C-130. We were wheels up in ten minutes.

Chapter Fifty

The House of Screams, Isla Dos Diablos
Sunday, August 29, 12:43 A.M.
Time Remaining on Extinction Clock: 83 hours, 17 minutes

The compound was never silent. Even here in the middle of the night there was noise. Cries of the jungle parrots, the incessant buzz of insect wings, the rustle of leaves as the breeze pushed its way through the palms. And the screams.

Eighty-two crouched in the dark and tried to remember if he had ever heard real silence here, if there was ever a time when someone wasn't shouting, or weeping, or screaming. He was sure there must have been times, but he couldn't recall. It wasn't like living at the Deck. Sure, there were screams there, too, but not all the time. Eighty-two had watched a lot of TV—even regular stuff he downloaded from satellite feeds—and he knew that hearing screams was not part of ordinary life.

Then again, he already knew he was a freak.

After he'd snuck out to recover the stone, Eighty-two had climbed back into his bedroom so that he'd be there for the midnight bed check. When the nurse and guard—there were always two of them—were sure he was in bed and asleep, they closed and locked the door. That left him four hours until the next bed check.

Eighty-two lifted the corner of his mattress and removed a small tool kit. The cover was part of a leather work apron he'd picked out of the trash, and the individual tools were things he had collected over the last two years. None of them were proper tools, but each of them was carefully made. Eighty-two was very good with his hands. He had learned toolmaking by the time he was ten and had even assisted Otto in making surgical instruments for Alpha. It wasn't something the boy enjoyed, but then again there was almost nothing he enjoyed. Toolmaking had been a thing to learn, and Eighty-two never passed up an opportunity to learn something. He believed that his willingness—perhaps his *eagerness*—to learn was one of the reasons Alpha hadn't let Otto kill him.

Alpha had hopes for him. Eighty-two knew that much, although he didn't know what those hopes were or *why* Alpha held on to them with such aggression. It wasn't out of love; the boy knew that much from long experience. There were a lot of other boys at the Deck, and Eighty-two had seen Alpha's mood change from approval to disapproval of many of them over the years. Alpha's disapproval was terrifying. Six weeks ago, Alpha had made Eighty-two and a dozen other boys sit and watch as One Thirteen was fed to Isis and Osiris. One Thirteen had not been clever enough at numbers, and his hand sometimes trembled when he held a scalpel. Alpha had been very disappointed in him.

Eighty-two used a pair of metal probes to undo the lock to his bedroom door, slipped out, and relocked the door. Then like a ghost he drifted along the empty corridors of the main house and along an enclosed walkway that led to the guardhouse. Twice he passed crosswalks that had cameras mounted on the wall, but he kept to his memorized timing schedule and no one saw him. To get to the House of Screams he had to pass through the guardhouse or go outside—and that wasn't likely with the dogs out there. From his window Eighty-two had seen four of the dogs—two big tiger hounds and a pair of some new breed he didn't know and didn't want to know. No thanks.

The guardhouse smelled of beer, sweat, sex, unwashed clothes, and testosterone. Eighty-two would love to have doused the place in gasoline and tossed in a match. Or thought he would. It was easy to think of doing that because the guards made him so mad.

But could he ever do that? Take lives?

He knew he was expected to. He knew that soon he'd be asked to. Told to. Made to.

God.

He slipped inside and hid in the shadows by the door, watching the rows of beds, listening to the snores.

There was a sound to his left—soft and weak—and he edged that way. It wasn't a male sound, not a guard sound. He thought he knew what it might be.

She was there, lying on the floor in a puddle of moonlight.

The female.

She was naked, knees drawn up to her chest, head half-buried under her arms. Her red hair was sweat soaked and tangled; her hunched back was crisscrossed with welts. Belt marks, with cuts here and there from the buckle. Eighty-two recognized them.

Carteret.

The female shivered despite the heat. The boy could smell urine and saw the glint of light on a small puddle. The female had wet herself. Either too afraid to move or too hurt, she just had wet herself. Eighty-two felt his heart sink. He knew that when Carteret woke up and saw the mess he would hurt her some more.

There was an expression Eighty-two heard in a couple of movies: "Damned if you do, damned if you don't." That's what the female must have felt. What she must feel now. There was no way to be right, to act right, to do right, in the eyes of the guards. Even obedience was sometimes punished. It was all about the punishment, about the breaking of the will. Eighty-two knew this, and he knew why it was important to Otto and Alpha, why they encouraged the guards to do whatever they wanted to the New Men. Especially when other New Men were watching.

The female opened her eyes and looked at him. The naked clarity of her gaze rooted Eighty-two to the spot. Her eyes searched his face and he could tell that she recognized him. Then her gaze shifted away toward the cot where Carteret slept, lingered for a moment, and shifted back to the boy. Slowly, being careful of her injuries and not to make a sound, she raised her hand, extended a finger, and touched it to her cheek. Then she drew the finger across as if wiping away a tear. Eighty-two instantly recognized the gesture—it was what the two male New Men had done after they'd seen him wipe away a tear after the female had been beaten.

Eighty-two's mouth went dry. He reached into his pocket and removed the black piece of volcanic rock and held it in a shaft of moonlight so she could see it. Her eyes flared wide in horror and she cringed, but Eighty-two shook his head. He closed his hand around the rock and mimicked throwing the stone at the sleeping Carteret. Eighty-two then pretended to be struck with a stone and reeled back in a pantomime of cause and effect.

The female's eyes followed his actions and he was sure she understood what he meant, but she slowly shook her head. Fresh tears filled her eyes and she closed her lids and would not look at him again.

Eighty-two watched the female shiver and he wanted to do *something*, but he made himself move away. He felt ashamed for scaring her and furious that she would not fight for herself, not even when Carteret was helpless. There was a sound like cloth tearing behind Eighty-two's eyes and the shadows dissolved into a fiery red around him as rage drove him suddenly to his feet and he raised the rock high above his head, muscles tensed to hurl it at the guard's unprotected head.

Eighty-two had never wanted to kill anyone or anything before. Not truly.

Until now.

But he didn't. His whole body trembled with the

effort of not killing this man. It took more strength than Eighty-two thought he possessed to lower his arm.

Not yet, he told himself. *Not yet.*

There was other work to be done.

He forced himself to move away, but as he did he saw the female watch him. She didn't plead with her stare; there was no flicker of hope that he would rescue her. All Eighty-two saw was a bleak, bottomless resignation that came close to breaking his heart.

Anger was a burning coal in his mind. He cut a final glance at Carteret's sleeping, drunken, naked body sprawled on the bed, and Eighty-two forced himself to put the stone back in his pocket.

Not yet, he told himself again. *But soon.*

He made it all the way to the end of the guardhouse and undid the lock and slipped into the House of Screams. Eighty-two had a plan, but it was a dreadful risk. He had tried once by sending the hunt video.

There was one more thing he could try. But if he got caught . . .

He did not worry as much about his own skin—he never expected to grow up anyway. Most of the other boys were already dead by the time they were his age. He had to be careful so that he could do something about Carteret.

Eighty-two made it to the House of Screams and slipped inside, evading all of the cameras, and found what he was looking for. A laptop sitting on a technician's desk. Eighty-two had seen it yesterday and hoped it would still be here.

Eighty-two opened it and hit the power button. It seemed to take a thousand years for the thing to boot up, but when it did there was a clear Internet connection. He licked his dry lips and tried not to hear the deaf-ening pounding of his beating heart. He pulled up a browser page, typed in the address of Yahoo, logged into the same e-mail account, and set to work. He was half-way finished composing his note when he saw that the laptop had a built-in webcam.

For the first time in weeks, Eighty-two smiled.

Chapter Fifty-One

In flight
Sunday, August 29, 12:44 A.M.
Time Remaining on the Extinction Clock: 83 hours,
16 minutes E.S.T.

I'm a damaged person. I know that about myself, and it's part of the reason that my best friend is also a shrink. We met because of Helen.

Helen had been my girlfriend when I was in junior high. One September afternoon a bunch of older teen-agers who were high on whiskey and black bombers cornered us in a field near where we lived. The boys stomped me nearly to death, rupturing my internal or-gans and breaking my bones, and while I lay there bleeding I could do absolutely nothing while the sons of bitches raped and sodomized Helen. Physically we'd both healed from the assault. Psychologically . . . well, what do you think? I got lost in frustration and impo-tent rage, and Helen just went inside her own head and got lost somewhere in the dark.

For the rest of her life Helen was under regular med-ical and psychiatric care. Rudy took over her case when Helen and I were twenty-one, and over the years it seemed like Helen was making some progress. Then one day I went to her apartment to check on her and she was gone. Her body was there, but she was already cold.

What can you do when they turn out all your lights?

Well, for my part, I learned to *use* the darkness. I'd joined a jujutsu dojo a few months after the assault and over the years learned every vicious and dirty trick I could. I made myself get tough. I never competed in tournaments; I just learned how to fight. When I was old enough I enlisted in the Army and after that I joined the Baltimore cops. Rudy knew what the attack had done to Helen and me. It had destroyed both of the people we had been. I lost a lot of my humanity that day and lost more of it after she killed herself. The process fragmented me into at least three different and occasionally compatible inner selves: the civilized man, the cop, and the warrior. The civilized part of me was, despite everything, still struggling to be an idealist. The cop was more cynical and less naïve—and luckily for all of us he's usually in the driver's seat. But when things got nasty, the warrior wanted to come out and play. As I sat in the noisy darkness of the C-130 I could feel the cop sorting through the available data, but the warrior wanted to slip into the shadows and take it to the bad guys in very messy ways.

I knew that I should probably talk to Rudy about what I was feeling. About Big Bob, about the firefight in Deep Iron, and about the things we'd found in Haeckel's bin. I could feel my self-control slipping notch by notch. I know I'm a professional soldier and a former police detective and a martial arts instructor—all roles that require a great deal of personal discipline and control—

but I was also damaged goods. Guys like me can never assume that self-control is a constant.

Rudy was working as a police psychiatrist before he got hijacked into the DMS. It's his job to keep his eye on a whole bunch of front liners—men and women who have to pull the trigger over and over again. As Rudy is so fond of pointing out, violence, no matter how justified, always leaves a mark. I'd killed people today, and I wanted to find more people to kill. The urge, the need, the *ache*, to find the people responsible for this and punish them boiled inside of me, and that is not the best head space to be in before a fight.

Not that I wanted to lose my edge, either, because the damage I owned also made me the kind of fighter that had brought me to the attention of Church. It left me with a useful kind of scar tissue, a quality that gives me an edge in a fight, especially when the fight comes out of nowhere.

You see, we don't always get to pick our battles. We don't often get to choose the rules of engagement. Sometimes a nasty bit of violence comes at us out of the blue, and it's not always of our making. We neither ask for it nor subscribe to it, but life won't ask you if it's fair or if you're ready. If you can't roll with it, if you aren't programmed to react when the hits come in on your blind side, then you go down in the first round. Or you can cover up and try to ride it out, but getting beaten into a corner is no way to win a fight. The sad truth is they won't tire when they're winning and so you'll still lose, and you'll get hurt more in the process.

Then there are those types who thrive on this sort of thing. If someone lands a sucker punch they dance out of the way of the follow-up swing, they take a little taste of the blood in their mouths, and then they go after the bad guys with a wicked little punk rocker grin as they lunge for the throat. It's hard to beat these guys. Real hard. Hurting them never seems to work out, and threats aren't cards worth playing. They're wired differently; it's hard to predict how they'll jump. You just know they will.

The bad guys have to kill them right away or they'll turn the whole thing around and suddenly "hunter" and "prey" take on new meanings. These types don't bother with sucker punches—they go for the kill. They're addicted to the sweet spot.

I understand that kind of person. I get what makes their fractured minds work.

I should.

I'm one of them. The killer in me was born in a field in the backstreets of Baltimore as booted feet stomped on me and the screams of an innocent girl tore the fabric of my soul.

I closed my eyes and in my head the face of the warrior was there, his face painted for war, his eyes unblinking as he peered through the tall grass, waiting for his moment. He whispered to me, *Take it to them. No mercy, no quarter, no limits.*

It was bad thinking.

But try as I might, I couldn't find fault with it.

The plane flew on through the burning August skies.

Interlude

Conrad Veder stood in the shadows beneath one of the arches in the courtyard of the Old Castle in Stuttgart. He chewed cinnamon gum and watched a pigeon standing on the plumed helmet of Eberhard I, Duke of Württemberg, a wonderful statue sculpted by Ludwig von Hofer in 1859. Veder had read up on the Old Castle before coming here, partly as research for this phase of the job and partly out of his fascination with German history. He was a man of few abiding interests, but Germany had intrigued him since the first time he'd come here thirty-four years ago. This was his first visit to Stuttgart, however, and this morning he had whiled away a pleasant hour on the Karlsplatz side of the Old Castle in a museum dedicated to the memory of Claus Schenk Graf von Stauffenberg, a former resident of Stuttgart who attempted to assassinate Adolf Hitler in 1944. A couple of years ago Veder had seen the movie *Valkyrie*, based on the incident. He thought Tom Cruise was a good fit for Stauffenberg, though Veder liked neither the actor nor the traitor who had failed in what should have been an easy kill.

After reviewing all the data, including floor plans of the site of the attempted assassination, Veder concluded that he would have done it differently and done it correctly.

He checked his watch. Almost time.

He took the gum from his mouth, wrapped it in a

tissue, and placed it in his pocket. Veder never left useful traces behind. Veder had little respect for police intelligence, but their doggedness was legendary.

A group of tourists came ambling past—fat Americans in ugly shirts, English with bad teeth, haughty French. It was no wonder stereotypes persisted. As they passed, Veder melted into the crowd. He was dressed in jeans and a lightweight hooded shirt with the logo of the VfB Stuttgart football club embroidered on the right chest and the emblem of the Mercedes-Benz Arena on the back. There were at least five other people in the square with similar shirts. He wore sunglasses and a scruff of reddish gold stubble on his jaw. His gait was slouchy athletic, typical of the middle-aged ex-athlete who resented being past his prime. It had taken Veder only a few days to identify the personality subtype among the crowds in the city. He saw hundreds of them and now he was indistinguishable from any of the others who wandered in and out of the shops and museums around the Old Castle.

He followed the crowd into the Stauffenberg museum. Veder was not dressed this way when he had visited the museum earlier that day. The other costume had been similarly based on a common Stuttgart *look*, and like this one it was equally at odds with Veder's true appearance.

It was possible, even likely, that he could have wrapped this job up during his early visit, but he liked the distractions and confusion that a group would provide. Earlier the attendance at the museum had been sparse. If someone very smart was to have watched the security tapes from the morning they might have been able to make some useful deductions about Veder's true physical appearance. But amid a sea of tourists he was virtually invisible.

The crowd was made up of three different tours, and the tour guides herded the people into one of the rooms to await a brief lecture by Stellvertretender Direktor Jerome Freund, the professor who was the assistant director of the museum. Freund came out of the back, walking slowly and leaning on a hardwood walking stick with a flowery silver Art Nouveau handle. Veder knew that the limp had been created by a high-powered bullet smashing Freund's hip assembly. That shot had been one of the very few misses Veder had ever made, and he disliked that he had failed in the kill. That at the time he had been bleeding from two .22 bullets in his own chest did not matter. It was one of three botched jobs—all related to the work he had done for his former "idealistic" employers.

Freund was a tall man with a Shakespearean forehead and swept-back gray hair. His spectacles perched on the end of his nose and arthritis stooped the big shoulders, but Veder could still see the wolf beneath the skin of a crippled old man.

The speech Freund gave was the same one he had given that morning. Even the professor's gestures were the same. *Ah,* Veder thought, *there is nothing so useful as routine.*

He waited until the professor began describing the day of the assassination attempt. If this was all rote to the man, then he would raise his cane and use it to point to the large photo that covered one wall, tapping the photo with the cane tip to indicate where Stauffenberg and Hitler had each stood. All throughout the talk Veder pretended to take photos with his digital camera.

Sure enough, the professor turned and began tapping the wall.

If Veder was a different kind of man, he might have either taken pleasure in how easy it was or been disappointed that it did not challenge his skills, but Veder had the cold efficiency of an insect. Insects are opportunistic and they don't gloat.

He pressed the button on the camera and the tiny dart shot out of a hole beside the fake lens, propelled by a nearly silent puff of compressed gas, traveling at a hundred feet per second. Freund flinched and swatted the back of his neck.

"Moskito," he said with a laugh, and the hot, sweaty tourists chuckled. It was hot and flies, gnats, and mosquitoes were everywhere. The lecture continued, the moment forgotten. Veder remained with the tourists until they finished the tour, and as the crowd boiled out into the courtyard he detached himself and strolled idly across to the opulent market hall. He bought clothes in different stores, changed in a bathroom, and became another kind of tourist who vanished entirely into the crowd.

Veder had no desire to linger. He did not doubt the efficacy of the pathogen on the dart, and he had no need to see his victim fall. He would read about it in the papers. It would make all of the papers. After all, how often does a German scholar die of Ebola?

By the time the first symptoms appeared, Conrad Veder was on a train to Munich. He was asleep within twenty minutes of the train leaving the station. By then Jerome Freund was already beginning to feel sick.

Part Three
Gods

*If the gods listened to the prayers of men, all human-
kind would quickly perish since they constantly pray
for many evils to befall one another.*

—EPICURUS

Chapter Fifty-Two

Hecate and Paris stood together on a small balcony that jutted out from a metal walkway built above and around the central production floor of their primary facility. Below them over a hundred employees moved and interacted with the mindless and seamless choreography of worker bees. It was an image they had discussed and one they always enjoyed. Everything was color coded, which added to the visual richness of the scene. Blue jumpsuits for general support staff, white lab coats for the senior researchers, green scrubs for the surgical teams, orange for the medical staff, charcoal for the animal handlers, and a smattering of pastel shades for technicians in different departments. Hecate liked color, Paris liked busy movement.

The production floor was circular and a hundred feet across, with side corridors leading to labs, holding pens, design suites, bio-production factories, and computer centers. The lighting made it all look like Christmas.

Rising like a spike from the center of the floor was a statue of the tattoo each of the Twins wore in secret: a caduceus in which fierce dragons were entwined around the shepherd's staff to form a double helix. Dragons were each carved from single slabs of flawless alabaster, the milky stone a perfect match for their skin. The central staff was marble, and the wings were made from hammered gold. The Twins had no personal religion, but to them the statue was sacred. To them it revealed aspects of their true nature.

Paris leaned a hip against the rail and sipped bottled water through a straw. He and his sister always drank from a private stock of Himalayan water. The general staff was provided with purified water. Their dockside warehouse, however, was filled to the rafters with bottled water from the bottling plant in Asheville owned by Otto on behalf of Cyrus. No one at the Dragon Factory was allowed to drink any of those bottles. Hecate and Paris certainly wouldn't.

Generally the water shipments went directly from the bottling plant to the customs yard and then by ship to ports all over the world. The current store was scheduled for distribution to several islands here in the Bahamas. The cargo ship was scheduled to dock in ten hours.

"You really think Dad put something in the water?" asked Paris.

"Don't you?"

He shrugged. "Like what? We've tested it for toxins, mercury, pollutants, bacteria . . . it's just water."

"Maybe," Hecate said neutrally. "Maybe."

"If you're that concerned with it, then dump it into the ocean and fill the bottles with tap water."

"We could," she said. "But wouldn't you like to know what's in it?"

"You ordered a battery of new tests as soon as we got

back. Let's leave it until our people finish their analysis." He narrowed his eyes. "Or . . . do you think you know what's in it?"

She took his bottle from him and sipped it. "Know? No, I don't know, but I have some suspicions. General suspicions . . ."

"Like . . . ?"

"Genetic factors."

Paris looked at her in surprise. "Gene therapy?"

"It can be done in water. It's difficult, but Dad could do it. *We* could do it."

"What kind of gene therapy?"

"I don't know. If Dad was just a corrupt businessman I'd think he was adding something to create an addictive need for the water. For that particular brand of water."

"We tested for hormones. . . ."

"No . . . Dad's all about genetics these days. And viruses."

"We checked for viruses," Paris said nervously.

"And found none, I know. That's why I'm having the water tested for DNA."

"What do we do if we find something in there?"

"Well, Brother . . . that depends on what the gene therapy is intended to accomplish. If it's just an addictive component, then we let it slide but ask for a bigger cut of the water market."

"What if it's something bad?"

" 'Bad'?" She smiled at that. "Like what?"

"Like something destructive. Something that will kill people."

Hecate shrugged. "I don't know. Why? Are you getting squeamish?"

"After what the Berserkers found in Denver? What if I am?"

"God! It's a little late to start developing a conscience, Paris."

His eyes met hers and then shifted away. "I've always had a conscience. Something like a poison or a plague . . . that would be different."

She shrugged.

Paris said, "The stuff we recovered from Denver. That's Nazi death camp stuff. That's . . . that's wrong on a whole different level from anything we've done."

"It's fascinating."

"Christ! It's gruesome. I can deal with some slap and tickle. And, yes, I can deal with a little snuff . . . but the systematic torture and extermination of *millions* of people?"

His sister gave another dismissive shrug.

"Why the hell does Dad want that crap?"

"Why would any geneticist?" she asked.

"I don't want it."

"I do. I wish we had the Guthrie cards. Hundreds of thousands of blood samples, all neatly indexed with demographics. They'd be useful for collecting genetic markers."

He shook his head. "I don't think I'd like to build our empire on those kinds of bones."

"What . . . you don't like being an evil mastermind?"

"This isn't a joke, Heck."

"I'm not joking. And don't call me that."

"Is this how you see us? I mean, really? Do you think we're evil?"

"Aren't we?"

"Are we?"

Hecate handed back the water bottle. "We've killed people, sweetie. A lot of people. You yourself have strangled two women while you were screwing them. Not to mention all the people the Berserkers have killed. I never saw you shed a tear. Evil? Yes, I think that pretty much covers it."

"We're corrupt," Paris said, almost under his breath. "Corruption isn't actually evil."

"It's certainly not a saintly virtue."

He crossed to the other side of the balcony and stared out through a big domed window at the warehouse on the dock. The doors were open and he could see the pallets of cased water. "Is there a line? Between corruption and evil? If so . . . when did we cross it?"

Hecate studied her brother's profile. She had suspected that this was coming, but she hadn't expected to hear this much hurt in Paris's voice. "What's going on with you? You've been in a mood ever since we left Dad's place."

"Dad. *Alpha*." Paris snorted. "If we're evil, Hecate, it's because he made us that way. He's a monster. We're . . . by-products."

"The apple and the tree, Paris."

Paris shook his head.

Hecate frowned. "What are you saying, that if you had a choice you'd have done things differently? That you would have chosen a different path than following in Dad's footsteps?"

"I don't know. And I don't want to get into a whole nature-versus-nurture debate, either," he snapped. When she said nothing he leaned on the rail and stared out over the water as if he could already see the freighter. "I enjoyed what we did. I know that about me, and in a way

I'm comfortable with it because I know that it serves my appetites. So . . . maybe there's a level of corruption—of *evil*—that I'm okay with. Maybe even a level I want to be part of what defines me."

"But . . . ?" she prompted.

"But I don't know that I want to believe that I have no limits. That my darkness has no limits."

"That's a little grandiose, Brother."

He turned and spread his arms. "Look at me, Hecate. Look at *us*. We're grand. Everything about us is larger than life. None of it's real, a lot of it's not even supposed to be possible . . . but here we are, and we've begged, borrowed, and stolen so much science that we've made the impossible *possible*. There's never been anything like us before in history. Dad calls us his young gods, and in ways he's not far wrong. We bend nature to our will." She opened her mouth to speak, but Paris gave a curt shake of his head. "No, let me finish. Let me say this. Hecate, we've always been the Jakoby Twins. People would actually kill to be with us. People would kill to be *near* us. You know that for a fact because men have killed each other over you on two continents. We're legends. We also know we're not normal. We're not even true albinos. This skin color is too regular, too pure white. Our bodies are without a single genetic flaw. We have blue eyes and perfect eyesight. We've never even had cavities. We're stronger than we should be; we're faster. And we're almost identical twins despite being of different genders."

"Yes, we're genetically designed. Big surprise, Paris . . . our father is probably the smartest geneticist on the planet. He wanted genetically perfect children, and that's what he got. He also made sure that we're gorgeous and really fucking smart. Smarter than anyone else except maybe the occasional freak. He tweaked our DNA to make us better, to try and create the 'young gods' that he's always dreamed of. So what? This isn't news."

"There's a fine line between genetic perfection and freakism," Paris said. "And no matter what you or Dad says, we are definitely freaks. If we did nothing else, nothing new or innovative, people will write books about us and talk about us for the next century. Maybe for a thousand years. We broke through boundaries of science no one has dared push."

Hecate folded her arms under her breasts and said nothing.

"So . . . what does that mean to us?" Paris continued. "We've been raised by Dad to believe that we are elevated beings. We're gods or aliens or the next phase of evolution, depending on which of Dad's personalities is doing the talking. Whether he's right or wrong, the truth is we're not normal. We're like a separate species."

"I know. . . ."

"So, is that why we do what we do?" he demanded, his voice quick and urgent, almost pleading. "Is that why we can kill and steal and take without remorse? Are we above evil because evil is part of the human experience and we're not quite human?"

"What do you want me to say?"

He shook his head. "I don't know. I . . . don't want to feel bad about what we're doing, Hecate, and yet it's tearing me up inside. It was bad before we saw Dad, and now it's worse. Maybe because when I see him I think,

There . . . that's true evil in its purest form. Or maybe it's that I think that all of this is bullshit rationalization and that we're just a couple of psychotic mass murderers who have no right to live."

"Jeez, Paris," Hecate said with a crooked smile, "when you get a case of existential angst you don't screw around." She came over to him and took Paris in her arms. He returned the hug sluggishly and tried to pull away, but Hecate held him fast. For a moment it seemed to him that she was stronger than he was. Hecate leaned into him, her lips by his ear. "Listen to me, sweet brother. We *are* gods. Not because Dad says or the *National-* fucking-*Enquirer* says so. We're gods because we say so. Because *I* say so. And, yes, we're evil. Our souls are as black and twisted as the Grinch's, but there's no Cindy Lou Who in Whoville that's going to turn us into good guys in the third act. We're evil because evil is powerful. We're evil because evil is delicious."

Her arms constricted around him with crushing force, the pressure making him gasp.

"We're evil because evil is strong and everything else is weak. Weak is ugly; weak is stupid. Evil is beautiful."

She purred out that last word. Then she kissed Paris on the cheek and pushed him away. He staggered back and hit the rail. If he hadn't grabbed the rail, he might have gone over. Paris stood there, his knees weak, gasping and startled.

"What the fuck . . . ?" he breathed. "What the hell was that all about?"

Hecate smiled at him. Her blue eyes were dark and deep, the irises flecked with tiny spots of gold that he had never noticed before.

"What the hell are you?"

"I'm your sister," she said softly. "And, like you, my sweet brother, I'm evil. I'm a monster."

Hecate licked her lips.

"Just like you."

Chapter Fifty-Three

The Warehouse, Baltimore, Maryland
Sunday, August 29, 4:09 A.M.
Time Remaining on the Extinction Clock: 79 hours, 51 minutes

We landed at a military airport, and the cargo—paper and human—was shifted to an MH-47G Chinook helicopter that swung us over to what had become my home. The Warehouse had been the base of a group of terrorists that had been raided by a joint police/Homeland task force on which I'd served. It had been that raid that had brought me to Church's attention, and I was recruited a couple of days later. That was the end of June, and we were still a week away from the end of August. So much had happened that it seemed like I'd been part of the DMS for at least a year. In the last two months I'd only spent three or four nights at my apartment. Even my cat, a chubby marmalade tabby named Cobbler, lived at the Warehouse. All of the operators on Echo and Alpha teams had rooms there, though a couple of them also went home—occasionally—to families.

As the big helicopter touched down I saw a squad of armed guards waiting for us—and two people who stood slightly apart. Rudy Sanchez and Grace Courtland. My heart did a little happy dance in my chest when I saw Grace. In the interests of professional decorum I kept it off my face.

She was the first bright spot in this whole mess, and she came to meet me as I exited the chopper. She strolled toward me without hurry, a mild smile on her lips, but I knew her well enough to know that the devilish light in her eyes meant that she was just as happy to see me as I was to see her. I wanted to drag her out of sight behind the row of parked Black Hawks and kiss her breathless. And I knew from experience that she could leave me just as breathless. Rudy hung back, tactful as ever.

"Home is the sailor home from sea, and the hunter home from the hill," she said with a grin.

"Wrong branch of the service. I was a Ranger."

"I don't know any poems about Rangers."

We shook hands because everyone was looking, but as she released mine her fingers gently stroked my palm. It sent heat lightning flashing through my veins.

We headed toward the door and Rudy fell into step beside us.

"How goes the war?" he asked, picking up the thread of our earlier conversation.

"Bullets are still flying, Rude. How are things around here?"

He grunted. "Welcome to the land of paranoia. It's amazing what persecution by the entire National Security Agency can do to the overall peace of mind of a group of government employees. I suggested to Church that he make some kind of statement to the troops here and via webcam to the other facilities. They all look to him for more than orders. His calm—you could almost say emotionless—manner—"

" 'Almost'?" Grace murmured.

"—has a soothing effect on the DMS staff. He's so clearly in command that no matter how wildly the feathers are flying, as long as Church is in control—"

"—and munching his frigging vanilla wafers," I said.

"—the staff will stay steady," Rudy concluded.

I nodded. It was true enough. Church was a master manipulator, and Rudy had marveled at the scope and subtlety of Church's tactics. It was there in everything from the choice of paint color on the walls to comfortable private bedrooms. And it was in Church's attitude. Most of us had seen him in the thick of it, blood on the floor, gunsmoke in the air, screams all around us, and he looked cool in his tailored suits, tinted sunglasses, and total lack of emotionality. Church made Mr. Spock look like a hysterical teenager with a pimple on prom night.

"Look, Joe," Rudy said. "I wanted to say goodbye before I headed out. Church wants me out in Denver. We haven't heard anything for sure about Jigsaw Team, but Church isn't optimistic. He said that he wants me there in case some bad news comes in."

"Damn. I hope he's wrong," I said, but it sounded lame. "Church thinks a lot of you if he's sending you all the way out there."

He shrugged. "I'm a tool."

I said nothing. Grace laughed.

"Okay," Rudy said, "I heard it. What I mean is that Church regards me as a useful instrument."

" 'Tool,' " said Grace.

"God, are you two in kindergarten?"

We shook hands and he trudged off to the helo that was waiting to take him to the airport.

"Is Church here?" I asked Grace as we pushed through the security door to the Warehouse.

"Yes," Church said. I nearly walked into him. He was standing just inside, looking like he just walked out of a board meeting. He offered his hand and we shook. "Glad to have you back safe and sound, Captain."

"Glad to be safe and sound. What's the latest on Big Bob?"

"Stable."

"Look, about that . . . I met Brick and I know he lost his leg in the line of duty. If Big Bob pulls through this I know he won't ever work the field again, but I don't want to hear about him getting kicked to the curb. That shit happens with Delta Force and—"

"Let me head you off at the pass, Captain," said Church. "This is the DMS. I'm not in the habit of abandoning my people."

"Fair enough. On the flight I had a chance to think this through, and I have about a million questions."

"Glad to hear it, but first things first. I want to take a look at the material you recovered in Denver, Captain. Dr. Hu is preparing a point-by-point presentation of everything we have. We'll meet for a briefing in one hour. Until then I suggest you spruce up and then get some rest."

Without another word he headed out to the landing area.

I glanced at Grace, who was frowning. She saw my look and shook her head. "That's about all he's said to me, too. I've tried a dozen ways to open him up, but he's been playing things pretty close to the vest."

"This meeting should be pretty interesting. It's go-

ing to be real interesting to compare notes . . . but first
I have to find a shower and some fresh clothes."

There were a lot of people around, so she gave me a
curt nod and we went our separate ways.

Chapter Fifty-Four

The Residence of the Vice President, Washington, D.C.
Sunday, August 29, 4:11 A.M.
Time Remaining on the Extinction Clock: 79 hours, 49 minutes

Vice President Bill Collins sat alone in his study looking out at the trees in the garden. His fist was wrapped
tightly around his fifth neat scotch. His wife was upstairs asleep, as if nothing was wrong in their world.

After leaving the Walter Reed, he kept expecting a
knock at the door. Secret Service agents. Or, if the universe was in a perverse mood, the NSA.

Maybe he had dodged the bullet. Maybe the President had swallowed the whole can of lies. There was no
way to tell, especially with this President. All the talk
in the press about how calm and unflappable he was did
not begin to scratch the surface of the man's calm control and his cold ruthlessness when he held the moral
high ground in a conflict.

Unless this thing blew over Collins without leaving
so much as a whiff of illegality, Collins knew that the
President would quietly, neatly, and ruthlessly tear him
to pieces.

He gulped more of the scotch, wishing that it
could burn away everything to do with Sunderland, the
Jakobys, or any of their biotech get-rich-quick schemes.

Everything that had seemed so smart and well-planned before now felt like pratfalls and slapstick.

The bottle of McCallum had been full when he'd come home, now it was half gone. But Vice President Collins felt totally empty. He poured himself another drink.

He sat in his chair and waited for the knock on the door.

Chapter Fifty-Five

The Warehouse, Baltimore, Maryland
Sunday, August 29, 4:14 A.M.
Time Remaining on the Extinction Clock: 79 hours, 46 minutes

My quarters were an office that had been remodeled into an efficiency apartment. There was a bed, stand-up closet—I didn't have enough personal effects to call it an armoire—and a work desk with a secure laptop. A small bathroom with a tiny shower was built into what had once been a storage closet. Cobbler met me at the door and entwined himself sinuously around my ankles as I entered. He's a great cat with a purr that sounds like an industrial buzz saw.

I squatted down and scratched his fur for a few minutes while I took stock of my life. Two months ago I was a police detective with aspirations of going to the FBI academy. Sure I'd worked on the Homeland task force, but I never thought that I'd be playing secret agent. It still felt unreal and vaguely absurd. After all, who was I? Just another working schlub from Baltimore with a few jujutsu tricks and a steady gun hand. Big deal. How did that qualify me to do this sort of thing?

Cobbler gave my hand a playful nip and dialed up the volume on his purr.

I got to my feet and the room suddenly did a little Irish jig as if some internal hand had thrown a switch to dump the last of the adrenaline from my system. Exhaustion hit me like a truck and I tottered into the bathroom, turned on the shower, and adjusted the temperature to "boiled lobster." I was still dressed in the soiled clothes I'd worn since my escape from the NSA at the cemetery. A lot had happened since then, and none of it made me smell like a rose. I stripped down and turned the shower to broil, but as I was about to step under the spray I heard a knock on the door.

Cursing under my breath, I grabbed a towel and knotted it around my waist and then jerked open the door, expecting to have to tell Rudy or one of my guys from Echo Team to piss off, but my growl turned into a smile.

Grace Courtland stood there.

Her green eyes met mine and then did a theatrical up-and-down evaluation of my state of near undress.

"I was just about to take a shower," I said. "And believe me I *need* one."

"I don't care if you're filthy," she said with a wicked smile, "because I've got a seriously dirty mind."

She looked quickly up and down the hall to make sure it was empty, then pushed me inside and kicked the door closed behind her. I pulled her to me and we kissed with such heat that the air around us seemed to catch fire. With one hand she helped me with the buttons of her uniform blouse; with the other she pulled apart the knot on my towel. We left a trail of clothes from the door to the middle of the bathroom floor. I popped the hooks of her bra and she shrugged out of it as she slammed me back against the wall.

"I couldn't really tell you earlier, not properly," I said as she kissed my throat and chest, "but I missed you."

"I missed you, too, you big bloody Yank," she said in a fierce whisper, and her breath was hot on my skin. A minute later we were in the cramped confines of my shower stall. We lathered each other up and rinsed off together and never stopped kissing. When she was aroused her green eyes took on a smoky haze that I found irresistibly erotic. I lifted one of her legs and pulled it around me and then hooked my right hand under her thigh and hoisted her up so that I entered her as she leaned back against the tiled wall of the shower. That moment was a scalding perfection of animal heat that made us both cry out. The day had been filled with stress and death and heartbreak and tension, and here amid the wet steam we reaffirmed the vitality and reality of our lives by connecting with the life force of each other.

When she came she bit down on my shoulder hard enough to break the skin, but I didn't care because I was tumbling into that same deep abyss.

After that it all became slow and soft. We stood together for a long time under the spray, our foreheads touching as the water sluiced down our naked limbs, washing away the stress and loneliness that defined us and what we did. We toweled each other off and then lay down naked on my bed.

"I'm knackered," she whispered. "Let me sleep for a few minutes."

I kissed her lips and her forehead and propped myself on one elbow. She was asleep almost at once. Her dark hair was still damp and it clung to her fine skull and feathered along the edges of her lovely face. Her eyes were closed, her long lashes brushing smooth cheeks. Grace's body was slim, strong, curvy, and fit. She looked more like a ballet dancer than a soldier. But she had a lot of little scars that told the truth. A knife, a bullet, teeth, shrapnel. I loved those scars. I knew each and every one of them with an intimacy I know few others had shared. Her scars—amid the otherwise flawless perfection of her—somehow humanized her in a way that I'm not articulate enough to describe. They made her more fully human, more potently female, more of a fully realized woman than any misdirection of fashion or cosmetics could ever hope to achieve. This was a person who was equal in power and beauty and grace to anyone and in my experience second to none. I loved that about her. I loved her.

And that fast my mind stopped and some inner hand hastily stabbed down on the rewind button so that I listened to what I'd just thought.

I loved her.

Wow.

I'd never said it before. Not to her. *We'd* never said it to each other. Over the last two months we'd shared trust and sex and secrets, but we'd both stayed at minimum safe distance from the *l* word. Like it was radioactive.

Yet here, in the semi-darkness of my room, in the midst of a terrible crisis, after hours of sleeplessness and stress, my unguarded heart had spoken something that all of my levels of conscious awareness had not seen or known.

I *loved* Grace Courtland.

She slept on. I pulled the sheet up to cover us both,

and as I wrapped her in my arms she wriggled against my chest. It was such an innocent—perhaps primal— act. A need for security and closeness dating back to those long nights in the caves while the saber-toothed cats and dire wolves screamed in the night. *Just that*, I told myself.

As exhausted as I was, I couldn't sleep. The conference was in twenty minutes anyway, so I lay there and thought about the enormity of those three little words.

Love is not always a goodness, its arrival not always a kindness or a comfort. Not between warriors. Not when we lived on a battlefield. Not when either or both of us could be killed on any given workday.

Not when it could become a distraction from focus or a cause for hesitation. Love, in our circumstances, could get people killed. Us and those who depended on us. It was careless and unwise and stupid.

But there it was. As real and present in my heart as the blood that surged through each chamber.

I loved Grace Courtland.

Now what do I do?

Chapter Fifty-Six

The Dragon Factory
Sunday, August 29, 4:31 A.M.
Time Remaining on the Extinction Clock: 79 hours,
29 minutes E.S.T.

They breached the compound from above, coming out of the night sky in a silent HALO drop. There were two of them, one big and one small, falling through the darkness for miles before opening their chutes and deploy-

ing the batwing gliders that allowed them to ride the
thermals as they drifted toward the island. The big one,
Pinter, took the lead as they glided under the stars, and
Homler, his smaller companion, followed. They were
clad head to foot in black. Pinter scanned the coastline
and jungle and compound with night-vision goggles that
sent a feed that posted a miniature image in one corner
of Homler's left lens. The smaller man had his goggles
set to thermal scans as he counted bodies, his data similarly shared.

Pinter's left glove was wired to serve as a Waldo so
he could control the functions on his goggles while still
maintaining a steering grip on his glider. He triggered
the GPS and angled down and left toward the predesig-
nated drop point they had chosen from satellite photos.
Nothing was left to chance.

They drifted like great bats along the edge of the
forest, in sight of the compound but equal to the tree line
so that they vanished against the darkened trees. Their
suits were air-cooled to spoil thermal signatures, and the
material covering their BDUs and body armor was non-
reflective. Pinter keyed a signal to Homler and together
they angled down and did a fast run-walking landing.
Quick and quiet. They hit the releases on their gear and
dropped the gliders, collapsed them, and stowed them
under a wild rhododendron. Then they did mutual equipment and weapons checks. Both men were heavily armed
with knives, explosives, silenced pistols, and long guns.
Nothing had a serial number; nothing had fingerprints.
Neither man had prints on file in any computer database
except that of the Army, and in that system they were
listed as KIA in Iraq. They were ghosts, and like ghosts
they melted into the jungle without making a sound.

They followed the GPS to the edge of the compound, to the weak point they'd recognized from long-range observation. The compound had a high fence set with sweeping searchlights, but there was one spot, just six feet wide, where no light was shining for nineteen seconds every three minutes. It was an error that would probably be caught on the next routine systems check, but it worked for them.

They knelt just inside the jungle and watched the searchlights for five cycles, verifying the nineteen-second window.

They wore muzzled masks that allowed them to speak into microphones but muffled any sound from escaping. A sentry ten feet away wouldn't have heard them.

"Okay, Butch," said Homler, "I got a sentry on the wall, fourteen meters from the east corner. He's moving right to left. Sixty-one paces and a turnaround."

"Copy, Sundance." Pinter raised his rifle and sighted on the guard. "On your call."

"Bye-bye," said Homler, and Pinter put two into the guard. The distant scuffle of the guard falling to the catwalk was louder than the shots.

"Second guard will be rounding the west corner in five, four, three . . ."

Pinter sighted, dropped the guard as he made the turn.

They waited for reactions or outcry, heard nothing, and moved forward, running into the dead zone between the spotlights. They made it to the base of the wall and froze, counting the seconds until the next gap. Then they raised grappling guns and shot into the base of the corner guard tower. On the third dead zone they activated the hydraulics. The guns didn't have the strength to lift their whole weight, but it took enough of the strain to allow them to run like spiders up the wall. They clambered over the low wall of the guard tower and crouched down, waiting and watching.

"Thermals?"

"Nothing. We're clear."

They dropped fast ropes and slithered to the ground and ran fast and low across the acre of open ground. Sensors in their gear listened for traps, but if there were motion sensors or other warning devices they were not broadcasting active signals.

The two men made it all the way to the wall of the first building in the compound. They had the layout of the entire compound committed to memory. Twenty-six buildings, ranging from a guard shack on the dock to a large concrete factory. Except for the factory, all of the buildings were built of the same drab cinder block with pitched metal roofs. From the aerial photos the place looked like a factory in any third world country, or a concentration camp. It didn't look like what it had to be. Homler and Pinter knew this and understood that there was probably much more of the facility built down into the island's bedrock. Their employer had insisted that the central facility had to be at least four or five stories in order to accommodate the kind of work being done there. Between the two of them they carried enough explosives to blow ten stories of buildings out into the churning Atlantic.

They moved in a pattern of stillness broken by spurts of fast running. An infiltration of this kind was nothing new to either of them. They'd done a hundred of them, separately and as a team. Over the last four years "Butch and Sundance" had become the go-to guys for covert infiltration. They never left a mark if it was an "in and out" job, and when assigned to a wet-work mission they left burned-out buildings and charred corpses behind.

Homler dropped to one knee, his fist upraised. Pinter, a half-dozen steps behind him, froze, eyes and gun barrel focused hard in the direction his partner was pointing.

Five seconds passed and nothing happened.

"What?" whispered Pinter.

"I caught a flicker of motion on the scope. There and gone. Now—nothing."

"Camera on a sweep?"

"Negative. It had heat."

"Nothing there now. Let's *dīdī mau*."

They moved very quickly, angling toward the main building, making maximum use of solid cover—trees, other buildings—to block sensor sweeps.

They were forty feet from the rear wall of the factory when the lights came on.

Suddenly four sets of stadium lamps flared on, washing away every scrap of shadows, pinning the two men like black bugs on a green mat. They froze in the middle of a field, too far from the forest line, away from the shelter of buildings.

"Shit!" Homler growled, wheeling left and right, looking for an exit, but the lights were unbearably bright. They blinded the men and their sensors, and even though their night vision was cued to dim in the presence of a flare, this light crept in through the loose seal of their goggles.

"Remain where you are!" demanded a harsh voice that bellowed at them from speakers mounted on the light poles. "Lower your weapons and lace your fingers behind your heads."

"Fuck this," snarled Pinter, and opened fire in the direction of the nearest set of lights. He burned through half a magazine before the bulbs began exploding in showers of sparks.

Homler stood back-to-back with him and fired at the lights on the opposite side. He and Pinter moved in a slow circle, blasting the lights, waiting for the crushing burn of return fire.

The last of the lights exploded and the sparks drifted down to the grass as darkness closed in over them.

Instantly they were in motion, running like hell toward the fence, swapping out their magazines as they ran. They didn't care about stealth now. Homler punched a button on his vest that began pulsing out a signal to a pickup team in a Zodiac somewhere out beyond the surf line. If he and Pinter could make it to the water, they could get the hell out of this place.

Pinter caught movement on his right and fired two shots at it without breaking stride. There were no friendlies to worry about on this island. There was no return fire, though. A miss or a mistake—it didn't matter.

They could see the fence ahead and Homler reached it first. He leaped at it from six feet out, stretching for the chain links. Then he was snatched out of the air and flung ten feet backward by something huge and dark that seemed to detach itself from the shadows.

Homler crunched to the ground, rolled over onto hands and knees, tore off his mask and vomited onto the grass. Pinter wheeled and fired at the shadow, but there was nothing there. He spun and chopped every yard of foliage on either side of the fence, but nothing screamed and his night vision showed nothing. Pinter fitted in a new magazine as he backed up and knelt beside his partner.

"Sundance," he hissed. "How bad you hit?"

Homler tore off his goggles and turned a white, desperate face to Pinter. "I . . . I . . ." Whatever he tried to say was cut short as Homler's body suddenly convulsed.

Pinter stared down at his partner for a second and saw a deep puncture on the side of his neck. A dart? A snakebite? Pinter put two fingers against the side of his friend's throat, felt a rapid heartbeat. Homler's entire body was rigid now; white foam bubbled from the corners of his mouth. Pinter recognized the signs of toxic shock, but whether this was poison or some natural neurotoxin was uncertain. All that was clear was that he had to escape and he could not carry Homler over the fence.

Pinter felt bad about it, but self-preservation was a much stronger drive.

"Sorry, Sundance," he murmured, and as he rose and backed toward the fence he swept his rifle back and forth, searching the shadows with night vision. The grass stretched away before him, and except for wildflowers blowing in the wind, nothing moved. It made no sense. What had attacked his partner?

When Pinter felt the metal links of the fence press into his back he turned and started climbing. He made it all the way to the top before the darkness reached out of the trees and took him.

Chapter Fifty-Seven

We gathered around a conference table you could have landed an F-18 on. Grace and I on one side, Dr. Hu across from us, Church at the head, and a dozen department heads and analysts filling out the other seats. We all had laptops and stacks of notes. As usual there were plates of cookies on the table as well as pitchers of water and pots of coffee.

Church said, "We have a lot to cover, so let's dig right in. Yesterday was a very bad day for us, and not just because of the acrimony of the Vice President and the unfortunate injuries sustained by Sergeant Faraday. Yesterday none of us were playing our A-game. We reacted to the NSA issue as if it was the only thing on our plate. Our operational efficiency was so low the numbers are not worth discussing."

Hu started to say something, but Church shook his head.

"Let me finish. I think we've been played." He studied how that hit each of us. "As you know, I'm not a big believer in coincidences. I am, however, a subscriber to the big-picture approach. When I say that I think we've been played, I mean that too many important things happened at the same time, and all of it was timed to coincide with our need to pull back virtually all of our resources. Imagine how things might have played if the NSA had succeeded in either obtaining MindReader or forcing us to shut it down. It would have been the same as being handcuffed and blindfolded." He looked around the room. "Does anyone disagree?"

We shook our heads. "Actually, boss, not to sound like a suckup, but this is what I've been thinking. It's what I wanted to tell you before I left Denver."

He nodded as if he'd already guessed that. "Do you want to venture a guess as to what's happening?"

"No. Or at least not yet," I said. "There are still some blanks that need filling in. You told me a little about the Cabal and some Cold War stuff. That has to be tied to this, so why don't you bring us up to speed on that and then I'll play a little what-if. That work for you?"

"It does." He poured himself some coffee and addressed the whole group. "Based on what Captain Ledger found in Deep Iron, I think we're seeing one thing, one very large case. Because we've been out of the loop and off our game, we haven't caught a good glimpse of it. It's like the story of the three blind men describing an elephant. However, we don't yet know if this is something that has years to go before it becomes a general public threat or if it's about to blow up in our faces. My guess? There's a fuse lit somewhere and we have to find it."

"How do we start?" asked Grace.

He took a cookie from the plate, bit off an edge, and chewed it thoughtfully for a moment. "To the general public the Cold War was about the struggle between democracy and socialism. That's the kind of oversimplified propaganda that both sides found useful to perpetuate. What it was in fact was a struggle for power during a time of massive political and technological change. During the war there was a massive spike in all kinds of scientific research, from rockets to medicine.

Those decades saw the development of everything from the microchip to the cell phone. Some of the most groundbreaking work for the development of many of today's scientific marvels, however, predated the Cold War to the thirties and early forties in Germany."

"Absolutely," interrupted Bug. "There was wild science-fiction stuff going on back then. Z1, the first binary computer, was developed by Konrad Zuse in Berlin in 1936, and his Z3, developed in 1941, was the first computer controlled by software. People today seem to think computers started with the PC."

"Exactly," said Church. "And there were similar landmark moments in medicine and other sciences. After the fall of Berlin there was a scramble to acquire German science and German scientists. Even people who should have been tried as war criminals were pardoned—or simply disappeared—by governments that wanted these scientists to continue their work. Openly or, more often, in secret. There are many—myself included—who believe that all of the information gathered by Nazi scientists should have been destroyed. Completely. However, governments often don't care about the cost of information so long as the information itself has value."

Grace said, "So, you're saying that we kept that stuff . . . and used it?"

"Sadly, yes."

"Sure," said Dr. Hu. "Most of what we know about how the human body reacts to fatal or near-fatal freezing comes from research done in the camps. Virtually all of the biological warfare science of the fifties, sixties, and seventies has its roots in experiments done on prisoners at the camps and by Japan's Unit

Seven Thirty-one—their covert biological and chemical warfare research and development unit."

"We pay the Ferryman with the Devil's coin," said Grace.

"Indeed we do," said Church.

"You'd think we'd learn, but my optimism for that died a long time ago. Many of the doctors and scientists involved in these experiments were given pardons. Much of this research was intended for use by the military and intelligence communities, though some had more directly beneficial uses for the common good. Some became the property of corporations which exploited the beneficial aspects of these sciences in order to bring lucrative products to market."

"Big Pharma," said Grace with asperity.

"Among others," Church agreed. "There were also groups within governments or formed by like-minded people from various countries, who desired to see less savory lines of science carried through to their conclusions, and that's where our story begins."

Church pressed a button and a dozen photographs appeared on the big TV screen. The faces were all of white men and women, and some were clearly morgue photos. I recognized none of them.

"There was a very powerful group active from the end of World War Two all the way to the last days of the Cold War. They called themselves the Cabal, and their individual biographies are in the red folders you each have. They belonged to no nation, though many of their members had strong ties to the Nazi Party. At least three of the Cabal members were themselves former Nazis, while others may have been sympathizers but were actually citizens of the United States, Great Britain, Italy,

Argentina, and several other countries. These were all very powerful people who could draw on personal and corporate fortunes to fund their goals."

"And what were those goals?" I asked.

"They had several. Ethnic cleansing was one of their primary goals. They waged an undeclared war on what they called the 'mud people,' which is a blanket phrase for anyone who isn't descended from a very specific set of Caucasian bloodlines."

"Guess no one bloody well told them that we all evolved from a bunch of apes in Africa," said Grace.

Church smiled. "They would not be the first—or last—group to view evolution as a 'theory.' One of the key players in the Cabal, a brilliant geneticist known only by the code name 'Merlin,' apparently believed that humankind had been visited by aliens, angels, or gods— accounts of his beliefs vary—and that the purest human bloodlines are descended from those celestial beings."

"Oh brother," I said, and even Hu gave me a smile and nod.

"The Cabal made hundreds of millions by exploiting science stolen from Berlin after the fall, or from science that was begun in Germany during the war and continued uninterrupted by scientists who fled before the Allies won. Using a variety of false names and dummy corporations and relying on support from a few of the world's less stable governments, they were able to amass great wealth and possess some of the most advanced technology of their time. When they came onto the radar of one country or another they would close up shop, change names, and vanish only to reemerge again somewhere else."

"You said that they had been taken down," I said. "How and by whom?"

"Each of the world's major intelligence networks caught glimpses of the Cabal, but no one country saw enough of it to make an accurate guess as to its full size, strength, and purpose. It was only after a number of agents from different countries began tripping over each other that it became clear they were all working on aspects of a single massive case. Naturally when these agents individually brought their suspicions to their governments it was not well received. Partly because of the sheer scope of the case, their story was doubted. The agents were forced to waste time and resources to bring in proof that their governments could not ignore.

"These agents eventually formed a team of special operators working under joint U.S., Israeli, German, and British authority. This predates DMS and Barrier by quite a long way. Officially this group did not exist. The only code name ever used was *the List*. The List came into it much as we are now—catching glimpses of something already in motion—and like our current matter there were some losses before the List was able to make the transition from outsiders to active players.

"Once the existence of the Cabal was proven, the threat it posed shook the foundations of the superpowers. There are some—a visionary few—who understood then, as now, that the end of World War Two did not mean the end of this enemy. All that changed was the nature of the war. Instead of tanks and troops and fleets of warships, the Cabal waged its war with germs, weapons of science, and enough money to destabilize governments. Instead of using armies to slaughter groups they considered to be racially inferior, the Cabal financed internal conflicts within troubled nations in ways that sparked ethnic genocide."

The room was totally silent as Church spoke. I was leaning forward, hanging on his words, and in my head I could feel the pieces tumble into place one by one. The picture forming in my mind was dreadful.

"Over a period of several years the List managed to identify the key players in the Cabal, and one by one they were taken off the board. It was an undeclared war, but it was definitely a war." He paused. "And we took our own losses. More than half of the members of the List were killed during the Cold War. Some new players joined the team, but the core membership dwindled through attrition. Shortly before the collapse of the Soviet Union, the List mounted a major multinational offensive on the Cabal, and at that time we were convinced we had wiped them out. We acquired their assets, eliminated or imprisoned their members and staff, and appropriated their research records."

"Sir," said Grace cautiously, "I'm no scholar, but I'm enough of a student of modern warfare to wonder why I haven't heard any of this."

"None of this ever made it to history books, and the official records of this have long ago been sealed. Some have been expunged."

"Expunged? How?" she asked.

"I'll bet I know," I said, and everyone turned to me. "I'll bet a shiny nickel that one of the members of the List created a computer system specifically designed to search for and eliminate just those kinds of records."

Church said, "Close. A computer scientist named Bertolini developed a search-and-destroy software package for the Italian government, but before he could deliver it he was murdered and the system stolen. The program, known as Pangaea, was decades ahead of its time. The Cabal took Pangaea and used it to steal bulk research material from laboratories, corporations, and governments worldwide. That's what allowed them to have access to so much cutting-edge science. They didn't have to do the research: they stole the information, combined it to form a massive database, and then went straight into development."

"And Pangaea . . . ?" Grace prompted.

"A member of the List retrieved it. It was being guarded by Gunnar Haeckel, one of a team of four assassins called the Brotherhood of the Scythe. The other members were Hans Brucker, Ernst Halgren, and Conrad Veder."

"Hold on a sec," I said. "Brotherhood of the *Scythe*." I drew a rough sketch of a scythe on my notepad. The blade was facing to the left of the page. I thought about it and erased the blade and drew it facing to the right. "Haeckel's code name was 'North,' right? And the others were East, West, and South?"

Church nodded toward my sketch. "Yes, and you're on the right track. Finish it."

I added the three other scythes, each at a right angle to the preceding one. North, East, South, and West. Church reached over and gave the sketch a forty-five-degree turn.

I looked down at the drawing. The four scythes looked like they were churning in a circle. The image they formed was a swastika.

I heard a few gasps, a grunt, and a short laugh from Dr. Hu.

"Oh, that's clever," he sneered.

"It wasn't subtle then, either," Church said. "Probably one of those inner-circle ideas that sound good in a candlelit enclave."

"Jeez," I said.

"During the raid on the Pangaea lab," Church said, picking up his narrative, "Haeckel was shot repeatedly, including two head shots. He was definitely dead at the scene, which makes his presence in the video so disturbing. However, Pangaea was recovered and the List put it to better use: searching down and destroying all of the information the Cabal had amassed."

"Which member of the List retrieved that computer system?" I asked.

I didn't expect Church to answer, but he surprised me. "I did," he said.

He waited out the ensuing buzz of chatter.

"And I suppose you've given it a few upgrades over the years," mused Grace dryly. "And a name change?"

"Yes. The modern version, MindReader, bears little resemblance to Pangaea except in overall design theory. Both computers were designed to intrude into any hard drive and, using a special series of conversion codes, learn the language of the target system in a way that allows them to act as if they *are* the target system. And both systems will exit without leaving a trace. The similarities end there. MindReader is many thousands of times faster, it has a different pattern recognition system, it clones passwords, and it rewrites the security code of the target system to leave no trace at all of having been there, and that includes tweaking time codes, logs of download time, the works. Pangaea's footprint, though very light, can be detected by a few of the world's top military-grade systems, but even then it often looks like computer error rather than computer invasion."

"Mr. Church," Grace asked, "you said that the information taken from the Cabal was destroyed. I'm as cynical as the next lass, but I find it hard to accept that the governments for whom the List worked would allow all of that research to be eradicated."

"We all thought that way, Major. We met in secret to discuss the matter and we took a vote about whether to destroy the material without ever turning it over or to turn it over equally to all of the governments so that no one nation could prosper from it. The vote hung on the fact that there was real cutting-edge science hidden among the grotesqueries the Cabal had collected. Much of it would certainly have benefited mankind; of that we had no doubt."

"What did you do?"

"The seven surviving members of the List took our vote, Major," Church said. "The vote was seven to zero, and so we incinerated it all. Lab records, tons of research documentation, test samples, computer files . . . all of it. We left nothing. Naturally our governments were furious with us. Some of the members of the List were forced into retirement; others were reassigned to new duties that amounted to punishment."

"You survived," I said, "so I'm guessing that you found yet another use for MindReader."

He ate a cookie but said nothing.

"Okay," said Hu, "so I can see how this Cabal was the Big Bad Wolf for the Cold War, but that was then. How does it relate to the mess we're in now?"

"Because we're receiving information in a way that parallels the way the List first discovered the Cabal thirty years ago and several of the key players are caught up in things." He tapped some keys and a different set of faces appeared on the screen behind him. Twenty-two in all, most of them young men and women in their thirties. Five images were of people in their sixties or older. The last two image squares were blacked out.

Church said, "Most of these people died during the Cold War. The others retired from the intelligence services."

"What about the last two?" Grace asked, nodding toward the blacked-out boxes.

"Aunt Sallie and me." He smiled. "You already know what we look like."

Actually, I'd never seen Aunt Sallie or even visited the Brooklyn headquarters of the DMS, but I let it go.

Church pressed keys that removed all but the five middle-aged faces.

"These were the other surviving members of the List. Lawson Navarro and Clive Monroe of MI6, Mischa Gundarov of Russia's GRU, Serena Gallagher of the CIA, Lev Tarnim from Mossad, and Jerome Freund, who was a senior field agent with Germany's GSG Nine."

He paused.

"In the last six weeks all six have been murdered."

Chapter Fifty-Eight

Pinter sat on a hard wooden chair, his hands cuffed behind him, the chain fed through the oak slats of the backrest. He was naked and they had doused him with bucket after bucket of icy water. The air-conditioning was turned to full, and the temperature of the room was a skin-biting forty degrees. Pinter shivered uncontrollably, but he kept his jaws clamped shut to stifle the screams that clawed at the inside of his throat.

There were four people in the room with him. Three of them were alive. The fourth was a red ruin of twisted limbs and torn flesh that no longer resembled anything human. It was meat and bone. Two hours ago the meat had been Pinter's partner. But then the Jakoby Twins and their assistant had gone to work on him. They never even asked Homler any questions. They just began a program of systematic beatings that reduced the man to red inhumanity. Before they began, Hecate switched on video and audio recorders, and now that the actual screams had ceased and the body was inert the whole thing played out again on four big LCD screens mounted on each wall.

Pinter scrunched his eyes shut, but he could do nothing to block out those high, piercing screams.

It went on and on until Pinter felt cracks forming in his mind.

Then Hecate walked slowly across the room and

pressed a button that dropped the entire room into a well of silence. She turned like a dancer and walked back, passing in front of her brother and trailing her finger-nails across his stomach. Paris looked away. He had not participated in the torture, preferring to linger by the door, arms folded across his chest, his body deliberately out of the path of flying blood. His eyes followed his sister; his mouth was small and unsmiling.

Pinter licked his lips. His throat felt hot and full of nails.

Hecate leaned back against a wall and crossed her ankles. She wore a pair of capri pants and a bikini top. She was covered in blood from her polished tonails to her full underlip. Her eyes were bright with a predatory fever, and her chest heaved with exertion and passion.

"You know who I am?" she purred. It was the first thing anyone had said.

Pinter said nothing.

"And you know my brother. . . ."

Pinter cut a look at Paris, who studied his nails.

"And our large friend here is Tonton."

Tonton grinned. His teeth were bloody. He was a biter.

"Your weapons and equipment are American. You want us to believe that you and *this*"—she reached out and jabbed a toe into what was left of Homler—"You and your friend want us to think that you're special ops. Delta Force, SEALs, something like that."

Pinter said nothing.

"Which would be fine if I'd woken up stupid this morning." She smiled and Pinter thought that her teeth looked unnaturally sharp. The witch's eyes were a strange mix of dark blue and hot gold. "Now . . . we both know how this is going to end."

Pinter looked left and right as if there was some chance of escape. Hecate watched him and smiled. She pushed off the wall and came toward him with a slinky sway of hips that made Pinter see a big hunting cat rather than a woman. He thought he could feel the heat from her eyes. Then she raised a leg and straddled him, sitting astride him so that his face was inches from her chest.

"We all know that you'll tell us everything. Everything. The only question is whether you'll be smart and earn a quick release or play it stupid and make us work for this. The end will be the same. Tonton is very good at a quick kill when I want him to, but he doesn't like it. He has a bit of animal in him. Truth is . . . so do I."

Hecate reached behind her back and undid the strings of her bikini top. She pulled it off and let the straps slide through her bloody fingers. Her nipples were erect, her breasts flushed pink. She leaned forward to brush her nipples back and forth across his chest.

"I'd prefer that you make this slow and difficult. We have the time." She bent forth and whispered huskily into his ear, "I *like* the slow burn. But I'm fair. Play it straight with us and this will be over before you know it."

He held out for a long minute, grinding his teeth together to keep his mouth shut, but when Hecate opened her smiling mouth and licked the blood from his chin he broke.

Pinter threw his head back and screamed. Not in pain but with an atavistic dread that was so deep that it was beyond his ability to comprehend. It was primitive and unthinking, filled with need and desperation and a total hopelessness.

The echo of the scream bounced off of the walls and swirled around him like a poison vapor. He collapsed forward, his head against her breasts, his chest heaving with as much passion as Hecate's, but of a totally different flavor.

"You can die pretty," she said. "Or you can die ugly."

Hecate bent and hooked a finger under his chin, leaned toward him, and kissed him on the mouth. Pinter could taste the salty blood on her lips. He gagged.

"Tell me . . . ," she whispered.

He told her everything.

Chapter Fifty-Nine

The Warehouse, Baltimore, Maryland
Sunday, August 29, 5:04 A.M.
Time Remaining on the Extinction Clock: 78 hours, 56 minutes

The room was absolutely silent.

"The most recent victim was Jerome Freund, who worked as the assistant director of a historical museum in Stuttgart, Germany. He retired from active service with the Grenzschutzgruppe Nine eleven years ago and was involved in no active cases. He was not even a consultant, but he was assassinated apparently as a preventive measure by whoever has resurrected the Cabal."

"How long ago did these murders occur?" I asked.

"They've been spaced out over the last couple of months. I have a contact in Germany—Captain Oskar Freund, the son of Jerome Freund—who has been investigating this for me. Oskar is an active member of GSG Nine and it was he who first brought much of this to my attention. He called me this morning to tell me of his father's death." Church picked up a cookie, looked at it for a moment, and then set it down. It was the closest to agitated that I've ever seen him, and when he spoke I understood why. "Jerome Freund was my closest friend. My oldest friend. He was a good man who served his country and the world through very dark times. Despite the work he did while a member of the List, he was essentially a kind and gentle person, and over the last eleven years he has carried no gun, arrested no criminals, did nothing to warrant what happened to him. And yet he was murdered with deliberate care and in a manner that would ensure that he suffered greatly."

"How was he killed?" I asked.

"Someone dressed as a tourist came to the museum where he worked and shot him in the back of the neck with a glass dart. Oskar's review of the security cameras revealed that the weapon was a gas dart gun disguised as a camera. I believe that the choice of weapon was deliberate, because that type of weapon was used by his father during the Cold War, back when he was a member of the List."

"What was in the dart?" Dr. Hu asked with great interest.

"Ebola."

Hu actually broke into a grin and the word "cool" was forming on his mouth when I shot him a look that promised slow, agonizing death. He suddenly found his fingernails very interesting.

Grace said, "Effing hell! I didn't hear about any outbreak—"

"There was no outbreak," Church said, "and no one else was infected. The doctors were able to identify the symptoms quickly enough to get Jerome into isolation.

Oskar was only able to observe him via video camera. Afterward the German government put a security clamp over the whole matter. If the true cause of death surfaces at all, it will be as an accidental exposure of some kind. No one but Oskar, his superiors, and us in this room—and the killer—know that this was a murder. Oskar even managed to get the museum security tapes without raising any alarms."

"That was smart," Bug said.

"Oskar had already been looking into the killings of the List members at the behest of his father, and when he brought the information to me I discovered a very deliberate pattern." Mr. Church stood and crossed to the flat screen. He touched the first image. "Lawson Navarro, late of MI6, was killed in a car accident. While working with the List he arranged the deaths of several Cabal members by tampering with their cars, setting car bombs, or staging high-speed driving accidents."

He tapped the next picture.

"Clive Monroe, also of MI6, was the most skilled sniper of the List. He was shot with a high-powered rifle at Sandown Racecourse."

And the next.

"Serena Gallagher of the CIA died in a fall while hiking. Her method had to been to arrange 'accidents' for her targets."

Then the last.

"Lev Tarnim, one of Mossad's most celebrated field agents, was one of a dozen people killed by the suicide bomber in Tel Aviv last month. Until now the blame had been put on HAMAS. However, Tarnim was the List's explosives expert."

"So," said Grace, "this isn't just a matter of former

agents being killed . . . each person was killed in a way appropriate to the kind of damage they did to the Cabal."

"Exactly," agreed Church.

I said, "What about Jerome Freund?"

"Jerome did a number of selected eliminations using various biological agents."

"Jeez," said Bug.

"There is another thing," said Church, "and it's possible that this contributed to the specific choice of weapon used against Jerome. There are many disease pathogens that can kill . . . but Ebola was the weapon of choice. Jerome was a historian. He published several books on the war. He's best known for his book on the attempt to assassinate Hitler, because his father worked with Stauffenberg on that plot and was likewise executed. However, Jerome also wrote two books on the death camps, one of which was a general history of them and one in which he explored the cultural damage done to the German people because of what the Nazis did. Most people equate all Germans of that era with Nazism and believe that all Nazis were complicit in the attempts to exterminate whole races of people. That was never true. Many people opposed it, many were in denial about it, and many underwent irrevocable psychological damage because they were afraid to speak out against it. We Americans had a tiny dose of that following 9-11 when the public fervor was to go to war even though America had not been attacked by all of Islam. Hysteria and fear are terrible things."

"No joke, boss," I said.

"Jerome's next book, which was only half-written at the time of his death, was a history of the death camp program and the ideology—if we can call it that—

within which men felt both compelled and entitled to do so much harm to entire races of people. Jerome Freund postulated that the Nazi Final Solution served as the model for all subsequent ethnic genocide around the world, and particularly in Africa. He argued that the mass extermination of entire races, ethnic groups, and cultures that is running rampant nowadays would never have been so virulent had it not been for the thoroughly documented final solution campaign."

"And you feel that since he cited Africa so heavily an African pathogen was chosen?" Grace asked.

He nodded. "It seems to be in keeping with the Cabal's attempt at poetic justice. But that was only one-half of what drove the Cabal. They were also deeply dedicated to using cutting-edge science to restart and see to completion the eugenics program."

"*Dios mio!*" gasped Rudy.

"Wow," said Hu, a smile blossoming on his face.

"Shit," I said.

"What the hell are eugenics?" asked Bug.

Chapter Sixty

The Dragon Factory
Sunday, August 29, 5:30 A.M.
Time Remaining on the Extinction Clock: 78 hours,
30 minutes E.S.T.

Paris poured martinis for them both. Hecate was perched on the edge of a chair, her body tense, her eyes bright with anger. Paris set the pitcher down and slumped onto the couch.

"He was telling the truth," Paris said. "After what you

did to his friend he couldn't tell enough of the truth. He was begging you to believe him." Paris's face still wore a shadow of the disgust he felt. He did not mind killing and even liked a little recreational violence, but torture was not his cup of tea.

"I can believe this of Otto," said Hecate, "but not Dad."

Paris peered at her over the rim of his glass, one eyebrow raised. "Really? You can't believe that Dad—*our* dad—would resort to murder?"

"Don't be an ass," she snapped. "I know what kind of a monster he is. If you tally up all the nastiness in which we've indulged, we don't hold a candle to him."

"Then how on earth can you be surprised that he'd want one of us killed?"

She sipped her martini. "Because we're his children. His only children."

"Are we?"

She shot him a look. "What do you mean by that?"

"That kid . . . SAM. The one Otto called 'Eighty-two' before Cyrus bit his head off for it. I never saw a picture of Dad as a kid, but SAM looks like how I imagine he'd looked. Same eyes, same mouth and chin."

"Otto said that he was Dad's nephew."

"Sure. And we both know how much trust we can place in anything Otto says. Besides, I'm pretty sure the kid is a twin. A year or so ago I saw another kid at the Deck. He ducked out of sight pretty quick, but it looked a lot like SAM, and I'd just come from seeing Cyrus and SAM. Twins run in families."

She nodded, chewing her lip.

Paris said, "Cyrus probably has a legion of little bastards roaming around, ready to usurp our place."

"Even so . . . I can't believe that Dad would want us killed."

"Only one," Paris reminded her. "And it didn't matter which one, according to our late informant.

"I think we should be more concerned," said Paris, "with how he found us. Marcus said that no one came aboard our jet when we were at the Deck, and I believe him. But we were clearly followed. That means that Otto somehow managed to put a tracking device on the jet and also managed to have us followed. How? Where did Dad get the follow planes that Pinter fellow told us about? How did he hire assassins? Pinter said that this wasn't the first mission he'd done for Dad. How the hell is Dad managing all of this?"

She shook her head. "I guess we don't have as tight a control on him as we thought."

"Oh really? You think?" He sneered as he rose and refilled their glasses. "At this moment I don't know who we can trust. We certainly can't trust anyone at the Deck. I wish to Christ we'd gone through with the fail-safe device we talked about, 'cause right now I'd be happy to blow the whole fucking thing up. Dad, Otto, and everyone."

She nodded. They'd seriously considered boobytrapping the Deck during its construction but had ultimately decided against it. Back then they thought that they had Cyrus on an unbreakable leash. Now she felt like a fool.

"God, I hate being played."

"He's played us our whole lives," Paris said.

"But *how*? We own everyone at the Deck."

"Apparently he and Otto found better levers on them."

They lapsed into a long and moody silence.

"What do you think Dad would do if we sent him the heads of the two assassins?" Hecate suggested.

"Jesus, you're bloodthirsty," Paris said, but he pursed his lips. "Interesting idea, though. Dad would probably blow a fuse."

"What would that look like?"

He sipped his drink. "I don't know. If he controls the Deck, then he might be able to escape it. That means he'd be free to come at us any way he wants."

"Christ," she said as the possibilities that presented blossomed in her imagination. She stood up and walked to the window and looked out at the crews working to load the bottled water onto the freighter. "What should we do? Do we pretend this never happened and send that shipment out? And the next one, and the one after that?"

"Depends on whether we want to alert him. Right now he doesn't know that we know. At most he'll find out that our security team killed a bunch of intruders. We could play it like we don't know who came at us, or go with what he intended and play it like we're scared because the U.S. government sent a black ops team after us."

"He'll know we're lying," she said.

"So? As long as we keep the lie going it won't matter, and it'll delay any confrontation until we have a chance to look into this."

Hecate chewed her full underlip. Paris noted, not the for the first time, how sharp her teeth were, and he secretly wondered if she'd started filing them. It would be like her to do something freaky like that.

She ran her finger around the rim of the glass, over and over again until it created a sullen hum. A smile bloomed on her face.

"What?" Paris asked.

"I just had a wicked little idea."

"For Dad?"

"For Dad," she agreed. "Look . . . he now knows where we are. Okay . . . instead of counterattacking, why don't we really play up the innocent act and reach out to him like we're a couple of scared kids who need their daddy in a time of crisis?"

"I'm not following you. . . ."

"Why don't we *invite* him here?" she said with a wicked grin. "Tell him we're scared and that we could use his advice on how to protect the Dragon Factory from another attack."

"Ah . . . you sly bitch!" Paris said with a smile. "And once we have him here . . ."

"Then we put a bullet in Otto, lock Dad in a dungeon, and send a couple of teams of Berserkers to the Deck to, um . . . sterilize it."

"We don't have a dungeon."

"So," she said, "let's build one."

Paris looked at her for a long moment, his eyes glistening with emotion. "This is why I love you, Hecate."

Hecate pulled him close and kissed her brother full on the mouth.

Chapter Sixty-One

The Warehouse, Baltimore, Maryland
Sunday, August 29, 5:31 A.M.
Time Remaining on the Extinction Clock: 78 hours, 29 minutes

Dr. Hu turned to Bug. "Eugenics is in a bit of a gray area between social philosophy and evolutionary science. It was kicked off by Sir Francis Galton—Charles Darwin's cousin—in the late eighteen hundreds, and it's had a lot of high-profile supporters. We're talking people like H. G. Wells, George Bernard Shaw, John Maynard Keynes, a bunch of others. Its proponents advocate the improvement of human hereditary traits through intervention."

" 'Intervention,' " muttered Grace the way someone might say "anal probe."

Hu ignored her. "The theory is that by filtering out unwanted genetic elements, corruption, and damage, what emerges will be an elevated human being whose abilities and potential are beyond our current reach."

Before Bug could ask a question Grace cut in again. "Which is a very slippery way for some scientists—and I use that word with the greatest reluctance—to justify the worst kind of enforced social Darwinism. There are people right now who believe in eugenics and they hide behind causes that are very noble on the surface. For example, they'll point to a particular birth defect and in their grant proposals and lobbying materials they showcase the misery and suffering. They use talk shows and the media to gather support, and everyone falls in line."

Hu wheeled on her. "Of course they do! Who wouldn't want such a disorder eradicated? Any sane and compassionate person would agree—"

"And if the greater good were really the end goal of eugenics then I'd be campaigning for it," Grace cut in. "But—"

"Whoa, slow down," Bug said. "You lost me two turns back. Why are you getting so wound up?"

But Hu ignored him. "Don't tell me you're trying to make the case that all attempts to remove genetic defects have a master race agenda. That's unfair. A lot of solid genetic research is intended to prevent disease, increase health and strength, and lessen human suffering. And it's not just Big Pharma and Big Medicine that are behind it. Early funding for serious eugenics research was provided by the Rockefeller Foundation, the Kelloggs, the Carnegies—"

Grace looked like she wanted to spit. "Well, some of that was probably very well intentioned, I'm sure, but surely, Doctor, you can't be so effing naïve as to believe that everyone involved in medical research is altruistic and has the greater good at heart."

"Okay, let's try to keep our focus here," I interjected, holding my hand up like a traffic cop. "We don't have time to debate bioethics."

"No," said Church, "we don't, and this is beside the point. The research in those records wasn't intended to prevent harelips or autism. The Cabal was working to provide data that would justify state-sponsored discrimination, forced sterilization of persons deemed genetically defective, and the killing of institutionalized populations."

Grace's face was alight with triumph. "That's what I bleeding well said!"

Bug leaned toward me. "This is . . . what? Like trying to create a master race?"

It was Church who answered him. "Yes. We're talking about the ethnic-cleansing research of the Nazis in the hands of scientists who had access to advanced research and development methods and who wanted to see the eugenics program succeed."

Grace said, "And your lot—the List—sorted them out?"

"Yes," said Church.

Bug nodded. "So . . . the stuff from Deep Iron. Is that the eugenics research?"

"Not entirely. There is quite a lot of data from experiments in forced trauma—beatings and other abuse—as part of Mengele's study to determine the limits of physical endurance under traumatic circumstances. Ostensibly this was intended to help the German soldiers in the field, but few rational people believe that."

I noticed he cut a significant look at Hu when he said that, and for once Hu kept his mouth shut. Grace, to her credit, did not break into a smug smile.

Church said, "The experiments that Mengele performed, and those by other doctors in the various camps, were never intended to benefit the German soldier. They cared nothing for the man in the field. Jerome Freund did extensive interviews with camp survivors as well as those members of camp staff who were not executed after the Nuremberg Trials. What Mengele did—*everything* Mengele did—was fueled by his insanity and driven by his need to participate fully in the eugenics program."

"Why?" asked Bug. "What was his deal?"

"Mengele believed in the master race concept. Through his experiments he tried to determine the physical vulnerabilities of the different races. It's one of the reasons he and his masters picked Jews and Gypsies for much of their work, because those groups married within very limited family bloodlines. It allowed Mengele to work with a group who shared many common physiological traits, and that in turn allowed him to make intuitive jumps. The collection of statistics is more than just how the body reacts to trauma but how the bodies of specific races reacts. Think about the use for that when waging a war on what they believed were the lesser race. They believed that by researching common bloodlines they would find vulnerabilities that would give them weapons against the entire race."

Grace growled out a comment that would have shocked a stevedore, then said, "Yes . . . and we can thank God that Mengele was not a geneticist."

"Why?" asked Bug.

Hu fielded that one. "Because there are diseases and disorders that affect certain genetic lines. Tay-Sachs, for example, is a genetic disease that affects Jews whose bloodlines can be traced back to a certain region. Predominantly the Ashkenazi Jews of Eastern Europe. 'Ashkenaz' is a word from medieval Hebrew that refers to the Rhineland in the west of Germany."

Hu was starting to show off, so Church stepped in. "If Mengele had known about Tay-Sachs and had access to genetic science . . . there's no telling what kind of mass slaughter he might have perpetrated. It's not inconceivable that, given time, the Nazis might have developed genetic weapons that could indeed wipe out all of the world's Jews."

"Holy God," said Bug, looking aghast.

I had a very bad thought and I looked at Church. "The Cabal records that you destroyed . . . what were their lines of research?"

Church was silent for so long that I knew the answer would be bad.

"They were working on a way to weaponize genetic diseases. And, yes, that included Tay-Sachs. They wanted to create a version that could be *given* to people rather than inherited."

Grace shook her head. "Bloody maniacs."

Church punched some keys that put the letter I'd

found up on the screen side by side with the English-
language translation I'd written out during the flight
back from Denver.

"This was written during Mengele's tenure at Auschwitz. The reference to 'Herr Wirths' would be to Dr.
Eduard Wirths, the chief SS doctor at the camp. He was
Mengele's superior and was a fiercely dedicated Nazi.
Wirths was a highly trained physician who specialized
in communicable diseases, and his appointment to the
camp was made so that he could try and stop the typhus
epidemic that was affecting SS personnel at Auschwitz.
He was successful in that and stayed on to oversee other
areas of research. We don't have complete records of
what he did, but we know from camp survivors that he
was particularly interested in any prisoner who demonstrated symptoms of communicable diseases. It was
Wirths who recommended Mengele for promotion to a
senior doctor at the camp."

"Sounds like a right charmer," said Grace.

"Strangely," Church said to her, "Wirth had a repu-
tation for protecting inmate doctors and even improving some of the health care provided to inmates at
Auschwitz."

"Which is on a par with giving a man a nice cold
glass of water before shoving him into a pit of fire," I
said.

Church nodded. "Wirths was a complicated man. He
insisted that the deaths at the camp were 'natural deaths'
and not state-sanctioned executions. Jerome Freund
viewed him as a villain because of Wirth's unflinching
dedication to the three spheres of Nazi ideology: the
goal of revitalizing the German race, the biomedical
path to a perfected master race, and the belief that the

Jews were a significant threat to the immediate and long-term health of the Germanic race. So, he was no hero by any stretch, even if certain inmates praised his compassion during the trials."

"What happened to him?"

"He was taken into British custody in 1945 but shortly thereafter hung himself. Whether to escape punishment or out of remorse is anyone's guess. However, it is because of men like Wirths and Mengele that we now have the Nuremberg Code of research ethics and principles for human experimentation."

"What's 'noma'?" I asked.

"It's a disfiguring gangrenous disease that was sweeping through the camp," said Hu. "It's triggered by malnutrition and is still a significant threat in Africa and other third world countries. Anywhere you find poor food sources, inadequate health care, and unsanitary conditions."

I asked. "Okay, and what's 'zoonosis'?"

Hu took that one, too. "It's the category for any infectious disease that's able to be transmitted from animals to humans. HIV, bird flu . . . that sort of thing. Usually there isn't a species jump, but sometimes contamination, a botched experiment, or someone getting jiggy with the livestock will do it."

"Sorry," I asked, "how's that tie into Nazi research?"

"It's rumored that they experimented with it," said Hu, "but luckily, nothing much came of it."

"The Cabal were doing a lot of research in that area," said Church. "Their scientists were investigating zoonoses like measles, smallpox, influenza, and diphtheria to see if reintroduction to animals would strengthen the diseases so that they could then be weaponized and used against humans."

"Christ on the cross," said Grace. "I'm very glad your 'List' put those pricks down."

If they did, I thought. I had my doubts.

"What about the reference to 'twins'?" Grace asked.

"Mengele was obsessed with twins," said Church. "He removed them from the general population of the camps, gave them better treatment . . . though few actually survived the camps. No one really knows what the ultimate point was of those experiments . . . if Mengele even had a point."

"He was probably just batshit crazy," suggested Bug.

"He was evil," said Grace.

Hu gave her a condescending look. "Evil is an abstraction."

Church turned slowly toward him; there was a weird vibe in the air. "I assure you, Doctor, evil exists. Everyone here at this table has seen it. My friend was murdered by a dart filled with Ebola. Insanity would have manifested differently: a bomb, a knifing, even abduction and murder, but to carefully craft a pathogenic weapon, hire an assassin, and deliver that weapon to a target shows a cool, perhaps cold, mind and a clear intent. That's evil."

"What if the killers believe that their ideology is sound?" Hu countered.

"Like the Nazi Party?" Church asked quietly.

"Sure. Like the Nazi Party. Your friend was German. Nazism emerged in Germany. Surely you're not saying that a huge chunk of the German people suddenly became 'evil.' "

"Of course not. Most people—in Germany as in every other country—are easily led, and easily corrupted by an extreme few. We've seen that with Muslim terrorists. Islam is neither evil nor corrupt, but it takes the rap for what some people do in the name of that religion. We can see that here in the states as well. And don't misunderstand, Doctor; I'm not calling every extremist 'evil.' I don't even use that term to label most terrorists. Many believe that what they are doing is the only means to a better end, or they believe in the words of their leaders, or in a specific interpretation of scripture. There are countless reasons why people take arms and do violence against one another. No, when I label someone like Josef Mengele as evil, I am speaking of a level of corruption that is fueled by self-awareness. Mengele wasn't a fanatic blindly following a cause. He was a monster. If he had not been born into Nazi Germany, then he might have become a serial murderer or some other kind of monster."

Hu looked unconvinced, but he didn't pursue the point.

Church selected a cookie and bit off a piece. "Now, as for the rest of the material you found, Captain Ledger, most of it is in code and we lack the code key. Our cryptographers are working on it now, but that could take days or weeks. However, from diagrams and charts it's clear that a third of the boxes deal with some aspect of genetic research, which means that it is information from well after the war. We have to face the very real possibility that the material includes copies of the material the List destroyed."

"Swell," I said. "And the bruisers who trashed the Russians made off with most of the microfiche copies and probably the damn code key."

Church nodded. "The book Jerome Freund was working on mentioned Heinrich Haeckel. The Haeckel family has had an association with biological science for over a century. Ernst Haeckel, who died in 1919, was a noted biologist who made significant positive contributions to natural science. However, his brother's son, Heinrich, was a monster. He was also a scientist, but his interest was eugenics, and through his research Jerome was able to determine to a great degree of certainty that Heinrich Haeckel was the scientist who sold Adolf Hitler on the concept of *Lebensunwertes Leben*."

"Jesus Christ," I breathed, and when Grace and Bug looked at me with a frown I translated it for them. The words hurt my mouth.

"It means 'life unworthy of life.' "

Chapter Sixty-Two

The Deck
Sunday, August 29, 5:32 A.M.
Time Remaining on the Extinction Clock: 78 hours,
28 minutes E.S.T.

"Why haven't we heard anything yet?"

Otto looked up from his computer. "Give it time, Mr. Cyrus."

"It's been more than enough time," Cyrus snapped. "Are you sure that they have the right location?"

"Of course we do. Everything's been verified and the team is probably on the ground now. This is a field operation, a covert infiltration, and that demands care and caution. We have to let them do their jobs."

"I want to know what's happening. And I want to be

informed the minute that either Paris or Hecate has been killed. The minute, Otto."

Otto nodded but didn't respond. It was an unreasonable and irrational demand. A sure sign that it was time for a fresh set of pills. That would be tricky, because suggesting it while Cyrus was in this frame of mind was sure to spark a murderous rage. Though Otto was not physically afraid of Cyrus Jakoby, there was a very real danger to the plan. In the past few years Cyrus's rages had resulted in damage to crucial equipment and the murder or maiming of key staff members, all of which impacted the smooth flow of production. That, in turn, harmed the launching of the Extinction Wave.

The upcoming date of September 1 had been selected during one of Cyrus's whimsical phases and celebrated the discovery of the asteroid Juno by German astronomer Karl L. Harding. Cyrus insisted that the asteroid had not been discovered prior to that date because it had not come into existence until God put it there as a sign. The previous date for the launch of the Wave had held far more personal significance for Otto—May 20, the anniversary of the beginning of construction of Auschwitz. Before that it had been April 30, the anniversary of Hitler's suicide. Otto was determined to make the September 1 deadline, even if the astronomical connection meant less than nothing to him.

The second and third Extinction Waves were already lined up, and both would be ready well before their initial planning dates. If they stayed with this schedule, then the global release of ethnic-specific pathogens would reach critical saturation by May of the following year. The computer models predicted that by September of next year the death toll among the mud people would be closing in on 1 billion. In five years there would only be a billion people left alive on the planet, and unless they possessed some currently unknown immunity, none of the survivors would be black, Asian, or Hispanic. The thought of that gave Otto a sexual thrill far more intense than anything he ever got from a woman. The New Order was not only a perfect plan; it was also within their reach.

Unless Cyrus went too long without his pills.

Once they seized the Dragon Factory, Cyrus would likely calm down. He would have so many new toys to play with. But while the likelihood of accomplishing that goal was still fluid, then Cyrus's moods would swing further out of balance.

Otto would have to think of something to get Cyrus to take his pills. If it came down to it, Otto could always hit him with a dart gun. It wouldn't be the first time.

Chapter Sixty-Three

The Warehouse, Baltimore, Maryland
Sunday, August 29, 5:33 A.M.
Time Remaining on the Extinction Clock: 78 hours, 27 minutes

"Life unworthy of life," Bug said slowly. "Man, that has an ugly feel to it."

"It's the core of Nazi eugenics," Church said. "It refers to those people—or groups of people—who they believed had no right to live."

"If these assholes have their way," Bug said softly, "half the people at this table won't make the cut. We're not 'master race' material."

"Is anyone?" asked Church. "The idea of a master

race belonged to the Nazis . . . it was not and is not part of the cultural aspirations of the German people."

"So that's why Haeckel was corresponding with an asshole like Mengele," Bug said, putting it together now. "They were all playing for the same team."

"But how did his records ever make it out of Germany?" demanded Grace. "Wasn't Haeckel considered a war criminal?"

"No," said Church. "His involvement with the Nazi movement was never fully established even after the war. He was supposedly a dealer in medical instruments and even did work with the International Red Cross. He was sly enough to stay off the political radar, and it's very likely that he fled the country when things started going bad for Germany. A lot of Nazis were able to read the writing on the wall. They were losing the war, but many of them were so dedicated—or perhaps fanatical— that they wanted to lay the groundwork for their research so that it could start up again somewhere else. Haeckel might have gone to South America or even come directly here."

"How the hell could he swing that?" asked Bug. "No way a Nazi could just come waltzing into the U.S. during the war."

Grace shook her head. "Don't be naïve, Bug. There was active communication and even some under-the-radar commerce between Germany and some U.S. corporations during the war. Very low-key, but definitely there. There are people who always have what they call a 'big picture' view that basically lets them justify anything because they know that wars end and countries usually kiss and make up. Nowadays you Yanks are chums with Germany, Russia, Japan, even Vietnam."

"It can't be that easy," Bug said stubbornly.

"It's not," said Church, "but when there's enough money on the table a way is always found. Heinrich Haeckel disappeared from the public before the end of the war. Either he never made it out of Germany and was among the nameless dead or he came here and set up under a different identity. I'd place my money on the latter. From the way things have played out, it's likely he died here before passing along the records in his possession; otherwise the Cabal would have sought them out decades ago. My guess is that his nephew recently uncovered some reference to it among family papers and that started the race to Deep Iron."

"I can see why Haeckel and his Nazi buds would want the records," I said, "but who's the other team? The guys I tussled with in Deep Iron?"

"Unknown. Possibly a splinter faction, or freelancers looking to steal the material and sell it on the black market. We don't know enough yet to make a solid guess."

"Was Gunnar a scientist, too?" Grace asked.

"No," said Church. "He was muscle."

"You thought you killed him," I said, "but now he's alive and well in Brazil, where he's taking Rotary Club lunkheads on safaris for mythological animals."

"Yeah," said Bug, "how's that stack up to a grave threat to humanity?"

"The unicorn," I said, and Hu nodded agreement.

"Okay, I'm missing something, so spell it out for me."

Church said, "Science has come a long way since the Cold War, and genetics is a booming field. However, there are limits to what can be discovered during modern research. International laws and watchdog organizations are moderately effective, and a master race research program would need a huge database, including a massive number of tissue samples and test subjects. That would be virtually impossible nowadays without the cooperation of an entire government."

"Right," Hu said. "The Nazis had the cooperation of an entire government during World War Two, and they had millions of test subjects. Everyone who passed through the camps. Those records you found probably include extensive information on ethnic background, gender, age, and many other variables. The boxes of index cards with brown fingerprints . . . those are blood samples. Thirty years ago DNA mapping wasn't possible. The first DNA typing was accomplished in 1985 by Sir Alec Jeffreys at the University of Leicester in England. The Cabal had been torn down by then. What we stopped was a first step in gathering information that could be used when science caught up to the dreams of a master race."

"Can we do DNA typing from dried blood?" Grace asked.

"Sure," said Hu. "DNA typing has been done from Guthrie cards, which are widely collected at birth for newborn screening for genetic diseases and saved by many states. I read about a case where the paternity of a car accident victim was determined using blood from a seventeen-year-old Band-Aid."

"So those cards and the records help them regain their info on bloodlines," Grace said.

"Yes. Crafting a race of genetically perfect beings is the core ideal in eugenics," said Hu, "but it isn't quick. It's extreme social Darwinism, which means that it's a generational process. Quicker than natural evolution, but by no means quick. Unless, of course, you have access to genetic design capabilities that include transgenics. By remodeling DNA they could create more perfect humans in one or two generations."

"Unicorns . . . ," Bug prompted.

"Captain Ledger already sorted that out," said Church. "It's a moneymaking scheme not out of keeping with the Cabal mentality. Charge the superrich millions to hunt a trophy no one else can possibly have. It satisfies certain desires and it provides vast operating capital for a group like the Cabal. But more important, it demonstrates the advanced degree of genetic science they have at their disposal."

"The bloodline information, the advanced science, the money," I said. "It not only looks like the Cabal is back . . . but now they have a real shot at accomplishing what it took a world war and forty years of the Cold War to try and stop."

"Yes," said Hu. "These maniacs may well have the science to accomplish both challenges implicit in the eugenics ideal."

"Which are?" Bug asked.

"Not only do you have to make one race stronger," Hu said. "You have to make the other races weaker."

Grace gave us a bleak stare. "Or you have to remove them entirely."

We sat in horrified silence for a long moment before Bug asked, "How do we stop it? We don't even know who's involved, or how far along they are, or—"

Before he could finish, the phone rang. Church answered, and even with his typical lack of emotion I could tell that it wasn't good news.

Chapter Sixty-Four

Lt. Jerry Spencer, head of the DMS forensic investigation division and former Washington police detective, sat on the edge of a desk in the main office of Deep Iron. He felt old and tired and used up. He held his cell phone in one hand and drummed the fingers of his other hand in slow beats on the plastic shell. His eyes were bloodshot from working the Deep Iron crime scene—which was really a collection of related crime scenes—for a dozen hours, and that had been on the heels of working the ambush scene in Wilmington. There was a call he had to make, but his heart had sunk so low in his chest that he didn't think he could do it.

He sighed, rubbed his eyes, and punched in the numbers.

Mr. Church answered on the third ring.

Spencer said, "I found Jigsaw Team."

He said it in a way that could only mean one thing.

Church's voice was soft. "Tell me."

Chapter Sixty-Five

Church set down his phone and placed it neatly on the table. Then he stood up and walked to the far end of the room and stood looking out at the choppy brown water of the harbor. His back was to us, and I could see his broad shoulders slump. We all looked at one another.

"That was Jerry Spencer," Church said without turning. "They found Jigsaw."

We waited, not asking, not wanting to hurry bad news.

"Spencer found sets of tire tracks out in the foothills. He figured the Russian team drove to within a mile and walked in, and he followed the tracks back into the hills and found their vehicles. The Russians had come in a couple of vans. But there were two DMS Hummers there, too. Spencer said it looked like both Hummers had been taken out with RPGs. Hack Peterson . . . his whole team. They never had a chance, probably never saw it coming. The vehicles had been sprayed down with fire extinguishers—probably so the smoke wouldn't attract attention—and then covered with broken tree branches."

"*Dios mio*," murmured Rudy. Bug looked stricken, and even Dr. Hu had enough humanity to look upset.

Grace closed her eyes. Her hands lay on the tabletop and slowly constricted into white-knuckled fists. Hack Peterson was the last of the DMS agents who had worked for Church as long as Grace had. They were friends who had shared the line of battle fifty times. Without any bit of exaggeration it was fair to say that together they had saved America—and a big chunk of the world—from some of the most dangerous and vile threats it had ever faced. Hack was a genuine hero, and those were in damned short supply.

I took her hand. "I'm so sorry," I said softly.

She raised her head. There were no tears, but her eyes were bright and glassy, her face flushed with all the emotion I knew she would not release. Not here, not on the job. Maybe not at all. Like me, she was a warrior on the battlefield.

"God," she murmured, "it's never going to stop, is it? Are we going to go on and on fighting this sodding war until we kill everyone and everything? We're a race of madmen!"

I squeezed her hand.

Church turned back to face us. His tinted glasses hid his eyes, but his mouth was a tight line and muscles bulged and flexed in the corners of his jaw. Just for a moment, and then his control fell back into place with a steel clang.

"Spencer said that he also discovered how the other team escaped. He followed the blood trail from the Haeckel unit. He said that there were two sets of spatters, one that fell from at least five feet, which is probably the one you stabbed in the mouth, Captain, and the other showed heavy blood loss that fell with less velocity from a lower point. Spencer figures it for a leg wound. They took an elevator up to the surface. Spencer figures in Haeckel's bin you'd have been too far away to hear the hydraulics. Then they climbed up through the air vents to the roof and dropped down the side opposite where Brick was positioned. Spencer was able to follow the blood trail for half a mile to a side road, and from there tire tracks led away. He found two sets of footprints. Size twelve and size fourteen shoes. He's doing the math on the impressions, but he estimates that the men were well in excess of two hundred pounds . . . probably closer to three."

I said, "That's pretty nimble for big guys, even if they weren't hurt."

Grace nodded. "If they left a blood trail that long, then they must have been bleeding badly . . . so you have heavy men who, even if they are very muscular and fit, had to climb up air shafts, scale walls, and run into the hills while injured. And this *after* they'd killed a dozen men with their bare hands. I'm finding this all a bit hard to accept."

"Maybe not," said Church. "I'm leaning toward Captain Ledger's exoskeleton idea. Some kind of enhanced combat rig that gives them strength and supports their weight."

"We're not living in a science-fiction novel," said Hu. "We're years away from that sort of thing."

Bug stared at him. "Um, Doc . . . you're defending scientists who can make unicorns and you call an exoskeleton sci-fi?"

Hu conceded the point with a shrug.

"I can't believe Hack's gone . . . ," said Grace hollowly. "For what? For nothing!"

"That's not true, Grace," I said. "We may not know the full shape of this thing yet, but we will . . . and that means that their deaths will matter, because they are part of the process of stopping and punishing whoever did this."

"Why? To clear the way for some other bloody maniac to do even more harm?"

"No," I said, "because what we do matters. We take the hits so the public doesn't. We save lives, Grace. You know that. It's what soldiers do, and Hack Petersen knew that better than anyone. So did everyone on Jigsaw Team."

Grace turned away and I knew that she was struggling to control her emotions. "All we ever see is the war," she said bitterly. "All we ever do is bury our friends."

I said nothing. The others in the room held their tongues.

There was a knock on the door and the deputy head of our communications division leaned into the room. "Mr. Church . . . we have another video!"

Chapter Sixty-Six

The Dragon Factory
Sunday, August 29, 5:38 A.M.
Time Remaining on the Extinction Clock: 78 hours,
22 minutes E.S.T.

Hecate was both amused and disgusted by her brother's weakness. He should be stronger and wasn't. They were both aware of it, though they never openly spoke of it. By ordinary human standards Paris was a monster of superior skill: smart, careful, vicious, inventive, and cruel. By the standards of their family, he was the weak sister while Hecate was the true predator. Paris had directly murdered six people and had shared in the murders of several women during sex play. Hecate had personally murdered fifty-seven people, not counting the sex partners. Paris knew of nine of her kills. The others were not his concern, though she did nothing outrageous to hide them. Paris knew only as much as he had a stomach to know.

The playtime with the two operatives sent by Alpha and Otto had shown Hecate how weak her brother had become. He hadn't participated at all. For a while she thought he was going to disgrace himself by throwing up. Even that muscle-brain Tonton had seen it. He asked Hecate about it later, in bed.

"What's with Mr. Paris?"

Tonton lay under her, his massive frame covered with scratches and red pinpoint bruises. She had used teeth and nails on him. He liked the intensity, and when she could coax a yelp of real pain from him it made Hecate come. She'd come over and over again.

Sitting astride the big man, Hecate shrugged. "Paris has other tastes."

Tonton ran his rough hands over her small breasts. Her white skin was still flushed to a scalding pink from her last orgasm. He was on the edge of exhaustion, but she still had that fire in her eyes.

"He's not like you," murmured Tonton. "No one's like you."

Hecate smiled, thinking about how right he was. There was no one on the earth quite like her. Not anymore.

Tonton was only semi-erect, but Hecate moved her hips in a way that had three times changed that. It was taking longer this time. She smiled to herself, thinking, *Men are weak.*

She decided to throw Tonton a bone. "No one's quite like you, either, my pet."

"Nah," he said. "I'm just another grunt." It was feeble humility. Though it was true that there were hundreds of Berserkers now, it was equally true that he was physically far stronger than the others. The gene therapy Hecate had given him had brought him to a different level. His muscle mass was 46 percent denser than an ordinary man's. He was six feet, eight inches tall and carried his 362 pounds of mass as easily as an Olympic athlete. He could do one-arm chin-ups in sets of fifty and he could do those for hours. He could bench-press a thousand pounds without straining. He could climb a redwood tree and snap a baseball bat in half in his bare hands.

Tonton loved his strength. So did Hecate. He was the only one of the Berserkers she allowed into her bedroom, and over the last few weeks he'd gotten that call from her at least four times a week.

"How come Mr. Paris isn't like you?" he asked as she moved slowly up and down on him. He was hoping to distract her long enough for her to switch off. She may not have limits, but he did.

Hecate had her eyes closed, concentrating on what she was doing, and Tonton thought she wouldn't answer, but then she murmured, "We're like lions, my pet."

"I don't get it. . . ."

"The males are dumb and lazy and they lay around while the females do all the wet work. We hunt; we kill. We're the real pride leaders."

Tonton said nothing.

Hecate opened her eyes and the blue irises were

flecked with spots of hot gold. She smiled—at least Tonton thought it was a smile—and in the uncertain glow from the candles her teeth looked strangely sharp. More like a cat's teeth than he remembered them being.

Hecate said, "All the males do is look pretty and fuck."

She ran her sharp fingernails over Tonton's throat and increased the rhythm of her hips.

Tonton understood the message, and tired or not, he did his best to serve the needs of the leader of his pride.

Chapter Sixty-Seven

The Warehouse, Baltimore, Maryland
Sunday, August 29, 5:38 A.M.
Time Remaining on the Extinction Clock: 78 hours, 22 minutes

Church logged into his old e-mail account from his laptop and his fingers flew over the keys.

"Same sender as the hunt video," he said. To the communications officer he said, "Track this back and find out where the user logged on. Do it now." The officer sprinted out.

We were still reeling from the shock of the news about Jigsaw, but the fact that we might have another clue was like a shot of pure adrenaline. I wanted a scent I could chase down. I wanted someone in my crosshairs. I wanted someone's throat in my hands. I wanted it so bad I could scream.

Church sent the video to the conference room server and punched keys to display it on the flatscreen. The screen popped with white noise, faded to black, and then we saw the face of a young teenage boy, maybe fourteen. Dark hair, rounded face, a slight gap between mildly buck teeth, and brown eyes that held a look of such comprehensive despair that it chilled me.

"If he finds out that I sent this, he'll kill me," said the boy. It was recorded with some kind of stationary camera, maybe a webcam. Grainy and dark, with a weak streaming image. "But I had to try. If you got the other file I sent, then you know what's going on from what the two Americans said."

"But the sound kept cutting out," Bug said. "We could hardly—"

"Shhhh," said Hu.

"You have to stop them. What they're doing . . . it's . . .'' The kid shook his head, unable to put his horror into words. "I don't have much time. I stole one of the guards' laptops, but I have to get it back before they notice I took it. I read Otto's file, so if you're who I think you are, then you have to do something before everyone in Africa dies. And maybe more than that. You got to stop them! If you can't find this place, then see if you can find the Deck. That's the main lab; that's what you have to find. I know it's in Arizona someplace, but I don't know where. Maybe you can find that out when you get here. And then you have to do something about the Dragon Factory. I don't know where that is, but Alpha thinks it's in the Carolinas. I don't think so because I heard Paris tell his sister that they had to get back to the 'island.' I just don't know which island."

He paused, looking desperate.

"I don't even know if I'm making sense. Oh. . . . *wait*!" He obviously spotted something and darted out of shot. We heard the rustling of paper and then he was back, with a big piece of white paper in his hands. He turned it in a few different directions, trying to orient it, and then turned it around toward the camera. "Can you see this? I think this is us; I think this is the Hive."

He suddenly stiffened, lowered the paper, and sat with his head cocked in an attitude of listening.

"Someone's coming. I have to be quick. If you get this, if you come . . . then broadcast on this frequency." He read off the numbers. "It's only short range, but I made it myself. If you're here, I can help you get past the guards . . . but you have to be careful of the dogs. The dogs *aren't* dogs."

He turned his head again.

"Oh no! I have to go."

And with that he punched a button and the screen went blank.

Without waiting for comments Church ran it again and then froze the image on the map.

"Bug," he shouted, "download that image and find me that island. Now!"

"On it."

"Grace," Church said, "prep the TOC. By the time Bug locates that island I want birds in the air."

The Tactical Operations Center was the mission control room. It had MindReader stations, satellite downlinks that fed real-time images, and was networked into every branch of the military and intelligence network. And I don't mean just ours. . . . MindReader didn't give a crap about nationality.

Grace hesitated. "I want to—"

"I know what you want, Grace," he said, "but it looks like we're going to have multiple targets. This site . . . Arizona, and maybe the Carolinas or an island. I need you to prepare Alpha Team for a trip out west."

As she hurried out, she threw me an evil look. "Teacher's pet."

Church looked at me. "You're up, Captain."

I leaned across the table. "Church . . . the kid said that the answers were on the hunt video, but that file sucked and we got maybe one word in twenty. Can you get someone who reads lips? Maybe they can pick up something. . . ."

"Good call. Now—*go!*"

But I was already running for the door.

Chapter Sixty-Eight

The Deck
Sunday, August 29, 5:38 A.M.
Time Remaining on the Extinction Clock: 78 hours,
22 minutes E.S.T.

Otto Wirths stood at the foot of the bed, his hands clasped behind him so that he could feel the comforting outline of the pistol holstered at the small of his back. He was patient but cautious, and he didn't say a word. Not while Cyrus Jakoby was throwing a fit. The floor around the bed was heaped with torn bedding; down stuffing was scattered like snow, and tiny feathers floated past Otto's impassive face. Cyrus had already smashed the twenty-seven vases and ground the exotic flowers under his bare feet. He even had destroyed the portrait of his beloved rhesus monkey. Now he knelt on the floor and used a salad fork to stab one of his doubles to death. And it wasn't even Tuesday.

The double had long since stopped screaming, though he wasn't dead yet. Otto thought a salad fork to be an inefficient weapon but conceded that outright murder was not as important to Cyrus as inflicting hurt. Otto waited it out, one finger hooked under the hem of his smock in case he needed to pull the gun.

Cyrus stabbed down again and again.

Then, as if his internal passion triggered some pressure valve, the rage abruptly stopped. Cyrus sagged and slumped, the fork tumbling from his trembling fingers. The double coughed one more time and then he, too, settled into stillness.

Otto took this as his cue to step around the edge of the bed. He caught Cyrus under the arms and gently lifted him to his feet. Cyrus was as passive as a sedated old man and allowed himself to be led over to an armchair. Otto fetched him a glass of water and produced two pills from a cloisonné case he carried at all times in his pocket. One for heart and one for head.

"Take these, Mr. Cyrus," he murmured, and held the glass as Cyrus washed them down.

Cyrus gasped and shook his head. "I can't believe it! All of them? Dead?"

"All of them," Cyrus confirmed. The news had come back to the Deck from one of their pursuit craft. Both infiltration teams had been lost at the Dragon Factory, and the Zodiac with the extraction team had been taken out with a rocket-propelled grenade. The hit was a complete wash.

"Were any of the team taken alive?" All of Cyrus's people had tiny transponders implanted under their skin. The devices were the size of rice grains and they sent two signals: one for the GPS and another to a biotelemeter. As long as the wearer's heart continued to beat, the second signal was sent.

"None of the units are still active," said Otto.

"God damn it! How did the Twins know?"

"Who is to say if they knew at all? They're quite capable of reacting to an unexpected attack, and we should not be concerned until we know they have connected the attack with us."

"They're too smart, damn it."

Otto tut-tutted him. "Oh, please, Mr. Cyrus . . . we're so much smarter than those children. They don't even know who we *are*!"

It took a moment for Cyrus to shift gears, but eventually he nodded.

"So!" said Otto sharply. "We have much work to do."

Cyrus nodded and glanced over at the dead man on the floor. "I'm sorry I killed him," he said. "Kimball was the best of the doubles."

"He's replaceable."

"Oh, I know that . . . it's just that I was saving him for a special occasion."

"Today is special, Mr. Cyrus."

Cyrus looked up at him, momentarily confused.

"Today we discovered where the Dragon Factory is located. So what if we didn't breach it or kill one of the Twins? We know where it is now. Which means that by one method or another we will take it from your young gods and with their computer resources . . . well, we'll remake the world."

Cyrus's eyes sharpened and he bared his teeth. "I want that facility, damn it, and I want it right now."

Otto straightened. "Then what do you want to do?"

"Contact your Russian friend. I want as many men as he can provide. Don't haggle, Otto. Pay him whatever he's worth, but I want to hit the Dragon Factory with an army. I want to *take* it away from the Twins."

"That will take at least a day or two."

"I want to do it tomorrow at the latest. At the *latest*, Otto. Do you understand me?"

Otto Wirths smiled. "Yes, Mr. Cyrus, I understand perfectly. But you need to understand that in a full-out assault we can't guarantee the safety of the Twins. Neither of them."

Cyrus answered with a sneer. "Then so be it. I made them; I can make more. And I still have the SAMs."

"Very well."

"And contact Veder. I want him in on the assault."

"He doesn't do team hits."

"What is the line from that movie? 'Make him an offer he can't refuse.' "

"If we pull him now, then it'll delay the final hits. Church and that bitch who calls herself Aunt Sallie."

"So be it," Cyrus repeated. "Taking the Dragon Factory is more important. All we need is access to their computers and six or eight hours to trans-load all of their data via satellite to our off-site networked hard drives our friend is supplying. Once that's done we can hide it even from MindReader."

Otto looked pleased. "Fair enough." He looked at his watch. "I'd better make some calls. I'll have to wake up the Russian."

Chapter Sixty-Nine

Top and Bunny were still loading their gear into a Black Hawk when my earbud binged and I heard Grace's voice: "Joe—Bug located the island. MindReader matched the geography to Isla D'Oro, a small island in the Pacific, forty miles due west of Playa Caletas."

"Where's that?" I asked.

"Costa Rica. I'll have him download everything to your PDA. You have flight clearance to the Air National Guard Base at Martin State Airport. From there you'll switch to an Osprey."

"They're slow as hell—"

"Not this one. It's a prototype being developed for the Navy. Has a cruising speed of six hundred kilometers per hour and a twelve-hundred-mile range, which means you'll be refueling midair."

"Where'd you find something like that so quickly?"

"Mr. Church has a friend in the industry. The Osprey is on its way to the air base and should be refueled by the time you touch down."

"Do we have any local support?"

"I called one of my mates at Barrier and he said that the carrier *Ark Royal*'s in those waters. The Osprey will put you on their deck, and then you'll go to the island in a Westland Sea King. You can also have Royal Marines, Harriers, and anything else you need."

"That's fast work, Major. I'll take the ride, but for

now let's go with me, Bunny, and Top. Until we know what's what, I don't want to bring in the Light Brigade."

"I'd rather you took the whole fleet," she said. "But I can see your point."

It was clear she wanted to say more, but this wasn't the time and certainly wasn't the place. So instead she simply held out her hand. I took it and if we held our clasp a few seconds too long, screw it.

"Good hunting," she said.

"Thanks."

The Black Hawk was in the air in under five minutes.

I spread out a map and we gathered around. "This is Isla D'Oro. Gold Island. Supposed to be uninhabited except for a biological research station funded by Swiss grants and managed by a team from the Instituto Tecnológico de Costa Rica. We're looking into that to see if it's legit. Satellite images tell us there's a compound with buildings on the island that match with the construction plans filed by the university. Thermals are tricky because the island is mildly volcanic."

" 'Mildly volcanic'?" echoed Bunny. "That anything like 'somewhat pregnant'?"

"It hasn't popped its cork in over a century, but there are vents and geothermal activity, so thermals won't give us a reliable body count. We'll probably be relying on what we see rather than gadgets." I tapped the map. "Choppers from the *Ark Royal* will set us down here. The terrain is rocky with thick foliage. Combat names for the mission and keep the chatter down. Full team on channel two, direct to me on channel one. The TOC command channel is channel three. Call signs only once we hit the ground."

"What's the op?" asked Bunny.

"Mission priorities are flexible," I said. "We look first. If we can find the kid who sent the videos, then we extract him. Everything else after that is based on what we find."

"Rules of engagement?"

"Nobody gets trigger-happy," I said, "On the other hand, we're not flying two thousand miles to take anyone's shit."

"Hooah."

"The USS *George H. W. Bush* is heading this way in case this really turns into something. The *Bush* will be in fighter range about two hours after we make landfall. That means ninety fixed-wing and helos ready to pull our asses out of the fire if it comes to it."

"Wow . . . it's nice when Washington *likes* us," said Bunny. "Say, boss, what do we do if we run into any of those guys with the body armor?"

"Aim for the head," said Top. "Always been a fan favorite."

"Works for me."

Top took a slow breath. "Cap'n . . . about Jigsaw . . ."

"Yeah."

"We don't know which team took them out. Russians or the other guys."

"No."

"I'm of two minds. On one hand, I want to know who did it and nail their hides to the wall, feel me?"

"Completely."

"On the other hand, I get either side in my sights I'm not sure I'm going to indulge in a lot of restraint. You have any issues with that better tell me now and make it an order."

I considered how best to answer that. "Top . . . Church and the geek squad are working on connecting the dots. We got some new info off the second video, and he has a lip-reader working on recovering info from the hunt video. We're all hoping that by the time we put boots on the ground in Costa Rica we know who the bad guys truly are."

"Wasn't goons in exoskeletons put Big Bob in the ICU," said Bunny.

"Uh-huh," agreed Top. "And it wasn't the goons who killed the staff at Deep Iron. Now . . . I don't see how Russian mercs tie into a buncha assholes who still think Hitler's a role model, but I'm leaning toward them being the ones who need their asses completely kicked."

"Probably so, but we have to be open to any possibility. Church sent us on an infil and rescue, not a wet work."

"Okay, Cap'n, loud and clear."

"Bunny?" I asked.

"You're the boss, boss."

For the rest of the flight we went over the information from the conference and I played the second video. I watched their eyes when the kid said, "You have to do something before everyone in Africa dies. And maybe more than that. You got to stop them!"

Top leaned back, folded his arms, and said nothing. Bunny looked at me. "Holy shit. Is this for real?"

"We'll find out."

Top took a toothpick from his pocket, put it between his teeth, and chewed it. He didn't say a word for the rest of the flight.

Chapter Seventy

Aleksey Mogilevich, nephew of Semion Mogilevich, who was the lord of the Red Mafia in Budapest, looked at the name on the screen display of his phone and smiled. He waved away the redhead with the platinum nipple rings and flipped open the phone.

"Hello, my good friend." He never used names on the phone and preferred calling everyone "friend." Repeat customers were always his "good friends."

"Hello, and how is the weather?" asked Otto Wirths. The question referred to the security of the line and any prying ears where Aleksey was.

"Fine weather. Not a cloud in the sky. I hear that you've used up all the products I sent."

"Yes. Unfortunate."

"There are always more."

Of the twenty ex-Spetsnaz operatives leased to Otto by Aleksey only one was still alive, but as he was merely a coordinator his value was negligible. Neither Aleksey nor Otto was very broken up over the losses. Assets were assets, to be used and either disposed of or replaced depending on need.

"I'm glad to hear you say that," said Otto, "because I do need more."

"How many and how soon?"

Otto told him, and Aleksey whistled. The two girls sunbathing topless on the forward deck of the *Anzhelika* looked up, thinking that he was signaling them, but he shook his head. He got up and walked along the rail and gazed out into the vastness of the sea.

The yacht was an elegant 173 footer with a 37-foot beam, built by Perini Navi of Italy. The first time Aleksey had been aboard it had been a charter for which he'd paid $210,000 for a single week. He liked it so much he bought the boat after the trip was over. It had a crew of eleven, and though it was slow—twelve knots—Aleksey never needed to be anywhere fast. His business was conducted by satellite and cell phones and computer.

The *Anzhelika* currently floated in the wine dark waters thirty miles off the coast of Cyprus.

"Can you supply those assets?" asked Otto.

"There is a surcharge for overnight delivery, you understand."

"I understand."

"Then . . . yes. I have assets in Florida who will do nicely."

"If the assets fulfill my patron's needs, Aleksey, I'll send you a five percent bonus on top of that."

"Ah, it's always heartwarming to know of the generosity of my good friends."

They discussed a few details and hung up.

Aleksey watched the beautiful water and the pure white gulls and thought about how wonderful it was to be alive. Then he sat on a deck chair and made calls that would send several dozen of the most vicious and hardened trained killers he knew to the rendezvous point with Otto Wirths. As Aleksey made the calls he never stopped smiling.

Chapter Seventy-One

The chopper from the *Ark Royal* flew just above the waves and put us down on the far side of the island. We jumped out and faded into the green shadows of the trees until the chopper was far out to sea. We were in full combat rig, with all of the standard equipment plus a few special DMS gizmos. We crouched behind a thick spray of ferns until the jungle settled into stillness. Ambient sounds returned as the birds and bugs shook off their surprise and resumed their perpetual chatter. We waited, ears and eyes open, weapons ready, watching to see if anyone came to investigate.

No one came.

I switched on my PDA and pulled up a satellite image of the island. There was a cluster of buildings on the other side and nothing but dense rain-forest foliage wrapped around a terrain so rough and broken that it looked like an obstacle course designed by a sadist. Gorges, cliffs, broken spikes of old lava rock, ravines, and almost no flatland. All of it sweltering in 102-degree heat and 93 percent humidity. Fun times.

I dialed my radio to the frequency the kid gave us but got nothing but static. Then I tapped my earbud for the TOC channel.

"Cowboy to Dugout, Cowboy to Dugout."

"Dugout" was the call sign for the TOC. Immediately Church's voice was in my ear. The fidelity of our equipment was so good it felt like the spooky bastard was right behind me.

"Go for Dugout. Deacon on deck."

"Down and safe. No signal yet from the Kid." Not an imaginative call sign for the boy who'd contacted us, but it would do.

"Our friends from abroad wanted me to remind you of their offer of support."

The *Ark Royal* and its attendant craft could invade and take a small country, and if we got into a real jam I had no problem calling on them for support.

"Nice to know. Tell them to keep the fires lit, Deacon."

"Satellite feeds are updated on five-second cycles. Negative on thermal scans. Too much geothermal activity."

"Copy that. Cowboy out."

Bunny said, "Wait. . . . I thought this was a dead volcano."

"No, I said it hadn't blown up for a while."

"Swell."

We set out, moving in a loose line, mindful of the terrain and wary of booby traps. The rain-forest foliage was incredibly dense, and I could see why it would draw the attention of biologists and whoever wanted to hide from prying eyes. There were hundreds of different kinds of trees and thousands of species of shrubs, and I swear there was a biting bug or stinging insect on every single goddamn leaf. I must have lost half a pound of meat and a quart of blood in the first three miles.

"This is some serious bush," muttered Bunny. He was the only one of us who hadn't been jungle trained, and he was streaming with sweat. His entire term of service had been in the Middle East. He was also carrying a lot more mass than Top, who was a lean and hard 170, or me at 210.

I kept my radio tuned to the Kid's channel, but by the time we were five miles in there was still no answer.

Then suddenly the static changed to a softer hiss and a shaky voice said, "Is this Mr. Deacon?"

"Not exactly, Kid. But I work for him. Who are you?"

"How do I know that you work for him?"

"You don't, but you dealt the play."

"Tell me something," he said.

"You first. Say something to let me know I'm talking to the right person."

After a moment the Kid said, "Unicorn?"

I muted my mike. "Talk to me, Top."

He was looking at his scanner. "Definitely originating from the island, Cap'n. Three-point-six klicks from here." He showed me the compass bearing.

With the mike back on, I said, "Okay, Kid."

"Now tell me something," he said. The Kid was a quick study.

"Anyone listening?"

"No."

"Okay . . . you sent the hunt video from a cybercafe in São Paolo. Second video was from this island."

"Um . . . okay."

"How do you know Deacon?" I asked.

"I don't. I just know the name. From an old file I stole a look at. Otto and Alpha really hate that guy, so I figured if they hated him that much then he had to be their enemy."

"The enemy of my enemy is my friend," I suggested.

"Old Arabian saying," the Kid said without pause.

"Though it could be Chinese, too. They say it as 'it is good to strike the serpent's head with your enemy's hand.' "

"You know your quotes."

"I know military history," the Kid said, and I noted that he changed the phrasing. He didn't say, "I know *my* military history," which would have been the natural comeback. I filed that away for now.

"Where are you?" he asked. "Are you close?"

"Close enough. You got a name, Kid?"

"Eighty-two."

"What?"

"That's my name. But Alpha sometimes calls me SAM."

"SAM's a name at least."

"No," the Kid said, "it's not. It means something, but I don't know what. Alpha calls a lot of us 'SAM.' "

"Who's Alpha?"

"My father, I guess."

"You're not sure?"

"No."

"Is Alpha his first name or last name?"

"It's just a name. He makes everyone call him that. Or Lord Alpha the Most High. He's always changing his name."

"What's his real name?"

"I don't know. But he sometimes goes by 'Cyrus Jakoby.' I don't think that's real, either."

The name Jakoby rang a faint bell with me, and I signaled Top to confirm that this was all going straight back to Church at the TOC. He gave me a thumbs-up.

"Does Alpha run this place?"

"Him and Otto. But they're not here right now."

"Who's Otto?"

"Otto Wirths is Alpha's—I don't know—his manager, I guess. Foreman, whatever. Otto runs all of it for Alpha. The Hive, the Deck . . . all of it."

My pulse jumped. Otto Wirths. There had been a reference to a "Herr Wirths" in Mengele's letter. Could this guy be related? There had to be some connection. We were actually getting somewhere, though I still didn't know exactly where. Bug kept scanning the woods around us for thermal signatures, and the readings stayed clean.

"How old is this Otto character?"

"I don't know. Sixty-something."

Too young to have been at the camps. Son, nephew, whatever.

I glanced at my team. They were all listening in and I saw Bunny mouth the word, *Eighty-two*.

"Why don't I just call you Kid for now? A call sign. You know what that is?"

"Yes. That's okay. I don't care what people call me."

"And you're sure no one else can hear this call?"

"I don't think so. I made this radio myself. I picked the frequency randomly before I sent that e-mail."

"Smart," I said, though in truth anyone with the right kind of scanner could conceivably find the signal. However, they would have to be looking, and in the digital age not as many people scan the radio waves. Even so, I said, "Okay, Kid. Call me Cowboy. No real names from here on out."

"Okay . . . Cowboy."

"Now tell us *why* we're here. What's this all about?"

A beat.

"I already told you—"

"No, Kid, you sent us a video with almost no audible sound. We saw the 'animal,' but that's all we know."

"Damn!" the Kid said, but he put a lot of meaning in it. "You don't know about Africa? About Louisiana? About any of it?"

"No, so tell us what you want us to know."

"There's not enough time. If you come get me, maybe we can take the hard drives. I'm sure everything's there. More than the stuff I know about. Maybe all of it."

"You're being a bit vague here, Kid. If you want us to help you, then you have to help us out. We know where you're broadcasting from, but we need some details. Are there guards? If so, how many and how are they armed? Are there guard dogs? Electric fences? Security systems?"

"I . . . can't give you all of that from here. I'll have to sneak into the communications room. I can access the security systems from in there and can watch you on the cameras."

"Go for it. How long do you need?"

"You don't understand," he said. "Once I'm in there I'll have to lock myself in. They'll know I'm there. They'll break in eventually. If you don't get here by the time they get to me, then I'm dead."

Kid had a point.

"Terrain's rough. It'll take us forty minutes to get to your location safely. How far out are the first cameras?"

"Six hundred yards from the fence."

Top held out his PDA. He magnified the satellite display of the compound so we could see the thin lines of a double fence.

"Okay, Kid, what's our best angle of approach? What will keep us safe and give you the most time?"

"I can't describe it—"

"We're looking at a satellite image of the compound. Describe a building and I can find it."

"Oh. Okay, there's three small buildings together on the top of a hill and a bunch of medium-sized buildings in a kind of zigzag line sloping down toward the main house."

"Got 'em."

"That's all maintenance stuff. Come in on the corner of the fence. The camera sweeps back and forth every ninety-four seconds, with a little twitch when turning back from the left. I think it has a bad bearing. If you wait for it to swing to the left, you should be able to get from the jungle wall to the fence. The camera is angled out, not down."

"That's pretty good, Kid. Better get off the line. Contact me again when you're in place," I said. "And, Kid . . . good luck."

"You, too." He paused, then added, "Cowboy."

Chapter Seventy-Two

The Deck
Sunday, August 29, 2:31 P.M.
Time Remaining on the Extinction Clock: 69 hours, 29 minutes E.S.T.

Otto Wirths sat on a wheeled stool and watched as Cyrus Jakoby's fingers flowed over the computer keys. Cyrus was the fastest typest Otto had ever seen, even when he was writing complex computer code, inputting research numbers, or crafting one of the codes they used to protect all of their research. It was hypnotic to see all ten fingers merge into a soft blur that was streamed like water. Otto found it very soothing.

They were at their shared workstation, which could be invisibly networked to any and all stations here at the Deck or at the Hive but which could also be hidden behind an impenetrable firewall when the need for secrecy was greatest.

Like now.

The sequences Cyrus was currently writing were the distribution code that would be sent to key people positioned around the world. People who were poised to accomplish certain very specific tasks. Some would begin the distribution of bottled water as part of the faux promotional giveaway to launch a new international competitor in the growing bottled-water market. The company was real enough, and there were several hundred employees on the payroll who truly believed they worked for MacNeil-Gunderson Water-Bottling. Legitimate advertising companies had been hired to create a global campaign for the release of the water under a variety of names, including Global Gulp, GoodWater, Soothe, Eco-Splash. Celebrities had been hired to endorse the water, including two Oscar winners who were widely regarded for their support of the environment and a dozen professional athletes from six countries. Hundreds of thousands of gallons of the water had been promised to fledgling sports teams in developing countries and in the inner cities throughout the United States. After the initial "free giveaway," a portion of the regular sale price of the water would be donated to several popular ecology groups. Those payments would actually be made . . . until the world economy began to collapse and chaos set in. The IRS could audit any of the companies connected with MacNeil-Gunderson Water-Bottling and every cent would be accounted for.

Another group of key people would receive a code command from Cyrus to distribute bottles of water at specific locations throughout Africa, Asia, and the Americas. And then there were the operatives who would dump gallons of pathogen-rich fluid directly into rivers, lakes, and reservoirs.

And codes would be sent to the team of software engineers who had designed what Cyrus called the Crash and Burn e-mail virus that would send hundreds of thousands of infected e-mails to the CDC, WHO, the NIH, FEMA, and dozens of other disaster response and management agencies. The viruses were unique and poised to launch in waves so that as one was taken down another would go out. None of the organizations would be totally disabled, but all that was required was confusion and slower reaction time. Once the Wave was in motion it would no longer matter what those organizations did. It would be too late.

In all, 163 people would receive a unique coded "go" order sent by the trigger device. The go order would arrive in a coded form, and if no cancel order was sent the program embedded in the message would automatically decode the message and present a clear and unambiguous order to proceed with the release. The fail-safe had been Otto's idea. There had been too many delays to rely on an absolute go/no-go code signal. And Cyrus was, they both had to admit it, mad as a hatter. A lot of careful planning would be ruined by Cyrus sending a release order during one of his radical mood swings.

The code Cyrus was writing would be saved on a

flash drive that had a miniature six-digit keypad. The keypad code on this trigger device would be changed daily by Otto, whose memory was sharper than Cyrus's, and they both knew it. They still had to decide between them who would wear the trigger device on a lanyard around his neck. Cyrus felt that as the Extinction Wave was his idea it should be him. Otto agreed that Cyrus deserved to be the one to activate the trigger, but he did not trust Cyrus's mood swings. The last thing they needed was for Cyrus to fly into a rage and smash it with a hammer or on a whim feed it to one of the tiger-hounds.

That could be sorted out later.

At the moment, however, Otto let himself become lost in the flow of Cyrus's clever fingers as they constructed the release code and built its many variations. Otto smiled a dreamy smile as he watched this little bit of magic that would serve as the link between the dream of the New Order and its reality.

Chapter Seventy-Three

Isla D'Oro
Sunday, August 29, 2:57 P.M.
Time Remaining on the Extinction Clock: 69 hours,
3 minutes E.S.T.

The terrain directly around the compound was less treacherous, so it only took twenty-two minutes to get into position. There was nothing from the Kid, so we waited. The next eight minutes crawled by. We listened for shouts or screams from inside the compound; we listened for gunfire; we listened for anything that would indicate that SAM had been discovered. The jungle, though far from silent, simply sounded like a jungle. And then suddenly there was a wail of a siren.

Then SAM's voice whispered to me, "Cowboy . . . ? Are you there?"

"We're here, Kid. Where are you?"

"In the communications room. I started a fire in the laundry room at the other end of the compound. Everyone went running. I don't have a lot of time before they come back."

"Then let's move this along."

"All the cameras are on, but I can't see you. Can you stand up or something?"

"Not a chance." But I signaled to Bunny to shake a tree. He grabbed a slender palm, gave it a couple of quick jerks, and then moved off away in case it drew fire.

"Was that you?" the Kid asked.

"Yes. Now what do we do?"

"I'm the only one watching the monitors. You can rush the fence. Don't worry; I just turned off the electricity."

"We're taking you on a lot of faith. You'd better not be screwing with us, kiddo," I said. I didn't mention that U.S. and British warplanes would reduce this island to floating debris if this was a trap. The boy seemed to have enough to worry about.

"I'm not. I swear."

"Hold tight. Here we come."

We came at the fence at a dead run, running in a well-spaced single file. Top reached the fence first and ran a scanner over it.

"Power's definitely off. No signs of mines."

Bunny produced a pair of long-necked nippers and

began cutting the chain links. We repeated this at the second fence, then ran fast and low toward the cluster of utility sheds.

"There's a stone path by the sheds," SAM said, "but the guards always make sure not to step on it. I think it's booby-trapped."

Bunny flattened out by the flagstones and nodded up at me. "Pressure mines. Kid's sharp."

"We get through this," Top said, "we can chip in and buy him a puppy."

"Guards are coming," SAM said in an urgent whisper. "To your right."

We flattened out against the sheds. I had my rifle slung and held my Beretta 92F in both hands. It was fitted with a sound suppressor that you won't find in a gun catalog. Unlike the models on the market, this had a special polymer baffling that made it absolutely silent. Not even the nifty little *pfft* sound. A toy from one of Church's friends in the industry.

Two guards came around the corner. They were dressed in lightweight tropical shirts over cargo pants. They each carried a Heckler & Koch 416 and they were moving quickly, eyes cutting left and right with professional precision. An exterior grounds check was probably standard procedure with any emergency, and the fire SAM started must have been big enough to inspire caution.

I shot them both in the head.

Top and Bunny rushed out and dragged their bodies behind the sheds.

"Holy Jeez!" the Kid said.

"What's our next move . . . ?"

"There's a door right at the corner of the first building. All of the buildings are connected to that one by hallways. I cut the alarms on all the doors and blanked out the cameras inside the buildings."

"You're making me like you, Kid. What do we do once we're inside?"

"Um . . . okay, there are colored lines painted on all the floors. The blue line will bring you to the communications room, but you're going to have to go through the maintenance pod and then the common room. It's like a big lobby, with chairs and soda machines and a coffee bar. If you go straight across that, you'll see the colored lines start again. Keep following that."

"Roger that, Kid."

"Wait!" There was some rustling noise and then he came back, breathless. "I think they're coming back!"

"Can you lock yourself in until we get there?"

"The door's just wood. They'll kick it in."

"Is your radio portable?"

"Yes. I rigged a headset."

"Then get your ass out of there. Find someplace to hide. We're going to have to make some noise."

"God. . . ."

"Are there any civilians we need to worry about? Any good guys?"

"Yes!" he said immediately. "The New Men. You'll be able to spot them . . . they're all dressed the same. Cotton pants and shirts with numbers on them. Please," he begged, "don't hurt any of them."

"We'll do our best, but if they offer resistance . . ."

"Believe me . . . they can't."

He said "can't" rather than "won't." Interesting.

"Anyone else?"

"No . . . everyone else here is involved."

"Then get out of there."

"Okay, but . . . Cowboy? Watch out for the dogs."

"What breed and how many?" I asked.

But all I got from the radio was a hiss of static.

"Okay," I said to Bunny and Top, "pick your targets and check your fire. If anyone surrenders, let them. Otherwise, it's Bad Day at Black Rock."

"Hooah," they replied.

"Now let's kick some doors."

Chapter Seventy-Four

The Hive
Sunday, August 29, 3:08 P.M.
Time Remaining on the Extinction Clock: 68 hours,
52 minutes E.S.T.

The exterior door was steel, so I stepped back as Bunny put a C4 popper on the lock with one of Hu's newer gizmos—a polymer shroud that was flexible enough to fold into a pocket but strong enough to catch shrapnel. It was also dense enough to muffle the sound, so when Bunny triggered it the lock blew out with a sound no louder than a cough. The door blew open in a swirl of smoke.

No alarms. Kid's still batting a thousand so far.

I led the way inside.

The hallway was bright with flourescent lights and stretched sixty feet before hitting a T-juncture. There were doors on both sides. Everything was conveniently marked, and it was clear that this corridor was used by groundskeepers and technicians. Most of the rooms were storage. The left-hand rooms had bags of chemical fertilizer, shovels and garden tools, racks of work clothes. The right-hand rooms included a small machine shop, a boiler room, and a changing room for support staff. There were plenty of clothes and I debated having my guys change into them, but I didn't. My gut was telling me that we were fighting the clock here, so we tagged each doorway with a paper sensor pad set below the level where the eye would naturally fall. The sensors had an ultrathin wire and a tiny blip transmitter. We peeled off the adhesive backing and pressed them over the crack in the door opposite the hinge side. If anyone opened the door, the paper would tear and a signal would be sent to our scanners. Simple and useful.

We found one room in which a large piece of some unidentifiable equipment hung from a chain hoist. From the scattering of tools and the droplight that still burned it looked like a work in active progress. There was no one around. Everyone must have gone to investigate the fire the Kid had set and, like most employees would, was probably stalling before heading back to work.

I still had the Beretta in my hands and we moved through a building that was empty and silent.

That all changed in a heartbeat.

Two men rounded the right-hand side of the T-juncture while we were still twenty feet away. Both wore coveralls stained with grease, and I knew they had to be the mechanics working on the equipment. They were deep in conversation, speaking German with an Austrian accent, when they saw us. They froze, eyes bugging in their heads, mouths opened in identical "ohs" of surprise as they stared down the barrels of three guns. I put the laser sight of my Beretta on the forehead of the bigger of the two men and put my finger to my lips.

All he had to do was nothing. All he had to do was stay silent and not try to be a hero.

Some people just don't get it.

He half-turned and drew a fast breath to scream and I put one through his temple. Top took the other with two side-by-side shots in the center of his chest. They hit the floor in a sprawl.

If Lady Luck would have cut us a single frigging break we'd have been past them and into the complex within a few seconds. But she was in a mood today. There were other people behind them, out of our line of sight, farther down the side corridors.

People started screaming.

Then people started firing guns.

A moment later the alarms sounded.

So much for stealth.

Chapter Seventy-Five

The Dragon Factory
Sunday, August 29, 3:17 P.M.
Time Remaining on the Extinction Clock: 68 hours,
43 minutes E.S.T.

The three businessmen from China stood wide-eyed and slack jawed, all pretenses at emotional aloofness lost in the moment. Behind the glass, perched on the twisted limb of a tallow tree, its wings folded along the sleek lines of its sinuous body, was a dragon.

The creature turned its head toward them and stared through the glass for a long minute, occasionally flicking its flowing whiskers. It blinked slowly as if in disdain at their surprise.

One of the men, the senior buyer, broke into a huge grin. He bowed to the dragon, bending very low. His two younger associates also bowed. And just for the hell of it Hecate and Paris bowed, too. It might help close the deal, though both of them knew that this deal was already closed.

"Does . . . does . . . ," began the senior buyer—a fat-faced man named Chen—"can it . . . ?"

Paris smiled. "Can it fly?" He reached out and knocked sharply on the window. The sudden sound startled the dragon, and it leaped from its perch, its snow-white wings spreading wider than the arm span of a tall man, and the creature flapped away to sit in a neighboring tree. The enclosure was designed for maximum exposure, so even though the dragon could move away, it couldn't hide.

Chen murmured something in Mandarin that Paris did not catch. Neither of the Twins could speak the language. All of the business with these buyers had been conducted in English.

"How?" said Chen in English, turning toward the Twins.

"Bit of a trade secret," said Paris. He was actually tempted to brag, because the creation of a functional flying lizard was the most complicated and expensive project he and Hecate had undertaken. The animal in the enclosure was a patchwork. The wings came from an albatross, the mustache from the barbels of a Mekong giant catfish, the horny crest from the Texas horned lizard, and the slender body was mostly a monitor lizard. There were a few other bits and pieces of genes in the mix, and so far the design had been so complicated that most of the individual animals had died soon after birth or been born with unexpected deformities from miscoding genes. This was the only one that appeared healthy and could fly.

The really difficult part was designing the animal for flight. It had the hollow bones of a large bird and the attending vascular support to keep those bones healthy. They'd also had to give it an assortment of genes to provide the muscle and cartilage to allow it to flap its wings. Unfortunately, they had not identified the specific gene—or gene combinations—that would give it an instinctive knowledge of aerodynamics. So they'd spent hours with it in an inflated air room of the kind used at carnivals and kids' parties, tossing the creature up and hoping that it would discover that those great leathery things on its back were functional wings. The process was frustrating and time-consuming, and the animal had only recently begun flapping, and the short flight it had just taken was about the extent of its range. More like a chicken thrown from a henhouse roof than a soaring symbol of China's ancient history. The heavy foliage in the enclosure helped to mask the awkwardness of its flight. The entire process had been a bitch. A forty-one-million-dollar bitch. And the damn thing was a mule, unable to reproduce.

But at least it was pretty, and it more or less flew. Paris hoped it would live long enough for them to sort out all of the genetic defects so they could actually sell one. This one was display only. A promise to get the Chinese to write a very, very large check.

Paris thought he could hear the scratching of the pen even now.

The three Chinese buyers stood in front of the glass for almost half an hour. They barely said a word. Paris was patient enough to wait them out. When the spell finally lifted—though they still looked quite dazed—Paris ushered them to a small table that had been set with tea and rice cakes. The table had a view of the dragon, but it wasn't a great view. That was Hecate's suggestion.

"If they can't see the damn thing," she'd said, "they'll get impatient. They'll want to close the deal so they can go back and gape at it."

Paris liked the tactic.

Before the tea was drunk, before it had even begun to cool, the buyers had placed an order for three full teams of Berserkers. The total purchase price was the development price of the dragon with a whole extra zero at the end. The Chinese had been too dazzled and distracted to do more than token haggling.

The deal closer was Paris's promise to provide them with a dragon of their very own. Just as soon as they managed to make another one. Which, as far as he was concerned, was a couple of days before Hell froze over.

Chapter Seventy-Six

The Hive
Sunday, August 29, 3:26 P.M.
Time Remaining on the Extinction Clock: 68 hours, 34 minutes E.S.T.

Four guards rushed the corner and they did it the right way, laying down a barrage to stall us and then putting just enough of themselves around the corner to aim their guns high and low. It was nice.

I threw a grenade at them.

We ran through the smoke and screams and took the corner ourselves. The side corridor was choked with people who were fleeing back from the blast, tripping over one another, trampling the fallen, getting in the way of armed resistance. The opposite side corridor led to a ten-foot dead end and a closed door.

"Pick your targets!" I called as I aimed and fired at a guard who had taken a shooter's stance and was bringing his weapon to bear. My shot spun him as he pulled the trigger and his first—and only—shot punched a red hole through the leg of a hatchet-faced woman who was screaming into a wall-mounted red security phone. The woman shrieked in pain, but as she fell she pulled a .32 from a hip holster. Bunny put her down for the count.

I heard a yell and a barrage from the other end and then I was too busy for chatter as more security began forcing their way through the flood of panicking workers. These boys had shotguns and H&K G36s and they opened up at us even though some of their own people were in the way. A whole wave of civilians went down in a hail of bullets, and we had to duck for cover because there were ten of the sonsabitches.

"Frag out!" yelled Top and he and Bunny threw a pair of M67s. Most soldiers can lob the fourteen-ounce grenades up to forty feet, and then they'd better take cover, because the M67s have a killing radius of five meters, though I've seen them throw fragments over two hundred meters. We hunkered down around the corner and the blast cleared the hallway completely.

When I did a fast-look around the corner I saw drifting smoke, tangles of broken limbs, and no movement at all.

We got up and ran, leaped over the dead, avoided the

dying, blocked out the screams, and plowed through the clouds of red-tinged smoke. A man leaned against a wall, trying to hold his face on with broken fingers. The blast had torn his clothing and blood splashed the rest, so I couldn't tell if he was a technician or guard. He threw us a single despairing look as we passed, but there was nothing we could do for him.

The corridor opened into a big central lobby set with exotic plants and cages of wild birds. Technicians were running everywhere creating a wild pandemonium, tripping over couches and jamming the exits so that no one got through. A knot of a dozen guards burst through a set of double doors. A big blond guy with a lantern jaw and killer's eyes was clearly in charge, and he knew what he was about. He used the noncombatants as human shields to close with us and we had to either shoot the technicians or take unanswered fire.

I don't remember seeing "martyr" in my job description, but even so I didn't want to kill anyone who didn't need to die. It was a terrible situation that got very bad very quickly.

"Boss . . . ?" called Bunny.

The guards were taking shooting positions behind the screaming staff members.

If we fell back and got into a range war with these jokers we could be here all day, and we had no idea how many more shooters they could call on. It was balls out or beat it, so I did the one thing the guards did not expect: I attacked them, up close and personal. I knew my team would follow my lead.

The blond guy was behind a pair of women who crouched and plugged their ears and screamed, but he was too far away, so I zeroed the closest gun and I rammed my gun into his gut and fired twice. The impact jerked him a foot off the ground and I grabbed a fistful of his shirt and spun my body hard and took him with me. He hit the guy behind him hard enough to put them both on the cold terrazzo floor, and I stamped down on the second guy's throat.

To my left Top had closed to zero distance with a pair of shooters, and he used the same stunt as them—keeping the staff between their guns and his skin. When he was close he chucked a technician hard under the chin with the stock of his M4, and as he collided with the shooters Top shot over the falling man and hit one guard dead center. The other guard lost his gun in the collision, but he tossed the technician aside and lunged out and grabbed Top by the throat. I could see Top actually smile. Here's a tip: never grab a good fighter with both hands, because he can hit back and you can't block. Top dropped his chin to save his throat and put the steel-reinforced toe of his combat boot way too far into the bad guy's nuts. Bones had to break on that kick. Top slapped away the slackening grip on his throat and chopped the stock of the rifle down on the back of the guard's neck. Knocking him out was probably a mercy.

I saw movement to my right and I pivoted and ducked as one of the guards came around a thick potted fern and tried to put his laser sight on me. His face exploded and I saw Bunny give me a wink.

More people were flooding into the lobby. It was like trying to stage a firefight in the middle of a soccer riot. There had to be a hundred screaming people around us.

I dropped two more guys and my slide locked back. I dropped it and was reaching for another mag when the big blond guard and two others came at me in a fast three-point close. If I retreated they'd have closed around me like a fist, so I drove right at the closest of them, a red-haired moose with missing front teeth. I slapped his gun hand aside with the back of my gun hand and then checked the swing to chop him across the bridge of the nose with the empty pistol. That knocked him back into me, and as his back hit my chest I pivoted like an axle, whipping us both in a tight circle that allowed me to throw him at the man in the middle. It would take the redhead a second to disentangle himself and I used that second to lunge forward and bashed him in the crotch with my pistol. I didn't care if that hurt him, but I wanted to stall him in place; then I slammed the butt of the pistol down onto the top of his foot, feeling the metatarsals snap. Before he could even scream I shot back to my feet and put every ounce of weight and muscle I had into a rising palm strike that caught him under the chin and snapped his head back so far and so fast that he was out before he hit the ground. Maybe hurt, maybe dead, maybe I didn't give a shit.

The middle guy—the big blond—pushed his companion away. He'd lost his gun in the collision and as he stepped toward me he whipped a Marine KA-BAR out of a belt holster. I have a whole lot of respect for that knife, and he held it like he knew how to use it.

The KA-BAR has an eleven-and-three-quarter-inch blade with a seven-inch sharpened clip. The point was a wicked dragon's tooth that could pierce Kevlar like it wasn't there. The Marines and Navy have been using it since World War II, and in the hands of an expert it has all the bone-cutting force of a Bowie knife, coupled with wicked speed. I whipped my Wilson Rapid Response folding knife out of my pocket and with a flick of the wrist snapped the blade in place. Yeah, I know it only has a three-and-three-quarter-inch blade that looked like a nail file compared to the KA-BAR, but like they say, it's not the size of the ship but the motion on the ocean.

The blond guy—he had a name tag on his shirt that read: "Gunther"—began circling right and left, trying to force me to move with him. He kept cutting his angles and each time he changed direction he bent his elbow a little more to make me think he was staying at the same distance while actually moving closer. It was a nice trick that I'd used myself.

He suddenly lunged, taking a very fast half step forward and jabbing at my knife arm with the point of his blade. It was an expert's trick. Idiots try to stab in a knife fight, and though they can sometimes bury a blade, it leaves the other guy free to deliver cut after cut before the wound takes them. This guy went for a "pick," a micro-jab to try to injure my knife arm and take away both my offensive and defensive capabilities right away. He was lightning fast and I had to really move to evade the pick.

I circled left and he tried it again, this time going lower and deeper before flipping his blade up, the idea there being to cut me with the clip as he pulled his blade back. Another smooth move.

I was ready for him, though, and as he lunged in and back I did a tap-down with the curve of my blade. My knife was very light, so I had to use a wrist flick to give it enough weight to cut, but I could feel the edge tap bone. Blood drops danced in the air as he pulled his hand back.

The pain and surprise showed on his face, but he went immediately into another attack, this time doing a double fake and pick that caught me on the elbow and left a burning dot of pain where the flesh was thinnest.

The panic still roiled around us, but if either of us split his focus he was a dead man. I knew that my squad was doing their job. Top and Bunny were in the thick of it, but it took a whole lot of guys to outnumber that duo.

Gunther's eyes held mine, and I knew that he was relying—as I was—on peripheral vision to pick his moves and his targets. We stayed in motion, always on the balls of our feet, moving like dancers in a complex and dangerous piece of choreography. When he moved, I moved; when I moved, he moved. The blades flicked out and back. Twice steel hit steel, but each time it was a glancing parry.

When you're fighting an expert you can win if the other guy gets emotional, if he makes a mistake, or if you bring something to the game that he doesn't. So far Gunther wasn't letting his emotions drive the car, and he hadn't made a single mistake. He was bleeding from three nicks; I was bleeding from four.

He shifted to the right and then faked back and tried for a face slash, turned that into another fake, and went into a half crouch to try to slash me across the femoral artery. The high fake almost always makes you lean backward to slip the cut, and that raises your guard away from your lower torso, exposing groin and thigh. It was beautiful; it was textbook.

It wasn't the right move to use on me.

When he went for the face cut I knew it was a fake. Gunther hadn't made a mistake—he just picked the wrong guy to try this move on. As he dropped low and went for the long reach toward my thigh I dropped with him so that his blade skittered across the gear hanging

on my belt. I mirrored the arc of his cut with my own,
shadowing his recoil so that my knife followed him all
the way back, but I went deeper and drove the tip of my
knife into the soft cleft between the bottom of his inner
biceps and the upper edge of the triceps. My blade only
went half an inch deep, but that was enough to open a
pinhole in his brachial artery. From the way pain flashed
across his face I knew that I'd nicked the medial nerve,
too.

Gunther tried to switch hands, and maybe he was a
good left-handed knife fighter, too, but he knew as well
as I did that the moment had moved away from him. It's
a terrible thing when one feels his combat grace desert-
ing him. It takes the heart out of you in an instant.

He shuffled backward to make the hand-to-hand exchange, but I jumped forward and my cut was deep and
long and it took him across the throat. I had to spin out
of the way of the arterial spray. He went down and I
spun back into the fight, shaking off the knife, scanning
the floor for my pistol, bending, pulling a new magazine,
slapping it in, and all of it before Gunther had finished
falling.

Chapter Seventy-Seven

The Deck
Sunday, August 29, 3:28 P.M.
Time Left on the Extinction Clock: 68 hours, 32 minutes E.S.T.

An aide came tearing down the hallway to the private
alcove where Cyrus and Otto shared a huge and complex computer workstation. Intruding into this area was
forbidden without a call or advance warning via e-mail,

and more than one employee had been summarily executed for an infraction of one of Cyrus's strictest rules. However, the words the aide shouted as he pounded on the door wiped all thoughts of punishment out of their heads.

"They're attacking the Hive!"

Otto and Cyrus leaped to their feet demanding answers.

"It's on the central channel!" cried the aide, and Otto hit the buttons that sent the audio feeds to his speakers.

". . . message repeats . . . a team of armed men is attacking the Hive. They've penetrated the perimeter and are in the building. We're taking heavily casualties. Please advise; please advise."

Cyrus gasped. "It's the Twins! It has to be. . . ."

"How could they—?"

"They must have taken the team that we sent. Pinter and Homler both know about the Hive."

"They're trained operatives," argued Otto. "They'd never talk."

"That witch Hecate . . . my *darling* daughter . . . could make Satan himself give up the secrets of Hell and you damn well know it."

Otto waved the aide away and slammed the door to the alcove.

"We have to move fast," Otto said.

"But we have to make the right move," countered Cyrus. "This will be a team that they've sent. If they're doing this much damage, it must be one of the Berserker squads."

Otto nodded. "Then they won't be there in person. Paris doesn't have the balls for fieldwork, and Hecate is too smart. Even so, the Berserkers aren't totally stupid.

They're smart enough to tear a hard drive out of a computer. We can't allow the Twins to see what's on those computers. I don't trust that they'd let the Extinction Wave go forward."

"I know they wouldn't. They're not truly gods," Cyrus said with grief and regret in his voice. "We have no choice; we have to use the fail-safe. . . ."

Otto stepped around the workstation and put his hand on Cyrus's shoulder.

"Mr. Cyrus," he said kindly. "My friend . . . Eighty-two is at the Hive."

Cyrus's eyes went wide for a moment and then he closed them as the reality of that drove nails of pain into his heart.

"No. . . ."

Otto squeezed Cyrus's shoulder and sat down. With a few keystrokes he called up the security command screen that would activate the Hive's fail-safe system. He sent two sets of code numbers to Cyrus's screen. One activated the fail-safe and the other simply detonated the communication centers and hardlines that connected the Hive to the Deck.

"It's come down to this," he said softly. "Either we let the Twins see what we've been doing and risk having them stop us—and they *could* stop us—and then the mud people get to survive and the dreams of the Cabal and everything we've worked toward for seventy years will be wrecked, or you choose the boy who will make you immortal. That's the choice. The Extinction Wave or the boy."

Cyrus shook his head. He stared blindly at the screen, tears in his eyes.

"Eighty-two has my heart," he said. "He has my soul."

Otto said nothing.

"Please, God . . . give me a choice between the Twins and Eighty-two, but not this. . . ."

"We're going to run out of time," Otto said. "You have to make a choice."

Cyrus wiped the tears from his eyes and sniffed. When he lifted his hands to place his fingers over the keyboard they felt like concrete blocks.

"Cyrus . . . ," murmured Otto.

Cyrus used the cursor to select one of the codes.

He closed his eyes, squeezing them against a fresh wave of tears.

And hit "Enter."

Chapter Seventy-Eight

The Hive
Sunday, August 29, 3:38 P.M.
Time Remaining on the Extinction Clock: 68 hours,
22 minutes E.S.T.

It was a slaughterhouse. I went through another magazine with the Beretta before holstering it and switching to the M4. More guards crowded into the lobby from the far side, but they paused for a moment when they saw that the floor was littered with bodies. Some of them were people who had wisely dropped and covered their heads to stay out of the line of fire; the rest were dead. Bunny laid down some cover fire for me as I made a dash for a heavy counter on the far side of the lobby. I felt the wind and heard the buzz of a few close shots from guards who were crouched down behind a conversational grouping of couches and overstuffed chairs. I jumped into a diving roll and came up into a kneel, pivoted, and laid my shoulder against the side of a hardwood counter. Bunny was behind a Coke machine and Top had faded to the far side of the lobby and was shooting from behind a decorative column.

Echo Team formed three sides of a box, with the guards at the far corner. There were seven of them, and for a moment all we exchanged were wasted bullets. I had one fragmentation grenade left and a couple of flash bangs, but the lobby was half the size of a football field. To reach them I'd have to stand up and really put some shoulder into it, and I didn't like my chances of being able to walk away from that. The remaining guards were dishearteningly good shots.

I tapped my earbud. "Who has a shot?"

Nobody did.

Bullets tore into the counter, knocking coffee cups into the air and splashing me with hot coffee and creamer. The coffee burned, but none of the bullets penetrated. I knocked on it. Steel in an oak sheath. I shoved my shoulder against the counter and was surprised when the heavy piece of furniture moved almost two inches. Not bolted down, and it must have had little casters on it. Sweet.

"I'm trying something," I said in the mike, "so make sure I have cover fire when I need it." I threw my weight against the counter. It slid easily and moved four feet, the metal casters sounding like nails on a blackboard.

"Copy that, boss."

The guards saw what I was doing and concentrated their fire at me, but to little effect. The steady bullet impacts slowed me, but I kept going, shoving the counter across the terrazzo floor. I kept praying to whichever god was on call that these guys didn't have any genades.

"We got a runner, boss," said Bunny and I peered around the edge to see one of the guards break from cover and race to the far wall. There was a series of pillars there and if he could get to them he could inch his way up on my blind side.

"Got him," said Top, and the runner suddenly spun sideways and went down. With all of the other gunfire I never heard the shot.

I kept pushing the counter until I was thirty feet out. None of the other guards tried the same end-run stunt, but I could hear the squawk from walkie-talkies and I knew that they were calling up all the reinforcements they could. This was taking way too long,

"It's fourth and long," I growled. "Make some noise."

My guys really poured on the gunfire and for a moment it forced the guards down behind their cover. A moment was all I needed. I pulled the pin on the frag grenade and risked it all as I rose to a half crouch and threw it. Then I flattened down just as the blast sent a shock wave that slammed the counter into me.

There was one last burst of gunfire as a guard, blind from shrapnel and flash burned, staggered out on wobbling legs and emptied his gun in the wrong direction. Top put him down and the lobby was ours.

"Move!" I yelled, and I scrambled out from behind the counter and made a dead run for the far end of the lobby. Bunny was behind me and Top came up slower, keeping a distance so he could work long-range visuals.

At the far end of the lobby we peered down a wide hall that curved around out of sight. Now that the thunder of the gunfire was over I realized that the alarm Klaxons had stopped. The lobby and hallway were eerily silent.

I tapped the command channel. "Cowboy to Dugout."

There was no answer. Bunny tried it, same thing.

Top looked at his scanner. The little screen was a haze of white static.

"We're being jammed."

Two things happened in short sequence, and I didn't like either one.

First the lights went out, plunging the lobby into total darkness.

And then we heard something growl in the darkness. Behind us.

Chapter Seventy-Nine

The House of Screams, Isla Dos Diablos
Sunday, August 29, 3:40 P.M.
Time Remaining on Extinction Clock: 68 hours,
20 minutes E.S.T.

The man on the radio—the one who called himself Cowboy—had told him to run and hide. He almost did. When he heard the voices in the hallway, Eighty-Two grabbed his portable radio and fled the communications center and ran down two side corridors and across the veranda, back in the direction of his room.

The problem was that the guard quarters were between the communications room and the main house. He skidded to a stop at a juncture of corridors, torn by indecision. In the distance he heard gunfire and then screams. And then alarms. These weren't the fire alarms that had gone off when he'd sent his diversionary fire. No, these were the heavy Klaxons to be used only in the more extreme emergencies.

The Americans were attacking.

The thought sent a thrill through Eighty-two's chest. He started toward his quarters again but stopped after a single step.

What if he ran into Carteret on the way? When this alarm was going off, Eighty-two was under orders to remain in his room. Everyone on the staff knew that. Guards would probably be at his room now, wondering where he was, and his absence would be relayed to the head guard. Carteret. How could Eighty-two explain his presence on the far side of the compound, in the wrong building? Carteret wasn't stupid. He'd put the pieces together: a small fire to distract everyone and then a full-scale invasion.

Would Otto have given Carteret orders to kill Eighty-two if there was a danger he'd be taken?

No. Alpha would never allow that.

Then a second thrill went through the boy's chest and this time it wasn't excitement—it was terror.

If there was an invasion by government forces—American or otherwise—then their guards would almost certainly have other orders. Orders more crucial to Alpha and Otto's plans than the life of Eighty-two.

The boy looked down one corridor toward the sealed computer rooms. In there, in the very heart of the Hive, were records of all of the research done here on the island. Years upon years of study of genetics and transgenics, of special surgeries, of breeding programs, of the rape and perversion of nature. Evidence that would put Otto and Alpha away forever. Maybe have them executed.

Then Eighty-two turned and looked down the opposite corridor, back to the House of Screams. That's where the labs were, and that's where the bunkhouses for the New Men were.

The Americans were here because of what was in those computers. Even though Cowboy had told Eighty-two that the audio on the hunt video was bad, they must know that something terribly evil was being done here on the island. They'd come to find out what and to stop it. The computer records could save millions.

On the other hand, Otto and Alpha could never risk having the New Men fall into the hands of any government. The worldwide outcry would be like the shouts of outraged angels.

And there was the female.

In Eighty-two's pocket the stone felt as heavy as an anvil.

He stood and looked down the corridor toward the computer rooms, chewing his lip in dreadful indecision. Then he made his choice.

He turned toward the House of Screams and ran.

Chapter Eighty

The Hive
Sunday, August 29, 3:42 P.M.
Time Remaining on the Extinction Clock: 68 hours,
18 minutes E.S.T.

We flattened out against the walls and flipped down our night vision. I dropped to one knee and pivoted as I heard a second growl. The lobby went from absolute blackness to eerie green.

"What do you see, boss?" hissed Bunny, who was facing the other way.

"Nothing," I said, but I could *feel* something moving in the shadows. We'd left a lot of wreckage behind us, but everything looked still. But there was something and my senses were jangling. The after-echo of the growl played over and over in my head. It wasn't a dog growl. More like a cat, but not a cat, either. Whatever it was, the growl had been heavy, deep chested. Something big was back there, and it was ballsy enough to stalk three grown men.

"Move," I said, and began backing away from the lobby. We moved backward five feet, ten, following the curve of the hallway until the lobby was lost to view.

Just as we moved out of sight I thought I caught movement at the extreme range of the night vision, but it was too brief a glimpse. Just a sense of something huge moving on four feet, head low between massive shoulders.

Way too big for a dog.

"What the hell's on our asses?" Bunny asked in a jittery voice.

"I don't know, but if it comes sniffing down here I'm gonna kill it."

"Works for me."

"Let me know if you get a signal, Top."

"Roger, but we're still dead."

"Lousy fucking choice of words," muttered Bunny.

The thing behind us screamed.

It was a huge sound, high-pitched and filled with animal hate. Like a leopard, but with too much chest behind it. Then I heard the sharp click of thick nails on the tile.

"Run!" I yelled, and the two of them pounded down the hallway, but I held my ground, raised my Beretta in a solid two-hand grip, and clamped down on the terror that was blossoming in my chest. In the microsecond before the creature rounded the bend the image of the unicorn flashed through my head. If these maniacs could make something like that, then what other horrors had they cooked up in their labs? Horrific images out of legend and myth flashed before my mind's eye, and then something moved into my line of sight that was far more terrifying than any monster from storybooks or campfire tales.

It ran like a cheetah, with massive hindquarters thrusting it forward as long forelegs that ended in splayed claws reached out to tear at the tiled floor. The monster's face was wrinkled in fury and its muzzle was as long as a Great Dane's but contoured like a panther. The eyes were glowing green orbs in the night-vision lenses, but I could see feline slits. It snarled with a mouthful of teeth that were easily as long as the blade of my Rapid Release knife.

I had never seen, never imagined, a creature like this. It was easily as big as a full-grown tiger. From the points of those fangs to the tail that whipped the air behind it, the monster had to be twelve feet, and when it was five yards away it launched more than seven hundred pounds of feral mass into the air right at me.

I heard myself screaming as I fired. I pulled the trigger and fired, fired, fired as I threw myself down and to one side. The creature's mass was already in the air and it couldn't turn to track me, but I could feel the wind of its passage over me and I saw the dark blossoms as bullet after bullet punched into it, the big .45 slugs exploding through muscle and meat. I hit it six times and then it was past me, landing hard on the floor, skidding, sliding down the hall in the direction my men had taken, snarling, its claws tearing up floor tiles, smearing the walls with blood.

The monster scrambled to a violent turn and got to its feet, turning fast to face me.

How the hell was it still standing with six bullets in it?

The monster hissed at me and I could see its monstrous shoulders bunching to make another run.

I put the laser sight on its left eye and the creature flinched.

But not soon enough. I put my seventh shot through its eye and my eighth and ninth through the heavy bone of its skull. My slide locked back, the gun empty.

A terrible scream tore the air as the creature fell.

The sound did not come from the dying monster.

This scream came from right behind me.

These animals hunted in pairs.

I threw myself backward, dropping the magazine and clawing another out of my pocket as the second animal came at me out of the swirling darkness. I slapped the magazine into place, but this beast was bigger, faster, and it hit me like a freight train before I could get a round in the chamber or bring the gun to bear.

The impact drove me backward so fast and hard that I had no time to do anything but roll with it and try to hang on to my gun. Claws ripped across my chest, tearing open my heavy shirt and gouging chunks out of the

Kevlar. The creature's own weight kept me alive because it continued to tumble over and past me. I didn't try to get to my feet; I just jacked the round as the monster twisted around with a screech of claws on tiles and pounced. It landed on me with all of its weight, knocking my night vision off so that the world was black and full of teeth and claws. The sheer weight of it drove the air from my lungs, but I jammed the barrel up until it hit something solid and I pulled the trigger, over and over again.

I heard other shots, the reports overlapping mine, and the monster shrieked in terrible rage and pain.

Then all of its weight slammed down on me.

Chapter Eighty-One

The House of Screams, Isla Dos Diablos
Sunday, August 29, 3:43 P.M.
Time Remaining on Extinction Clock: 68 hours,
17 minutes E.S.T.

Eighty-two ran as fast as he could. Gunfire echoed through the halls and he thought he heard the screams of the tiger-hounds *inside* the building. There were eight of them on the island, including two mated pairs that were bigger than Siberian tigers. If they got past the guardhouse and into the House of Screams they would slaughter every last one of the New Men. It had been genetically bred into them to react to New Men as their primary source of prey—something Eighty-two had heard Otto discuss with one of the animal handlers. It allowed them to sell the animals to anyone who had bought sufficient numbers of New Men.

The building was in panic now. White-coated scientists ran past him; cooks and house staff scrambled for any way out of the compound. The sound of gunfire was continuous and there were explosions, too. Eighty-two knew the sounds of arms and ordnance. He recognized the hollow pops of small-arms and rifle fire and the heavy bark of grenades. This was a full-out assault, but there was no way to know who was winning.

He ducked into a closet long enough to try his radio, but all he heard was a high-pitched squeal. A jammer. That would be an automatic response initiated by the compound's auto defense systems, and the controls for that were in the guardhouse. He'd never be able to shut it off.

Eighty-two shoved the radio back into his pocket and dove back into the hall, turning right and heading for the dormitories where the New Men would be huddled. He could imagine their terror and uncertainty at what was happening. The alarms, the gunfire, the screams of the tiger-hounds.

Would *she* be there? Would the female be back in the dormitory, or had she been taken to the infirmary after Carteret had finished with her? Doubt made Eighty-two slow from a run to a walk.

And that's when the man who was following Eighty-two grabbed him by the hair.

Chapter Eighty-Two

Before my guys would risk trying to pull the monster off of me, Top stepped close and put his M4 to its head.

"Firing!" he warned, and popped two through its skull. The body gave a last twitch and then its weight settled even more crushingly down on me. It took Bunny and Top pulling with all their strength and me shoving with hands and feet to rock it sideways so I could scramble out. I felt flattened, and taking a deep breath was a challenge.

Bunny switched on a flashlight and we all stared at the two creatures.

"What the *hell* are they?" Bunny breathed.

"Dead," murmured Top.

"Somebody's been playing with his Junior Gene-Splice Kit," I said as I swapped magazines. My night vision was damaged and my helmet had been battered into an unwearable shape. The creature's claws had torn the chest out of my Kevlar and severed two of the straps, and my shirt was covered with blood. I removed the shirt and the Kevlar simply fell to the ground. Great. Now I was in hostile territory in a tank top. That would inspire a lot of personal confidence.

On the upside, the layers of material had kept me from being turned into sliced pastrami. Even so, I was starting to get a case of the shakes. Adrenaline does wonders for you in the heat of the moment, but when the cognitive processes kick in and you realize the enormity of what just happened, that can really do some harm. In the last ten minutes I'd been in a deadly firefight; I'd killed people with guns and a knife and was then attacked by a pair of animals that should exist only in nightmares. None of this felt completely real to me, at least not to the civilized man inside my head. The cop was trying to make sense of it but was having a hard time accepting some of this as real. Only the warrior part of me was calm and in control. The warrior had tasted blood now, and all he wanted to do was take it to the bad guys over and over again.

Bunny nudged one of the dead creatures with his booted toe. "And to think forty-eight hours ago I was playing volleyball on the beach at Ocean City with two blondes and a redhead."

"Well, at least your life ain't boring," said Top. "This here's an actual monster. Girls love monster slayers. Might get you laid one of these days."

"Only when you can tell them about it," Bunny said. "They ask me what I do for a living and I have to actually make up boring shit. And it's hard to make boring stuff up because, let's face it, fellas, since we signed onto this gig we haven't exactly been bored."

"I could use some boredom," said Top. "I could use a nice long stretch where nobody wants to burn down the world."

"There's a train leaving for the nineteenth century," I said.

Before moving out, we checked our surroundings. The lobby and hallway were totally still. We moved down the hallway. Nothing and no one confronted us this time, and I wondered if the staff had all fled, knowing that the mutant guard dogs were being let off the leash. I wished we still had an operational commlink. This would be a really nice time to ask our British friends on the *Ark Royal* to send a couple of helos full of backup. They could already be inbound for all I knew. Church was running the TOC, and I doubted he was sitting there watching Dr. Phil, not with our communication down during a firefight.

Around the bend we stopped at a set of heavy double doors. We checked them for trip wires and found nothing, so I cautiously pushed the crash bar and opened one door an inch. The door must have had a tight seal, because once it was open we could hear shouts and commotion. A couple of gunshots, too.

In this part of the building the emegency lights had come on, so we had more than enough illumination. The halls were empty, but there was the kind of debris that indicated panic and urgent flight: dropped clipboards, one low-heeled woman's shoe, dropped coffee cups. Here and there were smears of blood, probably from people fleeing the lobby fight.

The hallway ran forty feet to another set of heavy double doors that stood open. On the far side of the doorway there were three bodies. They were dead but not from gunfire. Their bodies had been ripped open and torn apart. Big red footprints trailed off down the hall.

"More of those whatever-they-weres," said Bunny.

"The Kid told us to watch out for dogs," Top reminded him. "He wasn't screwing around."

"Not sure if 'dogs' is the word that comes to mind here, Top." Bunny patted his pockets to reassure himself of his spare magazines. He glanced at me. "What the shit have we stepped into, boss?" asked Bunny.

"I don't know," I said. "So let's find that kid and get some goddamned answers."

Chapter Eighty-Three

The Deck
Sunday, August 29, 3:45 P.M.
Time Left on the Extinction Clock: 68 hours, 15 minutes E.S.T.

Cyrus Jakoby stood wide legged on the observation deck, his hands clasped behind his back. Grief had given way to cold fury.

The Twins had betrayed him.

The Twins had raided the Hive, had tried to steal his secrets.

The thought twisted like a serpent in his heart. It did not matter that he had sent spies and assassins to the Dragon Factory. It was his right to do as he pleased. He had *made* the Twins. Gene by gene, he had made them. He owned them and they were his to do with as he pleased. It was bad enough that they thought he was insane and laughable, that they believed that all this time they had held him captive here at the Deck. They had sent Drs. Chang, Bannerjee, and Hopewell to "oversee" his work without having the sense to realize that Otto and Cyrus already *owned* those men. Just as they owned everyone at the Deck. Those employees of the Twins Otto could not bribe were eventually won over by Cyrus's charisma and the grandeur of his purposes. The only thing the Twins had kept from him had been the

Dragon Factory, and they had been so careful to never let anyone who had ever worked on-site at that facility come to the Deck.

The war of secrets had been waged between Cyrus and his children for seven years, and now it had come to this. The Twins had sent hired mercenaries to invade the Hive.

"Bastards," he snarled to himself. "Ungrateful little bastards."

It was not merely the affront that tore at him. He had endured—and pretended not to notice—a thousand slights over the years. The Twins always treated him as if he was a pet scorpion—dangerous but contained. He was disappointed in their dimness of vision. No, the real hurt was that an attack on the Hive meant that the Extinction Plan was in serious jeopardy.

And that Cyrus Jakoby could not allow.

Cyrus felt Otto's presence and turned. The wizened Austrian looked more predatory than usual.

"Well?" Cyrus demanded.

"I've sent the orders. We can put two hundred troops on the ground at the Dragon Factory in twenty-four hours."

"Good. I want the computer records and then I want it burned to the ground."

Otto cleared his throat. "The Twins have been handling the distribution of the bottled water. We have to make sure that we can account for every copy of their distribution records. That's paramount, Mr. Cyrus."

"Then make it happen," snapped Cyrus with such heat that even Otto took a half step backward. "Then destroy every stick and stone of that place."

"What about the Twins?"

Cyrus leaned on the rail and stared down at the animals in the zoo for a long time, and Otto let him work it through. There were times when Cyrus could be handled and even pushed, and there were times when that was like reaching into a tiger's mouth.

"Try to capture them both, Otto," Cyrus said at last.

"And if we can't?"

"Then bring me their heads, their hearts, and their hands. Leave the rest to rot." His voice was barely a whisper.

A passenger pigeon landed on the rail inches from Cyrus's hand. Cyrus reached for it and picked the bird up gently. The pigeon tilted its head and stared up at Cyrus with one ink black eye.

"We're doing God's work," whispered Cyrus. "Man is such a polluted and corrupted animal. I'd hoped that Hecate and Paris would be the answer, the next step in the evolution from the trash that humanity has become to the ascended level where he needs to be in order to serve God's will. I can see now that they are not all that I'd hoped."

"I—"

Cyrus stopped him with a shake of his head. "No, let me talk, Otto. Let me say this." He stroked the pigeon's delicate neck. The bird did not struggle to escape but seemed to enjoy the contact. It cooed at Cyrus, who smiled faintly. "Do you know what makes me saddest, Otto?"

"No, Mr. Cyrus."

"It's that I don't think the Twins would ever understand why we're doing what we're doing. They see things in terms of product and profit, and they've become mired in that mind-set. It actually matters to them; it actually motivates them. They have no grand schemes. Their highest aspirations to date have been to twist genetics in order to make themselves rich. I . . . I long ago lost my ability to communicate with them."

"To be fair, sir, you play a role in that—"

"Yes, but they should have seen through it and glimpsed the higher purpose. Just as we glimpsed through the foolishness of politics and war making to see the divine beauty of eugenics. Clarity is a tool, Otto, just as perception is a test. The Twins were bred to have greater intelligence. Their IQs are on a par with Einstein, with da Vinci. With *mine*. But . . . where is their Theory of Relativity? Where is their masterpiece? You might say that they've done what no one else has done, that they've twisted DNA and turned it to their will, but I say, 'So what?' They were given the gift of higher intelligence by design. I started them on a higher level and they should have aspired to more than clever toys for rich fools. There's no higher purpose in anything they've done, or anything they've imagined, and by that standard they are failures."

"We could breed them," offered Otto.

"Mm. Maybe. But that presents its own risks. No, Otto . . . I think we were both so enamored of their beauty and by their precociousness that we lost sight of our own plans for them. They are not the young gods of our dreams. Of my dreams." He drew a breath and let out a long sigh. "If they are both taken, then we'll harvest his sperm and her eggs and enough DNA to begin the next phase. If either or both are killed, then we'll have to start with the DNA alone and hope that we can use it for gene therapy on the SAMs. I know this is vain, Otto, but we may not live long enough to see the true race of young gods become flesh. It may be two or three generations away, and it may be the SAMs alone who witness it."

"I know," said Otto, and he patted Cyrus on the shoulder.

"Of course," said Cyrus with a flicker of his old mad delight, "at least we will be here to clear the way for the new gods. We will be here to see the mud people—the blacks and Jews and Gypsies and all of those disgusting mongrel races—wiped away. Not just reduced, but gone for good. We will live to see that!"

Otto glanced at his wristwatch. The numbers were matched to the Extinction Clock. He showed the numbers to Cyrus. *"Die Vernichtungs Welle."*

The Extinction Wave.

Those words and the numbers on the clock worked a transformation in Cyrus, whose face changed in a heartbeat from clouds of sadness to a sunburst of great joy.

"Nothing can stop it now," murmured Cyrus.

"Nothing," agreed Otto.

Chapter Eighty-Four

The Hive
Sunday, August 29, 3:51 P.M.
Time Remaining on the Extinction Clock: 68 hours, 9 minutes E.S.T.

The hallway we followed was long and narrow, with doors only on the right-hand side. In one room we found another corpse. The victim was small and thin and had been partially devoured. The head was gone.

"Jesus," said Bunny, "I hope that ain't the Kid."

"I think it's a woman," said Top. "*Was* a woman," he corrected. "That ain't our boy."

Clustered around the body were more animal prints. They were scuffed, but it looked like there were two sizes of them. I pulled the door shut and we kept moving, following the blue line that was supposed to lead us to the Kid. Only I'd told the Kid to go hide, so we might be heading in the wrong direction and we had no way to get in touch with SAM and arrange a better rendezvous. I thought about the headless corpse and hoped Top was right.

We cleared all of the rooms and found no one who looked like a teenage kid. Three times guards came at us. Three times we put them down. And, luckily, we saw no more of those freaking dogs. Or whatever they were.

Suddenly I heard a harsh buzz in my ear and then a voice.

"The jamming stopped. Scanner's up," called Top. "Commlink's back online."

I switched to the command channel.

"Cowboy for Dugout, Cowboy for Dugout."

Immediately Grace Courtland's voice was in my ear. "Dugout here, Cowboy. Amazing on the line. Effing good to hear your voice!"

"Right back atcha."

"Deacon here, too, Cowboy," said Mr. Church. "Sit rep."

I gave it to him in a few terse sentences.

"Medical team and full backup are inbound," Church said. "Say fifteen minutes."

"Haven't found our local friend," I said, "but contact is iminent. Tell arriving medical staff to watch for animals of unknown type. They look like dogs but are bigger than tigers. We took down two, but they are very—I repeat—*very* dangerous. This ain't a petting zoo, so shoot on sight."

"Roger that," said Church, and in the background I heard Grace mutter, "Effing hell." "Cowboy, we have additional intel for you. We put a lip-reader on that hunt video. Most of what we got was worthless, comments on the hunt, the weather, and the mosquitoes. But we hit gold on one conversation when the men in the video had stopped to take a drink from their canteens. We don't yet understand what we got, but the content is alarming. Sending a transcript to your PDA now."

"I'll look later—"

"Unless you are under immediate fire, look now," said Church.

"Roger that," I said more calmly than I felt. I pulled my PDA from my pocket and hit some keys. The transcript came up right away. It was a snatch of a conversation between one of the unidentified Americans and Harold S. Sunderland, brother of the senator. It read:

NOTE FROM TRANSLATOR: The unnamed person was smoking a cigarette, which complicated the translation. Illegible and unclear words have been marked.

UNKNOWN AMERICAN: Where are you going to be during the Wave?

HAROLD SUNDERLAND: Shit. Anywhere but Africa.

UNKNOWN AMERICAN: [illegible] . . . not like it'll happen overnight. [illegible] . . . months for the [illegible] to kill that many niggers.

HAROLD SUNDERLAND: Sure, but what if it jumps? All we need is some white guy who can't keep it in his pants banging some jig and we—

UNKNOWN AMERICAN: [Shakes head] Otto said it don't [illegible] like that. Otherwise they'd have to [illegible] half of South Africa.

HAROLD SUNDERLAND: Yeah, well, they said AIDS couldn't jump from a monkey to humans, and then some faggot bones a chimp or—

UNKNOWN AMERICAN: It was a rhesus monkey, Einstein, and I don't [illegible] it just jumped. I asked Otto about that and [illegible] me a sly-ass wink like he knew something.

HAROLD SUNDERLAND: Yeah, well, that Kraut fuck had better be right about that, 'cause I am not dying of some jigaboo disease.

UNKNOWN AMERICAN: I hear you. [The next sentence is illegible as he has his hand on the cigarette, blocking his lips.]

HAROLD SUNDERLAND: Me, too.

UNKNOWN AMERICAN: I'm sure as hell going to stay [illegible] until after September 1.

HAROLD SUNDERLAND: I thought you trusted Otto.

UNKNOWN AMERICAN: I do, but I don't like taking chances. When that frigging Extinction Wave hits I don't want. . . .

NOTE: Remainder illegible.

While I read every drop of my blood had turned to greasy ice water in my veins. I tapped my earbud.

"Is that all there was?"

"Yes," said Church.

"I can see why the Kid thought we'd be interested."

"Comments, reactions?"

"It doesn't exactly fill me with pride."

"For being a white man?" Grace asked.

"For being a carbon-based life-form. I'd love to have some playtime with both of those jokers."

"Agreed."

"How sure was the translator about the phrase 'Extinction Wave'?"

"Very. What does it suggest to you?"

"The same thing that it suggests to you, boss. Someone's about to launch a major plague in Africa that will target nonwhites. Is there such a thing?"

"Dr. Hu is working on that. Most of the diseases that sweep Africa are based more on health conditions, lack of food, polluted water. That sort of thing. Diseases focusing on racial groups tend to be genetic rather than viral or bacteriological."

"The Otto he mentioned has to be Otto Wirths. What did you come up with on him?"

Church said, "Nothing at the moment. We've got MindReader working on it. However, we got a hit on the other name the boy gave you. Cyrus Jakoby. If it's the same man, he's the father of the Jakoby Twins."

"As in Paris and Hecate? Those albinos who keep showing up in the tabloids? She can't keep her clothes on and he's always getting thrown out of restaurants. Aren't they scientists of some kind?"

"They're geneticists, in point of fact. Superstars in the field of transgenics."

"Well how about that? Any ties to the Cabal or eugenics?"

"Nothing so far. And nothing much on Cyrus Jakoby except a few offhand references the Jakoby Twins made in interviews to the effect that their father was in poor health. MindReader has found twelve Cyrus Jakobys in North America and another thirty-four in Europe. The cross-referencing will take a while, but there are no initial hits or connections to anything that rings a bell."

"Very well. Let me fetch our young informant and see what kind of intel we can squeeze out of him."

"He seems to be on our side, Cowboy," said Grace. "Squeeze lightly."

"How lightly I squeeze depends on how forthcoming he is, Grace. The words 'Extinction Wave' don't exactly give me the warm fuzzies."

I signed off.

Bunny said, " 'Extinction Wave.' Holy shit. Who thinks up stuff like that?"

"When I meet him," said Top, "I'm hoping he'll be in my crosshairs."

"With you on that."

There was another burst of static and then a desperate voice said, "Cowboy? Cowboy, are you there?"

It was the Kid and we were back online.

"I'm here, Kid. Where are you?"

"I'm in the House of Screams."

"Say again?"

"The conditioning lab. Red district. Look at the floor. Follow the red line. It ends right outside where I am. I had to run and then they tried to grab me, but I got away. I—"

Whatever else he was going to say was suddenly drowned out by the roar of gunfire and the sound of a lot of people screaming. Then nothing.

"Kid! SAM . . . !"

But I was talking to a dead mike.

The red lines on the floor stretched out in front of us.

We ran.

Chapter Eighty-Five

The Hive
Sunday, August 29, 3:55 P.M.
Time Remaining on the Extinction Clock: 68 hours,
5 minutes E.S.T.

We crashed through another set of double doors that opened on an atrium that was thick with exotic plants and trees in ceramic pots. The plant leaves, the pots, and the floor were all splattered with blood. The floor was littered with shell casings. There were bodies everywhere. The dead were all strangely similar: short, muscular, red-haired, and dressed in cotton trousers and tank tops. None of the dead had weapons on or near

them. From what I could see in the split second I had to
take in details was that the entry wounds were on their
backs as if they'd been gunned down while fleeing.

The atrium was crowded with people. Scores of the
red-haired people were fighting to get through an open
doorway into a room labeled: "Barracks 3." A dozen
guards stood in a rough firing line, blasting away at the
fleeing, screaming people. One guard stood apart. He
was a big man with a buzz cut and an evil grin. He was
wrestling with a teenage boy who had to be SAM. The
Kid was screaming and kicking at the big guy but for
all his fury wasn't doing the guard a lot of harm. The
guard even looked amused.

SAM broke free and dug something out of his
pocket—a black rock the size of an egg—and then
leaped with a howl and tried to smash the guard's skull
with it. The guard swatted SAM out of the air like a bug.

All of this happened in a split second as we pelted
across the atrium. Somehow through the gunfire and
screams the guards must have heard us. They turned
and began swinging their weapons toward us.

"Take them!" I yelled. Easier said than done. With
the red-haired people on the far side and the Kid in
front, a gun battle was iffy, and we were right on top of
them. So we crashed right into them and it was an instant melee.

Bunny hit the line from an angle and it was like a
wrecking ball hitting a line of statues. The impact
knocked guards into one another, and that probably
saved all our lives because suddenly everybody was in
one another's way. Top and I both capped a couple of
the guards with short-range shots and then we were up

close and personal. Top clocked one guard across the jaw with his M4 and spun off of that to ram the barrel into someone else's throat.

I went for SAM, but the boy was once more grappling with the big guard. Another guard stepped up and put his rifle to his shoulder. If I'd been five feet farther back it would have been a smart move for him, but I was way too close. I grabbed his rifle and thrust the barrel toward the ceiling and pistol-whipped him across the throat, then gave him a front kick that knocked him down. The guard next to him swung his rifle at me and knocked my pistol out of my hand and damn near broke my wrist. I pivoted and broke his knee with a side-thrust kick, and as he sagged to the ground I chopped him across the throat with the edge of my other hand.

Bunny tore a rifle from one guard's hand and threw it away, then grabbed the guy by the back of the hair so he could hold his head steady while he landed three very fast hammer blows to the nose. The man was a sack of loose bones, so Bunny picked him up and slammed him sideways into the chests of two other men. Bunny's strategy was to keep destablizing the line. It was something we'd worked on in training. He was enormously strong and fast and he had a lot of years in judo, so he knew about overbalancing. Top, on the other hand, was lethal at close and medium range and his hands and feet lashed out with minimum effort and maximum efficiency. Top had done karate since he was a kid, and none of it was tournament stuff. No jump-spinning double Ninja death kicks. He broke bones and gouged eyes and crushed windpipes.

One of the guards came at me with a six-and-a-half-inch Fairbairn-Sykes commando knife. I took it away from him and then gave it back; he fell back with the blade buried in his soft palate.

SAM screamed in rage and pain as the big guard grabbed him by the hair and punched him in the face. The Kid's nose exploded in blood and his knees buckled. He would have fallen if not for the massive fist knotted in his black hair, but even so the Kid tried to swing that stone again. Kid really had spunk.

There was one more guard between me and the big guy and I wasn't in the mood to dance, so I grabbed the punch he was trying to throw and broke his arm, stamped on his foot, and then gave him a rising knee kick to the crotch that went deep enough to break his pelvis. He fell screaming to the floor and I closed on the big guy.

The guard saw me coming and swung the boy around to use him as a shield, locking a huge arm around SAM's throat.

"I'll pop his bleeding head off," the man said with a thick Australian accent.

I pulled my Rapid Response knife and clicked it into place.

"Let him go or I'll put you in the dirt," I said.

Around me Echo Team was tearing the last of his men to pieces.

The guard—his name tag identified him as Carteret— lifted SAM off the ground so that he was a better shield. The boy's face was going from rage red to air-starved purple.

"Killing the Kid's not going to make the day end better for you, sport," I said. "He's the only coin you have left to spend."

"Fuck you!"

I was about to rush him when SAM, oxygen starved

and battered as he was, swung both feet toward me and then bent his legs and swung them back and up so that both of his heels slammed into the man's groin. The guard's eyes went as wide as dinner plates and he let out a whistling shriek. I grabbed SAM by the front of the shirt and pulled him free.

The guard staggered back. I put him on the deck with an overhand right that knocked him cold.

I spun back to the fight, but there was no fight. Bunny and Top stood in combat crouches, both of them bruised and breathing heavy, but none of the guards were able to answer muster. Most never would.

SAM took a staggering step toward me. The lower half of his face was bright with his own gore and he hocked up a clot of blood and snot and spit it into Carteret's face.

It was a strange moment. Even with all of the vicious combat and murder around me, that act seemed to possess more real hatred than anything else that had happened here today. The boy was panting and crying.

"SAM—?" I asked.

He nodded. "Are you . . . Cowboy?"

"At your service."

The Kid pawed tears from his eyes with bloody fists and then turned toward the open door through which the last of the red-haired people had fled.

"We have to save them . . . ," he said thickly.

"Are there more guards?"

The Kid shook his head. "I don't know . . . but I heard the tiger-hounds roaring earlier."

"So, that's what they're called," said Bunny. "We put two of them down."

"Two? What about the other six?"

Christ.

"First things first," I said. "Who are the people the guards were shooting?"

"They're the New Men."

"Why do the guards want them dead?"

The boy shrugged. "To hide the evidence, maybe. I don't know."

" 'Evidence'?" asked Bunny. "Of what?"

"Of what Otto and Alpha have been doing here. The stuff in the computers is just part of it."

Bunny and Top moved among the groaning survivors and bound their wrists and ankles with plastic cuffs.

I gestured to the doorway through which the New Men had fled. "What's through there?"

"Dormitories. It's where they keep all the New Men."

"Are they dangerous?" Bunny asked as he picked up his fallen M4 and checked the action. "To us, I mean."

SAM shook his head. "They won't fight. They . . . can't."

"Where are the computers?" I asked.

"We can cut through the dormitories and go around back. It's faster than going back through the building . . . and besides, if the tiger-hounds are inside, then it'll be safer out there."

"Show us."

"Will . . . will you help the New Men?" he asked.

I didn't know how to answer that question, so I said, "We'll see what we can do."

He didn't look deflated, but there was a look of disappointment in his eyes that had a lot of mileage on it. I didn't know his story yet, but trust was not something he expected. That much was clear.

"Okay," he said as he picked up his rock. Almost as

an afterthought he took the knife from Carteret's belt and staggered toward the open door.

Like players in a bizarre drama, Echo Team and I followed.

Chapter Eighty-Six

The Hive, Barracks 3
Sunday, August 29, 4:06 P.M.
Time Remaining on the Extinction Clock: 67 hours,
54 minutes E.S.T.

We stepped into hell.

The barracks was vast, stretching into the shadows. There were hundreds of cots set in neat rows that fled away on all sides of us. Figures lay sprawled or huddled on the narrow beds, or sat in rickety chairs, or shuffled around with their heads down. Everyone wore the same kind of thin cotton trousers, tank tops, and slippers. The clothing was a sad gray that made the people look like prisoners, or patients in an asylum, and I had the sinking feeling that they were both.

Top said, "Holy Mother of God."

The New Men who had fled from the gunfire were clustered a few yards away. Several of them were wounded, and the others huddled around them, pressing their own wadded-up shirts to the bullet holes. None of them looked directly at us, though a few cut nervous glances our way, but each time we made direct eye contact with them they looked away. I saw no trace of anger, no rage at what had just happened. The only emotions that I could read on those faces were fear and a sadness that was endlessly deep.

All of the people in the barracks had red hair, though that varied from a bright orange to nearly brown. They were short, even the men, and all of them were heavily built. The most striking feature was their heads. Their skulls were large, suggesting a larger braincase, but it was lower and longer than normal. They had sloping foreheads, thick lips, and no chins.

"What the hell's going on here?" asked Bunny. "Who are these people?"

"They look like . . . ," began Top but left it unsaid, and none of us wanted to put a name to it, either.

"We have to get them out of here," said SAM. He turned and grabbed my arm. "We have to get them off the island."

I said nothing.

One of the New Men—a female—rose from the huddled group. She looked at SAM, then away, and then back. She looked scared, but she held the eye contact longer than any of the others. She was as brutish and ugly as the others, but there was an innocence about her that was touching.

"Master," she said in a voice that was higher-pitched than I expected from her muscular bulk. She turned toward the main barracks and shouted, "Master!"

The call was repeated over and over in that high voice. Suddenly everyone in the barracks was in motion. The New Men all got quickly to their feet and began moving forward.

"Boss . . . ?" murmured Bunny. He began raising his rifle, but SAM reached over and pushed the barrel down.

"No . . . it's okay. They have to line up. They're afraid not to."

Bunny and the others stared at the Kid and then

turned back to watch as the New Men shuffled forward, eyes and heads down, to stand in rows in front of their cots. Because they moved with their heads down they frequently collided with each other, but there were no grunts or growls of annoyance, no harsh words. After each collision they would separate and bob their heads as if each automatically took responsibility for the mistake, then continue toward their assigned spot. We stood rooted to the spot, unable to speak, as five hundred of these strange people formed into lines and slowly straightened as much as their stooped and muscular bodies would allow. One of them—an older man with gray in his red hair—who stood at the first cot in the line called, "Master!"

All of them dropped to their knees and bowed until their heads touched the floor.

Bunny wheeled on SAM and grabbed a fistful of the Kid's shirt and lifted him to his toes. "What the fuck is this shit?" Bunny snarled in a dark and dangerous voice.

"Tell them to get up," I said.

"Stand!" SAM yelled. "Stand."

The New Men climbed to their feet, but their heads were still bowed like whipped dogs waiting for their master's approval. I felt sick and angry and deeply confused.

"Farmboy here asked you a question," said Top, leaning close to SAM, who was still up on his toes.

"Let the Kid go," I said.

Bunny opened his hand and pushed the Kid roughly away. SAM fell back against Bunny, who twitched his hip to push him away. The Kid looked up and saw a lot of hard faces staring down at him.

"Tell us," I said. "What are they? Why are they acting like this?"

"They have to. They're genetically designed to be servants."

"You mean slaves," said Bunny.

He nodded. "Yes. Slaves. They did gene therapy on them to remove genes that code for aggression and assertiveness. The idea is to create a race of people who will do anything they're told to do and . . ." His voice faltered, but he sucked it up and tried it again. "And accept any kind of abuse. No matter how bad you beat them or . . . degrade them . . . they'll just take it. Otto and Alpha call them the New Men."

"I didn't ask what they're called; I asked what they are."

"They—Otto, Alpha, and their science teams—they took old DNA and then rebuilt it to create them."

"They're not human. What *are* they?" I asked again.

SAM looked scared to even say the word.

"They're Neanderthals," he said.

Chapter Eighty-Seven

The Dragon Factory
Sunday, August 29, 4:09 P.M.
Time Remaining on the Extinction Clock: 67 hours,
51 minutes E.S.T.

"What is this stuff?" asked Tonton as Hecate injected a golden liquid into the IV line attached to the Berserker's arm.

"A gift from my father," said Hecate. She emptied the syringe and threw it into a red sharps disposal. "It'll make you feel better."

"I feel pretty frigging great right now," Tonton

growled. Even when he spoke in ordinary conversational tones, he had a deep voice that rumbled like thunder. Over the last few months the gene therapy had taken him a few steps further than the other Berkserkers. Tonton's brow had become more pronounced, his nose wider and flatter. He looked less like his natural Brazilian-German and more like a mature silverback gorilla. Hecate had even noticed that Tonton's back hair was starting to fade from black to silver. It was one of the things that troubled Paris, because they hadn't given the Berserkers the genes for hair coloration or facial deformity and yet the traits had emerged anyway.

Hecate found it fascinating and wildly sexy.

It also reflected some of the changes she was experiencing with her own covert experiments. The gene therapy she used on herself was nowhere near the scale used on the Berserkers, and it drew on feline traits from the *Panthera gombaszoegensis*, the European jaguar, a species extinct for a million and a half years but whose DNA was recovered from a German bog. Her goal had been to enhance her strength by making her muscles 20 percent denser and to heighten her senses. She could not achieve feline sensory perception, but already she realized that it would soon become necessary to start wearing tinted contact lenses to hide the pupilary deformation and color changes. Her teeth were growing sharper, too, and that was absolutely not part of the plan. Hecate accepted the reality that these would need to be filed soon, but for the moment she liked the extra bite.

"So . . . what's it do?" growled Tonton.

Hecate gave him a playful slap across the face. "It'll keep you and your boys from going *apeshit* during missions."

He stared at her, then got the joke. They both cracked up.

"Yeah," he said at length, "some of the boys do get a bit rambunctious. In Somalia . . . Alonso and Girner were really fucked up. I had to stomp them a bit to keep 'em from eating people. Dumb sonsabitches."

"It's not their fault," Hecate said. "The therapy has some wrinkles, but my father had some ideas on what to do."

"And I'm the guinea pig?"

"Yes."

"Jeez."

"You scared, big man?" she purred.

"Scared? No. Who'd be scared with a crazy bitch like you pumping God knows what into me based on the advice of a total whack-job."

Hecate slapped him again. Harder.

He grinned at her. There was a trickle of blood at the corner of his mouth and he licked it up. The cut was deep, though, where the vulnerable flesh of his inner mouth had been smashed against his teeth. A new bead of blood formed, and Hecate pushed Tonton back in the chair, climbed on him, straddling him with her white thighs, and then bent and licked off the trickle of blood.

"Is the door locked?" he asked.

"Yes," she said huskily.

"Good," Tonton said with a growl. A second later they were tearing at each other's clothes.

Chapter Eighty-Eight

"Wait—*what*?" said Bunny.

"Neanderthals," SAM said again.

"Slow down," Top said. "There are no Neanderthals. Not for—"

"Not for over thirty thousand years," SAM said. "I know. And I guess these aren't *true* Neanderthals, but they're close enough. Otto and Alpha started with mitochondrial DNA recovered from old bones and then mapped the genome. Then they repaired any damage with human and ape DNA. These people are the first generation. By studying them the science teams will know how to improve the model in the next generation. And they're working on adjusting performance and attitude with them through gene therapy and conditioning."

"What do you mean by 'conditioning'?" Top asked.

"The guards . . . they're told to do anything they want to the New Men. Beat them, torture them, rape the females. Some even rape the males."

"For the love of God—*why*?" demanded Bunny.

"Part of it is a test to see if the New Men will ever talk back, or strike back, or rebel. Or try to escape. The sales brochures claim that they're perfect servants, with zero ability for insubordination."

Bunny gaped. "They have sales brochures for this shit?"

SAM nodded.

"Who are the buyers?"

"Rich people, mostly. Some corporations have bought them for work that's too dangerous or expensive for human labor. Mining, unskilled labor around radioactive materials, toxic-waste handling . . ."

Top opened his mouth to say something, then bit down on it, unable to let those words have voice. I felt fevered and light-headed, like this was some weird dream and I was lost in it.

"Is this all of them?" I asked.

SAM shook his head. "No. There are three barracks in the compound. Barracks one and three are the same. Five hundred in each. Barracks two is the nursery."

" 'Nursery'?" Top's eyes closed and his face fell into sickness. "God save this sinner's soul."

I stared at the rows of New Men.

At the rows of *Neanderthals*.

The word was jammed into my brain like a knife.

"SAM . . . how do I tell them to relax? To . . . stand down?"

"They're trained for code words. If you want them to relax but still listen, you say 'community'; if you want them to do what they were doing, you say 'downtime.' "

" 'Downtime,' " said Bunny. "Christ. Hey, I have an idea. Can we tell them to go out and find the rest of the guards and tear them into dog meat?"

"No," said SAM. "They're incapable of violence. Otto and Alpha made sure of that. There are certain genes for aggression that were—I don't know, removed or deactivated. But they just won't get violent no matter what. There's one . . . a female . . . who was hurt by that guy Carteret."

"The one you went after with your rock?" I asked.

"Yes." He told us about the female who had been brutalized over the dropped rock. "Otto says that a dedicated program of humiliation erodes the will and rewrites the instincts to accept all forms of abuse as a natural part of life."

Bunny said, "Boss, I really want to spend some quality time with this asshole, Otto."

"Stand in line, Farmboy," Top growled. "I got a few things to say to him myownself."

"Okay, Kid," I said, "time for answers. What's happening in Africa on September 1, and what the hell is an 'Extinction Clock'?"

"Didn't you watch the video?"

"I already told you. Sound was bad on most of it and we just translated a fragment." I showed him the transcript on my PDA. "September 1 is a couple of days from now. Tell me absolutely everything you can."

"The two guys talking during the hunt was an accident. If Hans had heard them, he'd have done something bad to them."

"Who's 'Hans'?"

"The guy leading the hunt. Hans Brucker. He's here at the Hive."

Top flicked me an inquiring look, but I shook it off.

"Who exactly is Otto Wirths? Is he any relation to Eduard Wirths?"

"From Auschwitz? I think so. There are portraits of Eduard Wirths here and at the Deck."

"Where's the Deck and what is it?"

"It's short for the 'Dodecahedron.' That's Alpha and Otto's lab in Arizona. I don't know exactly where. In the desert and mostly underground."

"Alpha . . . he's Cyrus Jakoby?"

"Yes." He looked at Bunny. "Can I have my stone back?"

Bunny glanced at me; I shrugged and nodded. The kid put it back in his pocket.

"Okay, big question now, Kid," I said. "What's the Extinction Wave?"

"I don't know much, but it has something to do with the release of some kind of disease—or maybe a couple of diseases—that's supposed to make all of the . . ." SAM cut a look at Top and then back at me. "Um . . . all of the black people in Africa sick. Really sick. With something that could kill them."

"Just the black Africans?" Top asked.

The Kid flinched when Top addressed him. Top saw it and knew that I did, too. File that away for later.

"Yes. Just the . . . um . . . blacks."

"And it'll be released on September 1?"

"Well . . . yes. That and the other stuff."

I said, "What *other* stuff?"

"Other diseases."

"In Africa?"

SAM shook his head. "All over the place. I heard something about Jews in Louisiana, but I don't know what exactly will happen there, or how they'll be released. That's why I needed help. We have to find out and stop them."

"Yes, we do," I said. "I need you to show me where the computer rooms are and the right labs. I need information and proof."

"Okay."

"Kid," asked Bunny, "why's Otto got such a hard-on for black Africans?"

The boy edged slightly away from Top as if he expected to be hit for what he was about to say.

"You have to understand," he began in a trembling voice. "These are their words, not mine, okay? Otto and Alpha. It's not how I think."

Top smiled his warmest smile. He was the only one of the Echo Team who had kids. "Kid, you're helping us out here. If you were one of *them,* then you wouldn't be here with *us.*"

I liked the way he leaned on the words "them" and "us," and I could see how the subliminal hooks softened the Kid.

SAM nodded.

"Otto and Alpha always separate people into three groups. There's the Family, the white race, and the, um . . . mud people." He looked at Top as if expecting the genial smile to melt, but Top gave him a nod and a light pat on the shoulder.

"Yeah, Kid, I've heard that sort of thing before. Heard worse. Bet you have, too . . . living here with people like that."

SAM's eyes filled with tears and he looked down at his shoes. "A lot worse," he said softly. "Heard and seen. You don't understand . . . you don't know."

"Then show us, SAM," Top said. "Show us what we need to see so that we can stop this."

"It's all in the computer rooms."

"Take us there," I said.

SAM looked desperate and he turned back toward the New Men. "You're going to help them, aren't you?"

"Those records are first priority."

"But you *will* help them?"

I nodded. "Yeah, Kid . . . we're going to help them. Bet on it."

SAM searched my eyes for a lie and didn't find one.

Tears rolled down his bruised and bloody face, but eventually he nodded. "Okay, then I'll take you to the computers."

He turned back to the waiting New Men.

"Downtime!" he cried, and immediately the New Men fell out of line and shuffled back to their cots and chairs and the wretched reality of their lives. Only the one female lingered. Once more she raised her head and stared at SAM. Then she touched her face with a finger and drew it to one side as if she was wiping away a tear. SAM stared at her and then did the same motion.

When he led the way out of the room SAM was sobbing.

Chapter Eighty-Nine

The Hive
Sunday, August 29, 4:14 P.M.
Time Remaining on the Extinction Clock: 67 hours, 46 minutes E.S.T.

We found the computer room without incident, but there was a nasty surprise inside.

The computers were slag.

Every last one of them. Rows of networked supercomputers leaked oily smoke. Puddles of melted plastic and silicon had formed around each one.

"Son of a *bitch*," growled Bunny. He slipped a prybar from his pack and forced open the front panel on one unit, but the insides were a melted mass that looked like a surreal sculpture.

Top poked at the melted goo. It was still soft and hot.

"This just happened. We missed it by a couple of minutes."

No one said anything, but we were all aware that while we were in the New Men barracks we could have been here. *Should* have been here. A few minutes might have changed everything.

"What's the call, Cap'n?" asked Top quietly.

"We better hope we can find some disks or paper records," I said. "And I mean *now*. You two work on that."

"Where you going, boss?"

"I want to go have a talk with our boy Carteret."

"He won't help you," said SAM. "And you can't threaten him. He's a mercenary. He's really tough."

"Then I'll have to ask him real nice," I said with a smile.

I headed out alone, watchful for guards and tiger-hounds and any other bit of nastiness that the Hive might have to throw at me, but the halls were empty. My heart was sick at the thought of losing all that computer data. If that meant that we wouldn't be able to stop the release of a pathogen designed for ethnic genocide . . .

God, I didn't even want to think about that.

Chapter Ninety

Tactical Operations Center
Sunday, August 29, 4:27 P.M.
Time Remaining on the Extinction Clock: 67 hours, 33 minutes

"Copy that, Cowboy," Church said. "Deacon out."

Church leaned back in his chair and pursed his lips. Grace, Bug, and Dr. Hu surrounded him, each of them waiting to learn what had happened down in Costa Rica.

"Every time I think we have a handle on the definition

of evil," Church said, almost to himself, "someone comes along to prove that we're shortsighted."

"As a conversational opener," Bug said, "that makes me want to run and hide."

"The computers at the Costa Rica facility have been destroyed. Some form of thermite-based fail-safe device. Captain Ledger thinks it was remote detonated. However, Echo Team has found some paper records and a handful of flash drives and disks. There was also one laptop that wasn't networked in and it did not receive the self-destruct code, so we may get lucky there."

"That's something," said Grace.

But Church shook his head. "At first glance all that Captain Ledger has found are references to the Extinction Wave, and the date, but most of the paper records are coded and we don't have the code key. Without that we don't know how many pathogens, their exact names and strains, or any information to tell us where, how, and by whom they will be released. Africa is a big continent."

"Effing hell." Grace punched Bug on the shoulder. "I thought your lot were supposed to be able to crack any bloody code."

"First . . . *ow!*" he said. "Yeah, given time we can crack it. But time's not our friend here. I got all forty of my guys—here and at the Hangar—on this thing. Plus we're having to scan in tens of thousands of pages, and the stuff in Costa Rica will have to be scanned. I think we might even be dealing with several different codes. I've seen that sort of thing before, where there are individual codes for different aspects of an operation. Whoever set this is up is good."

"Better than you?"

Bug didn't rise to the bait. "Maybe. But I have better

toys, so I'll crack it. Big question is whether we crack it in time to do any good. Be nice to find the code key, or—if there are multiple interrelated codes—a master code key."

"Birds from the *Ark Royal* should be there soon," Grace said. "We can prevail upon them to get that material here as fast as possible."

"True," Bug said, "but it's already August 29 and the Extinction Wave is set for September 1. We not only need to break the code; we need to devise a response and then put it into place."

"We should probably bring World Health and the CDC into it now," said Hu. "And CERT, National Institutes for Health . . . a few others."

Church nodded. "Yes, but carefully. We don't know if any of those organizations have been compromised."

Grace studied him. "I have a feeling that there's more. Care to drop the other shoe?"

Church nodded. "This, perhaps more than anything, will give you a window into the souls of the people we're up against."

He told them about the New Men.

Chapter Ninety-One

The Hive
Sunday, August 29, 4:46 P.M.
Time Remaining on the Extinction Clock: 67 hours,
14 minutes E.S.T.

I found Carteret where we'd left him. He was awake and furious and had wriggled his way across the floor and had rolled onto his back so that he could kick open the door to the New Men's barracks.

"Come on, you slope-headed fuckers!" he screamed. "Come out here and cut me loose."

I came up quietly and saw through the small door glass that several of the New Men were indeed shambling toward his cries. Even now, even after he'd brutalized them and tried to exterminate them, they were obeying the conditioning that had removed all traces of free will. It made me furious. If I didn't need answers, I think I might have just slit Carteret's throat and called it a job well done.

Instead I grabbed him by the plastic band holding his ankles together and dragged him away from the door.

"Hey!" he yelled. "What the bloody 'ell do you think you're playing at?"

"Shut the fuck up," I said quietly. I went back to the door, opened it, and called, "Downtime!"

The single word burned like acid on my tongue, and the sight of the New Men slowing to a confused stop, then turning without question and heading back to their cots made me heartsick. Carteret was still yelling when I turned back to him, but the look on my face quieted him for a moment.

I dragged him by the heels past the dead or unconscious bodies of the other guards and into an adjoining room, then closed the door.

"Who the bloody hell are you?" he demanded.

I flicked the blade on my Rapid Response knife and knelt over him.

"Steady on, mate," he said quickly. "Let's not do something we both regret."

I held one finger to my lips. "Shhhhh."

With two quick flicks of the knife I cut his plastic bonds. As I cut the bands on his wrists I saw that he had numbers tattooed on the back of each hand: 88 on his left and 198 on his right. I recognized the code from some gang work I did while on the cops. *H* was the eighth letter of the alphabet, so 88 stood for "HH." Shorthand for "Heil Hitler." The other one broke down to "SH." "Sieg Heil." Our friend Carteret was a neo-Nazi. No surprise, but it made what I was going to do a little easier.

"Get up," I said as I rose and backed away. I laid the knife on a table.

He got slowly and warily to his feet, rubbing his wrists and studying me, but I could see the effort he put into keeping his eyes from flicking toward the knife.

"You're a Yank," he said.

"You're a genius," I said.

"You working for the Twins?"

I said nothing.

"No . . . you look the military type. You're Special Forces, am I right?"

I said nothing.

"I did my time in the service. Don't suppose you'd like to look the other way while I scarper? Little professional courtesy?"

"Doesn't seem likely. What I'd rather do," I said, "is beat some answers out of you. How's that sound for an afternoon's entertainment?"

He sneered. "This is a private facility, mate, and we're in international waters. Check the map; we're three miles outside of Costa Rican—"

"Which means no one's watching, Sparky."

"You think you're going to strong-arm me? You'd better have a lot more than a knife."

"I have what I need."

He tried a different tack. "I thought you Yanks didn't do torture anymore."

"Torture is something you do to the helpless. Like the stuff you did to those New Men."

"Boo-fucking-hoo, mate. They ain't even people."

"Not all that sure you are," I said.

"Arrest me or whatever, but I'm not saying a bloody word."

I slapped him across the face. It was fast and hard, but I was going for shock rather than damage. He blinked in total surprise. Slaps hurt so much because the palm strikes so many square inches of face and all those facial nerve endings cry out in surprise.

He put his hands up.

I faked with my right and slapped him with my left. Carteret backed up a step. He was surprised by the speed but more so by the sting. No matter how tough you are, there is a certain primitive reaction to being slapped that brings out the essential child self. The eyes start to tear, and that sparks certain emotional reactions that are not necessarily valid but almost impossible to control.

I smiled and moved toward him, slow and steady. He threw a head cracker of a hook punch. He was pretty good. Nice pivot, good lift of the heel to put mass into the blow.

I kept my smile in place as I slipped it and slapped him right-handed.

Carteret reeled back, caught himself, and tried to rush me, but I stopped him with a nonthrusting flat loot on his upper thigh. It's like running into one of those half doors. It stopped his lower body and made him tilt forward farther and faster than expected. I slapped him with my left, blocked a combination, and slapped him with my right.

His cheeks glowed like hot apples. All those nerve endings were screaming at him.

In other circumstances Carteret would probably be a formidable fighter and I usually don't screw around like this, but I needed to make a point. And it's at times like this that I'm glad I study jujutsu rather than karate or tae kwon do. No slight on those other martial arts—after all, Top's a karate expert and he can deconstruct an opponent like nobody's business—but I wasn't trying to destroy Carteret. I wanted to defeat him. Break him. Jujutsu is all about controlling an opponent. Evading, destabilizing, using mass and motion against the attacker. It has roots in grappling arts of ancient China and India coupled with the Japanese dedication to economy of motion.

When Carteret rushed me again I parried his outstretched arm to one side and shifted out of the path of his incoming mass. As I did so, I lightly swept his lead leg just as he was stepping down toward me. It made him stumble into an awkward step and collapse into a clumsy sprawl. He immediately tried to right himself, but his arms were pinwheeling for balance, so I reached between them and slapped him again.

He was panting now, eyes wide and wet, chest heaving with the runaway rage of complete frustration. Once he was upright he tried to kick me with a vicious Muay Thai leg sweep that would have broken my knee had it landed. I checked with with the flat of my shoe while I reached out with both hands and swatted down his guard. I slapped him fast left-right-left.

"Stand and fight!" he screamed, and his voice broke mid-shout.

I kept smiling.

"Tell you what . . . I'll let you hit me. How's that? Just to make it fair." I patted my gut.

"Fuck you!" Spit flew from from his lips as he snarled, but he also took the opening and threw everything he had into an uppercut that was probably his favorite deal closer. I sucked my gut back and shifted ever so slightly with bent knees so that only some of the impact hit my tensed abs, but most of the real force was defused. I knew that it wouldn't feel that way to him. In fact, he'd feel the firmness of contact, feel the shock of the impact in his knuckles and wrist. It simply wasn't anywhere near as hard as he thought it was. I learned that trick from a West Baltimore boxer named Little Charlie Brown. Hell of a sweet trick. The guy slams you one and he's convinced that he nailed you, but aside from some sting you aren't hurt.

I slapped Carteret across the face and stepped back, lightly patting my gut. I put a look of amused disappointment on my face. If I'd used my fist and beaten him to a pulp he would have had a totally different reaction. That was big pain; that was a warrior being defeated in battle. He would have manned up and endured and stonewalled. This was different. It made him a different person because it disallowed anything connected to his adult strength.

Down on the primal level, in the logic centers of the lizard brain, he knew he could not beat me. He believed that he couldn't hurt me. He'd given me his best and it hadn't even put a twitch on my mouth. Carteret's face was a mask of pain. His subconscious mind kept scrambling to assign emotional cause to the tears in his eyes. I could see the tension grow in his face but leak out of his muscles; his shoulders began to slump.

I slapped him again. Quick and light, like a period at the end of a sentence.

"You're all alone out here," I said.

He tried to slide past me toward the door. I shifted into his path, faked him out, and slapped him with my right. He made an attempt at a block, but it was weak—he was already telling himself that it wouldn't work.

"And you're going to tell me everything I want to know."

He looked past me at the knife lying on the table. He lunged for it. I pivoted off of his lunge and used my turning hip to send him crashing into the wall. While he was getting to his feet I folded the knife and put it in my pocket. Then I kick-faked him and slapped his right and left cheeks.

Tears were streaming down his face. The skin on his cheeks was a ferocious red.

"The people you work for can't help you."

Another slap.

"And they'll never know you told me."

Slap.

"But it's the only chance you have left."

Slap.

"Stop it!" he said, but his voice was as broken as his spirit.

Slap. A bit harder, sending a message about insubordination. Carteret collapsed against the wall. He tried to push himself off. I moved to slap him again and his knees buckled. He slid down the wall, shaking his head, weeping openly now.

I stood over him, within reach, the dare implied in my distance to him, but my smile was the promise of what would happen if he tried and failed.

He didn't try. His cheeks were so raw there were drops of blood coming from his pores. It looked like he was weeping blood.

I stood there. "Look at me."

He shook his head.

"Look at me," I said more forcefully, putting terrible promise in the words.

Slowly, warily, he raised his head. I would like to think that at that moment he was taking personal inventory of the things he'd done, of the abuse he'd heaped upon the helpless New Men. That would be sweet, but this wasn't a TV movie. All he cared about was whether he could save his own ass—from the immediacy of further harm and ultimately from whatever kind of punishment I chose to inflict. He was using what wits he had to sort through his options. How to spin this. How to survive the moment. How to spin a deal.

"I want immunity," he said. I don't know what court he thought would grant it. He was right; these were international waters. Maybe he was afraid I'd turn him over to the Costa Ricans, or take him back to the states, or maybe put him in the dock in some world court. It didn't matter. He wanted something that he thought would save him, and in exchange I knew he'd tell me everything.

"I want immunity," he said again. "Or I won't tell you anything."

"Sure," I lied.

Interlude

Conrad Veder was unhappy.

The private jet was luxurious, the food excellent, the cabin service first rate, but he was not pleased. His contact, DaCosta, had reached out to Veder using a private number to a disposable phone that he carried for single-use communication.

"There's been a change of plans," said DaCosta.

"What change?"

"My client would like you to put your current assignment on hold."

"Why?"

"He didn't tell me."

"This is irregular," said Veder.

"I know. But he was insistent."

"Does that mean the contract is canceled?"

"Canceled?" DaCosta sounded surprised. "No. No, not at all. Apparently there is another matter he would like to discuss with you. A side job."

"And you don't know what it is."

"No. He said he would like to discuss it with you."

"I can give you a phone number—"

"No . . . he wants to discuss it with you face-to-face."

"I don't do face-to-face. You know that."

"I told him."

"Then why are we having this conversation?"

"He told me to say that he will provide a bonus equal to half the agreed price of the current contract if you meet with him."

That was three and a half million dollars. Even so, Veder said, "No."

"He said that he would wire the money to your account *before* the meeting."

Veder said nothing.

"And he said to tell you that if you accept the side job, he will double the entire amount of the original contract."

Veder said nothing.

"On top of the meeting bonus."

Veder, for all of his deep-rooted calm, felt a flutter in his chest. That would mean that this entire job would net seventeen and a half million dollars. He thought about that for a long minute, and DaCosta waited him out.

"Where and when?"

"He'll send a private jet." DaCosta told Veder the location and time.

"You know I'll assess the situation," Veder said. "If this is a trick or a trap, then I'll walk away."

"My client knows that."

"And I'll hold you responsible for setting me up."

This time DaCosta said nothing for almost thirty seconds.

"It's not a setup. Check with your bank in thirty minutes. The money will have been wire transferred."

Veder said nothing.

"Are you there?" DaCosta asked.

"How do I know that this will even *be* the client?"

"He told me that you'd ask. He said that if you did I was to say this: you are needed in the West."

Veder said nothing. It was the right code. The client

had to be either Otto Wirths or Cyrus Jakoby. Veder had already determined that they were the ones who had been paying him to assassinate the remaining members of the List. They were the only people—apart from Church and the woman named Aunt Sallie—who knew about the Brotherhood of the Scythe and of his code name: West.

Veder did not like it. It meant stepping out of the antiseptic world of clean kills with no emotional connection and back into the muddier world of politics and idealism. Veder held both in contempt. Thirty years ago he had been recruited into the Brotherhood for his skills, and back then he was susceptible to idealistic rhetoric and flattery. The Brotherhood was to be the world's most deadly alliance—the four greatest living assassins. It had been done with the ostentatious ritualism of the old Nazi Thule Society. The members of the Brotherhood wore masks when they met. They swore blood oaths. They promised fealty to the Cabal and all it stood for.

How silly, he thought. He was privately embarrassed to have been coaxed into the group, though admittedly they had provided great training, excellent intelligence, and lots of money. And in a very real way they had made him the man he was, because as the List systematically dismantled the Cabal, Veder had learned habits of caution that became the framework for the rest of his life.

Since then he had intentionally distanced himself from any connection to political or social agendas. He did not like being drawn back into it now.

But the money . . .

Veder was detached enough to realize that Wirths and Jakoby were using money now in exactly the way that they had used idealism and flattery back then. It was trickery and manipulation.

What made Veder the most unhappy as he sipped green tea in luxurious comfort aboard the private jet was that the manipulation worked.

Part Four
Monsters

He who fights with monsters must take care lest he thereby become a monster.

—FRIEDRICH NIETZSCHE

Chapter Ninety-Two

Grace Courtland lay naked in my arms. She was gasping as hard as I was. Our bodies were bathed in sweat. The mattress was halfway off the bed and we lay with our heads angled downward to the floor. The sheets were soaked and knotted around us. Somehow we'd lost all of my pillows and the lamp was broken, but the bulb was still lit and it threw light and shadows all over the place.

"Good God . . . ," she said hoarsely.

I was incapable of articulate speech.

Grace propped herself on one elbow. One side of her face was as bright as a flame from the shadeless lightbulb, the other side completely in shadow. She looked at me for a long time without speaking. I closed my eyes. Finally she bent and kissed my chest, my throat, my lips. Very softly, like a ghost.

"Joe," she said quietly. "Joe . . . are you awake?"

"Yes."

"Was it terrible?"

I knew what she meant. After I'd interrogated Carteret and brought him back to the computer room, we heard more gunfire and the *whump* of explosions. I handcuffed Carteret, and Top, Bunny, and I rushed out to investigate. What we found was indeed terrible. The remaining staff members of the Hive had fled to the far side of the compound. A guard sergeant named Hans Brucker herded them all into a secure room, telling them all that they could seal it and that they'd be safe until Otto sent a rescue team. Once they were all inside, Brucker and two other guards had opened up with machine guns and threw in half a dozen grenades before slamming the doors. There were no survivors. No one who could talk, no one who could help us.

Brucker then shot the two other guards and put his pistol in his mouth and blew the back of his own head off.

It was insane.

It was also confusing, because Brucker was clearly the man who had led the unicorn hunt. Despite what Church had thought, it wasn't Haeckel. When I told Church this via commlink he ordered me to scan the man's fingerprints.

They matched Haeckel.

No one had figured that out yet.

Shortly after that the Brits arrived and we headed back to the states with what records we had, with SAM, and with Carteret. The remaining six tiger-hounds were gunned down by soldiers from the *Ark Royal*. The New Men were gathered up and brought aboard the carrier, but they were so terrified that several of them collapsed. One died of a heart attack. The ship's doctor ultimately had to sedate them all, and the incident left the crew of the *Ark Royal* badly shaken.

Everyone else at the Hive was dead.

It had been terrible indeed.

"It was bad," I said.

"There are so many monsters . . . and we keep hunting them down." She laid her cheek against mine. "What if we can't beat them this time?"

"We will."

"What if we can't? What if we fail?" Her voice was small in the semi-darkness. "What if we fall?"

"If you fall, I'll be there to pick you up. If I fall, you'll be there for me. That's the way this works."

"And if we both fall?"

"Then someone else will have to step in and step up."

She was silent a long time. It was a pointless conversation and we both knew it. The kind of convoluted puzzle that the mind plays with in the dark, when pretenses and defenses are down. There was no one else on earth with whom Grace Courtland could ever have had this conversation. Same with me. There are some things too deep, too personal, to even share with Rudy.

I wrapped my arms around her and pulled her tight.

"One way or another, Grace," I said, "we'll get through it. With what we got from Carteret and the files we brought back from the Hive, Bug thinks that he'll crack this in no time. Maybe even by morning. And then we'll strap on the tarnished armor, take up our battered old broadswords, give a hearty 'tallyho' and head off to slay some dragons."

"Monsters," she corrected.

"Monsters," I agreed.

We lay there on the slanting mattress, the sweat of passion cooling on our naked skin, and listened to the sound of our breathing becoming slower and slower. I reached over and pulled the plug on the lamp and we were instantly cocooned in velvety darkness. We lay like that for a long time. I thought Grace had drifted off to sleep when she whispered to me.

"I'm sorry," she said.

I turned my head toward her even though she was invisible in the darkness. "Sorry? For what?"

She didn't answer at first. Then, "I love you, Joe."

Before I could answer her hand found my mouth and she pressed a finger to my lips.

"Please," she said, "please don't say anything."

But I did say something.

I said, "I love you, Grace."

We said nothing else. The meaning and the price of those words were too apparent, and they filled the darkness around us and the darkness in our hearts. The battlefield is no place to fall in love. It makes you vulnerable; it tilts back your head and bares your throat. It didn't need to be said.

I just hoped—perhaps prayed—that the monsters didn't hear our whispered words.

Chapter Ninety-Three

The Dragon Factory
Monday, August 30, 5:02 A.M.
Time Remaining on the Extinction Clock: 54 hours,
58 minutes E.S.T.

Hecate and Paris lay entwined on the bed they had shared for ten years. The young black woman they had enjoyed lay between them, her chocolate skin in luxuriant contrast to the milky whiteness of theirs. The woman lay with her head on Paris's arm, but she faced Hecate and her dark hand rested on Hecate's flawless flat stomach.

Paris and the girl were asleep, but Hecate lay awake long into the night. Her blue eyes were open, fixed on the infinity of stars that she could see through the wide glass dome above their bed. The endless rolling of the waves on the beach outside was like the steady breathing of the slumbering world. In this moment Hecate was at peace. Her needs met, her appetites satiated, her furies calmed.

Except for one thing. Except for a small niggling item that was like a splinter in her mind.

Six hours ago she had finally let Paris talk her into inviting Alpha to the Dragon Factory. The conversation had been brief. He had sounded so happy, so flattered that they were inviting him, and he accepted their conditions without reservations because they were small: the windows of the jet would be blacked out. She teased Alpha, saying that he had taught them to always be careful and she was being careful. Alpha agreed to everything.

Too easily.

"He knows," Hecate said to Paris after the call was ended.

"He doesn't know," insisted Paris. "He *can't* know."

"He knows."

"No way. If he knew, then he'd never agree to come here, never allow himself to be that much in our power."

"He knows."

"No, sweetie. Alpha doesn't know a damn thing. But he will once he gets here. I can promise you that."

That had been the end of it. Hecate had to accept that Paris was too much of an idiot to recognize the subtle brilliance that made Alpha who and what he was. Not that she knew exactly who and what Alpha was—but she grasped the essence of their father in a way that her brother seemed incapable of managing.

"He knows," she murmured to the infinite stars.

Yet he was coming all the same.

Chapter Ninety-Four

Eighty-two sat in the dark and looked out at the black water of the harbor. He'd never been in Baltimore before. Except for the Deck, he'd never been anywhere in the United States before. He felt strange. Lonely and scared, and alien.

Everyone here had treated him well. His nose was tended to, he was clean and dressed in new clothes: jeans, sneakers, a T-shirt with the logo of a baseball team. They even let him keep his rock. He'd been allowed to eat whatever he wanted. He'd had pizza for the first time in his life, but he wasn't sure if he liked it. They gave him a bedroom that had a TV with cable. He was allowed to watch whatever he wanted.

But he knew that he was a prisoner. No one had used the word, but what other word was there? Before they let him go to his new room they'd taken his fingerprints and samples of hair and blood and swabs from inside his cheek. They asked him to pee in a cup. It wasn't all that different from what the scientists at the Hive did, though these people smiled more and said "please" and "thank you." But they weren't really asking his permission to do their tests.

The night was long and he didn't want to sleep. The big man who called himself Cowboy had promised that the New Men were being taken care of, but nobody explained what that meant. All Eighty-two knew was that ships from the British and American navies had converged on the island. Beyond that, he knew nothing and no one would tell him anything about what was being done to the New Men. He never saw the female again, not after Cowboy had rescued him.

Eighty-two felt more alone than he had ever been.

How strange it was, he thought, that he felt more alone, more alien, more apart, here in this place, here among the "good guys," than he ever had before. He realized bleakly that he no longer had a place. He could not go home again even if he wanted to, which of course he did not, and he certainly didn't belong here. He belonged nowhere.

He was no one.

The darkness stretched on forever before him.

Chapter Ninety-Five

The Warehouse, Baltimore, Maryland
Monday, August 30, 5:04 A.M.
Time Remaining on the Extinction Clock: 54 hours, 56 minutes

Mr. Church sat behind his desk. He hadn't moved at all in over half an hour. His tea was cold, his plate of cookies untouched.

On his desk were three reports, each laid out neatly side by side.

On the left was the coroner's report on Gunnar Haeckel that included DNA, blood type, body measurements, and a fingerprint ten-card. In the middle was a brief report on Hans Brucker that included preliminary information and a fingerprint card. The blood type was a match; the basic body specifications were a match. That was fine. There were a lot of people of that basic size, build, weight, and age with O Positive blood. The troubling thing were the two fingerprint cards. They were identical. Church had ordered the prints scanned and compared again, but the results had not varied. Not even identical twins have matching fingerprints, but these were unquestionably identical.

But it was not the inexplicable match of fingerprints on the two dead men that troubled Mr. Church. For the last half hour he had barely looked at those reports. Instead all of his attention was focused on the brief note he had received from Jerry Spencer, who was now back at the DMS and ensconced in his forensics lab. The note read: "The prints taken from the boy are a perfect match for the unmarked set of prints you forwarded to me. The only difference is size. The unmarked set are larger, consistent with an adult, and there are some minor marks of use such as small scars. However, the arches, loops, and whorls match on all points. Without a doubt these prints come from the same person. There's no chance of a mistake."

When Mr. Church first read that note he called Spencer and confirmed it.

"I thought my note was clear enough," said Spencer. "The prints match, end of story."

But it was by no means the end of the story. It was another chapter in a very old and very twisted story. It painted the world in ugly shades.

Mr. Church finally moved. He selected a cookie and ate it slowly, thoughtfully, thinking about the boy called Eighty-two. The boy who had reached out to him, who had risked his life to try to save millions of people in Africa and to save the lives of the genetically engineered New Men.

Church picked up the boy's fingerprint card and turned it over to study the photograph clipped to the other side. It had been taken during the physical examination of the boy. Church looked into the child's eyes for long minutes, searching for the lie, for the deception, for any hint of the evil that he knew must be there.

Chapter Ninety-Six

The Deck
Monday, August 30, 5:05 A.M.
Time Remaining on Extinction Clock: 54 hours,
55 minutes E.S.T.

"I think she suspects," said Cyrus. He sipped his wine and held the Riesling in his mouth to taste its subtleties.

"About?"

"The Wave. Not that she could know anything with specific knowledge, but I think she suspects that we have some sort of global agenda."

"Of course she suspects," said Otto. "Wouldn't you be disappointed in her if she didn't?"

Cyrus nodded. It was true enough.

"But," said Otto, "she can only be guessing. She can't know."

"No."

"Not like we know."

"No."

"You'll be able to see for yourself when you visit the Dragon Factory tomorrow."

They thought about that for a while, and then they both laughed.

"Are you surprised that they invited me?" asked Cyrus.

"A little."

"Do you think it's a trap?"

"Of course. Our misdirection with the assassins probably only fooled Paris," said Otto. He pursed his lips and added, "Though my guess is that this is a fishing expedition more than anything. She wants to look you in the eye when she talks about the attack. She probably believes that you'll give something away."

Cyrus laughed again. Otto nodded.

"She's very smart, that one," said Cyrus, "but I think we can both agree that she doesn't know me as well as she thinks she does."

"No."

"So . . . a fishing expedition with a trapdoor if she doesn't like what she sees? Is that what you think?"

"More or less. Probably not as rigid as that. Hecate likes wiggle room. If she's not one hundred percent sure that you sent the assassins, then I expect she'll give you some heavily edited version of a tour. Letting you see only what she thinks would appeal to you and perhaps flatter you. She's her father's daughter in that regard."

"No, Otto . . . I think she gets that from you."

Otto shrugged. "I believe that's her plan."

"And if she becomes convinced that I *am* responsible for the assassins? Do you think she'll try to have me killed?"

"No," said Otto. "Not a chance. She may torture you a bit; I think she'd be very happy to do that."

"Let her try."

"As you say. But ultimately I think Hecate would

want you alive. She's smart enough to know that you're smarter. She and Paris have stolen more science then they've pioneered. You, Mr. Cyrus, *are* science. Hecate is too much your daughter to throw away such a valuable resource."

"She'd want you dead, though," Cyrus said.

"Without a doubt. And I would like to think that she's too smart to risk torturing me. She learned the art from me, and she knows that turning it around is something I daresay *I've* pioneered. No . . . if Hecate gets the chance she'll put a bullet in my brain."

"If we let her," said Cyrus.

"If we let her," said Otto.

They smiled and clinked glasses.

They sat in lounge chairs that had been brought outside. All of the Deck's exterior lights had been turned off, and they were miles from any town. There was nothing to mute the jeweled brilliance of the sky. They could even see the creamy flow of the Milky Way.

"Veder is on his way," said Otto. "He'll be here before the Twins' jet arrives for you. Do you want him to accompany you? We can say that he's your valet."

"No. He can go in with the team. But once your Russians have breached the walls I want Veder to find me. I want him protecting me throughout."

"Easy enough."

They lapsed into a longer silence.

Several times Otto looked at Cyrus and opened his mouth to speak, but each time he left his thoughts unsaid. Finally Cyrus smiled and said, "Speak your mind before you drive me crazy. You want to know about the Hive. About how I feel?"

"Yes. We lost so much. . . ."

460   Jonathan Maberry

"We lost nothing that matters, Otto."

"The New Men. The breeding stock . . ."

"The Twins will have them somewhere. They're smart enough to recognize what the New Men are. They would want to experiment with them. Once we take the Dragon Factory we'll get them back. Or we'll get enough of them back so that we can start again."

"And Eighty-two?"

"I don't think the Twins will have killed him. I think he's alive. I *feel* it. If he's at the Dragon Factory and unharmed, I might even show the Twins a degree of mercy."

Otto did not need to ask what Cyrus would do—or to what extremes he would go—if Eighty-two was dead. No amount of pills would be able to control Cyrus if that happened.

But then Cyrus surprised him by saying, "But in the end it doesn't matter."

Otto gave him a sharp look.

"Somehow I feel like we've moved past that," said Cyrus. "As we get closer to the Extinction Wave, so many of the other things are becoming less important."

"The New Men fill a necessary role. A master race needs a slave race."

"Maybe."

"Those are your own words, Mr. Cyrus."

"I know, and I believed them when I said them. But they don't feel as valid now. We're doing a great thing, Otto. We're doing something that has never been done before. Within a year a billion mud people will have died. Within five years—once the second and third Waves have had a chance to reach even the remotest parts of Asia—there will only be a billion people on the planet. When we created the New Men we conceived them as a servant race during an orderly transfer of power. But . . . do you really think things will *be* orderly?"

Otto said nothing.

"I think we have lit a fuse to chaos itself. As the mud people die, the white races will not unify as a single people. You know that as well as I do. That was Hitler's folly, because he believed that whites would naturally form alliances as the dirt races were extinguished. You and I, Otto . . . we're guilty of being caught up in fervor."

"Why this change of heart? Are you doubting our purpose?"

Cyrus laughed. "Good God, no. If anything, I have never felt my resolve and my focus—my mental focus, Otto—to be stronger. With the betrayal of the Twins I feel like blinders have been removed and a bigger, grander picture is spread out before me."

"Are we having an incident, Mr. Cyrus? Should I get your pills?"

"No . . . no, nothing like that. I'm in earnest when I say that I have never been more focused."

"Then what are you saying? I'm old, it's late, and I'm tired, so please tell me in less grandiose terms."

Cyrus nodded. "Fair enough." He sipped his wine and set the glass on the cooling desert sand. "I have been reimagining the world as it will be after the Extinction Wave—*Waves*—have passed. There will be no reemergence of old powers. The Aryan nations will not rise. That was a propaganda that we both believed, and we've believed it for so long that we forgot to think it through; we forgot to allow the ancient dream to evolve even while we evolved our plans as we acquired new science.

The deaths of five billion people will not bring a paradise on earth. It will not create an Aryan utopia."

"Then what will it bring?"

"I told you. Chaos. Mass deaths will bring fear. Fear will inspire suspicion, and suspicion will become war. Our Extinction Wave is going to plunge our world into an age of total global warfare. Nations will fall; empires will collide; the entire planet will be awash in blood."

Otto was staring at him now.

Cyrus looked up at the endless stars.

"We were born in conflict, Otto. Our species. Darwin was right about survival of the fittest. That's what this will become. Evolution through attrition. We will light a furnace in which anything that is weak will be burned to ashes. True to our deepest dreams, Otto . . . only the strong shall survive. It is up to us to ensure that strength is measured by how skillfully the sword of technology is used. But make no mistake, we are about to destroy the world as we know it." He closed his eyes. "And it will be glorious."

Chapter Ninety-Seven

The Warehouse, Baltimore, Maryland
Monday, August 30, 9:14 A.M.
Time Remaining on the Extinction Clock: 50 hours, 46 minutes

When I woke, Grace was gone. She left like a phantom early in the morning. I looked for her, but every time I found her she was busy. Too busy to talk, too busy to make eye contact that lasted longer than a microsecond. It hurt, but I understood it. Those three little words we had whispered to each other in the dark had been like fragmentation grenades tossed into our professional relationship. This morning was like the deck of the *Titanic* twenty minutes after the iceberg.

A pretty hefty dose of depression was settling over me as I made my way to the conference room for my seven o'clock meeting with Church and Dr. Hu.

They were both there. Church studied me for a long moment before greeting me with a wordless nod; Hu didn't bother even looking up from his laptop. I poured a cup of coffee from a pot that smelled like it had been brewing since last month.

"Please tell me we're ready to roll," I said. "I feel a strong need for some recreational violence."

"Switch to decaf," Hu murmured distractedly.

"Have we checked out those New Men? I mean . . . does the Kid's story hold water about them being Neanderthals?"

"Too soon to tell," said Hu. "We're running DNA tests now, but you forgot to bring me a blood sample or bring back a specimen."

"By 'specimen' you better mean a urine sample," I said, "because if you're referring to those people as specimens I'm going to—"

"They aren't people," said Hu. "If they are Neanderthals, then they are not human. No, wait, before you leap over the table and kick my ass, think for a minute. You're going to make the argument that Neanderthals evolved from *Homo erectus* just like we did and therefore common ancestry makes them human. Whereas I can applaud your hippie granola we're-all-one-big-family sensibilities, the fact is that they were distinctly different from modern humans. They may not have even interbred with early humans, and our last common ancestor died out about six hundred and sixty thousand years ago. Besides, the Kid was wrong when he said that they were reclaimed from mitochondrial DNA. The mitochondrion only has a little over sixteen thousand DNA letters that code for thirteen proteins. To reclaim and grow an extinct species you'd need DNA from the nucleus, which has three billion letters that produce more than twenty thousand proteins."

"Who the fuck cares?" I yelled. "They're *people*. They talk; they think; they look like people. . . ."

"I don't know what they are, Ledger, but they're still scientific oddities. Not people."

"Enough," said Church quietly. He looked at me. "The New Men will be transported to a U.S. military facility in Central America."

"You mean an internment camp?"

"No. They will receive medical attention and assessment to determine how we can best integrate them into society, if they can be integrated into society, and with the heavy conditioning and genetic manipulation they've undergone we may have to face the reality that they cannot be successfully integrated into our culture."

"So what will happen to them?"

"Ultimately? I don't know. I've made a strong case on their behalf to the President, and he agrees that this needs to be handled with the utmost care and the greatest concern for their well-being and their rights."

"Rights?" asked Hu. "What rights?"

Church turned to face him and Hu withered under the cold, hard stare. "The President agrees with me that they are to be treated as liberated prisoners of war. Their basic human rights will be addressed first, and at some later point wiser people than us will determine how best to serve their needs." He paused. "Terrible things have been done to these people, and in many ways this is as great a human rights atrocity as the death camps."

"Sure," said Hu. "Fine. Whatever." He went back to work on his laptop, and I drank my coffee and poured another cup.

Hu brightened. "Okay, maybe I got something. . . ."

"Got what?" I asked. "A conscience?"

Church interrupted, "We've had a busy night collating the information from the Hive. We still haven't pinned down the location of the Deck, but Bug thinks that will happen this morning. First Sergeant Sims is already prepping Echo and Alpha teams for a full-out assault. If the facility is in Arizona, then we can get ground support from the L.A. office. Unfortunately, Zebra and X-ray teams are still in Canada. If this morning goes well for them, then they'll close out that matter and we can put them on the ground."

"What about the teams from the Hangar?" The Brooklyn facility had four field teams. Baltimore and L.A. had two each, Denver and Chicago had one. I knew that the Chicago team had been chopped down in a mission two weeks ago that had killed the team leader and four of the six operators. They were vetting new candidates from Delta and the SEALs.

"Tango and Leopard are overseas. Hardball is in the process of moving to Denver to replace Jigsaw. They're on standby."

Unlike traditional branches of the military the DMS didn't use the standard A, B, C code names for all of the teams. They did originally, but as teams were wiped out they were replaced by teams with new names that started with the same letter. If Grace and I ever came up for air we were supposed to start building new B and C teams to replace the original Bravo and Charlie Teams massacred during a major terrorist action in late June.

"We'll also have National Guard support and if necessary a squadron from the Three Hundred and Fifty-fifth Fighter Wing out of Davis-Monthan Air Force Base in Tucson." He measured out a half smile. "We're taking this very seriously, Captain. I had a long talk with the President last night and again this morning. He's put enough assets and resources at our disposal to wage a war."

"That's what this is," I said.

"Yes," he said. "That's definitely what this is."

"Where do we stand with intelligence?"

"Sit and I'll go over it. The full intelligence packet is being downloaded to your PDA, but here are the talking points, and there are some real speed bumps." He tapped a key and the LCD screen behind him showed a picture of the man the boy SAM had identified as Hans Brucker.

"This is Gunnar Haeckel," said Church. He tapped another key and a second photo appeared. It was a scan of an employee ID photograph. "This is Hans Brucker." He hit some keys and two fingerprint ten-cards appeared, one beneath each photo. "Here are their prints. Now watch." He tapped keys and the cards moved together and the computer program corrected the angles of each so that they overlapped. Brief lights flashed every time a loop or whorl aligned. It was like looking at a string of firecrackers. One by one each separate fingerprint image flashed white to indicate that a complete comparison was finished. All ten prints were perfect matches.

"Yeah, you told me that there was a screwup. Someone's screwing with the fingerprint index."

"No," said Church. "These are the correct prints from each man."

Hu looked up finally, grinning. "We're also running a high-speed DNA profile on Brucker. Guess what?"

"You look too pleased with yourself, Doc. This isn't going to be good news, is it?"

"It's about the coolest thing I've seen in a while," Hu said. "What we got here is a new chapter in the second *Star Wars* movie."

"Huh?"

"Second *Star Wars* movie. After *Phantom Menace*, before *Revenge of the Sith*."

It took me a moment to fish through the raw geek data in my brain.

"Oh shit," I said.

"Yep," said Hu, grinning fit to bust. "*Attack of the Clones*!"

"Oh . . . come on. . . ."

"Sadly," said Church, "Dr. Hu is correct." I noticed a little twitch in his voice when he said "Dr."

"Well," I said, "we already have unicorns and tiger-hounds. Why not clones?"

Hu looked a little deflated, as if he expected a bigger reaction from me. Truth was that I'd toyed with that concept on the flight back from Costa Rica, after learning that the fingerprints matched. I'd dismissed it mostly because I didn't want to believe it.

"We have any aliens or crashed UFOs?" I asked.

"Not at the moment," Church said dryly.

"Okay, then what about the Extinction Wave? What do we know about that?"

"That's the real problem," said Church. "Doctor?"

Hu said, "It looks like our mad scientists have been trying to take diseases that are normally genetic—meaning passed down through bloodlines—"

"I know what 'genetic' means," I said.

He sniffed. "They've been trying to take genetic diseases and turn them into viruses. It's wacky and way out on the cutting edge. Essentially they're rebuilding the DNA of certain viruses to include the genes that code for Tay-Sachs, sickle-cell, Down's syndrome, cystic fibrosis, certain types of cancer . . . that sort of thing."

"So this is the Cabal," I said. "This was what they were working on during the Cold War days."

"Definitely the same agenda," said Church, "and some of the same players."

"The difference," Hu said, "is now they can actually do this stuff. They've cracked the process for turning genetic diseases into communicable pathogens."

"And the Extinction Wave is going to be a coordinated release of these pathogens?" I asked.

"Yes," said Church.

"How the hell do we stop them?"

"That's what you're going to find out for us when you raid the Deck. We have a glimmer of hope—"

"Not much of a glimmer," Hu cut in, but Church ignored him.

"—in that we found several matching lists of the countries and regions where the pathogens will be released."

"That's great! We can warn—"

"I've also been on the phone with the State Department. Embassies in each country have already been put on standby. There's an issue of delicacy here," Church said. "We have to keep our awareness of this under the radar until we've taken down the Deck and the people responsible. We can't risk a leak that might lead to this new Cabal going dark and starting up again at a later date and in new locations."

I nodded.

"From everything we've read," Hu said, "there's a specific release code that needs to be sent out. Your dancing partner, Carteret, said that the release code was programmed into a trigger device that is always kept by either Otto Wirths or Cyrus Jakoby. He said he thinks it's a small device about the size of a flash drive but with a six-digit keypad on it."

"He didn't say any of that to me," I said.

Church adjusted his glasses. "He told me," he said. "He was quite willing to unburden his soul."

"What did you do to him?"

Church ate a cookie and didn't answer.

Hu said, "So we have to get to Wirths or Jakoby and get that trigger device before the code is sent to agents around the world who would then release the pathogens."

"Only that? Swell, I'll see if I can work it into my day," I said sourly. I reached over and took a cookie from Church's plate. "We're going to have to go in quietly. Otherwise, they'll just trigger the device at the first sign of an invasion. Quiet infils take time to set up, and I can hear that frigging clock ticking."

"I have an idea about that," said Hu. "This trigger device probably *is* a flash drive. A device of the kind Carteret described isn't big enough to have a satellite uplink. It probably doesn't have any kind of transmitter. I asked Bug about this. He agrees that the trigger device probably needs to be plugged into a USB port and then the code sent out via the Internet. It's the smartest way to do it, and it would allow for individual codes for each launch."

"Okay, so what's the plan?"

"An EMP," he said. "Right before you rush the place, or maybe after you're inside, but before you start going all Jack Bauer on everyone, we pop an E-bomb on them."

"What the hell's that?"

"An electromagnetic bomb," he said. "Very cool stuff. It's a bomb that creates an electromagnetic pulse. It won't kill people, but the EMP fries anything electrical and should wipe out their computer systems. Unless they're ruggedized . . . but that's a risk."

"We have this stuff?"

"The Navy was playing with them during the first Gulf War," said Church. "And we used one to take out Iraqi TV during the 2003 invasion. If we can locate the deck I can arrange to have an E-bomb dropped."

"Friend in the industry?" I asked.

"Friend in the industry," he agreed.

"Then that's our edge," I said. I stood up and reached across the table to Hu. "Nice work, Doc."

He looked at my hand as if I was offering to beat him to death with it. After a few seconds' hesitation he took my hand and shook it.

"What about the Jakoby family?" I asked. "The Twins. SAM said that they were involved. He told me that they were the ones who genetically engineered the unicorn for the hunt and they treat Cyrus as if he's their prisoner rather than their father. SAM doesn't know them that well, but he said that they have a lab somewhere and that Cyrus has been trying to find it for years. The Twins call their lab the Dragon Factory."

"Wonder if they've engineered a dragon?" Hu mused.

"There was nothing in the recovered records that gives any indication of the location of the Dragon Factory," Church said. "And MindReader has not been able to pin down a recent location for either Paris or Hecate Jakoby. They were last seen at an art show in London a week ago. We have nine of their known residences under surveillance by police in four countries. At this moment, beyond providing animals for the hunts we don't know the scale or depth of their involvement. We're poised to seize all of their known holdings and assets, however, but that move won't be made until we're sure it won't interfere with our attempts to find that trigger device."

"And their dad?"

"There are no photos of Cyrus Jakoby anywhere. No personal details of any kind other than when the Twins mentioned him in passing during press interviews. If he's being kept as a prisoner, then it might explain why he's so conspicuously off the radar. There was a sensational news story about the birth of the Twins, but none of the papers carried photos of the father."

"Sounds like he doesn't want his face publicly known," I said. "That squares with the assumption that 'Jakoby' is not his real name. Could be anything from a drug lord on the lam to someone in witness protection."

"It covers too much ground for easy speculation. Bottom line is that we don't know who he is, and it is remarkable that MindReader cannot dig up a single piece of verification on him."

"If he's tied to the Cabal, could someone have used that old system—"

"Pangaea," he supplied.

"—to erase records of him?"

"Yes. And considering the connections to the Cabal that already exist in this case I think that's what has happened."

"How about Otto Wirths?"

"Same thing. Nothing. The names are probably aliases. However, there is another possible tie to the death camps. Eduard Wirths, the senior medical officer at Auschwitz, was nicknamed 'Otto' as a child. Some of his close adult friends still called him that, though in all the official records he went by Eduard."

"So, you're thinking that Otto is what? Son, grandson? Named after Eduard's nickname?"

"It's worth considering."

Hu said, "Or he could be a clone of Eduard Wirths. Hey, don't look at me like that, Ledger. If we're playing with clones, then we have to factor them into all of this. And it's been thought of before. You know, *The Boys from Brazil*. Ira Levin book. Movie with Gregory Peck—"

"They were cloning Hitler."

"Why not? Maybe someone's cloning the whole upper echelon of the Nazi Party. Or a whole army of Hitlers!"

"Don't even joke," I said.

"Okay, but if we run into an army of short guys with toothbrush mustaches and undescended testicles don't say I didn't warn you."

I shook my head and turned to Church. "How's the Kid?"

Church did not answer right away. "We're doing some additional testing."

"I want him to go with me when we raid the Deck."

"Why?"

"He used to live there. We don't have time to learn the layout and intricacies on our own. I don't like taking a kid into a combat situation, God knows, but we're short on advantages."

Church nodded. "We can wire you with a camera and have the boy online with you from the TOC. But he doesn't go into the field." He paused. "I don't entirely trust the boy," he said.

"Why the hell not? If it wasn't for him we wouldn't be *anywhere* with this."

"I'm sensible of the debt we—and the world—owe him. But his connection to the key players behind this makes me uneasy. We can discuss it more later. Dr. Sanchez is with him at the moment."

"Rudy's back?"

"Yes. He flew in early this morning at my request. He's been with the boy for several hours now. I'd like to hear his assessment on the boy before I—"

The door burst open and Bug rushed in. He was grinning from ear to ear. Grace was a half step behind him. She shot me a quick, excited look, but it had nothing to do with last night.

"We have the buggers," she said. "Captain Smythe from the *Ark Royal* just called. There was a small plane in a hangar at the Hive. One of Smythe's pilots searched the plane and checked the controls and mileage, gas usage—the lot."

Bug said, "I matched the mileage log against traffic control records, using Arizona as a probable location. I

think we found the Deck. It's definitely Arizona. A nowhere spot near Gila Bend, just over the border from
Mexico."

"Never heard of it," said Hu. "Are you sure?"

Bug slapped a satellite printout onto the table. It
showed a small cluster of buildings in the middle of a
desert landscape. Smack dab in the center was a struc-
ture with twelve sides.

"Son of a bitch," Hu said.

I clapped Bug on the shoulder. "Outstanding!"

Church said as he got to his feet, "Captain Ledger,
Major Courtland . . . get your teams ready to roll. Alert
all stations. I'll get on the horn and find us an E-bomb."
His face was hard and colder than I'd ever seen it. "We're
going to war."

Chapter Ninety-Eight

Southwest of Gila Bend, Arizona
Monday, August 30, 5:19 P.M.
Time Remaining on the Extinction Clock: 42 hours,
41 minutes E.S.T.

I was alone in a world of heat shimmers, scorpions, biting flies, and nothing else. The Sonoran Desert may not
be the Sahara, but it has its moments. The temperature
at one o'clock in the afternoon was 122 degrees, and
there was not so much as a wisp of cloud between its
furnace heat and me except camouflaged BDUs and a
thin film of sunscreen. Bunny and Top were in the air-
conditioned back of an FBI van that was painted to look
like a Comcast Cable TV truck out on a dirt road that
led from nowhere to nowhere. Grace and Alpha Team

were somewhere in a Black Hawk helicopter on a mesa fifteen miles to the northwest. Somewhere up in the wild blue yonder was the 358th Fighter Squadron, ready to rain hell and damnation down on the Deck if I gave the word. One of those planes carried an E-bomb. The upside was that we could get one; the downside was that my own electronics might not survive it. The ruggedized unit I had in my pack was supposed to be able to withstand the EMP, but as has been pointed out to me so many times since joining the G, it was a piece of equipment built by the lowest bidder.

A westerly breeze did nothing but push hot air past barrel cactus, water-starved junipers, jimson weed, and tumbleweed. I shimmied through the hard pan to the lip of a ridge that looked down on a small cluster of buildings nestled in a shallow basin between two nondescript ranges of small mountains. According to the Pima County Assessor's Office, the buildings were commercially zoned for "scientific research and development." The IRS told Bug that all appropriate taxes had been paid by Natural White, a company doing research on a cure for "vitiligo," a pigmentation disorder in which melanocytes—the cells that make pigment—in the skin are destroyed. As a result, white patches appear on the skin in different parts of the body.

Very cute. I guess even psychopathic white supremacist assholes can have a sense of humor.

There were several names on the IRS and deed forms, and so far they all checked out as citizens of the United States with no criminal records. With an organization as large as the Cabal, there was probably no shortage of members willing to lend their name to a dummy corporation.

Bug and his team were working on locating all assets and accounts tied to Natural White so they could be frozen when we made our move. Sometimes you do more to cripple the beast by picking its pocket than putting a bullet in it.

I shielded my PDA from the sun and studied the satellite image of the facility. The central building was, as SAM had said, shaped like a dodecahedron. There was a long, flat road to the east of the building that didn't seem to go anywhere but was just about the right width and length to serve as a decent airstrip.

I tapped my earbud.

"Cowboy to Deacon."

"Go for Deacon."

"I'm in position. Ask the Kid if they use the eastern road as a landing strip."

"He says yes. The Twins use it for their Lear and he's seen other small craft land there. He says there is a hidden hangar as well. We're sending you thermal scans. They're enlightening."

My PDA flashed with a new image that showed thermal scans of the basin. The Deck was the hot center point, but there were radiating lines of heat going out in all directions to form a pattern that had nothing to do with what the naked eye could see. One long corridor ran half a mile from the center of the Deck to another hot spot that was nearly as big.

"Ninety percent of this place is underground," I said.

"Yes."

He didn't say anything and I knew that he was giving me a chance to change the mission, to back out or ask for backup. But I didn't want to do that, because we could not risk tipping our hand too soon.

"Wish me luck," I said with as much jauntiness as my nerves could afford. "Keep the Kid handy."

"I'm here, Cowboy," SAM said.

"Roger that. I'm proceeding inside."

I took a small high-power camera and clipped it to my topmost buttonhole. I wasn't wearing full combat rig, no tin pot with a helmet cam. The lapel cam was one of Bug's toys, and it fed images to a satellite that relayed them to the TOC. With that in place, I crept down the side of the basin in an uneven rhythm. If a tumbleweed moved, I moved. When the wind died and everything stood still, so did I. SAM said that he didn't think that there were any motion detectors, but there were cameras. He'd written out a timetable that was impressive bordering on obsessive-compulsive. When I'd commented on the precision, SAM shrugged and said that he had a lot of time to himself, then, after a long contemplative pause, added, "Besides . . . the only way to really be alone in that place is to become invisible, and that means staying out of the camera cycle."

He blushed when he said it, realizing that it sounded weird. Actually, I thought it sounded very sad.

It took forty minutes to make my way to the first camera.

SAM's voice guided me through the security maze.

"The first camera's in the dead cottonwood tree twenty yards ahead and to your right," he said. He and Church were watching my progress via the clip-on camera and a real-time satellite. "Wait for it to swing past, then run. Go straight to the red rocks and stop. Great! Now the next camera is on that pole coming up out of the ground right ahead. It does a three-hundred-and-sixty-degree sweep, so once it moves you can follow it almost all the way around. There's an old wooden picket fence. See it? Drop down behind that and count to fifty, then get up and run to the first building."

I followed every step, moving, stopping, dropping, running, and made it to the building.

"The doors need swipe cards," he said.

"No problem, Kid." I crouched by the door and fished out the first of a bunch of gizmos Dr. Hu and Bug had given me. The unit was the size and shape of a pack of stick gum. I peeled off a plastic strip to expose the adhesive and pressed it gently onto the key-swipe mechanism. Adhesive was safer than magnets in case the unit had a magnetic detector. Downside was that they weren't recoverable, so there was a timer inside that would release a tiny vial of acid in an hour—just enough to fry all of the internal works—the chemical reaction would also neutralize the adhesive and the thing would fall off.

Once the unit was secure, I tapped in a code and waited. The unit was remote linked to MindReader; it raced through possible code combinations while MindReader's stealth software instantly erased all traces. It was designed for keycard systems that trigger alarms if the wrong card or a failed card is used too many times.

"Got it," I heard Bug say over the commlink.

"Copy that," I whispered, and removed a master key-card that had now received from MindReader the proper code. I swiped it and all the little lights above the lock flashed a comforting green. I opened the door and stepped inside, staying low per SAM's instructions.

"I'm in a tractor shed," I said. "No visible doors other than the one I came in and the big garage door."

"There are four operational modes for the Deck," said SAM in way that sounded like he was reciting back a training orientation speech. "The Daily Mode maintains a security-neutral appearance for all exterior buildings, but there are a lot of extra security steps to keep unwanted guests out. All secure entrances to the Deck are closed. There's a Work Mode, which leaves only crucial doors locked, but there would be guards everywhere. Then there's a Visitor Mode, which is what they do when the Twins come—it hides stuff inside as well as out. And last is the Defense Mode. I've never seen that."

"Let's hope we don't. What's next?"

"Do you see the droplight on the other side of the tractor?"

"Roger. It's turned off."

"The security camera is mounted on the ceiling in the left-hand corner. It has a motion sensor, but if you crawl under the tractor and come up on the other side it won't trip."

"I feel like I'm in a video game."

"Yeah, but there's no reset button," said SAM. A sober warning that I took to heart as I slithered under the tractor and crawled out on the far side.

"Reach for the droplight. Press the off button twice. It opens a wall panel with a second keycard. The same key code will open this and the next two doors. Don't try it on the door marked with a white circle."

I did as he instructed and a wall calendar from a tractor company slid up to reveal a recessed space with another keycard. Cute. My master keycard tripped it and a door-sized section of wall slid noiselessly aside to reveal a sophisticated steel security door. I key-coded it and stepped into a large metal cubicle with another security door. There was a line of pegs on the left side on which hung lab coats in various colors.

"The picture's fuzzy, I can't see you," SAM said. "Where are you?"

"Between two security doors."

"Are there jackets on the wall?"

"Lab coats, yes."

"Put on an orange one. That's for the computer maintenance staff. There's like a million of them, and they can go almost anywhere as long as they have the right keycards. No one will look twice at you."

"Works for me."

I slipped into an orange lab coat, but there was nothing I could do about my camo fatigue pants. I clipped the minicamera to the jacket and hoped no one would notice it. If you didn't peer too close at it, the thing looked like a slightly oversized button.

I passed through the next security door and walked a long hallway that fed off into rooms marked: KITCHEN, LAUNDRY, DRY GOODS, and a few others. None of these doors had keycard locks, but there were security cameras mounted at both ends of the hallway. No way to bypass them, but SAM said that it was all about what color lab coat you wore. As I walked, I peeled the adhesive off of another of the code-reader doohickeys, and when I reached the door I surreptitiously pressed it in place.

I faked a sneezing fit and made a show of patting my pockets for a tissue. I pretended to wipe my nose on my sleeve and Bug said, "You're good to go."

I removed the newly recoded master keycard and opened the door.

No problems.

I was inside the Deck now.

"The image feed is back," said SAM. "You're right near a big hallway that runs the length of the upper level. The staff calls it Main Street."

The doorway led to a wide central corridor that was packed with people wearing a rainbow assortment of lab coats and coveralls. Most people ignored me. No one cared about my pants or boots: I saw everything from sandals, to sneakers, to high heels. Several people in orange lab coats passed by and they were the only ones who appeared to notice me, but they gave me nods and went about their business.

Then SAM walked right past me.

I was so surprised I began to say something to him, but I immediately clamped my mouth shut. This boy was at least a year older than SAM. He looked just like him, though. Same gap in his front teeth, same soft chin and dark eyes. I tried to turn the camera his way, but there were too many people.

When the boy was gone I discreetly tapped my earbud. "Hey, SAM . . . I think I just saw your brother."

"I don't have a—," SAM began to say when suddenly there were three long, harsh bleats from an alarm system. Everyone froze in place.

I began to slip under my lab coat for my gun, but then a hugely amplified voice blared from speakers mounted in the ceiling, "The Deck is going into Visitor Mode. Please prepare to receive visitors."

It repeated several times and suddenly everyone was in motion. Wall panels shifted to close off whole wings of the building; scores of staff members filed through hidden doorways that closed behind them so seamlessly it was as if the people had vanished from this reality. The blaring message repeated and repeated.

Then Church's voice was in my ear: "Cowboy . . . there is a small commercial jet inbound to your location."

"I know," I said. "We're about to have visitors."

Chapter Ninety-Nine

The Deck
Monday, August 30, 6:13 P.M.
Time Remaining on the Extinction Clock: 41 hours,
47minutes E.S.T.

Hecate and Paris were all smiles as they stepped down from their jet. Cyrus and Otto were dressed in suits that were ten years out of style, and a stack of suitcases was piled on an electric cart. A tall, austere man in a modern suit stood next to them.

"Alpha!" cried Hecate, and ran to her father. Instead of bowing, she hugged him and buried her face in the side of his neck. Cyrus was momentarily nonplussed, but after a hesitation he hugged his daughter. "Alpha . . . Daddy . . . ," she murmured.

Cyrus looked wide-eyed at Paris, who adjusted his own expression from a glad smile to one of concern. "Alpha . . . ever since we were attacked Hecate's been very upset. So have I, as a matter of fact. If the government is sending black ops teams against us then we're out of our depth. We—"

Hecate cut him off. She had tears in her blue eyes. "We *need* you. Daddy . . . we *need* you."

"I—" Cyrus looked truly at a loss.

"She's right, Alpha," said Paris, stepping close so he could pat Hecate's back. "We're afraid of losing everything. We're . . . well . . . we just don't know what to do. I can't tell you how grateful we are that you're willing to come to the Dragon Factory. We need to know how to make it more secure, and if we have to abandon it . . . then we need your advice on how to preserve our research."

Hecate leaned back from the embrace, staring deep into her father's eyes. "If we have to . . . if you don't think we're safe there . . . can we transfer our data to your computers here? We have to keep it safe."

"We have to keep it in the family," said Paris.

Cyrus looked at Otto, who raised a single eyebrow. The tall man with him wore no expression at all.

"Why . . . certainly," said Cyrus, though his voice was anything but certain.

Hecate threw herself back into Cyrus's arms and wept with obvious relief. Paris closed his eyes as if the weight of the world had been lifted from his shoulders.

"Thank you," he murmured. "Alpha . . . *Father* . . . thank you."

Eventually they climbed aboard the jet.

Otto Wirths and the other man lingered for a moment before following them.

"Those are his children?" the man asked, a note of skepticism in his voice. "Those are the Twins?"

"Yes," said Otto.

"They're more effusive than I expected."

"Aren't they."

"Mr. Jakoby brought me all the way out here because of them?"

Otto wore a smile that did not reach as far as his eyes. "We are being played, Mr. Veder."

Conrad Veder smiled thinly. "No kidding."

They climbed aboard. Once the jet was refueled, it taxied in a circle and took off for the Dragon Factory.

Chapter One Hundred

The Deck
Monday, August 30, 6:14 P.M.
Time Remaining on the Extinction Clock: 41 hours,
46 minutes E.S.T.

"The Deck is in Work Mode," said the voice from the speakers. "All duty personnel return to assigned tasks."

There was a pause and then, "Supervisor protocols are in place."

The doors and hidden panels shifted again and the multicolored swarms of people emerged. I found a men's room and ducked inside. Once I made sure I was alone I said, "What was that all about?"

Church said, "A Learjet owned by White Owl, a dummy company that MindReader traced back to Paris Jakoby, just landed and picked up three passengers. From the satellite image SAM thinks that the passengers were Otto Wirths and Cyrus Jakoby. We didn't get a good angle on the third man."

"Swell. Looks like I came to the wrong party."

"Amazing and Alpha Team are in follow-craft. They'll assess and take the next steps to find the device."

"What about me?"

"Your call. If the Jakobys are heading to the Dragon

Factory, then Amazing will infil and attempt to secure the device. Once she succeeds, the fist of God in the form of three DMS teams and National Guard units will pound the Deck."

It was a crappy set of choices. If I left I still wouldn't catch up to Grace before she caught up to the Jakobys. If I stayed here I might learn something, but I might also get caught.

"Keep SAM on the line and give me a quick tour. I'll see what I can see, and then I want to collect Echo and follow Alpha to the frat party."

"Roger that."

Chapter One Hundred One

In flight
Monday, August 30, 6:36 P.M.
Time Remaining on the Extinction Clock: 41 hours,
24 minutes E.S.T.

Maj. Grace Courtland sat hunched over her laptop watching a white dot move across the satellite image of the southern United States. The dot kept just inside U.S. airspace, cruising fifty miles north of the Mexican border as it crossed Arizona and New Mexico; then it cut across the Texas midlands and out over the Gulf of Mexico south of Houston.

She tapped her commlink. "Bug, have you gotten through to the FAA yet?"

"Just finishing with them now. The jet filed a flight plan for Freeport, Grand Bahama Island. The FAA have records of the same jet making the run twice monthly for the last few years."

"That's it, then. Brilliant, Bug."

Grace sat back and closed her eyes. It was going to be a couple of hours yet until touchdown, and there was nothing much she could do until then. She'd eavesdropped on the command channel while Joe infiltrated the Deck, and her heart had been in her throat the whole time. Partly because of the oppressively huge stakes they were playing for and partly for Joe.

Joe.

Early this morning, after making love, she had told him that she loved him. She'd said the words that she swore that she would never say to anyone as long as she wore a uniform. It was stupid, it was wrong, and it was dangerous.

Later that morning she hadn't said a word to him. She was too embarrassed and too frightened of the damage their pillow talk might reveal in the light of day. And then, of course, everything started happening.

Grace wished she could roll back the clock to this morning so she could take back those words. Or, failing that, to have had the courage to stay all night and talk with him later that morning. Instead she had fled— the one act of cowardice in a life filled with risk taking.

That morning, when she'd said those words, Joe should have given her the pat lecture on the dangers of getting too close to a fellow combatant. It was never smart and it usually worked out to heartbreak of one kind or another, and that included the very real possibility of getting drummed out of the DMS and shipped back to England with a career-ending reprimand in her jacket. She'd never work in covert ops again, not unless she wanted to gallop into battle behind a desk.

She felt sick and stupid for saying those words.

What made it worse . . . so very much worse, was that Joe had said them back.

I love you, Grace.

She could hear the echo of those words as if Joe was whispering them into her ear as her pursuit craft tore through the skies.

I love you, Grace.

"God," she said, and Redman—her second in command—glanced up.

"Major . . . ?"

She shook her head and closed her eyes again.

Chapter One Hundred Two

The Deck
Monday, August 30, 6:40 P.M.
Time Remaining on the Extinction Clock: 41 hours,
20 minutes E.S.T.

I moved through the Deck quickly but casually. I found a clipboard on an unoccupied desk and took it. Every time I saw someone who looked vaguely official I studied the clipboard and mumbled meaningless computer words to myself. Bug must have heard me, because I heard him chuckling in my ear.

SAM steered me through the common areas toward the research centers. His knowledge of the Deck ended there, but that was fine. I wasn't going to stick around very long. The Deck was multileveled and I took a combination of escalators, stairs, and moving walkways to get around. A couple of times I thought I saw SAM again—or the kid who looked like him—but each time there were other people around and I couldn't risk trying to make contact. It was another mystery to be solved later.

I reached a level that was marked: AUTHORIZED PERSONNEL ONLY, which I thought was kind of funny since this was the secret lab of a maniac out to destroy the world. But I guess there's bureaucracy everywhere.

I used another of Bug's sensors to reset my master keycard and then slipped inside the restricted area. Just inside was a glass-enclosed metal walkway that ran along all four sides of a huge room in which sat rows of big tanks in massive hydraulic cradles that rocked them back and forth. The tanks had glass domes with blue lights that filled the room with an eerie glow. There were at least thirty of the tanks connected to computers on the floor and a network of pipes and cables above. I leaned close to the glass and looked down to see a half-dozen technicians in hazmat suits adjusting dials, working at computer stations, or taking readings. There were huge biohazard warning signs everywhere.

"Are you seeing this?" I whispered.

Church said, "Yes." He didn't sound happy. "Walk around and see if you can get a better angle on the tanks."

I moved along, pretending to make notes on my clipboard, until I found a spot that offered the best view of the closest tank.

"Whoa!" It was Dr. Hu and for once he seemed disturbed rather than jazzed by something science related.

"What am I looking at?"

"Something that I've only ever heard talked about but never expected to see," he said. "This setup is like a gigantic version of a vaccine bioreactor. But the scale!"

"Bioreactor?"

"It's a device in which cell culture medium and cells are placed in a sterile synthetic membrane called a Cell-bag, which is then rocked back and forth. The rocking motion induces waves in the cell culture fluid and provides mixing and oxygen transfer. The result is a perfect environment for cell growth. I mean, GE was making these back in the mid-nineties but for a max of like five hundred liters. Those things are the size of . . . they must be able to hold . . ."

" 'Five thousand gallons,' " I said, reading it off of the side of the vat.

"Jesus . . ."

"I kind of doubt they're making vaccines down here," I said. "Could this be how they're mass-producing the pathogens?"

"It . . . could," Hu said hesitantly, "but if so, whoever designed this is heading off into some new areas of production science. That's some scary shit right there."

"Believe me when I tell you, Doc, I'm shaking in my boots."

"Captain Ledger," said Church, "get out of there. We have enough proof to shut this place down once we secure that trigger device. Get out of the building and rendezvous with Echo Team."

"I want Echo Team to provide backup for Alpha when they hit the Dragon Factory."

"That depends on timing. Alpha may not be able to wait until you arrive."

"Copy that. I'm out of here."

I wanted to run, but I had to play my role. I slowly made my way to the exit but then turned and looked back through the glass at the rows of slowly rocking tanks. At the absolute proof that evil existed in the world. Not as a concept, not as an abstraction, but as an irrefutable reality. Right here, brewing in those tanks. And I knew that if the Extinction Wave was set to hit in two days, then the pathogens for that were already gone, already distributed to Africa and God knows where else.

This . . . this was *more* of it. More evil, more danger brewing in a very real sense. Who was next? Who else were these madmen planning to kill? Was it to be all races except for some select few?

God, the rage that burned through my veins was unbearable.

How do you reconcile yourself to a world in which monsters like Cyrus Jakoby can exist? I stared at the handiwork of this man and struggled to grasp the enormity of what he'd done and the horror of what he was on the verge of doing. This man was willing to kill millions—tens of millions—to infect whole populations, to try to eradicate entire races.

How do you fight something like that? Hitler is seventy years in his grave and still the pollution of his dreams taints our modern world. What drives a man like Cyrus Jakoby to keep such an inhuman program going? The technology in this room spoke of enormous intelligence, imagination, and drive. He broke through barriers in genetics, virology, bio-production . . . aspects of science that could have benefited mankind, and why? To destroy? To exterminate people as if they were lice.

Hate. Now that's something I understand. At that moment, standing on the catwalk above the rows of bioreactors, I was filled with a degree of hate that took me beyond heat and into a strange cold space. I turned away and headed for the door. I needed to get out of here and into the air. I needed to be there when the DMS took Jakoby and the rest of the Cabal down, and if it was within my power I was going to see that it was taken down for good this time. Taken down, torn to pieces, and the bits scattered to the winds.

As I walked the halls and climbed the stairs I thought about what we would do if we caught Jakoby alive. How do you punish such as person? A bullet seems so simple. Too easy. A bullet and he dies; he's gone.

Torture?

Man, that was a can of worms. My personal politics are left of center, but I have my hardline moments. A guy like Jakoby, a man willing to slaughter every non-white in Africa . . . I hate to know this about myself, but I know that if I was alone in a room with that bastard I don't think I'd be Mr. Passive. If I could make it last for a year, keeping him in screaming agony, would that offer an adequate redress? When the crime is so vast that it spans decades of time, crosses all national lines, *changes* cultures, and devours the weak and strong alike, then what possible form of punishment could be appropriate? Where is justice in the face of true unalterable evil?

I could use his records, his confession, to launch a holy war against those who embrace the ideas of eugenics, ethnic cleansing, and the master race. I could light that fire—but what chance was there that the resulting firestorm would burn only the guilty? War is madness, and when bullets fly and bombs explode many people use the conflagration to settle personal agendas, or profiteer, or simply play blood games.

No . . . I could not do that.

But I had a better plan. It would bring neither peace

nor closure to the victims of Cyrus Jakoby, but it would do something no bullet or hangman's noose could do. It would *hurt* him.

With those dark thoughts burning in my brain, I made my way carefully out of the Deck, crossed the obstacle course of cameras, and then ran the rest of the way back to where Top and Bunny were waiting.

"The Brits are landing," Top said.

Chapter One Hundred Three

In flight
Tuesday, August 31, 1:27 A.M.
Time Remaining on the Extinction Clock: 34 hours,
33 minutes E.S.T.

"Mr. Church," said Grace, "I think we've found the Dragon Factory."

In Florida, Alpha Team had transferred to a Navy helicopter that was now sitting on the beach of a deserted cay fifteen nautical miles from Dogfish Cay. They were waiting for pickup from the USS *New Mexico*, a Virginia Class submarine that was patrolling these waters. Her team waited in the forward cabin of a large fishing boat owned by the DEA. The captain, an agent two years from retirement, got a "no questions asked" call from his boss and was happy to oblige. All he had to do was sit at anchor and pretend to fish.

"Tell me," Church said. He was at the TOC and had spent an hour on the phone with the President. Church sounded uncharacteristically tired.

"The Jakoby jet landed on Grand Bahama and they transferred to a seaplane which they flew to Dogfish

Cay. There's a dredged harbor and good deep water. The *New Mexico* will bring us to within a mile and we'll go in by water at zero dark thirty."

"Good. Captain Ledger and Echo Team will be in the water about ninety minutes behind you. Do you want to wait for him?"

"There's no time. He did his part at the Hive and in Arizona. I'd like to tear off a piece of this for myself."

"Be careful, Grace," Church said. "Joe had insider information; you don't."

Grace was startled by Church's use of her first name. He rarely did that and she found it both touching and mildly unnerving.

"I'll be careful. And I'll get that sodding trigger device if I have to cut off Cyrus Jakoby's head to do it."

"I'm okay with that scenario," said Church, and disconnected.

She went up on deck and then around to the wheelhouse where the captain was sitting with his feet up and a cold bottle of Coke resting on his stomach. He gestured to the cooler and she fished one out and sat in the co-pilot's seat. The sea was gorgeous, streaked with purple and orange as the sun set with majestic splendor behind a narrow ridge of clouds. Seabirds flew lazily back to land, and water slapped softly against the hull. Grace twisted off the cap and sipped the cold soda.

She said nothing and went into her head to prepare herself for what was to come. Her team was in peak condition and eager for a fight. So was Grace.

The captain cleared his throat.

"You call for a cab, Major?"

"What?"

He nodded to the waters off the port bow where a

huge hulking shape was rising with surprising and eerie silence from the depths. She went out on deck and watched the 377-foot-long vessel rise so that its deck was almost level with the flat ocean. Only the conning tower rose into the twilight air like a giant black monolith. The displaced water from the submarine's ascent rolled the fishing boat, and Grace had to grab a metal rail to keep her balance.

"Big boat," said the DEA agent. "But . . . I'm guessing that it's just my imagination that's making me see an attack submarine out there."

"Twilight over the ocean," said Grace. "It can play strange tricks."

"It surely can." He sipped his Coke. "Major, I don't know what's going on and I probably don't want to know, but your team don't look like trainees and they don't send out brand-new attack subs for just anyone. So . . . I'm not asking for any information, but can you at least tell me if there's something I should worry about?"

Grace considered for a long moment. "Are you a religious man, Captain?"

"When I remember to go to church."

"Then you might want to pretend this is Sunday," she said, "and say a little prayer. The good guys could use a little help tonight."

He nodded and held out his bottle. They clinked and he went back to his chair and pretended he didn't see all the weapons and equipment that were off-loaded from his boat to the waiting sea monster that floated in the darkening waters. Ten minutes later, he was alone aboard his boat and the sun was falling toward the horizon with such a spectacular display of colors that it looked like the whole world was ablaze. For the first time since he'd taken this job out here, he didn't like the look of that sunset. The reds looked like blood, the purples like bruises, and the blacks like death.

He keyed the ignition, fired up the engines, and turned in a wide circle to the northwest, back to Grand Bahama.

Chapter One Hundred Four

The Dragon Factory
Tuesday, August 31, 2:18 A.M.
Time Remaining on the Extinction Clock: 33 hours,
42 minutes E.S.T.

Even though it was the middle of the night, Hecate walked arm-in-arm with her father as she gave him a tour of the facility she and Paris had built. Her brother walked on Cyrus's other side but did not touch his father. Otto drifted behind them. Behind him were two unusual men: the cold and silent Conrad Veder—who had been introduced as a close advisor to Cyrus—and the hulking Berserker, Tonton. Though Veder was a tall man, Tonton towered over him, and reeked of sweat and testosterone.

"Daddy," purred Hecate, "we want to show you what we've done here. I think you'll be so proud of us." Since her emotional outburst at the Deck, Hecate had taken to calling Cyrus Daddy. Where this would normally earn a sharp rebuke, Cyrus seemed entranced by it. Or so Otto thought. All through the flight he had searched Cyrus's face for some sign that he wasn't at all taken in by the fiction of the Twins' newfound and childlike devotion, but Cyrus avoided making eye contact with Otto.

"Certainly, my pet," said Cyrus in a soothing and—

most shocking of all to Otto—a *fatherly* tone. "Let's see what you rascals have cooked up."

Their first stop was the warehouse.

"It's empty," said Otto.

"Yes, it is," said Paris with a proud smile. "The last shipments went out and everything is in place for your advertising campaign. It tickles me that your work is going to be largely funded by the sale of a legitimate product."

Cyrus smiled and nodded. Otto said nothing, but he wondered if the Twins had somehow discovered what was in that water. There had been plenty of time for them to have run DNA and biological tests on the water, but would they have thought to do so? He ran a thin finger along the scar on his face, making sure that Veder could see it. It was a prearranged signal to be extra vigilant. Veder scratched his ear. Message received and understood.

The night was soft and vast, and billions of stars sparkled down on them as they strolled from the dockside warehouse up the flower-lined path to the main facility. The moon had not yet risen, but the compound lights had not been turned on. Instead the path was lighted by flaming tiki torches on poles.

The main entrance of the Dragon Factory had a short flight of stone steps up to a glass front with ten-foot-high double doors. Berserkers in lightweight black BDUs stood at attention at the open doors. Cyrus gave them each a smile but made no comment as he passed inside, but Otto touched Paris's arm.

"These are the GMOs? Your 'Berserkers'?"

Paris nodded. "As is Tonton. These guards are from the second team."

"So, they've been field-tested?"

"Several times."

"And the matter you came to the Deck to discuss?"

"Oh," said Paris, "that's only a factor of fieldwork. During downtime they're quite affable." He gestured for Otto to enter the building. Veder, lingering behind Otto, caught the momentary flicker of a smile on Tonton's brutish face.

Inside the facility, Hecate led them through a series of labs, most of which held nothing new or of much interest to Cyrus, though he continued to smile and nod, as if this was all new and as exciting as a toy store. Several times he pointed to pieces of equipment and asked if he could have one for the Deck.

Hecate promised him everything. Cyrus was extremely pleased.

They passed through the main lab complex and Cyrus suddenly stopped, mouth open in awe at the statue that dominated the center of the room. A caduceus made from an alabaster pillar, hammered gold and jewels. Twin albino dragons coiled around the staff.

"Beautiful . . . ," he murmured.

Hecate and Paris exchanged covert smiles.

"Quite impressive," said Otto with a total absence of reverence. He could have been appraising a broken clamshell on the beach. His eyes were locked on Cyrus and doubt ate at him. Cyrus was unstable at the best of times, and now he seemed entranced by the wonders of the Dragon Factory. *Did the betrayal of the Twins knock something loose in Cyrus's mind?* Otto wondered. It was always a real possibility. Otto carried a pocketful of pills to handle different emotional extremes, but quite frankly, he didn't know which one would be needed here—or if a pill was needed at all.

"And now, Daddy," said Hecate as they stopped before a massive security door guarded by two more Berserkers, "we come to the real heart of the Dragon Factory. The Chamber of Myth. This is where we work our real magic!"

Cyrus clapped his hands.

Hecate placed her hand on a geometry scanner and waited as the laser light read every line, curve, and plane of her palm and fingers. A green light came on and a small card reader slid out of the wall. Hecate reached into the vee of her pale peach blouse and pulled out a swipe card on a lanyard. She swiped the card and heavy locks disengaged with a hydraulic hiss. One of the Berserkers gripped the handle and swung the door open. It was as thick as a bank vault door, but it opened without a sound.

Hecate stepped through and beckoned her father to follow. The whole party moved inside and there they stopped. Even Otto's cynical disdain was momentarily forgotten as they stared around them at the things the Twins had made. At the impossible brought to life.

The room was designed to look like a forest from a fantasy story. The walls were painted with photo-real mountain ranges. Holographic projections of clouds drifted across a sky that could have been painted by Maxfield Parrish. Thousands of exotic plants and trees were arranged on hills sculpted from real rock and soil. On the branch of a nearby tree a winged and feathered serpent crouched, watching them with amber eyes. It was a perfect interpretation of the Quetzalcoatl of Aztec myth. In the distance a pair of snow-white unicorns nibbled at sweetgrass. Several tiny people walked by, none of them taller than two feet. They wore green clothing and had pointed ears. As they passed they tipped their hats to Hecate, who curtsied. There was a gruff sound and the party turned to see a horse trot by, tossing its head haughtily. A pair of golden wings were folded against the horse's muscular flanks.

"Can . . . can that thing fly?"

"Not yet," admitted Paris, "but it's the first specimen in which the wings are fully formed. We have to significantly reduce the muscle density of the horses so we can give them hollow bones. Otherwise it's purely decorative."

Conrad Veder's insect coldness had fled and he stood smiling as a fat European dragon waddled by. It looked like a brontosaur with bat wings and was the size of a dachshund.

Paris smiled at him. "That's a prototype. Arthurian dragon. So far we've been able to make them in miniature. George here is the oldest of six that we have. He's four."

George the dragon trundled over to Paris and bumped his head against Paris's leg until he fished a treat out of his pocket and let the dragon eat it from his palm. "It's a granola snack. High protein and vitamins but with sugar, sesame, and nuts. He loves them, which is why he's so fat. C'mon, shoo, off with you. . . ."

The dragon ambled off, munching his treat.

A larger shape clopped past them on heavy hooves. The lower half was a powerful Clydesdale, but the upper half was a bull-chested man. He shot a frightened glance at the strangers and moved quickly away.

"You have human-animal hybrids?" Otto asked.

"A few," Paris said. "The centaur was one of our first, but he hasn't made the psychological adjustment. He's not a true specimen. There was a lot of surgery involved and extensive pre and postoperative gene therapy. We've sunk a lot of money into that line, but I think it might be a dead end. There are too many problems with genes that code in unexpected ways."

"Have you had any successes with animal-human transgenics? Besides the Berserkers, I mean."

"A few," Hecate said but didn't elaborate. "And quite frankly, they kind of freak out the buyers. People seem to want the animal exotics. Unicorns, miniature griffins, dragons, that sort of thing. The elves and kobolds are popular, though. Now that we're getting word of mouth we've been getting requests for a lot of exotics that we never thought of."

"Such as?" asked Cyrus.

"Oh . . . we've had a dozen requests for Cerberus. We haven't successfully made one, though. We did make a *samjoko*, a three-legged bird, for a Korean buyer. We made a Jersey Devil last year, and we have an order for a *chupacabra*. Gargoyles, too. We get a lot of requests for those."

"This is . . . ," began Veder; then he suddenly remembered where he was and why and left whatever he was going to say unsaid.

Paris smiled at him. "A lot of people are speechless. You should have seen the looks on the faces of a group of buyers from China when we trotted out an actual flying Chinese dragon. It was small, of course, but the buyers were entranced."

Cyrus walked a few steps away from the group and bent down to pat the head of a swan-sized sea serpent that had raised its head from a koi pond. The animal shied back at first, but Cyrus cooed at it until the animal came closer.

"That's our Nessie prototype. Pretty easy design. We want to get them to the size of a horse before we sell them."

"Wonderful," murmured Cyrus. "Absolutely wonderful. . . ."

Hecate beamed. Paris smiled.

Otto and Veder exchanged meaningful looks.

"Your clients are worldwide?" asked Cyrus as he tickled the sea serpent under the chin.

"Yes."

"How unfortunate."

"Sorry . . . ?" asked Hecate.

Cyrus smiled and without turning said, "It's unfortunate because in less than two days you're going to help me kill most of them."

"What?" said Paris.

"Our clients?" asked Hecate.

Cyrus turned his head and the smile he wore was no longer the vapid grin of a father pleased with the antics of his clever children. It was a death's-head grin of such naked malice that the Twins actually took a step backward from him.

"No, my young gods," Cyrus said softly, "at noon tomorrow—you and I—will launch the Extinction Wave. By this time next year I'm afraid most of your clients will be dead."

His hand darted out and caught the sea serpent by its slender throat, and with a vicious twist of his wrist he broke its neck.

"And the dead don't need fucking *toys*."

Chapter One Hundred Five

They moved silently through the night black waters of the North Atlantic. Nine figures in wet suits and tanks, each crouched over the cowling of a K-101 Hydrospeeder that plowed through the water at almost 10 miles an hour. The speeders were not the catalog versions—these new prototypes were being tested by Marine and Navy units in oceans and lakes around the world. Mr. Church had made a call and had a dozen of them flown in and lowered down to the deck of the USS *New Mexico*. Grace was sure that nobody else but Church could have made that happen this fast. The remaining three speeders were left behind on the submarine in case Joe and his team needed them.

Alpha Team set out from the sub thirty minutes after sunset. Divers from the *New Mexico* wanted to go with them and the boat's captain wanted to send them, but Grace made it clear that this was a less-is-more situation.

"But Captain," she added confidentially, "have your lads keep their suits on, because this will probably go from quiet to quite loud sometime this evening. At which point I'd like as much backup as you can send."

"You'll have it," the captain promised. He was an ex-SEAL himself who had gone back to subs when he got too old for special ops. The gleam was there in his eye, and Grace left the sub feeling confident that he wouldn't let her down.

Before she slipped into the water she made two last

calls. The first was to Church for an update on the main wave of close support.

"Major, be advised that there is a lot of boat activity in your vicinity. Watercraft of all kind. We're checking now to see if there's an unusual run of sport fish."

"No problem," she said. "We'll go in under them, but we'll be careful of nets and hooks. How's my backup coming along?"

"Every DMS agent in the continental United States is closing on your twenty, Major," said Church. "In one hour we'll have forty-six field operatives on the island. SEAL teams Five and Six are also inbound and we have twenty operators from Delta if we need them, but they're an hour and ten out. Joe and Echo Team will get there first, but he's still forty minutes behind you. He told me to ask you to save him something to do."

"Bloody Yank," she said, then added, "can I get a secure channel to him before we dive?"

Church hesitated. "How secure a channel?"

From the question, Grace knew for sure that Church was aware of the affair between his two most senior field commanders. She was glad Church wasn't there to read her face. *Sod it*, she thought. "Very," she said.

"I'll arrange it."

"Mr. Church . . . I don't want another pair of boots on this island until I have that trigger device. We can't risk showing our hand too soon, not when doomsday's a button push away."

"Roger that. But understand this, Major; if we don't get that signal from you within thirty minutes of you making landfall we're going to drop an E-bomb over the island. Your electronics will be fried along with every-one else's."

"So I'll send up a flare. Blue if I have the device, red if I don't."

"I'd rather see that blue flare," Church said, then added, "Grace . . . we can't let Cyrus send that code. If he's on that island and I don't see a blue flare at the agreed time, then the EMP may not be the only bomb I'll be forced to drop."

"I understand. There's no 'I' in 'team.'"

He laughed. "Good hunting, Major."

He disconnected, and Bug contacted her a minute later to say that she had a secure line to Joe Ledger.

"Go for Cowboy," Ledger said.

"Joe . . . this is a secure line," Grace said. "Just us. No ears of any kind."

"Wow," he said. "It's good to hear your voice."

"Joe, I'm sorry about this morning. I didn't mean to snub you—"

"Don't sweat it. Been a funky few days."

"About this morning . . . about what I said."

"Yeah."

"I . . . can we pretend I didn't say it? Can we roll back the clock and reset the system?"

"I don't know. Can we?"

"We have to."

"Do we?"

"You know we do."

Ledger said nothing.

"Joe . . . there's too much at stake. When you reach the island, you have to be smart about this. I'm just another soldier. So are you. We're professionals, not a couple of kids. If this gets hot tonight, then we have to follow procedure, stick to training, and not let any emotions interfere with our actions. End of story."

There was a five count of heavy silence; then Ledger said, "I hear you."

Grace said, "This . . . isn't what I want. You understand?"

"I do," he said sadly. "The mission comes first."

"The mission comes first. Joe . . . I'll see you there."

"I'll be there," he said. "And Grace . . . ?"

"Yes?"

"Good hunting, Major."

"Good hunting, Captain."

She disconnected.

That was an hour ago.

Now she lay on the Hydrospeeder as it cut through the water toward the Dragon Factory. Behind the clear glass of her goggles, Grace Courtland's eyes were the hard, heartless eyes of a predator. They were the eyes of a soldier going to war.

They were a killer's eyes.

Chapter One Hundred Six

In flight above the North Atlantic
Thirty-five minutes ago

I stood behind the pilot, and if my fingers were dug a little too tightly into the soft leather of his seat, then screw it. I stared out of the cockpit window at the blackness of the ocean below.

The pilot said, "Captain . . . wishing won't make this bird fly any faster."

"It might," I said, and he laughed.

The co-pilot tapped my arm. "You have a call coming in on secure channel two."

I went back into the cabin and screwed my earbud into place.

"Go for Cowboy," I said.

"The fish are in the water," said Church. "Two minutes to landfall. What's your ETA?"

"Bailout in twenty, then drop time."

"Good hunting, Captain."

"Yeah," I said, and switched off.

Top and Bunny were ready to go, their chutes strapped on and their weapons double- and triple-checked. All of us were heavy with extra magazines, frags, flash bangs, knives, and anything else we could carry. If we hit water instead of land, we'd sink like stones.

"Alpha Team will hit the island in under two minutes," I said.

"Wish we were with them, boss," said Bunny.

Top studied me for several seconds. "It ain't my place to offer advice to an officer," he said, "me being a lowly first sergeant and all."

I gave him a look.

"But I'm pretty sure there'll be enough beer left by the time we get to this kegger."

"There goddamn well better be," I growled.

Chapter One Hundred Seven

The Chamber of Myth
Tuesday, August 31, 2:21 A.M.
Time Remaining on the Extinction Clock: 33 hours, 39 minutes

Hecate and Paris stared in shock and horror as their father tossed the dead sea serpent aside and got to his feet.

"What . . . what are you talking about?" Hecate said.

Paris sputtered, unable to talk.

Cyrus mocked his son's startled stutter, "I-i-i-'m sorry, Paris, did I speak too quickly? Use too many big words? Or are you simply as stupid as I've feared all these years?"

If Paris had been on the verge of saying something, those words struck him completely dumb.

Cyrus turned to Hecate. "And you, you feral bitch. I'd held you in higher regard until now. Did you actually think you had me fooled. 'Daddy'?" He spit the distasteful word out of his mouth. "The day I become a fawning dotard I hope to God Otto puts a bullet in my brain."

Otto smiled and bowed, and then he and Cyrus laughed.

Hecate looked back and forth between them. "What . . . what's going on here?"

"I believe the Americans call it 'payback.' "

"For *what*?" Paris blurted, finally finding his voice.

"How much time do you have?" sneered Cyrus. "For all those years when you two thought you had me imprisoned at the Deck. For treating me like a vapid old fool. For the disrespect you show me in every action, even when you are faking respect. For trying to steal Heinrich Haeckel's cache of records. For trying to control me by staffing the Deck with your toadies."

Otto laughed.

"Wait—you sent the Russian team to Gilpin's apartment? And to Deep Iron?"

"Of course. Those records were supposed to come to me. It was an incident of mischance that Heinrich died before he could pass along the information about where the records were stored. Even his own family didn't know what he had stored or *where* it was stored. For years we thought that all of that wonderful research was lost. Then in one of those moments of good fortune that reinforce the reality of a just and loving God, Burt Gilpin approached one of Otto's agents with information about a cache of early genetics research. And what do we discover? That Gilpin used to work for the Jakoby Twins, that he was a computer consultant for them. Our Russian friends encouraged him to talk and he told us about how he helped the legendary Jakoby Twins install a revolutionary computer system called Pangaea. Did you know that he built himself a clone of Pangaea? That he used it to steal medical research in exactly the way you two were stealing it? Only he made the mistake of trying to sell the bulk research . . . and he tried to sell it to Otto."

Cyrus shook his head slowly. "Stealing the schematics for Pangaea from me was very naughty . . . though I do admire you for that much, at least. But you had to take a smart move and plow it under with a stupid one by getting into bed with that parasite Sunderland to try and steal the MindReader system."

"How—?"

"How do I know?" Cyrus cut in. "Because most of the people you trust work for me. I knew about the foolish plan to try and use the National Security Agency against the Department of Military Sciences. Were you on drugs when you conceived that idea? Did you think you could stop Deacon when the entire Cabal could not?"

Hecate and Paris looked confused.

"You don't even know what I'm talking about, do you? You don't know who the Deacon is, do you? You don't even know about the Cabal—about the thing that should have been your legacy. You're so goddamned stupid that you truly disappoint me. Do you think that I was *ever* your prisoner? Ever? I've owned every single person you set to watch me. From the outset. You think you are so clever—my young gods—but I'm here to tell you that you are playing children's games with adults."

"We never—," Paris began but Cyrus walked quickly to him and slapped him so hard across the face that Paris was knocked halfway around. He would have fallen had Tonton not stepped up and caught him.

"Don't ever make excuses to me, boy. That's all you've ever done. You were a disappointment as a child, and as a man you're a joke. At least your sister has enough personal integrity to say nothing when she has nothing useful to say."

As Tonton moved, Conrad Veder used the opportunity to shift his position. He had a plastic four-shot pistol in a holster inside his pants. The bullets were caseless ceramic shells that would explode a human skull. He could draw and fire in less than a second.

Hecate said, "What did you mean that you were going to kill our clients?"

Cyrus smiled. "You see, Paris? When she speaks she asks an intelligent question." He clasped his hands behind his back. "I'm sure you've wondered about the water. About whether there was something in it." When Hecate nodded, he said, "Did you test it?"

"Of course. We found no trace of poisons or pathogens."

"Naturally not. There are no pathogens in the water."

Hecate nodded. "Genes," she said. "You've figured out how to do gene therapy with purified water."

Cyrus looked pleased. "You were always my favorite, Hecate. Not nearly the total disappointment your brother has become. Did you do DNA testing?"

"We started to," she said. "We haven't finished."

"What did you think I put in the water?"

"One of the genes that encourage addiction. A1 allele of the dopamine receptor gene DRD2, or something like that."

"If I was a street nigger who wanted to sell crack cocaine maybe," Cyrus said harshly. "Have more respect."

She shook her head rather than give the wrong answer.

"Otto and I—and a few very talented friends—have spent decades weaponizing ethnic-specific diseases. Ten years ago we cracked the science of turning inherited diseases like Tay-Sachs and sickle-cell anemia into communicable pathogens. Anyone with a genetic predisposition to those diseases would go into full-blown outbreak after even minimal exposure to the pathogen."

"But there were no pathogens in the water!" Paris said.

"No. The pathogens are being released into lakes, streams, and reservoirs worldwide. The bottled water contains the gene for the disease. Drink a bottle of water . . . even brew a cup of tea with it . . . and specific ethnic groups and subgroups will develop the genetic disorder. Within a few weeks they will be vulnerable to infection from the pathogens in the regular drinking water. Or from exposure to anyone who has become infected. No one would think to look in the bottled water for the genes because no one can do gene therapy with bottled water."

"No one except us," said Otto. "Funny thing is . . . it wasn't as hard as we thought."

"But *why*?" demanded Hecate. "This is monstrous!"

"It's God's will," said Cyrus. "It's the beginning of a New Order that will purify the world by removing the polluted races. Blacks and Jews and Gypsies and—"

"Are you fucking crazy?" demanded Paris. "What kind of Nazi bullshit is this?"

Cyrus's smile grew and grew. "Nazi. Now . . . the moron shows a spark of intelligence by choosing exactly the right word."

Hecate looked confused. "Wait . . . you're a Nazi? Since when?"

"Since always, my pet. Since the very beginning."

"Since the beginning of what?"

"Since the beginning of *Nationalsozialismus*," Cyrus said, letting his German accent seep through. "Since the beginning of National Socialism in Germany. For me personally, I first embraced the ideals while working in the reserve medical corps of the Fifth SS Panzergrenadier Division Wiking. But it wasn't until I met Otto at Auschwitz that I discovered the full potential of the party ideals."

"What the hell are you talking about?" snapped Paris. "That's World War Two crap. You weren't even *born* then. . . ."

Otto and Cyrus laughed out loud. "Idiot boy," said Cyrus, "I was older than you when I came to work at Auschwitz. I was older than you when I made a name for myself that the world will never forget."

Paris shook his head, unable to grasp any of this.

"Father . . . you're rambling," said Hecate. "You were born in 1946."

"No," he said, wagging his finger back and forth, "Cyrus Jakoby was born in 1946. As were a dozen other cover names in six countries. But I was born in 1911."

"That's impossible!" said Paris.

Cyrus looked around. "We stand here in the midst of unicorns and flying dragons and you tell me antiaging gene therapy is impossible? Otto and I have been tampering with those genes for years. Granted there are . . . ," he gestured vaguely to his head, ". . . the occasional psychological side effects, but we're managing those."

"But . . . but . . . ," Hecate began. "If Cyrus Jakoby is an alias . . . then *who* are you?"

Otto said, "He's a man you should be on your knees worshiping. Your father is the boldest, most innovative medical researcher of this or any generation."

The Twins stared at him, and even Veder's eyes flickered with genuine interest.

Cyrus touched his face. "Under all of this reconstructive surgery, beneath the changes I've made with gene therapy to change my hair color and eye color . . . beyond the façade," he said, "I am the former Chief Medical Officer of the infirmary at Auschwitz-Birkenau. I am *der weisse Engel*—the 'white angel' that the Jews came to fear more than God or the Devil."

He smiled a demon's smile.

"I am Josef Mengele."

Chapter One Hundred Eight

The guard never heard a sound. He strolled back and forth along the footpath between the docks and the main building. He chewed peppermint gum and glanced now and again at the stars. Patrol duty was boring. Except for the night when the hit came in, the months of his service at the Dragon Factory were a huge ho-hum, and he'd been off-shift that night. The hit team had been taken out by a Stinger dog and one of the Berserkers.

The guard hated the Berserkers. Those ugly goons got all the perks. Everyone thought they were so cool. Fucking transgenic ape assholes.

He spit out his gum and began to turn to pace back to the dock.

He never heard a sound, never felt anything more than a quick burn across his throat when Grace Courtland came up behind him and slit his throat from ear to ear.

Grace dropped the corpse and two of her men dragged it into the bushes away from the light from the tiki-torches.

She ran like a dark breeze along the edge of the path. Grace sheathed her knife and drew a silenced .22, and as she rounded the corner she saw two guards—one bending forward to light his cigarette from the lighter held in the cupped hands of the second. Grace shot them both in the head, two shots each.

The path ended at the front of the building where two immense men stood guarding the tall glass doors. There was too much light from inside the building for a stealthy approach. Grace signaled to Redman, her second in command. She indicated the guards and gave a double twitch of her trigger finger. Redman waved another operative forward and they flattened out on either side of the path and flipped night vision over the scopes of their sniper rifles. Both rifles had sound suppressors. It would drop the foot-pounds of impact, but at this distance the loss of impact would be minimal.

Redman fired a split second before Fayed. Two shots, two kills. The big guards slammed against the glass doors and fell.

Grace Courtland smiled a cold killer's smile and ran forward.

Fifty yards behind her another group of shadows broke away from the wall of darkness under the trees. They were heading to the far side of the compound and did not see Grace and Alpha Team take out the guards or enter the building. Even if he had, the team leader, a harsh-faced man named Boris Ivenko, would have thought that he was seeing one of the many teams of Spetsnaz that were invading the island from every side.

Chapter One Hundred Nine

In flight
Sixteen minutes ago

"Eight minutes to drop, Captain," called the pilot.

About damn time, I thought.

Out of the corner of my eye I saw Bunny nudge Top and then the two of them share a look. I must have had quite an expression on my face. I turned away and hoisted my poker face on.

There was a *bing!* in my earbud and then Church's voice said, "Cowboy. Our spotters are seeing some activity around the island. Over two dozen small commercial fishing craft have closed on Dogfish Cay and launched boats."

"What the hell? Don't tell me the Navy's jumped the gun on this."

"No," he said. "They're not ours."

"Then who the hell are they?"

"Unknown at this time."

"Russians?"

"Possible, but there are a lot of them. Early estimates put the number at over one hundred."

"Christ. Any word from Grace? Do we have the trigger device?"

"She reported in just before I called you. She does not yet have the device. This situation is still fragile."

Shit.

"Okay . . . keep all of the backup on standby. I'm seven minutes from my drop. I'll get back to you with intel as soon as I'm on the ground."

Chapter One Hundred Ten

The Warehouse, Baltimore, Maryland
Tuesday, August 31, 2:21 A.M.
Time Remaining on the Extinction Clock: 33 hours, 39 minutes

Rudy Sanchez unscrewed the top of the bottle of ginger ale and poured a glass for the Kid. There was a plate of sandwiches that the boy hadn't touched and an open pack of cookies from which one had been taken, nibbled, and set aside. The boy looked briefly at the soda and then turned his head away and continued to stare at his own reflection in the big mirror that covered one wall.

"You couldn't sleep?" Rudy asked.

The boy shook his head.

"You probably have a lot of questions. About what's going to happen. About your own future."

A shrug.

"SAM . . . ?"

"That's not my name."

"Sorry. Do you prefer to be called Eighty-two? No? Is there another name you'd prefer? You have a choice. You can pick any name you want."

"That guy Joe called me Kid."

"Do you like that? Would you like people to call you that?"

A shrug.

"Tell me what you'd like."

The boy slowly turned his head and studied Rudy. He was a good-looking boy, but at the moment his eyes held a reptilian coldness. The brown of his irises was so dark that his eyes looked black, the surfaces strangely reflective.

"Why do you care?" said the boy.

"I care because you're a teenager and from what Joe's told me you've been in a troubling situation."

The boy snorted. " 'Troubling.' "

"Is there another word you'd prefer?"

"I don't know what to call it, mister."

Rudy said, "I also care because you're a good person."

"How do you know?" The boy's tone was mocking, accusatory.

"You took a great risk to warn us about the Extinction Wave."

"How do you know I wasn't just trying to save myself?"

"Is that the case? Did you take all of those risks to send those two videos and the map just to save yourself? You took great risks to help other people. That's very brave."

"Oh, please . . ."

"And it's heroic."

"You're crazy."

"No," said Rudy. "Do you know what bravery is?"

"I guess."

"Tell me."

"People say that being brave is when you do something even when you're afraid."

Rudy nodded. "I imagine that you were afraid. You were probably very afraid, and yet you took a risk to send us this information."

The boy said nothing.

"Why did you do it?"

"That's a stupid question."

"Is it?"

"It's stupid because I had to do it."

"Why did you have to do it?"

The boy said nothing. His dark eyes were wet.

"Why did you have to do it?" Rudy asked again.

"Because."

"Because why?"

"Because I'm afraid."

"What are you afraid of?"

Tears filled the boy's eyes and he turned away again. He sat for a long time staring at his reflection. The lights were low and that side of the room was in shadows. It distorted the boy's reflection, made him look older, as if the mirror was actually a window through which the boy could see his future self. A tear broke and rolled down one of his cheeks.

"I'm afraid I'm going to go to Hell," said the boy.

Rudy paused. "Hell? Why do you think that? Why would you go to Hell?"

"Because," said the boy quietly, "I'm evil."

Chapter One Hundred Eleven

The Chamber of Myth
Tuesday, August 31, 2:22 A.M.
Time Remaining on the Extinction Clock: 33 hours,
38 minutes E.S.T.

Hecate and Paris stood there, surrounded by the wonders they had created, and both of them felt as if the world had been pulled out from under them.

"Mengele?" Paris whispered. "I don't . . ." He shook his head, unable to finish.

"You still don't get it, do you?" said Cyrus, his eyes glittering. "Everything I've done has been toward one end. To purify the world. Tomorrow I'll send a coded message to operatives all over the world. Some will release the bottled water; others will release pathogens into the water supplies; others will send computer viruses out that will crash the CDC and other organizations. In one coordinated movement a process will be set into motion that cannot be stopped. Nothing on earth can prevent the spread of the pathogen once released into the populations of the mud people."

" 'Mud people,' " Hecate murmured. She looked dazed, her eyes glazed.

"Why?" asked Paris. "Why do . . . this?"

"To complete the work Otto and I began more than half a century ago. Otto, you see, is a nickname from his boyhood. His real name, his birth name, is Eduard Wirths. He was the Chief Medical Officer of the entire camp. He was my boss," Cyrus said with a laugh.

"Well, only for a while," said Otto. To the Twins he added, "Your father was and is brilliant. When he came to the camps as a young captain I was immediately entranced by his vision, by his insights. Every day we would work on the prisoners in the camps and then we'd talk late into the evening, reviewing our research, excited by the directions it was taking, by the possibilities it presented. We were doing the work that would make the dream of eugenics practical. But even then we knew that the science at our disposal was not adequate to the tasks. So we planned. We built a network of scientists and supporters who would continue the work long after Hitler's war was over. Even in the early days your father and I knew that the war would never be won by Germany. But it didn't matter. Our plan for the New Order of humanity was so much bigger than the aspirations of a single nation."

"We knew what we had to do," said Cyrus, taking up the thread of the story. "We hired spies to keep tabs on everyone who was doing work that would support our cause. Not just Germans, but Russians, and Americans. Even Jews. Anyone who was doing progressive research. When the war started going badly we had our friend Heinrich Haeckel smuggle copies of all of the research out of the country. Unfortunately, Haeckel suffered several strokes and was unable to communicate to us the location of the materials. Even then, though, we did not stop, did not falter. We built the Cabal—a network of scientists, spies, and assassins unlike anything the world had ever seen. Even today there are arms of the Cabal in every country, in every government. Your patron, Sunderland . . . his brother is a member of the Cabal; so is the man you called Hans Brucker, the man you hired to lead your hunts. Brucker is a product of our cloning program, along with many others who share his unique skill set."

Here Cyrus flicked a glance at Conrad Veder, but Veder missed it. He was watching Tonton, who had been very slowly edging toward a security phone mounted on the wall. If the big man took two more steps, Veder would shoot him.

Paris shook his head. "This is all . . . too much. Why do this? What could you possibly gain from killing so many people?"

"Change," said Cyrus. "The Extinction Wave will ultimately eliminate all nonwhites. All of them. And the whites who survive will have to fight for the right to dominate and rebuild the world."

"You're a fucking madman!" yelled Paris. "Both of you. You want to kill millions of people?"

"No, Paris," said Cyrus, "not millions. *Billions.* We've already killed millions."

"What . . . what do you mean?"

"The Extinction Wave is not our first attempt," said Otto. "If you count the attempts that yielded only moderate results, this is our tenth phase. Phase six was our biggest success."

"This will be much, much bigger," said Cyrus.

"What was phase six?" asked Hecate.

Otto smiled like a vulture. "Your father took a disease that had presented in several chimpanzees and rhesus monkeys and reengineered it to work on humans. He released it into certain test populations in the late 1970s. It didn't catch on as fast as we liked, but it gained a lot of traction in the eighties."

Paris paled. "God . . . you're talking about AIDS."

"HIV," Otto corrected, "but yes. It was introduced to homosexuals in the United States and Canada and then to the general population of Africa. It's been quite effective."

"You're insane."

"You keep saying that," said Cyrus. "And while I admit that I do have some 'moments,' if you call me insane again I'll have your hands cut off."

"Why didn't you tell us this before?" asked Hecate.

Cyrus shrugged. "I was waiting to see how you matured. We wanted to see if you had the qualities we hoped you'd have. The qualities we tried to build into you."

Hecate's lips parted as his words sank in. "We're part of your experiment, aren't we?"

"Everything I do serves the New Order."

Paris gagged. His eyes were wide and fever bright as understanding sank in.

Hecate looked at the white purity of her hand. "The story has always been that we were special. Cosmic children . . . all of that stuff. But we're just part of a breeding program to make superior beings."

"To make superior white beings," corrected Otto. "Let's keep perspective."

Paris whirled and threw up into the bushes. The

winged serpent on the tree branch hissed and flew away.

"I always said he had no stomach," Cyrus said to Otto, who inclined his head. "We knew fifteen years ago that you were weak, Paris. You were the evidence that breeding programs would not be the answer. Even with the genetic manipulation to give you extra strength and intelligence, you're still weak. That's why the SAMs are so important."

" 'SAMs'?" echoed Hecate. "The boy that looks like you, the one at the Deck. I'm sure I saw another one that looked just like him. Are they your sons?"

"No. Children have proven to be such a disappointment."

"Then . . . what?"

"He's *me*," said Cyrus. "That's why I call him SAM. That's why I call all of them SAM. SAM. It's an acronym."

Hecate shook her head.

"SAM. Same As Me."

She got it now and her eyes widened. "They're . . . clones?"

"Yes," said Cyrus. "And I have a lot of them. A whole family of them. Clones with transgenic enhancements. Superior beings. They will be the fathers of the new race, the race that will emerge from the chaos after the Extinction Wave has cleansed the world."

Chapter One Hundred Twelve

"Evil?" said Rudy. "Why do you think you're evil?"

"Because of who I am. Because of *what* I am." The boy shook his head. "That man you all work for, the one I thought was called 'Deacon,' he knows. You know, too."

"I suppose I do." Rudy kept his face bland. "You believe that you are a clone," he said.

"I am!"

"A clone of Josef Mengele."

"Yes." The word was as harsh as a fist on unprotected flesh. "There are a lot of us. That's why my name is Eighty-two."

Rudy pushed the glass of ginger ale closer to the boy. He didn't touch it. Rudy waited. The bubbles in the ginger ale popped. The second hand on the wall clock swept around in silent circles. Once, twice.

"I guess . . . ," began the boy. He coughed and then cleared his throat. "I guess my real name is Josef."

The boy wiped the tears off his cheeks with an angry hand.

"Do you know who Josef Mengele was?"

"He's me," said the boy.

"No," said Rudy. "You're fourteen. Josef Mengele was born a hundred years ago."

"It doesn't matter. We're the same person."

"Are you?"

"Yes."

"Was Josef Mengele a good person?"

"No!" the boy said as if Rudy was an idiot.

Rudy smiled. "Well, we agree on that. Was Josef Mengele the kind of person who would have risked his own life to help other people?"

A shake of the head.

"Would that man have done what you did to contact Mr. Church—the Deacon—and ask for help?"

No answer.

"Would he?"

"No. I guess not."

Rudy changed tack. "So there are eighty-two clones of Josef Mengele?"

"No," said the boy.

"I don't—"

"There are a lot more than that."

"And you're one of them?"

A nod.

"Are the others all like you?"

"We're all clones, I told you."

"No . . . I asked if they're like you. Do they have the same personality?"

"Some do."

"Exactly the same?"

No answer.

"Please," said Rudy. "Answer my question. Do they all have the same personality?"

"No."

"How can that be?"

"I don't know."

"How many of them would have done what you did? How many of them would have risked their lives to try and warn us?"

No answer.

"Are any of them cruel?"

"Yeah, I guess."

"Are you cruel?"

"No."

"Don't you enjoy hurting people? Don't you enjoy in-flicting harm and—"

The boy gave him a sharp, hurt look. "No!"

"You mind that I asked that?"

"Of course I do. What kind of stupid question is that?"

"Why is it stupid? You said that you were the same as Josef Mengele. You said that you were evil. And you said that you were going to Hell."

"I'm *him;* don't you get that?"

"I understand that you're a clone. I admit I've never spoken with a clone before, and until today I would have thought that a clone might carry some of the same traits and characteristics as the person from whose cells they were cloned. And yet here you are, a teenage boy who risked his life on several occasions to help stop bad people from doing very bad things. A boy who attacked a big security guard in order to try and stop the slaughter of unarmed people. A boy who could easily have done nothing."

The boy said nothing.

"You may be cloned from cells taken from an evil man. Our scientists will determine that through DNA testing. If it's true, then it changes nothing," said Rudy. "Josef Mengele was a monster. *Is* a monster, I suppose, if Cyrus Jakoby is really him."

"I'm pretty sure he is."

"He's such a terrible person . . . and yet you risked

everything to save the very people he wanted to destroy."

The boy looked at him.

Rudy smiled.

"You're *not* him."

"I am."

"No," Rudy said, "you're not. You've just proven something that people have been arguing over for centuries. In fact, you may be living proof of the answer to a fundamental question of our human existence."

"What are you talking about?"

"Well, there's the question of nature versus nurture. Is a person born with certain mental and emotional characteristics that are simply hardwired into him by genetics? Or do environment, exposure to other thoughts and opinions, and life experience determine who we are? I'd say that you are living proof that there has to be a third element permanently added to that equation."

"What?"

"Choice."

The boy looked at him for a long time and said nothing.

"There has never been a situation like this before. We've never had the chance to observe a clone and determine if that person is, or wants to be, exactly the same as the source entity."

"They wanted me to be. Every day I had to learn about Mengele's life and work. I had to learn surgery and about torture and war." Tears streamed down his face. "Every day. Day after day after day."

"And yet you chose a different path than the one they intended for you."

The boy was sobbing now.

"You're not him," said Rudy gently. "*He* would never do what you did. And you could never do what he did."

Rudy fished a plastic package of tissues from his jacket pocket and handed them to the boy, who pulled several out, blew his nose, wiped his eyes. Rudy did not try to physically touch the boy, not even a pat on the shoulder. It was an instinctive choice. The boy was solitary; comfort had to come from within.

They sat together in the interview room as the silent minutes burned away.

"There's one more thing for you to think about," said Rudy.

The boy looked at him with red eyes.

"Josef Mengele is one of the worst criminals of the last hundred years. A monster who has done untold harm to countless people and now wants to destroy a large percentage of the world's population. The records we recovered indicate that he started the AIDS epidemic, and the new tuberculosis plague in Africa. Even if we stop him today, he'll be reviled as the greatest mass murderer in history."

"I know."

"While you on the other hand . . . ," Rudy said, and smiled.

"What . . . ?"

"You are very probably going to go down in history as the greatest hero of all time."

The boy stared at him.

"We had no idea of the Extinction Wave," said Rudy. "No idea at all. If it had not been for your act of bravery, for the *choice* you made, millions—perhaps billions—would die. We didn't even know we were in a war until a little more than a day ago. You changed that.

You made a choice. You took a chance. And if we succeed, if Joe Ledger and Major Courtland and the other brave men and women who are fighting right now to stop this madness are successful, it will all be because of you."

"All I did was send two e-mails!"

"The value of choice is not in the size of the action but in its effect. You may have saved the entire world." Rudy smiled and shook his head. "I can barely fit my mind around the concept. You're a hero, my young friend."

"A 'hero'?" The boy shook his head, unable to process the word.

"A hero," Rudy agreed.

The boy wrapped his head in his arms and laid them on the table and began sobbing uncontrollably.

Mr. Church watched all of this on his laptop, which was positioned so that only he could see it. The noise and motion of the TOC flowed around him. He removed his glasses and polished the lenses with a handkerchief and put them back on.

"Well, well," he murmured to himself.

Chapter One Hundred Thirteen

The Dragon Factory
Ten minutes ago

Grace Courtland and Alpha Team moved quickly and quietly through the corridors of the Dragon Factory. They avoided people when they could, and when they couldn't they killed. Redman and the others dragged bodies into closets or hid them under office desks. The team moved on, searching for Cyrus Jakoby, driven by the certain knowledge that time was running out.

They saw two more of the massive guards standing on either side of a huge hatch that was the size of a bank safe. The hatch stood ajar and the guards were alert. Grace crouched down behind a bushy potted plant at the far end of the corridor and studied them through the magnification of her rifle scope. The guards were unnaturally large, more muscular and massive even than steroid-enhanced bodybuilders. They had similar features: sloping foreheads with overhanging brows, blunt noses, and nearly lipless mouths. These had to be the bruisers Joe had encountered at Deep Iron, and she could well understand why Echo Team had thought they were up against soldiers wearing exoskeletons. The guard on the left had to have a chest that was seventy-five inches around and thirty-inch biceps.

Redman leaned close and whispered, "What the hell are they?"

"Transgenic soldiers," said Grace.

"They look like gorillas."

"No kidding," said Grace dryly, and then Redman got it.

"Holy shit."

"Fun with science," Grace murmured. The hatch the soldiers guarded looked inviting, and she was willing to bet her next month's pay that whatever was inside was important. She was also willing to bet that Cyrus Jakoby was in there. The guards were hyperalert, their posture absolutely correct.

"I need to get in there," she said.

"We don't have enough cover for two snipers. Have to take them one at a time."

She shook her head. "No. That's not going to work."

She quickly outlined a plan that had Redman shaking his head before she was finished.

"It's not a suggestion," Grace hissed. "Do what you're bloody well told."

Redman nodded, but his face showed his displeasure.

Grace faded back around the bend in the corridor and quickly shrugged off her combat gear and jacket so that she wore boots, pants, and a black tank top. She removed the rubber band from her dark hair and shook it out. She slid a knife into her pocket and tucked her .22 into the back waistband of her fatigue pants.

"Be ready," she whispered to Redman, and then she walked out into the center of the hall and strolled up to the guards.

The guard on the left spotted her first and tapped his companion. They both turned to see the tall, slender, beautiful woman walking toward them. Grace put just enough hip sway into her walk to catch their attention, and as she drew close she smiled up at them.

"This is a restricted area, miss," said the right-hand guard.

"I know," she said. "But I wanted to tell you guys something."

"What?" asked the left-hand guard, but he leaned slightly forward, making no pretense of hiding the fact that he was looking down her top.

"Look what I have," Grace said in a conspiratorial whisper.

The guards bent closer still.

She drew her pistol and shot the left-hand guard through the eye. A split second later Redman put a bullet through the right-hand guard's forehead.

Grace smiled and waved her team forward, thinking to herself that men—even mutant transgenic ape soldiers—were all the same. Show them a little cleavage and they lose all sense.

She stepped to the edge of the hatch and peered carefully inside. She could see a group of people standing thirty yards down a foliage-lined path. She recognized the Jakoby Twins at once.

Suddenly warning buzzers began blaring overhead and a recorded voice blared from wall-mounted speakers, "Intruder Alert! Intruder Alert!"

Down the hall there was a rattle of automatic gunfire and immediately automatic fail-safes activated and the hatch began to swing shut. There was no time to think; Grace leaped through the hatch and ducked behind a thick shrub just as the huge portal slammed shut.

Outside, Redman yelled as the hatch clanged into place. Gunfire and screams filled the air and people erupted from rooms and side corridors. Some were unarmed staff; others had guns. Everyone was yelling, and then the guards spotted them and began firing.

More gunfire came from behind.

There was no more time to think. Redman and Alpha Team dove for what cover there was and returned fire.

Chapter One Hundred Fourteen

We glided through the night, silent as bats, our night vision painting the world below us in shades of green and black. The three of us had tumbled out of the plane miles above the island, and for a long time we fell in total darkness. Skydiving at night is deceptive; after you become accustomed to the rush of air, all sense of movement ceases and you feel as if you're floating. Without an altimeter to tell you the truth about how fast the ground is rushing up to meet you there is a very real chance you'll find out in a last microsecond of surprise.

There was almost no wind, so we deployed our glider chutes at ten thousand feet. There is a moment where the resistance of the chute jolts every bone in your body, and then the glider takes over and once more you feel like you're floating rather than falling. The glider has its own dangers built in because it doesn't feel like you're dropping down at all. It's so smooth and steady.

I went through Airborne training in the Army, so you'd think I enjoyed throwing myself out of airplanes. You'd be wrong. I'm good at it, but I do not like it. Both Top and Bunny were more experienced at this sort of thing. Top used to teach it, Bunny did it on his days off. Doing it at night with no lights to steer by, having started seven miles up, isn't my idea of a rollicking good time.

On the other hand, a high-altitude low open jump means that the bad guys usually don't know you're coming, so there are fewer bullets to try and dodge while you're in the air. Kind of a silver lining.

We saw the landing point we'd chosen from the satellite photos and I tilted my chute forward to spill air out of the back and drop down, but suddenly I saw a ripple of bright flashes and heard the hollow *pok-pok-pok* of automatic gunfire. In the same moment I heard Church's voice in my ear:

"Deacon to Cowboy, Deacon to Cowboy, be advised, the island is under attack. Identity and number of hostiles unknown. Estimate one hundred plus hostiles. Confirm; confirm."

"Confirmed, dammit." I tapped my earbud and identified myself. "Alpha Team, report location."

"Alpha Team is inside the complex and taking fire," Redman said.

"Hold tight," I said. Back on the command channel I yelled, "Deacon, are any friendlies on the grounds?"

"Negative. Alpha Team is inside, other assets inbound. No friendlies on the ground."

"Roger that." I tapped the earbud once more as we circled around the line of trees and headed back to our drop site. "Echo Team, zero friendlies on the ground. Let's rock and roll."

While I was thirty feet above the dark lawn I saw four men in the same nondescript BDUs we'd seen on the Russians in Deep Iron. They didn't see me. Sucked to be them.

I cut them down.

Gunfire flashed from our right, but I was below the tree line now. I stalled my speed and dropped to a fast walk, hit the release, and ran from my chute. There was no time to be neat and tidy. I headed straight for the cover of a close stand of palms, and I could hear rounds burning the air around me.

Bunny yelled, "Frag out!" and threw a grenade toward the muzzle flashes. I don't know if he got any of them with the burst, but it gave him and Top a clear moment to land. They split up and went into the trees on either side of me.

The main building was on our left, the lawn and another row of trees to our right. There was a stone path lined with torches nearby, but half of the torches had been knocked over or torn up by gunfire. I saw a dozen bodies littering the ground between here and the door, and more sprawled on the steps.

I turned and headed toward the building, zigzagging behind trees and shrubs, firing at anything that moved. I killed a couple of exotic ferns that got caught in a breeze, but I also took down several of the hostiles.

"Grenade!" Bunny yelled, and slammed into me with a diving tackle that rolled us both to the foot of the stone steps as a blast tore a hole a few feet from where I'd been standing. I'd never seen the throw. Top spun and chopped up the hedges and a man screamed and toppled to the ground.

The steps offered no cover, but the main glass doors were intact despite dozens of impacts from armor-piercing rounds. High-density bulletproof glass. I scrambled to my feet and ran inside, crouching instinctively as a line of heavy-caliber bullets whacked into the glass. It held. So I turned and knelt to offer covering fire as Bunny and then Top ran from cover and risked the open ground near the steps. A ricochet bounced off the open door and pinged around the lobby for a heart-stopping moment before burying itself in the wall six inches from Top's head.

"Jesus," he muttered.

I held the door while they checked the hallway behind me. A crash door opened and six men wearing security uniforms rushed the hallway. Top and Bunny put them down with short bursts and I rolled into the doorway and put half a magazine in the next four who were running up a flight of metal stairs to this level.

"Clear!" called Bunny, and I backed away from the doorway.

I tapped my earbud. "Cowboy to Amazing, Cowboy to Amazing."

No answer.

Then, "Headhunter to Cowboy." Headhunter was Redman's call sign.

"Go for Cowboy."

"We're hearing gunfire behind us. Sounds like M4s." He described his location.

"That's a roger," I said.

"We could use a quarterback sneak."

"Copy that. On our way."

We ran down the hallway, passing several bullet-riddled bodies and the signs of mass panic. A lot of people had fled this way, dropping coffee cups and clipboards and trampling the dead.

We slowed. If Redman had heard our gunfire and could tell the difference between M4s and either the H&Ks used by the Dragon Factory guards or the Kalashnikovs carried by the Russians, then so could whoever they were fighting. The corridor was a long curve and the ambush was exactly where you'd expect it to be— at the sharpest point of the curve where decorative potted trees provided cover.

Top and I tossed our party favors at them and the fragmentation grenades ripped the ambush to pieces.

"Hopscotch!" I called, giving today's code.

"Jump rope!" It was Redman's voice.

We moved around the bend as his people came out from behind the meager cover they had found. Only six of Alpha Team could walk. Two were badly wounded—one with multiple gunshot wounds to the legs and the other with a facial lacerations from flying glass. A third—a new transfer from the SEALs—lay in the kind of sprawl that only looks like what it is.

"Report," I said. "Where's your commander?"

Redman turned toward the heavy portal. "She saw something and went in there just as the alarms kicked in. The door swung shut automatically."

"Any sign of Cyrus Jakoby . . . ?"

"From the way the major went diving into that room, I think she must have seen something."

"Can you open it?" Top asked.

"Sure, if I had two hours and a lot of C4."

I pointed. "There's a keypad. Uplink to Bug and get him on it. If that thing has a computer control then let's put MindReader to work on it."

"Yo!" called Bunny from the sharp bend in the hallway. "We got company."

"How many?"

"A shitload. We're about to get outnumbered really fast."

I cast a desperate look at the closed hatch. There was no time to break through. Damn it to hell. The advancing Russians began firing and bullets tore through the air, the ricochets turning the hallway into a killing floor.

"Fall back!" I shouted, pulling on Alpha Team members and shoving them down the hallway toward a set of exit doors. Bunny picked up one of the wounded and ran with him as lightly as if the soldier was a little child. Two other Alpha Team operatives grabbed the second. We had to leave the dead for now. Alpha Team looked hurt and angry. They didn't want to leave Grace behind any more than I did, but there was no way we could hold this position.

We fired, we threw grenades, but we yielded ground yard by yard, letting ourselves be driven around the curving hallway until we could no longer see the hatch.

No bullets hit me, but as I backed around the corner I felt like I'd taken a fatal wound to the heart.

Grace.

Chapter One Hundred Fifteen

The Chamber of Myth
Tuesday, August 31, 2:23 A.M.
Time Remaining on the Extinction Clock: 33 hours,
37 minutes E.S.T.

Grace moved behind the rows of exotic plants, closing on the Jakobys in a wide circle. The artificial terrain was uneven, and at times she had to tuck her pistol into her belt in order to climb a rock or up and down a ravine. Mammals and birds scattered from her and at first Grace took no notice of them, but then a creature stepped briefly into her path that froze her heart and almost tore a cry of surprise from her lips. The creature had the twisted legs of a goat, a roughly manlike torso, black bat wings, spiked horns, and a grinning face that was out of ancient nightmares.

It was a gargoyle.

Grace stared, not knowing what to do. She forced

herself to remember where she was. These people made monsters. This was just another perversion of transgenic science . . . but a wave of atavistic fear gripped her heart as the monster climbed onto a rock and stared down at her with bottomless black eyes.

Then, in the space of a few seconds, Grace's perception changed. The gargoyle was three feet tall, and it moved with an awkward jerkiness of limb that looked clumsy and painful. As Grace moved slowly up the slope, the creature scuttled away, but it threw a single penetrating look at her before it disappeared under a fern. In that moment, though, Grace saw a human intelligence in the lustrous black eyes and a depth of horrified self-awareness that chilled her to the bone. In some grotesque way the transgenic animal was partly human, and that fragment of its mind was totally aware of its own wretched nature. Sadness crashed down on her as she stared after it. Then a moment later the sadness was overwhelmed by a burning fury as the enormity of this abomination of nature struck her. She set her jaw and drew her weapon and continued her hunt for the real monsters here in this chamber.

She tried to contact the TOC or Joe, but all she got from the earbud was a low-level buzz. A jammer. It must have kicked in when the building went on alert. Grace hoped that Church would realize what was happening and order the drop of the E-bomb.

Grace found a path that looked like it was used by the groundskeeping staff and she ran along this, circling closer and closer, trying to hear the conversation. Eventually she moved into a natural blind formed by the edge of a decorative waterfall and there she stopped. The waterfall was built over rock, but the back was clearly made from painted metal. She ran her hands along it and found the edges of a doorway fitted so snugly into the façade that it was virtually invisible. A door or an access panel of some kind. She filed it away for later.

Grace could see all six of the people in the room. She recognized the Jakoby Twins easily enough—tall, white as snow, and beautiful. The brute standing near them was one of the transgenic guards, though he was bigger than any of the others she'd seen. The two older men were strangers, but she felt that it was safe to guess that one of them was Cyrus Jakoby and the other possibly Otto Wirths. The last of the men there startled her and also made her feel like the earth was shifting under her feet.

If the photos Mr. Church had shown were correct, then this was Gunnar Haeckel.

Or Hans Brucker.

Both of whom were dead.

So . . . who was the tall man with the calculating expression? Another clone?

Clones, transgenic monsters, ethnic-specific pathogens.

She was surrounded by monsters.

Grace drew her pistol and leaned close to listen.

"—your little magic castle is about to come tumbling down," said Cyrus Jakoby.

Hecate sneered. "You may find that more difficult than you imagine, Father. We're not exactly vulnerable here."

"Which is why we brought enough muscle to sweep past whatever defenses you have," said Otto.

"Maybe," said Paris. "And maybe your guns for hire are about to encounter a few surprises."

"The teams know about your Berserkers. Ape DNA does not provide protection from armor-piercing rounds."

Paris smiled. "No, but the Berserkers are not the only defenses we have. You'll see."

Otto gave a small shrug. "Yes, we'll see."

"What I want to know," said Hecate, "is why you're doing this. Why attack us at all?"

"Retribution, Miss Jakoby. *You* attacked the Hive."

"The Hive? What the hell's the 'Hive'?" said Paris.

"In Costa Rica?" prompted Otto, but the Twins shook their heads.

Cyrus studied both of the Twins, checking body language and eye movement. He frowned. "You really didn't attack the Hive," he concluded.

"We still don't know what it is."

Cyrus didn't elaborate. His expression, at first bemused, quickly darkened. "Then what happened to Eighty-two? Who hit the Hive? Who took him?"

"It had to be a military hit." Otto frowned. "Question is . . . which government?"

"Could be Germany," suggested Cyrus savagely. "Our former homeland would love to see our heads on pikes. Or it could be the Americans."

"Then why didn't they hit the Deck, too?"

Cyrus shook his head. "If the military took the Hive, then it's possible that Eighty-two was killed along with the rest of the staff."

"It would be better than being taken." Otto's voice said one thing, but his eyes conveyed a different message. All of the psychological profiles that had been done on Eighty-two had indicated that the boy did not have a predatory nature, that he lacked the strength to be a killer. It was so anomalous a finding that Cyrus had refused to accept it, had killed the testing doctors, had made Otto try over and over again to prove that Eighty-two was truly a part of the Family, that the boy's loyalties were not a "given." Now this belief could possibly be put to the test under interrogation by the United States. The boy could already have broken. Military forces could be closing in on the Deck even now.

Cyrus looked deeply hurt and it took him a moment to master his voice enough to speak. "We have to move up the timetable for the release."

"The real question," interrupted Hecate, "is why *you* sent assassins here to kill us."

"Only one of you."

"Why?" she insisted.

"Call it a Darwinist experiment."

"What . . . you'd use the murder of one to identify which of us had the greater survival instinct and then try to bargain with the survivor?"

Cyrus applauded. "You see, Otto? I always said that she was the smarter twin."

"You miserable old prick," growled Paris. His hand strayed toward his pocket.

Instantly Conrad Veder pulled his pistol and pointed it at Paris. The movement was so fast and fluid that the weapon seemed to appear in his hand as if by magic.

"Make no mistake," said Cyrus, "Conrad will blow your head off if I tell him to. Now pull that dart gun with two fingers and throw it in the pond. You, too, Hecate. And tell your pet ape to stay exactly where he is."

Tonton curled his lip. "That little popgun won't do shit."

Veder's face was neutral. "There's a simple way to find out."

Cyrus chuckled. "Kill anyone who moves, Conrad."

The Berserker held his ground. Paris carefully removed his gas dart gun and threw it away as ordered. It made a splash near the dead sea serpent.

"Father," said Hecate, ignoring Veder's pistol and the order to dispose of her own, "what do you want from us? Why come here? Why tell us all of this now? Why spring it on us rather than bring us in?"

"Those are the right questions, my pet," said Cyrus, nodding approval. "I'll bet Paris didn't even think to ask. This is quite simple, Hecate. You have to make a choice. The Extinction Wave is going to launch." He fished a device from beneath his shirt, an oversized flash drive attached to a silk lanyard. "This sends the codes that will begin an irrevocable change. Truly only the strong will survive. Granted, you're white and you've been engineered to be immune to any of the pathogens or genetic diseases we're using, but afterward there will be war, as I said. The strongest will survive. Otto and I have prepared for the war. We will survive. If you join with us—willingly join with us—then you can share in the benefits of our protection, and together, as one Family, we can usher in the New Order."

"Join you?" said Hecate distantly.

"You're fucking nuts," said Paris. "You stand there and tell us that you started the AIDS epidemic. You brag about that? Then you say that you want to kill four-fifths of the people in the world?"

"More like six-sevenths," Cyrus said.

"Jesus Christ. You think this is a frigging joke? You're trying to destroy the world."

"We're not trying to do anything," said Otto. "We are *going* to remake it."

Paris spit on the ground in front of Cyrus. "I hate you," he snarled. "I hate that I have your blood in my veins. I hate—"

"Shut up, Paris."

Everyone turned toward the person who spoke.

Hecate.

Her blue eyes were laced with veins of hot gold.

"What . . . what did you . . . ?" Paris said.

"I told you to shut up," she said. "Father's right. When you open your mouth you embarrass yourself. You embarrass the *Family*."

Paris stepped close to her but pointed at Cyrus. "Have you lost your mind, too? Are you subscribing to this bullshit? Are you saying that you support this fucking monster—"

Hecate struck him across the face. It wasn't a slap. She punched him so hard and fast that he spun in place, his jaw knocked out of shape, teeth flying from between his rubbery lips. He stood erect for a trembling moment and then he collapsed to his knees, blood gushing from his shattered mouth. His eyes rolled high and white and he fell forward onto the grass.

Everyone stared at her in shock. Hecate stepped over her brother's body and walked over to her father and only stopped when their faces were inches apart. Veder shifted slightly to keep his weapon on her. Otto stood apart, his face still registering shock and uncertainty.

Hecate leaned close to her father until her lips were an inch from his ears.

"Father," she said. "Why wait until tomorrow? If we're going to burn the world down . . . why not start right now?"

And she kissed him on the cheek.

Cyrus Jakoby's chest hitched with a sob that broke the stillness of the moment. He threw his arms around Hecate and crushed her to his chest.

"My pet," he said, tears filling his eyes.

Grace courtland stepped out from behind the waterfall and raised her gun in a two-hand grip.

"This is all bloody touching," she said, "but you have two seconds to give me that bloody trigger device before I blow your twisted brains all over the landscape."

And then the lights went out.

Chapter One Hundred Sixteen

The Dragon Factory
Tuesday, August 31, 2:24 A.M.
Time Remaining on the Extinction Clock: 33 hours,
36 minutes E.S.T.

The exit doors were steel and we made our stand there. The Russians kept coming. The hallway was choked with them, and the front rank held ballistic shields. They advanced as far as the hatch and then held their ground. It was clearly their target and they had the manpower to take and hold it. I couldn't see what they were doing, but I heard the whine of a high-power drill. I never did find out if they brought it with them or found it on the premises, but they were attacking the hatch.

I tapped my earbud.

"Cowboy to Deacon."

"Go for Deacon."

"We're taking heavy fire and casualties." I gave him the bad news about Grace. "There's no way to know if the trigger device has been activated. If you have the cavalry out there, now's the time to blow the bugle."

"They're already inbound. Three DMS teams are on the island. Quicksilver Team has taken the south beach. India and Hardball teams are on the docks. SEAL team Six is five minutes out."

"The trigger device . . ."

"We can't take any more chances, Cowboy. We have to take out the electronics."

That would fry the active team communication as well, and we both knew it. But he was right. We were out of options.

"Do it!" I yelled.

Bullets hammered the metal doors and I had to shout to my men. "Church is launching the EMP. We're going to go radio dark in a few minutes!"

It was not good news. In the dark with no radio, in a firefight where everyone was wearing black BDUs, friendly fire was quickly going to become as much of a threat as enemy fire.

Top leaned close to me. "If those Spetsnaz sonsabitches get through that hatch . . ." He left the rest unsaid.

"We saw guards come up from downstairs," said Bunny. "Maybe there's a way to flank these bozos."

I grabbed Redman and pulled him close.

"Hold this position. I'm going to take Echo Team downstairs and see if we can come up on the far side, catch these assholes in a cross fire. DMS and SEAL teams are on the island and have been apprised of your position." He started to protest, but I cut him off. "Protect your wounded and hold this end of the hall. We have to get back to that hatch. Everything depends on it."

"Don't stop for coffee on the way, Captain," said Redman.

I gave him a wink and dashed down the stairs with Top and Bunny on my heels.

We went down two flights of metal stairs, going so fast that we pushed the envelope of safety on the corners. We knew our backs were protected, so all of us had our M4s pointed down. When a guard actually did step out we cut him to ribbons before he got off a single shot.

The security door on the next landing down was locked. Bunny tried to pick it, but even though the tumblers moved, the door held fast.

"Must be a drop bar or something," he said.

"Let's go one more level down and if that doesn't work we'll come back up and try to blow the door."

We moved down two more flights into the underbelly of the building. Maintenance level. Poorly lighted, the ceiling crisscrossed with pipes, big generators rumbling with subdued thunder. It was hot and moist down here, and water dripped from the ceiling. The maintenance floor had a security door, too, but it was propped open with a chair. An ashtray and a copy of *Popular Mechanics* lay on the floor. God bless the lazy janitors everywhere. Once inside we found a second door that was similarly blocked, but there was a draft here and the sound of distant gunfire. I shined my flashlight up and saw a long concrete utility ramp that went all the way to the surface.

"Wait here," I said, and ran up the slope. There was a heavy grilled outer door set with a pivoting drop bar, but the bar was in the upright position and the door stood up and open. I peered out and saw the backs of at least fifty Russians engaged in a firefight with some other force. From the ramp I couldn't tell if they were fighting the Dragon Factory guards or our own boys, and I was in no position to participate in this fight. So I retraced my steps and found Top and Bunny.

They stood back-to-back, pointing their guns into the bowels of the maintenance area, their bodies tense and alert.

"What is it?" I whispered.

"Don't know, Cap'n," said Top. "Heard something weird."

"Weird?"

Before he could answer there was a *clickety-click* sound somewhere near. Like toenails on concrete.

"Guard dog," Bunny said.

"He ain't barking," Top said.

"Not all of 'em do."

I sighted down the barrel and did a slow sweep. Suddenly something moved from left to right, breaking cover from behind the steel case of a big blower and darting behind a row of stacked crates.

"What the fuck was that?"

"Dog?" Bunny said, but this time he made it a question.

"Didn't look like no dog to me," Top said.

I had to agree. The silhouette was all wrong. The

body was big, about the size of a mastiff, with thick shoulders and haunches, but the head shape was wrong and the tail was . . . weird. Too big and curling all the way over its back to beyond its snout.

The scuttling sound came again. This time to our right.

"Two of 'em," Top said.

Then we heard it behind us.

"Three," Bunny said.

I turned. "More than that," I said. At least four of the weird shapes filled the darkness of the ramp that led outside. They ran toward us with frightening speed.

"Jesus Christ," Bunny said, and I turned as one of the creatures moved through a patch of light.

It was a dog. Or it had started out that way. God only knows what you'd call it now. The body was as broad and solid as a bullmastiff, the hair midnight black. The face was a twisted parody of a dog's, but the snout and head were covered with what I first thought was some kind of armor like they used to put on fighting dogs centuries ago. I could have dealt with mastiffs in armor. That was scary, but it wasn't nightmare stuff.

But as the creature moved back through the lamplight I saw that the armor ran all the way down its back and covered its sides, where it eventually thinned and blended with the dog's natural fur. The armor plating gleamed like polished leather. But what sent a flash of horror all the way down through my brain and heart and guts was what rose above the dog's back. It wasn't a dog's tail. The appendage that curled over the massive back and shoulders of the dog was a huge, segmented scorpion tail.

There were at least a dozen of them now . . . closing on all sides.

The one in the spill of light paused, its tail trembling above it, the stinger dripping hot venom. Its muzzle wrinkled back to show rows of sharp white teeth and it glared at us with eyes as black as the Devil's.

With a monstrous howl of unnatural hate, the creature ran at us.

And then the others rushed at us from all sides.

Chapter One Hundred Seventeen

The Chamber of Myth
Tuesday, August 31, 2:28 A.M.
Time Remaining on the Extinction Clock: 33 hours,
32 minutes E.S.T.

There was a sharp crack, and a bullet cut through the darkness so close that Grace could feel the heat. She threw herself to one side and crashed into a row of thorny shrubs. Needles jabbed her and plucked at her clothing as she rolled over the shrubs and scrabbled to find solid ground. She kept her pistol by sheer luck and was glad of the lethal promise of it as she fumbled her way through the absolute blackness. All around her exotic creatures screamed in voices never before heard outside of nightmares.

"What happened to the lights?"

"It's a fail-safe," Hecate said. "If there's gunfire in the building the whole facility goes into a forced lockdown."

"Did you hit her?" someone asked. Grace thought it was Otto.

"I don't know," came the reply. Both voices were off to her right, so Grace kept moving to her left. The ground sloped under her and she crouched low, using her free hand to feel for obstacles.

"The security lights will be on any moment," said Hecate, and as if to punctuate her words several overhead lights flared on. The light was weak but more than enough to see by. Grace dodged behind a mound of clover and flattened out.

Hecate led her father to a cleft in a rock wall. Otto squeezed in with them. Tonton and Veder found cover behind nearby foliage.

"Who was that bitch?" demanded Otto. "Was she one of yours?"

"No," said Hecate. "I thought she was one of yours."

"I don't care who she is," snapped Cyrus. "Veder, kill her."

The assassin moved off without a word, melting into the foliage and vanished without a trace.

"Tonton," said Hecate, "*hunt*."

The Berserker grinned broadly and ran in the direction where Grace had been. As soon as he reached the waterfall he stopped, bent low, and sniffed; then he turned and ran down the path.

"What's he doing?" asked Otto.

"He has more than ape strength," said Hecate. "We've been experimenting with them, giving them additional combat useful skills. His olfactory senses are much sharper than a human's. He'll sniff her out."

Grace heard the big man coming. She was down several rounds, so she quickly swapped out her magazine and found a spot with limited access from behind. She could command a three-sided view. While she shifted she processed what she had learned. One point was the name of the man who looked like Haeckel and Brucker. Cyrus had called him first Conrad and then Veder. Conrad Veder was another of the assassins of the Brotherhood of the Scythe.

A strange idea occurred to her and as she thought it she somehow knew that it was true. Haeckel and Veder were two of the four assassins of the Brotherhood. They looked identical, and it was no stretch under the present circumstances to accept that they were clones from the same cell line. It seemed likely that all four of the assassins of the Brotherhood were clones. The same level of skill because they were all, in essence, the same person. Was deadly accuracy and a coldness of heart hardwired into the genetic code? She didn't know and would have to explore that with Hu and Rudy one of these days.

At the moment she had to focus on the big killer who was coming her way. The one Hecate had called Tonton. The Berserker moved with a surprising economy of movement, leaping over rocks, climbing with simian ease, hopping from rock to rock across a stream. Grace steadied her pistol and waited until he was within perfect pistol range.

Tonton suddenly stopped and crouched low, his eyes scanning the ground. He followed the path the woman must have taken, and he knew where it led. If she got into the cleft by the south corner, then she would have solid rock at her back and a flat shooting platform. He smiled. If he'd taken three more steps, his head would have risen above the hump of the next hill and that would have been the ball game.

"Smart bitch," he murmured.

He turned and ran to his right into the brush. She may have the better position, but he knew every inch of the Chamber of Myth.

Veder had no intention of trailing the woman through the dense jungle environment of this chamber. It was foolish and it was a waste of his skills. Instead he scouted the terrain and picked out the three or four best places to set an ambush. If this woman was smart, she would be in one of them. Veder carefully surveyed the angles of each. They were all good, but there was one—a ledge that was partially screened by tendrils of Spanish moss—that offered an angle to the other two. If the woman was not there, then he could crawl onto the ledge and wait until that ape found her. If the Berserker killed her, so much the better. Veder wasn't being paid extra for this. If the woman killed the Berserker, then Veder would be able to find the spot from which she fired and then he'd take her out.

The decision was a practical one. Once he made it, Veder pocketed his pistol and began to climb.

Chapter One Hundred Eighteen

The Dragon Factory
Tuesday, August 31, 2:35 A.M.
Time Remaining on the Extinction Clock: 33 hours, 25 minutes E.S.T.

The creatures howled like demons as they closed on us. The nearest was thirty yards away and its tail whipped back and forth, clanging on the overhead pipes. I hit it with a short burst and the creature slewed sideways, blood and pieces of its shell flying into the air. The others stopped for a second, but then the wounded one hissed and scuttled forward, bleeding but far from dead.

"Oh, fuck," said Bunny, and opened up into the mass of them.

"Frag 'em!" I yelled. Our M4s were fitted with the new M203 single-shot 40mm grenade launcher mounted under the barrel forward of the magazine. It had a separate handle and trigger, so I grabbed that with my left while holding the primary rifle hand with my right. It gave me two guns at once—and I needed all of the immediate firepower I could muster. The downside was that the grenade launcher was a single-shot.

I aimed for the center of the biggest mass of them and fired.

The explosion tore three of them to pieces, and I suppose it was comforting to know that beneath the insect carapace there was a flesh-and-blood animal. Not sure if it could still be accurately called a dog, but it could die like one.

Top turned and fired up the concrete ramp. The confines of the ramp maximized the force of the explosion, and it tore the creatures apart and blew a hot, wet wind back at us that painted us with gore.

Far above us there was a rumble of thunder and all at once every light in the underground flared and then winked out.

"EMP!" I yelled.

"This is not a good fucking time!" bellowed Bunny. He dug desperately into his pockets to produce a handful of chemical flares. He broke and shook them and then threw some of them in all four directions. The creatures had been as startled by the darkness as we had, and I realized that their eyes were still canine. Dogs could see in poor light but were as blind as we were in total darkness.

"I think you just turned on the EAT AT JOE'S sign," I said.

The creatures immediately began rushing at us again.

"Frag out!" Bunny yelled, and threw his grenade. It hit the back of one of the animals just as it flicked its tail, and the round took a little hop as it burst. The downblast flattened one monster and tore the guts out of the pipes above. Water and steam showered the animals and there were even higher-pitched screams as they were scalded. In their confusion and fury two of the scorpiondogs turned on each other in a murderous frenzy, the stingers stabbing over and over again until they both staggered away on trembling legs and then collapsed, victims of each other's poison.

Top had his back to mine and we fired continuously as more of the creatures swarmed out of the darkness.

"Aim for the head!" I cried.

At first the sheer numbers of them that rushed toward us pushed along the corpses of the monsters we killed, but then Bunny got into the game and threw a hand grenade first to Top's side and then to mine. The blasts deafened us but decimated the creatures. On both sides the front ranks were blown to bits, and the creatures backed off for another hesitant second and then rushed us again.

"I'm out!" Top called, and Bunny started firing while Top switched magazines. As soon as he started firing I went dry and Bunny covered me.

There were ten left.

We emptied another magazine each.

Then there were seven. Fifteen feet away.

Too close for another grenade. Bunny opened up with his rifle.

Four. Ten feet.

Top burned through an entire magazine as they nearly reached our firing position.

Two. One whipped its tail at me and the sharp stinger stuck in the Kevlar chest protector.

Bunny jammed his rifle against its head and pulled the trigger.

It leaped at Top and bore him to the ground. The scorpion tail whipped around Top as he screamed and twisted to one side, then the other. I couldn't risk a shot, so I kicked the monster in the face, once, twice, drawing blood, hurting it, but it snarled in pain and fury and tried to bite my foot.

Then Bunny did something that was either incredibly brave or incredibly stupid. He jumped on top of the monster and used his body mass to pin the powerful tail to the dog's back. The stinger shook and twitched inches from Top's face.

"Get it off me!" Top screamed, and his voice was filled with pain. I couldn't tell how or where he was hurt. The mastiff—even without the ponderous tail—had to weigh 250 pounds of powerful muscle, and all of that mass was crushing down on Top. And Bunny's enormous body was piled on top of that. Fat drops of venom dripped from the stinger and splashed Top's forehead and cheeks.

I drew my leg back and kicked the brute as hard as I have ever kicked anything. I could feel its bulging side collapse under the impact. Ribs broke and the creature let out a disturbingly normal dog yelp, but the kick did the trick and the creature reeled sideways. I shuffled in and kicked it again, just as hard. The scorpion-dog fell over and Bunny pulled at it, forcing the thing away from Top. The big young man and the dog rolled over and over and then Bunny locked his arm around the monster's bull neck. He was growling more savagely than the dog. I could see his massive arm muscles swell under his shirt and then Bunny jerked his whole body up and back. The was a huge wet *crack!* and then the monster dog flopped into limp stillness.

Bunny rolled off it, gasping, saying. "Oh shit oh shit oh shit. . . ."

I knelt over Top, who was struggling to sit up. I was mindful of the venom on his face and I tore open a first-aid kit to find some gauze pads to dab it up.

"Are you hurt?" I asked.

"Yeah," he said with a wince. "Think my ribs are busted."

I undid the Velcro on the Kevlar and probed his sides. The hissed intakes of breath told us both the news.

"Your whole side's cracked. Five, six ribs."

"Fuck me," he said, and tried to reach his right hand across to feel for himself, and then another jab of pain shot through him. "God damn it. . . ."

I felt wetness under my fingers as I continued to probe. "You're bleeding."

Very gingerly I lifted his shirt and looked at his back. I was almost sorry I looked. The brown skin of his side was slick with red blood, and in the midst of it two white and jagged ends of bone had torn through flesh and muscle.

"Is it bad?"

"It ain't good."

"Tell me, Cap'n."

"You have a couple of compound rib fractures. I can stop the bleeding, but we can't set them right now."

"God damn it . . . I want to be *in* this fight."

"Dude," said Bunny, who was standing above us now, checking our perimeter, "you were just in a firefight with mutant monsters. You're going to be able to brag about this shit for—like—*ever*."

"If there's a world to brag to, Farmboy. We ain't caught up to them Nazi psychos yet, or did you forget?"

"Point taken."

"You want painkillers, Top?" I asked after I was finished with a quick patch job.

"Just say no to drugs," he grumbled.

"Let's see if you can stand."

We helped him up and there was no way to do it that didn't hurt. Top called us names I won't repeat. Bunny steadied him as he tried to walk. He could manage it, but there was no way he was going to get back into this fight. We all knew it.

"Look, Cap'n, you and Farmboy gotta get going. I'll guard the stairwell."

"You can't fire a gun—," Bunny began, but Top cut him off.

"I can shoot a pistol, son. Want me to show you? Bet I can kneecap you from here."

"Okay, okay," Bunny said, "grouchy old bastard."

"Clock's ticking," Top said to me. "You need to be gone."

"We are gone," I said, and turned away to head into the complex. After a moment I heard Bunny coming behind me.

I looked back once and saw Top standing there in the doorway. The dead monsters were all around him, and he looked like an ancient warrior on some battlefield out of legend. He sketched a small wave, and then Bunny and I rounded a bend and he was gone.

Chapter One Hundred Nineteen

The TOC
Tuesday, August 31, 2:39 A.M.
Time Remaining on the Extinction Clock: 33 hours,
21 minutes E.S.T.

"Blackwing Three to Deacon."

"Go for Deacon."

"Package has been delivered," said the pilot. "It's the night the lights went out in Georgia."

"Roger that. Well done, Blackwing."

Church leaned back in his chair and stared at the array of screens that had, until moments ago, relayed images from helmet cams of every DMS field operative on Dogfish Cay. Now all of the screens were dark except for the night-vision image from the satellite.

He heard someone come up beside him.

"What just happened?" asked Rudy Sanchez.

Church explained about the electromagnetic pulse bomb. "If we're lucky, then Cyrus won't be able to access a working computer terminal in order to send out the code for the Extinction Wave."

"If we're lucky?" repeated Rudy. *"Dios mio."*

The satellite image showed hundreds of bright dots, milling around across the island. Every few seconds a brighter spot would flare.

"What's that?"

"Thermal scans of the battle. Each dot is a signature for a combatant. The flares are explosions, probably grenades."

"Which ones are ours?"

"We've lost all telemetric feeds from the island," said Church.

"Which means what?"

"Which means we don't know which ones are ours."

The collision of the hundreds of dots made no sense to Rudy. Everyone seemed to be right on top of everyone else. All those soldiers, each person dressed in black, out of communication even with their own teammates. It was a frightening thought to him, and he could only imagine the terror the men on the island must be feeling.

"You're a religious man," said Mr. Church. It wasn't framed as a question, but Rudy nodded.

"Yes."

"Now would be a useful time for prayer."

Chapter One Hundred Twenty

The Chamber of Myth
Tuesday, August 31, 2:41 A.M.
Time Remaining on the Extinction Clock: 33 hours,
19 minutes E.S.T.

For the second time in twenty minutes the lights went out in the Chamber of Myth.

"What now?" growled Cyrus.

"I . . . don't know," said Hecate.

"It's that woman," said Otto.

"No. There's no bypass in here for the security lights. They'd have to be turned off from the security office. Your men must have done this."

"No," insisted Otto. "They are under strict orders to leave all systems in operation."

"Why?" Hecate asked, then answered her own question. "Oh . . . you need a working computer terminal for your device."

"Why don't you say that a little louder?" said Otto icily. "Just in case the female agent didn't hear you."

Hecate ignored him. Instead she said, "Listen . . . can you hear the blowers?"

They were all silent in the absolute darkness. "I can't hear anything except a few birds," said Cyrus.

"Damn it! The blowers are offline." Her voice was shrill with tension. "They're on a dedicated system with their own generator. The controls for that are in my office." She paused. "That means the main power is out as well as the security systems and auxiliary systems. All at once?"

Cyrus opened his cell phone. There was no light.

"Otto, try your phone. See if the light comes on."

"It's dead."

"Something took out all electronics in a single burst," said Cyrus, his voice low. "Either the island has been nuked or someone hit us with a precise EMP."

"Our teams don't have anything like that," said Otto.

"Then the Americans are on the island. If they used an E-bomb, then they know about the trigger device. Nothing else makes sense."

There was a distinct note of panic in his voice.

"We have to get out of here," said Otto in an urgent whisper. He fumbled in the dark until he found Hecate's arm and gave it a fierce squeeze. "We need to get out of here before they can stop us or we will have lost everything we've worked for."

"I have a ruggedized laptop in my office," she said. "It can withstand any kind of EMP and it's in a lead-lined safe along with a portable hard drive with our backup files."

"But how can we get to your office?" demanded Cyrus. "We're trapped in here."

Hecate laughed, a strangely feline sound in the darkness.

"I designed this place, Father. Do you think I would be so careless as to let it be my tomb?"

"Then get us out of here."

"I need to find the waterfall. The rear panel is false. There's a door that leads to a service tunnel. Now be quiet and let me get my bearings."

Conrad Veder took the darkness philosophically. He wasn't frustrated, because he was not emotionally invested in the kill. All it meant was that the change in circumstances required a new plan.

He remembered the process of climbing up to the ledge and climbing back down would be easy enough. But he didn't move right away. There was no immediate threat to him up here and the lights might come back on.

One of the greatest advantages of having a mind like an insect is that there is no tendency toward impatience.

Tonton did not like the total darkness. It was the only thing that made him feel vulnerable.

He could still smell the woman and if he was careful

he could track her. But what if she had night-vision goggles? How was she dressed? Fatigue pants and boots, a black tank top.

Did she have an equipment belt?

He didn't think so, but he wasn't sure.

A few seconds passed.

No, he decided. She hadn't been wearing an equipment belt. On the other hand, she may have had a pack and left it among the foliage. He hadn't seen her after she'd run into the brush. She might have had time to grab a pack and keep going.

So what did he do?

If he had one of the new recruits he'd have ordered him to stand up and then he'd see if the bitch put a bullet through his head. Tonton was not willing to risk his own head.

Miss Jakoby might have a trick. Tonton reached into his pocket for his cell, but the unit was dead. Not even a glow from the screen. What the hell?

Wracked with indecision, Tonton did nothing.

Grace Courtland did not fear the darkness. She would have preferred night vision or some useful light, but she didn't need it. There was too much of the predator in her to be stymied by darkness.

If she couldn't see, then neither of the men who were hunting her could see, either. And she understood the *why* of the darkness. Church had dropped the EMP, which meant that she had a little breathing room. But she also had a very specific purpose. There might be a hardened terminal or laptop on the island. She doubted there was one in this chamber, but that meant that she had to prevent Cyrus Jakoby from getting out of the chamber.

Her Special Forces training ran deep. Grace had been one of the very first women accepted into the SAS, and she'd been the first field team operator for Barrier. Church hadn't recruited her for the DMS because she was decorative. Church wanted her because she was the best of the best. Now was the time to live up to that, and in the absolute darkness Grace smiled.

If anyone had seen that smile—even a killer like Tonton—it would have given him pause.

She moved out of her niche, recounting the steps she'd taken. Her training taught her to remember directions, yards run, right and left turns, elevation. This wasn't a time for gunplay. She couldn't see a target, and the muzzle flash from a missed shot would give her position away. The gun went back into her waistband and she practiced drawing the fighting knife from her right-hand pocket several times until she knew that she could have it out and flick the blade into the locked position in under a second.

That gave her the confidence to keep her hands free while she retraced her steps. She paused briefly to feel along the ground for small rocks, and she put several of them into her left pocket.

Somewhere off to her three o'clock position she could hear the whispered voices of Cyrus, Hecate, and Otto. Their position sounded about right for where she thought she needed to go.

Her greatest care was in placing her feet, making sure that each step was featherlight until she was sure of her footing, and then she shifted weight in a flow from one leg to the other. It was like using Tai Chi to stalk her prey in the darkness—long, slow, controlled steps.

Tonton thought he heard something and he turned his head and sniffed at the darkness. The air was thick with the scent of fear from several of the transgenic animals that had panicked when the lights went out. It clouded his sense of smell, but he was sure that he'd just caught a fresh whiff of the woman. Humans don't smell like animals, and though Tonton did not possess the genes necessary for processing the thousands of individual scents that jungle apes had, he had trained for many hours to hone his olfactory skills.

He was sure that it was the woman. She'd moved.

There was a sudden sound far off to his opposite side and he turned suddenly, swinging his pistol around to point at the blackness. What had made the noise? The woman? Veder? One of the animals?

There was a second sound. Sharp and fast, like a stone dislodged by a running foot.

Then a third. All off to his right side.

It *had* to be her. Somehow she'd tricked him and was crossing the open field under cover of darkness instead of coming back along this path.

"Got you, bitch," he said with quiet malice as he rose from a prone position and got to his feet. He took a tentative step, then another.

And then something brushed against his leg and he spun, but as he spun he felt his thigh ignite with a white-hot burn. He smelled a confusion of scents. The woman—close!—and then the sharp, coppery tang of blood.

He swung a vicious a blow through the shadows, but all he hit was air.

There was another flash of burning pain across the back of his knee and suddenly he found himself tilting to that side, his knee buckling.

Tonton cried out as pain hit him in waves, a one-two burst of agony from thigh and knee. He scrabbled at his thigh and could feel wetness, and then he felt something hot splash against his palm. He was bleeding. Fast and hard. An artery.

The bitch had cut him!

She'd found him in the dark and cut him.

"You fucking cu—!" he started to shout, but he was struck across the face. His cheeks burned with unbearable pain, and when he touched his face he could feel something weird, something terribly wrong. His mouth seemed to stretch wide . . . absurdly wide. Where the corners of his mouth should be were two ragged double lines of torn flesh.

He flailed at the darkness as fear burst through him like fireworks. Then he felt fingers curl into a knot in his hair and his head was jerked violently backward. Then there was the hard edge of a blade against his throat. It pressed deep but did not cut.

Something brushed his ear and he realized it was a pair of soft lips.

"This is for those poor bastards in Deep Iron," the woman said in a murmur that was as soft as a whisper of passion.

He didn't understand. He hadn't been at Deep Iron. That job had been done by two of his men. He hadn't killed those people. He opened his mouth to tell her, to plead with her. Then there was a lava-hot line across his throat and he had no voice at all. Tonton heard a weak and distant gurgle that sounded like it came from underwater. He felt hot wetness in his mouth, and then he was falling forward into a darkness more complete and eternal than the temporary shadows of the Chamber of Myth.

Chapter One Hundred Twenty-One

The Dragon Factory
Tuesday, August 31, 2:44 A.M.
Time Remaining on the Extinction Clock: 33 hours, 16 minutes E.S.T.

If there were more of the scorpion-dogs down in the lower level we didn't encounter them. We did find a half-dozen guys in greasy overalls lying dead inside a shattered office. It looked like they'd tried to make a stand against the monsters by pushing a desk against the door and arming themselves with wrenches. They'd killed one of the transgenic creatures by smashing in its skull, but from the looks of the place the other monsters had swarmed in. The workers looked to have been stung dozens of times each.

"Poor bastards," Bunny said.

"Poor bastards who work for the bad guys," I said. My sympathy level was bottoming out.

We ran on, chasing our flashlight beams. The EMP had wiped out our night vision, but we each had a flashlight and extra batteries wrapped in lead foil for this purpose.

"Stairs!" Bunny said, pointing, and we cut right and went through the doorway as fast as safety would allow. The stairwell was empty, so we climbed, taking turns covering each other on the corners, never stopping. If Alpha Team still held the far end of the hall, then I was hoping to catch the Russians by surprise. A few flash bangs and then some frags would make the odds more even. They would literally be in the dark, so we'd use that against them.

We got to the main floor and opened the door cautiously. No sounds of gunfire from inside the building. No way to tell if that was good news or bad. I could hear sounds of a pretty heated exchange outside, though.

This next part would be tricky because we couldn't risk using our flashlight, but we had to get down that hallway.

I leaned close to Bunny and told him what I wanted to do.

"Roger that," he whispered.

I slung my rifle and drew my Beretta. Moving carefully, I found the far wall with my left hand; Bunny kept one hand on my shoulder. Like a couple of blind beggars negotiating an alley we walked forward. I let my fingers glide along the wall and never moved faster than my ability to recognize the terrain. Each time I found an opening—a hallway or a doorway—I stopped, tapped Bunny's hand twice, and then moved in a shuffle until my fingers made contact once more with the long, curving wall. Being in total darkness makes you realize how much of every action relies on sight. Sudden darkness for a sighted person opens up a feeling of great vulnerability. Movement is clumsy and slow. To overcome this you have to create a system of movement and constant analysis. Speed is an enemy to sightless orientation.

So, it took us a while to navigate that hallway, but the way we did it brought us all the way to the main doorway.

The big glass doors were closed, so I followed them to the other side and found the wall again. Now I knew where we were and how far from the hatch.

We went another forty yards and then stopped. I found Bunny's hand, tapped it three times—a cue that I was about to give instructions—and then followed his hand up his arm to his chest and then to the grenades hung on his battle rig. Then I found his big hand and drew a series of letters in his palm. He tapped my wrist every time he needed me to repeat one.

When I was done he gave my wrist two sets of two taps. Message received and understood.

We reoriented ourselves and moved farther along the hall until we could hear voices. Whispers from several men. Low, quiet, and in Russian. I could make out what they were saying, but there wasn't time to translate for Bunny. Besides, none of it was tactically important. One man asked another when the lights were coming back on, and a gruff voice—probably a sergeant or team leader—told him to shut the hell up.

I holstered my pistol and took two grenades from my harness. A flash bang in my left and a fragmentation grenade in my right. From the faint rustle I knew Bunny was doing the same.

"Light 'em up!" I hissed, and we pulled the pins on the flash bangs.

If the Russians heard me, it didn't matter. We sailed the grenades into the emptiness in front of us, squeezed our eyes shut, and covered our ears the best we could. Even so, the blast and starburst was like a hot knife through the brain.

It was far worse for the Russians.

The grenades burst in the air right above them and I

opened my eyes a second after the detonation. I saw them—maybe twenty in all—reeling back from the intense light, screaming at the pain in their ears, too shocked and confused to do anything. The last sparks of the flash gave Bunny and me perfect distance and angle.

"Frag out!"

We threw.

They died.

Not all of them. We had to shoot three of them.

But the rest took the shrapnel full in the face. The fools had been spooked by the dark and had grouped together for safety. It had been a stupid mistake, but they probably thought they owned this hallway.

Now it was their tomb.

The echo of the blast rolled up and down the hallway, and my head rang from the thunder. Even pressing your hands to your ears can only block out a portion of that noise.

I turned on my flashlight and swept the beam over the charnel house.

"God Almighty," said Bunny.

I cupped a hand around my mouth.

"Hopscotch!" I yelled.

A moment later the reply echoed back to us.

"Jump rope!"

It was Redman. Alpha Team had survived.

We converged on the hatch. We pulled chemical light sticks and threw them down so that we all met in a mingled blue and green glow. One of the Alphas came last, supporting Top, who looked ashy and ill.

"How you holding up?" asked Bunny, hurrying over to help.

"Just fucking peachy, Farmboy. Took you long enough."

"Yeah, we stopped at a titty bar for a few beers."

"Wouldn't surprise me."

Redman closed on me while I was examining the hatch. "First Sergeant Sims won't accept any painkillers. He threatened to kneecap the first son of a bitch who tried to give him morphine."

"He seems to be in that kind of mood. Leave him alone. We have other fish to fry. We need to get through this hatch."

Before he'd been promoted to Grace's number two, Redman had been the demolitions expert for Alpha. He ran his hand over the hatch and then crabbed sideways and knocked on the wall.

"Okay, Cap," he said, "we couldn't blow that hatch with an RPG, but the wall is just block. If we can knock a big hole in it, I can rig a compressed charge and maybe make us a doorway. We have just about enough C4 for that; it's the hole that's going to be the problem."

"I need solutions, not problems."

Redman looked at the dead Russians, then turned to one of the Alphas. "Beth—check the bodies. I need grenades and explosives. If they have any, it'll be Semtex. Detonators, too. Whoever has the most Semtex will have the detonators. Do it now."

Alpha Team moved with a purpose, and in under two minutes Redman had twenty grenades and four tubes of plastic explosive. Three of the four Russian detonators had been broken, but he said he only needed one.

He set to work rigging the grenades together over a wad made from half of the Semtex. He draped it with three layers of Hu's polymer blast dampening cloth, placed the detonator with great care, and started backing up, unspooling wire as he went. I chased everyone back to the sharp bend in the corridor and we all flattened out on the floor by the wall.

"Fire in the hole!" Redman called, and clicked the detonator.

The blast was massive. Smoke and dust blew over us, funneling around the curved corridor.

As soon as it was clear, I was up and running, a cloth pressed to my face, squinting through the smoke. There was a smoking crater in the wall that was at least eight inches deep, and fissures ran outward from side to side and floor to ceiling.

"Damn," Redman said, "I'm good."

He set to work on the second part of the job, gouging the cracked inner stone to make a tight crevice for his C4. He packed it tight. A compressed blast does far more damage, and we needed damage. We needed a doorway big enough for me to climb through.

Once he was done we repeated our retreat and he clicked the detonator.

This blast was bigger but not louder. A lot of the force went into the stone wall with such intensity that we felt the vibration run along the floor.

Again I was up and running, and as I approached the wall I knew that Redman had broken through. I could feel a breeze of moist heat coming at me through the smoke. I waved furiously at the cloud of dust and shined my light at the hole.

It went all the way through.

But it wasn't big enough.

Not for me. Not for any of us.

And we'd used all of our explosives.

Chapter One Hundred Twenty-Two

Grace moved away from the corpse of the Berserker and retraced her steps to the path. Ahead of her in the darkness she could hear the whispered conversation of Hecate and her father. It was no longer stationary. Grace crouched and listened, tracking the sound even though she couldn't make out the words. The sound moved from left to right in front of her. There were no points of reference to guess distance, especially with whispers, but it couldn't have been more than twenty yards.

What was to the right?

The sound told her. The soft hiss of the waterfall. That's where Hecate was going. She remembered that metal panel in the back. A door or access panel. Grace was willing to bet a lot on it being a door.

She adjusted her course, feeling ahead for the terrain. She found a line of small rocks and recognized them as stones that lined the path used by the groundskeeping staff. Perfect.

"—give me a second—"

It was a snatch of a comment and Grace froze. Whoever said it couldn't have been more than a dozen feet in front of her. She drew her pistol and listened.

"—here it is!" whispered Hecate. "There's a release right under the—"

Grace fired in the direction of the voice. She knew that her first shot would probably miss, but the muzzle flash would show her where to put the second shot.

After the absolute darkness the flash was eye-hurtingly bright, but it froze a picture in her mind. The back of the waterfall. Hecate reaching up under the overhang of moss, her lithe body stretching. Cyrus behind her, his fist clutched around something that hung from a lanyard around his neck. Otto Wirths in the foreground, bent in the direction of the panel.

A flash image. There and gone.

Grace smiled and squeezed off five more shots.

She heard a scream.

And then the wall five feet to her right exploded, showering her with debris. A chunk of rock the size of a fist struck her on the side of her shoulder, and her last shot was high and wide.

Grace fell over and her gun vanished into the darkness.

A moment later Hecate slammed into her, snarling and spitting with insane rage, grabbing her arms with insane strength.

"You fucking bitch!" snarled Hecate as she drove Grace Courtland into the dirt. They rolled over and over again through the darkness, tumbling sideways down the hill away from the waterfall, colliding with rocks and smashing through plants. Hecate snarled continuously and Grace could feel hot spittle on her face and throat. The woman was enormously strong, her fingers like iron bands crushing into Grace's arms with enough force to crush skin and muscle.

Grace jammed a forearm under Hecate's chin to keep

those sharp white teeth away from her throat. With her other hand she shoved back on the woman's shoulder, trying to create space. Grace twisted to bring her knee up between them, using the long thighbone as a strut to separate them.

What the hell was she fighting? Had this mad bitch used her own genetic science on herself? Everything about Hecate provoked an image of one of the big fighting cats. Hecate even hissed like a panther.

Hecate suddenly let go of Grace's arms and grabbed her throat. It was like being crushed by a vise. All at once Grace was unable to breathe.

Grace stopped pushing on Hecate's shoulder and immediately hit her in the face—once, twice, again, pounding on the side of Hecate's cheek and eye socket. The pressure eased by a tiny fraction. Grace dragged in a spoonful of air, but then Hecate tightened her grip, overlapping her thumbs to try to crush the windpipe. Grace pressed her chin down on the thumbs, forcing them against her sternum to slow the choke while continuing to hammer at Hecate. She cupped her palm and slapped Hecate over the ear.

Instantly Hecate howled in pain and toppled sideways. Grace pivoted on the floor and kicked out with both feet, catching Hecate on the hip and stomach, driving her farther away. Grace didn't want to escape; she needed to breathe and reorganize. She spun around and came up into a crouch.

Otto Wirths tore away the decorative vegetation and ran his hands over the panel. The moss had hidden four wing nuts and Otto grabbed the first one and tried to twist it. It resisted and he growled in fury and frustration—and then it moved. He spun it around and around until it reached the end of the thread and fell away.

"Hurry!" Cyrus urged. "They're breaking through the wall."

"I *am* hurrying, damn it." Otto attacked the second one, which was stuck just as firmly as the first. "What about Hecate?"

Cyrus was invisible beside him. He said, "She'll catch up."

The second wing nut began to turn. "And if she doesn't?"

"We have a large family, Otto."

Otto dropped the second wing nut and began turning the third. That one was looser and it yielded immediately. The fourth was harder, but he threw all of his strength at it and the nut turned.

"Otto . . . ," Cyrus hissed. "I hear something. . . ."

There was a second and much bigger explosion and debris flew outward into the chamber. A jagged piece of stone whistled through the air and struck Grace on the side of the head and she spun and fell facedown on the grass and did not move.

Chapter One Hundred
Twenty-Three

The moment I leaned close to the hole in the wall I heard a male voice yell, "They're breaking through! Get us out!. . . ."

A second male voice yelled, "Hecate . . . did you kill that bitch?"

"I don't know," a woman snarled from the darkness deeper in the chamber. "Otto, get my father out of here. Up the stairs. My office. The gray case."

"What about . . . ?"

"I'll make sure you're not followed. Go!"

Christ.

I could tell Grace was in trouble. Maybe dead. But the Jakobys were about to escape. There was no way for me to know whether a distraction at this moment would help or hurt. If Grace was still alive and hiding, then I could get her killed. On the other hand, I needed to know what the Jakobys were doing.

Grace's own voice echoed in my mind.

The mission comes first.

I knew what the mission required. I put the flashlight and the muzzle of the Beretta into the hole, which gave me only a few inches of extra space to see. I prayed I was making the right move.

I switched the flashlight on and pointed the beam in the direction of the male voices. The woman had told

Otto to get her father out of there. Cyrus was the one with the trigger device.

The flashlight beam swept over tropical foliage of all kinds and for a moment I saw nothing else; then I caught a momentary image of something at the edge of the beam of light. I immediately angled the beam back and saw a vulture-faced old man squinting at me through the glare. He held a piece of flat metal in his hands that he had obviously just lifted out of a rectangular hole in the wall. I fired at him and the first bullet hit the metal plate at an angle and whanged off into the darkness. I fired again as the man dropped the plate and tackled a second man who stood closer to the opening. Was that Otto and Cyrus Jakoby? It had to be. I fired and fired, sure that I hit at least one of them, but the tackle had sent them spilling into the opening. I fired the entire magazine and then tore the M4 from Bunny's hand, jammed it into the opening, and let it rip. I wanted to fill their bolt-hole with ricochets that would chop those maniacs to pieces.

I thrust the gun at Bunny to reload and I swept back and forth with the flashlight.

"Hopscotch!" I bellowed.

But if Grace heard my call, she was not able to shout back the countersign.

My heart sank in my chest.

I spun and grabbed Redman by the shoulder. "The DMS and SEALs are all over this island. Find them. Get all the C4 you can and blow me a fucking hole. Bunny— I'm going back to the stairs to see if I can find Hecate's office. Cyrus and Otto are on their way upstairs. Hecate said something about a gray case—"

"Shit . . . you think she has a ruggedized laptop?"

"Yeah, dammit, that's exactly what I think. I've got to find that office."

"I'm going with you."

"No . . . Redman's going to need muscle to fight through to our teams outside. We *need* that hole. As soon as he's secured, then come find me."

He wanted to protest, but I was already in motion.

Chapter One Hundred Twenty-Four

The Chamber of Myth
Tuesday, August 31, 2:57 A.M.
Time Remaining on the Extinction Clock: 33 hours,
3 minutes E.S.T.

It was the blood that woke Grace Courtland. It seeped from the gash in her scalp and curled in lines over her cheek and into her nose. She choked and the sudden spasm of a cough brought her out of her daze. She rolled over onto her stomach and coughed the blood out of her nose and mouth. Her head felt like it was ten times normal sized and stuffed with broken glass. Nausea was a polluted wind that blew through her stomach.

There was movement, noise, and light off to her right and she turned her muzzy head to try to make sense of it. Colored lights popped on and flew through the air and in her confusion Grace didn't understand what she was seeing, and then clarity returned to her. There was a hole in the wall to the Chamber of Myth and someone was tossing chemical light sticks inside. The Jakobys wouldn't do something like that. It had to be . . .

"Joe!" she called, but her voice was a hoarse croak.

Grace climbed shakily to her feet. Her gun was lost somewhere in the shadows. There was no sign of Hecate or the others.

"Effing hell!" she growled, and began climbing back up the hill toward the waterfall and the hole in the wall. Her feet were unsteady and from the dizziness she felt Grace knew that she had a concussion. It was hard to think, but she forced herself to remember where she was and what she had to do.

When she was ten feet from the hole she called out.

"Hopscotch!"

There was a pause and then a familiar voice called back, "Jump rope! Major . . . is that you?"

"Beth . . . thank God. . . ." Grace stumbled the last few steps and leaned on the wall. She saw Beth's eyes go wide and realized what a mess she must look. Her face was covered with blood.

"Beth . . . what happened? Where did the Jakobys go? Where's—"

Staff Sgt. Beth Howell, Alpha Team's number two, gave it to her in a few quick sentences.

Grace turned and reached for Beth's flashlight and shined it on the back of the waterfall, saw the open portal.

"Damn it."

"Give me a flashlight and your sidearm," she ordered, and Beth passed them through along with a spare magazine.

"It's the last one I have."

"If Captain Ledger or anyone else gets in touch, tell them I'm following the Jakobys."

"Major—Captain Ledger took the stairs. He's trying to find the Jakoby woman's office, too."

"Then I'd better bloody well beat him to it. Can't let Echo Team take all the glory."

Beth smiled, but she looked as stressed and nervous as Grace felt.

"Good hunting!" Beth called.

Grace said nothing. She racked the slide on the Sig Sauer, laid her pistol arm across the wrist of the hand holding the flashlight, and stepped through the opening. In her mind this wasn't a simple hunt. The bloody Jakobys weren't the only ones capable of extermination.

The stairs led upward into the darkness.

Gun in hand, Grace began climbing.

Chapter One Hundred Twenty-Five

The Dragon Factory
Tuesday, August 31, 2:58 A.M.
Time Remaining on the Extinction Clock: 33 hours, 2 minutes E.S.T.

I pushed through into the stairwell, cleared it, and then began climbing. There were two floors above the main level, and I would have to check them both. My heart was racing and my nerves were screaming at me. Images of Grace, alone and hurt in the dark, kept trying to climb into my head and I kept forcing them out.

The mission comes first.

The pressure I felt was almost unbearable because the cost of failure was too high to calculate. Global ethnic genocide. How is that concept even possible for a human mind to grasp, let alone attempt to undertake? Even if someone was a racist, the concept should be so alien to the mind that it would never form, and yet these maniacs were within minutes of setting it into motion. Evil should never be allowed to flourish, but this transcended evil. I don't know if there's even a word for what this was.

That's what put the power in my muscles; that's what gave me focus.

At the first landing I pushed the door open slowly and quietly. The hall was dark as pitch. I risked my flashlight, casting the beam up and down, and then shut it off and shifted quickly away from where I'd been standing.

No shots tore through the doorway.

So far, so good.

I turned the light back on and moved down the hallway at a light run. Seventy feet in I found a body. It was a Russian and even from ten feet away I could tell there was something wrong about him, but it wasn't until I was right on top of him that I could see that he had no arms. They had been ripped out of their sockets.

A second man lay against a wall a few yards away, and from the damage done to him and the smears of blood it looked like someone had beaten him to death with . . .

Holy shit.

Someone had torn the first Russian's arms off and used them to beat the second man to death. As soon as I understood it, I knew that it had to be—

Something hit me in the side hard enough to pick me up off the ground and send me crashing into the wall. My gun and flashlight went flying. I hit, dropped, and rolled away, and if I hadn't then a booted foot would have crushed my skull.

I scuttled backward as something huge and monstrous rushed at me from the shadows. It was roughly man shaped but way too big.

One of the Jakoby Twins' transgenic soldiers. A three-hundred-pound killing machine with the face of an ape and a chest twice as massive as Bunny's.

The soldier raised his foot to take another stamp and I swept his standing leg. He crashed with a sound like a clap of thunder, and I side-rolled back to my feet. My gun was on the floor fifteen feet away and I started to dive for it, but the ape-man grabbed my ankle and tripped me. As I fell he clawed at me with his other hand and grabbed a strap of my Kevlar.

I rolled sideways toward him and chopped him across the face with an elbow smash that cracked bone. It knocked his head back against the marble floor, and I pivoted on my back to bring my legs to bear and ax-kicked him on the mouth. The heel of my boot smashed in his front teeth and suddenly he was choking and gagging on bone fragments.

I got to my feet and drew my Rapid Response knife. I'm not one of those idiots who wait for their opponent to get back to his feet so there can be a round two. I threw myself at him and buried the knife into his eye socket. Then I cut his throat because I was having a bad fucking day.

Blood geysered up and splashed my face and arm. *Screw it.*

I got to my feet just as a second Berserker came running at me out of the shadows.

A gun would have been so much easier, but there was no time.

As he closed on me there was a moment when he

passed through the flashlight's glow and I realized that Bunny had been right and Top wrong when assessing the two men we'd fought in Deep Iron. These weren't exoskeletons. Bunny had simply used fists against something so damn big and strong that his blows did little useful harm.

We'd all been right, though, about the body armor. These guys were dressed head to toe in it. I doubted that it was anything cutting-edge that stopped the PSI of bullets. These guys just bulled through it. It wasn't that they were big—if they had ape DNA, then they were also much stronger and with far denser muscle tissue.

This passed through my mind in a microsecond. While those pieces were clicking into place I was moving forward to meet the brute.

He tried for a grab, but I figured him for something like that, so I dropped into a low crouch and drove the knife into the top of his foot and then slammed my shoulder into his crotch. He howled in surprise and pain and instinctively shoved at me. I kept a solid grip on the knife and yanked it free as his shove sent me skidding ten feet down the hall. At the end of the skid I brought my knees up and tucked into a backroll, so I ended up on my feet right next to the Russian's dismembered arm.

The Berserker took a step and his foot buckled. I scooped up the Russian's arm and threw it at the apeman and as he batted it aside I was already moving forward. I slashed him from eyebrow to jawline in a hard diagonal slice that cut right through his nose. He shrieked in pain and clamped both hands to his face. In the narrow gap between his forearms I lunged in and stabbed him in the throat, gave the blade a quarter turn, and tore it free.

He fell.

I picked up my pistol and slapped my pockets for magazines, found that I had one plus what was in the Beretta.

It would have to do.

I wiped and folded the knife, picked up the flashlight, checked the action on the pistol, and ran like hell.

I got to the end of the hallway without finding a single room that looked like an office. There were workrooms and a lunchroom and some computer labs but nothing else. *Shit.* At the far end I found a stairwell and crashed through. Hecate's office had to be on the top floor.

I was halfway up the stairs when I heard men shouting and screaming and firing. Flashlight beams cut back and forth and I risked a glance over the edge of the stairs. Two flights below, a group of Russians were fighting a losing battle against a pack of the scorpion-dogs.

"Son of a bitch," I muttered, and ran upward. If I'd had a grenade left I'd have sent it down as a "hello" from Uncle Sam. Pity.

I took the steps two at a time and then came out onto the top level. My flash showed a much more elegant hallway, with brass fittings, expensive art on the walls, and a décor that tended toward style rather than function. Hecate's office had to be here, but as I shone the light down the hall I could see at least twenty office doors.

My flashlight also swept across the simian faces of a half dozen of the Berserkers.

They saw me and grinned.

And then they rushed me.

Chapter One Hundred Twenty-Six

The Jakobys
Tuesday, August 31, 3:00 a.m.
Time Remaining on the Extinction Clock: 33 hours,
0 minutes E.S.T.

The spiral staircase that rose from the Chamber of Myth to Hecate's office was one of several bolt-holes she'd built into the architecture. Paris knew about most of them but not all. Paris had been unaware of this one and of one other that took Hecate down to a pneumatic tube in which she could take a capsule from the main building straight to the dock. There was a seaplane and a twenty-eight-foot ZT-280 Checkmate speedboat with 496-horsepower engine and a top speed of 74 miles per hour. A final private stairway led to a small lab she had ordered built during one of Paris's trips to the South of France. It was in that private lab that Hecate had worked with panther and tiger genomes for some personal gene therapy.

In lighter moods Hecate sometimes castigated herself for wasting the time and resources on the bolt-holes and for the paranoia that led her to create them. Now, as she followed Otto and Cyrus up through the dark, she felt a flush of vindication.

"I can't see a damn thing," growled Cyrus from above her.

"You don't need to see," she snapped. "Just climb."

"Wait . . . the ladder stopped. . . . I can feel a door."

"That's it. It opens into a closet in my office."

One by one they emerged from the spiral staircase into a closet that was as dark as everything else. Hecate felt her way past Otto and Cyrus to the door and let herself into her office. The room felt alien now that there were no points of reference, but she finally located her desk and from there oriented herself to the whole room. A few brief diffused flashes of light backlit the blinds, and Hecate moved to the window and peeked out.

"God! Look at this."

With the blind lifted even a bit, the flashes of automatic gunfire and explosions gave them enough light to cross the room to join her. They peered out. The lawn below was a battlefield. On one side were at least sixty of the remaining Russians. They had a very secure firing position among a tumble of decorative boulders. Well to their left were the guards from the Dragon Factory—normal humans and the genetically modified Berserkers. Neither of these two forces was firing at the other. Though there had been no opportunity for either Hecate or Cyrus to tell their forces to stand down, that the conflict between the two houses of Jakoby—the Deck and the Dragon Factory—was over, they had somehow worked out a temporary alliance against a common threat. The other side of the lawn was crammed with armed men. It was impossible to pick out any details from that distance, but the precision and tactics they observed told the tale. These were U.S. Special Forces. A lot of them.

Between the two opposing sides lay the burning wreckage of a Black Hawk helicopter. Whether it had been shot down by their own men or had crashed because of systems failure following the EMP was anyone's guess. The lawn was littered from end to end with bodies.

"This isn't a fight we can win," said Hecate.

"Where is the rest of your staff?" Otto asked.

"If they followed procedure then they're down in the caves below the maintenance level. They are instructed to remain there until they get an all-clear signal." In the dim light she gave a rueful smile. "Of course, if they made it to the caves and locked themselves in before the EMP, then that could be a problem. The computers control all life support."

Cyrus turned to his daughter.

"Listen to me, Hecate. . . . I cannot express how deeply your loyalty touches me. I would love to spend years and years working with you, side by side, to help reshape this world as the Extinction Wave cleanses it. But . . ." He nodded to the battle outside. "I can't see how we can get away from here."

"I have a boat. And a seaplane."

"And we've had an EMP," he reminded her.

Hecate closed her eyes. "Shit."

"We're not getting out of here," said Cyrus. "I think we can all agree on that."

Otto opened his mouth to say something, then sighed and nodded.

"We can try," insisted Hecate. "We can't just roll over and let them win."

"Win?" said Cyrus with a smile. "What makes you think they can win? The most they can do is kill us."

"But . . ."

He fished into his shirt and brought out the trigger device.

"In war people die," he said. "All that matters is winning. Now, my pet, let's get that laptop."

Chapter One Hundred
Twenty-Seven

I raised my pistol and fired.

All of them were wearing body armor, and they were fast. It was head shots or I was dead. The Berserkers screamed like mountain gorillas—not a human sound at all.

I hit the lead one in the forehead and he pitched back and dragged two others down. I fired three more shots and took down another. Another two shots for a third.

Then they started shooting at me.

I jumped sideways and crashed through an office door, hit the ground, rolled, and came up into a kneeling firing position as they tried to squeeze through the doorway. The window blinds were open, and rippling light from the pitched battle outside gave me enough illumination to see the Berserkers. Their bulk was against them as they fought one another to be the first to get to me. I fired and hit the lead one in the throat, but he opened up with a Škorpion vz. 61 machine pistol that chewed up half the room. He was still firing when he fell down dead.

Another of the Berserkers reached over him and fired. I twisted out of the way of the first round, but the second and third slammed into me and sent me flying. I could actually feel my ribs break. The pain shot through me like lightning as I hit the wall and slid down.

But I used the pain; I let it wipe my mind to clarity.

The Berserker stepped into the room and I shot him through the upper lip. The bullet punched through the back of his head and tore the ear off the Berserker behind him. I grinned and fired again. The one with the torn ear raised an arm to fend off the shot, and though the Kevlar deflected the round, I could tell from his howl of pain that the impact broke his arm. I didn't much care. I put two rounds into him. And fired my last at the remaining Berserker before the slide locked back.

I dropped the magazine and pulled my last one. Just doing that sent daggers of pain through my side. Everything that had happened over the last hour had drained me, and the damaged ribs weren't going to help. My head pounded from the noise of all the gunfire and I still hadn't found Grace or the Jakobys.

The last Berserker was wounded, but he was still growling as he hauled on the corpses that choked the doorway. He yelled threats in Afrikaans and English and promised to tear my head off. I think he meant it.

I struggled to my feet and braced my butt against the desk to help steady my aim. The broken ribs were on my right side. My gun arm.

"Come on, you ugly bastard!" I yelled.

He grinned at me with bloody teeth and poked a rifle barrel into the room. I put four shots into him before he could squeeze the trigger. His head seemed to disintegrate as he flew backward.

I headed for the door, but on the first step I realized that there was something wrong with my left leg. When I'd fallen I must have twisted something. Swell. I sucked it up as best I could and limped to the door. The Berserkers were slumped everywhere and I had to climb over them to get back to the hallway.

My flashlight lay on the floor. Bending to pick it up was no fun at all with busted ribs.

There were still a lot of offices to check. I had to find them.

The first office was empty. So was the second. And the third.

Just as I was reaching for the doorknob on the fourth office, the door opened and a Berserker punched me in the face.

Chapter One Hundred Twenty-Eight

The Jakobys
Tuesday, August 31, 3:02 A.M.
Time Remaining on the Extinction Clock: 32 hours,
58 minutes E.S.T.

Hecate swore and punched the wall beside the safe.

"What's wrong?" demanded Cyrus.

"I can't see the numbers on the dial. Look in my desk drawers . . . find a lighter, anything!"

Otto and Cyrus began tearing apart her drawers, throwing papers and pens everywhere. "Matches!" cried Otto. "I found a pack of matches."

Hecate crossed the room, navigating by the light from the battle. There was a scrape and a hiss and a small fire blazed at the end of a paper match. Cyrus snatched up a sheaf of reports and rolled them into a tube. Otto held the match to the roll, and as it caught, the glow flooded the room, pushing back the shadows.

Cyrus cried out in delight as if with all of the technology he and Otto had stolen or created, this simplest of man's tools—fire—was the wonder of the ages. He and Otto hurried over to the wall and watched as Hecate attacked the dial once again. This time the tumblers clicked one-two-three and she jerked the door open.

The safe was large and there were stacks of papers, bundles of currency, cases of jewelry, and several high-capacity flash drives banded together with oversized rubber bands. One whole side of the safe was taken up by a large briefcase with a corrugated metal cover. It was very heavy and Hecate grunted as she pulled it out and they carried it over to the desk. Otto swept the last of the papers onto the floor as Hecate set the case down and unlocked it. She punched the on button and they all held their breath.

A tiny green light popped on and the screen flashed from black to blue.

"Thank God!" said Cyrus.

"Lead case in a lead-lined safe," said Hecate. "My father taught me to be extra-careful."

Cyrus looked up at her and there was such a depth of love in his eyes that Hecate felt her own eyes growing moist. She said, "I want us to survive this."

"We can't. . . ."

"We can't escape the island," said Hecate. "But there are caves and tunnels all through this island. We may be able to find a place to hide until we can escape."

"What are the chances?" said Otto with a calculating coldness.

"Slim. But that's better than none."

Otto studied her and then nodded. "Your father and I have faced longer odds."

"Like when we faked my death in Brazil," Cyrus

said. "That was the first time one of the 'Family' had to be sacrificed for the cause."

"What do you mean?"

"We drowned a clone and let his body be found. By then we were in Cabo and reading about it in the papers."

The computer finished loading.

There was a sudden racket from outside. Yells and gunfire.

"They're here!" Cyrus cried, but when Hecate ran to the door and looked out she shook her head.

"No . . . it looks like a single soldier." She turned back, smiling. "I have a dozen Berserkers on this floor at all times. They'll tear him apart. We have time."

Cyrus dug the flash drive from under his shirt and lifted the lanyard over his head. He kissed it lovingly and handed it to Otto, who punched in the security code that activated the drive.

"How will we transmit?" asked Otto as he handed the drive to Hecate. "The EMP will have taken out your router."

"Satellite uplink," she said. She fitted the drive into a USB port and tapped a few keys. "The uplink's built into the computer. We can hack three different Mexican satellites from here." She turned the laptop around with the keys toward Cyrus.

"Good," said Cyrus. "The next steps are critical. I have to upload the release codes and then transmit. The signal also sends an automatic verification sequence. Unless I hand-enter a cancel sequence, then the release codes are unscrambled when the Extinction Clock reaches zero."

"When's that?" asked Hecate, caught up in the sorcery of her father's plan.

"Noon tomorrow."

The gunfire in the hallway was punctuated by hoarse death screams. Hecate chewed her lip. The screams sounded more like Berserkers than ordinary men. More soldiers must have reached this floor.

"What if those soldiers break in here and take the trigger device?"

"Doubting the unstoppability of your transgenic toys?" Cyrus said with a smile.

"I don't want to fail when we're this close."

"We won't. Once this is sent, all we have to do is . . . nothing. Unless they know the cancel sequence it won't matter."

"*I* don't even know it," said Otto. "Mr. Cyrus is the only one who can stop it, and . . . why would he?"

"It's all yours, Father," she said. "Let's change the world."

"Let's not," said a female voice.

They whirled to see Grace Courtland standing in the doorway to the closet.

Chapter One Hundred Twenty-Nine

The Dragon Factory
Tuesday, August 31, 3:04 A.M.
Time Remaining on the Extinction Clock: 32 hours, 56 minutes E.S.T.

I went down and I almost went out.

The only thing that saved me was my injured leg. As soon as I saw the Berserker lunge at me I shifted backward and my bad leg buckled under me. He still nailed me, but it wasn't full-power. It was enough, though, to knock me across the hallway and smash me into the far wall. My head felt like cracked church bells were ringing and fireworks burst in my eyes.

I heard the Berserker laugh.

He drew his sidearm as he came out of the office. I brought my gun up and fired over and over again, trying to aim through the haze and distortion filling my eyes. There's an Army saying that if you put enough ordnance downrange you're bound to hit something. I put half a magazine into the air where I thought his head should be.

He never returned fire.

I blinked my eyes clear and stared. The Berserker was leaning back against the door frame and he slowly . . . slowly sat down. His eyes were wide and filled with surprise, and there was a black dot above his right eyebrow.

I'd fired eight shots and hit him once.

Once was enough.

A voice inside my head said, *Tick-tock.*

I got to one knee. Then to my feet. My left leg felt like it was made from Silly Putty and a furnace had opened in my chest. My head was a bag of broken stones.

"Grace . . . ," I said.

I kept going down the hall. There was just one door left, and as I reached for the handle I heard shouts and then gunshots. I tried kicking the door open, but my bad leg collapsed under me and I fell.

"There!" someone yelled, and I turned to see more of the goddamn Berserkers pounding down the hallway toward me. I leaned against the office door, raised my pistol, and fired.

And then from the other side of the door I heard Grace Courtland scream.

Chapter One Hundred Thirty

Grace
Tuesday, August 31, 3:05 a.m.
Time Remaining on the Extinction Clock: 32 hours,
55 minutes E.S.T.

For Grace Courtland it had all come down to this. A single moment in time when what she did and who she was would matter most.

She had climbed up through the long darkness of the access stairs and emerged into the darkness of the utility closet in Hecate's office. She almost rushed straight out, but when she heard them talking about the trigger device she stopped to listen. She understood what had to be done.

"It's all yours, Father," said Hecate. "Let's change the world."

Grace stepped out and pointed her gun at Cyrus Jakoby's face.

"Let's not," she said.

The three of them froze, in shock, but their eyes were filled with sudden and immeasurable hatred.

"*Mein Gott!*" cried Cyrus.

Grace fired.

Not at Otto, or Cyrus, or Hecate. She fired at the laptop. But the lead-shielded computer was too tough and the bullet ricocheted off to punch a hole through Cyrus's left biceps. He screamed and fell back, clapping a hand over the bloody wound.

"No!" said Otto in a hoarse whisper.

He lunged for the keyboard and Grace shot him. The first bullet took Otto Wirths in the shoulder and spun him, and her second punched a wet hole in his chest. Otto crashed to the desk and then rolled off onto the floor, dragging the laptop with him.

And then Hecate threw herself at Grace. The albino woman leaped twelve feet across the office and drove Grace against the wall. With a snarl of inhuman rage Hecate bit down hard on Grace's shoulder. Grace screamed and reeled back and she struck her already-injured head on the corner of the closet doorway. The pain was almost unbearable, but she clubbed Hecate with the butt of her pistol. The blow barely slowed the woman. Hecate snarled at Grace, her lips red with the blood that pumped from Grace's torn shoulder. Grace hit her again and again, but Hecate backhanded her so hard that the world went white in the midst of all the blackness.

Grace hit the ground and her gun slid away from her. Hecate looked from Grace to the fallen pistol and was caught in a split second of indecision. Grace tried to focus her eyes, but there were two of everything. Even so she did not hesitate. She kicked hard and swept Hecate's feet from under her, and as she fell Grace rolled sideways toward her gun. Hecate sprang into a catlike crouch and lunged again, but Grace had her gun now. She fired from point-blank range and the bullet tore through Hecate's stomach.

"No!" cried Cyrus as his daughter was flung backward.

Grace struggled to her knees and pointed the gun at Cyrus.

"Step away from that fucking computer!" she ordered.

Someone began pounding on the office door and then came gunshots. Grace could not tell who it was—Special Forces, the Russians, the Berserkers—and she couldn't risk it.

"Step away or I will kill you!" Grace yelled. Her head injury was making her sick, and the double vision was getting worse.

Cyrus hesitated. His eyes were wild, mouth open, drool beginning to drip from his lower lip.

"You can't," he implored. "This is everything I've worked for my whole life. This is the *purpose* of my life!"

"Move away from the keyboard. . . ."

"You idiot . . . you're white! What I'm doing will be the saving of the entire race. Don't you understand that? This for the survival of the white race!"

Grace's eyes narrowed to icy slits. Her hands were trembling, but her voice was firm. "And this is for the survival of the human race."

She pulled the trigger.

There were two blasts.

The first caught Cyrus Jakoby high on the left side of his chest and spun him against the wall.

The second blast, which happened in almost the same instant, struck Grace Courtland in the back.

The impact threw her forward to the edge of the desk.

She hit it hard and collapsed to her knees. Shocked beyond understanding, she turned and saw a shape emerge from the shadows of the closet.

Conrad Veder. He held his smoking pistol in his hand and raised the barrel to point at Grace's head.

Chapter One Hundred Thirty-One

The Dragon Factory
Tuesday, August 31, 3:06 A.M.
Time Remaining on the Extinction Clock: 32 hours,
54 minutes E.S.T.

I fired three shots, two at the Berserkers, hitting one of them in the head, and then I pointed the gun at the door and blew the lock off. I threw my shoulder against it and saw a sight that nearly tore the heart out of my chest.

Grace was on her knees, half-collapsed over the front of a big office desk. In the pale glow of a laptop screen I could see that she was covered in blood. Her face was painted red; her back was slick and wet. Hecate Jakoby was crawling slowly along the floor toward the desk and she, too, was bleeding. Otto Wirths lay dead on the floor, and Cyrus Jakoby was climbing back to his feet, blood streaming from his arm and chest.

And one person stood on his feet.

I knew him as Hans Brucker and Gunnar Haeckel. But those men were dead. This was an exact copy. Another clone. And he held a pistol in his hand.

"Joe . . . ," said Grace in a ragged whisper. "The code . . ."

The assassin shot her.

I think I screamed. I don't remember. I could feel the gun buck in my hand. I saw the assassin duck backward into a closet, saw splinters rip loose from the doorjamb. I staggered into the room, screaming as Grace slid down to the floor.

I wheeled into the doorway of the closet, but it was empty. There was an open trapdoor in the floor and splashes of blood all around it. I'd hit him. But he was gone.

I spun back into the room and shot Cyrus Jakoby in the stomach. He fell backward and collapsed. Hecate stretched up a long arm from the floor toward the laptop. I shot her in the head. My slide locked back, my gun empty.

I could hear the Berserkers coming.

If I had any chance of saving Grace I had to do something. I looked wildly around. There was an adjoining office, and I stumbled to it. It was almost identical to Hecate's. Probably her brother's. I staggered back to Grace and pulled her to her feet. She was nearly unconscious. I grabbed the laptop with the other hand and somehow dragged us all into the next room. I eased Grace down into a chair and then rushed back, scooped her gun up off the floor as the Berserkers began crowding into the room. I shot the first one in the forehead, but I could see that there were more of them in the hallway.

I retreated to Paris's office, slammed and locked the door. There was a security crossbar on the door and I dropped it in place. Almost immediately the Berserkers began pounding on the door. The whole frame shook. I knew it wouldn't hold.

I staggered over to Grace. There was harsh white

light coming in through the window. One of the soldiers outside had set off a flare. Gunfire was constant.

Grace was slumped in the chair. She had been shot twice in the back, and the exit wounds on her stomach and chest were dreadful. I tore off my Kevlar and ripped my shirt to rags to staunch the flow of blood. Her head lolled and for a horrible moment I thought she was gone, but when I pressed my fingers against her throat I could feel a pulse. It was weak, but it was there.

"Grace" I said, pitching my voice sharply enough to wake her from the stupor of shock. "Grace, stay with me, babe . . . come on . . . stay with me."

She opened her eyes a little and licked her lips. "That's . . . *Major* . . . Babe . . . ," she said with a smirk.

"Yes, it is, honey; yes, it is."

The pounding on the door was incessant.

"Joe . . . the laptop . . ."

It was on the desk and I pulled it close. There were two words in a little gray box.

Message sent.

"Grace . . . did Cyrus send the code?"

"I—don't . . ." Her voice disintegrated into a fit of coughing. Blood flecked her lips.

"Grace, honey, stay with me. Help's on the way."

I hoped to God that I wasn't lying to her. I could hear helicopters in the air now, which meant that help was arriving from outside the EMP blast zone. Soon hundreds of troops would be landing. But was it all for nothing?

"Joe," she whispered, "listen. . . ." She reached up with a weak hand and gripped the front of my shirt, tried to pull me close. "Joe—if the . . . code . . . was sent . . . there's . . ."

She broke off into another fit of coughing. I used another strip of cloth from my shirt to dab the blood from her lips. I wanted to scream. I wanted to do anything to get out of this room, to get her to a medic.

". . . Joe . . . if the code was sent . . . there's still time."

"What do you mean, Grace? How can we stop it?"

"Cancel. . . . code. . . ." More coughing, more blood. "Cyrus knows. If not . . . MindReader. . . ."

The Berserkers were knocking plaster out of the wall. The whole room shook.

"Take the flash drive . . . to Bug . . . tell him." Her eyes drifted shut.

"Grace, come on . . . don't do this to me. Don't leave me. . . ."

Her eyelids fluttered open. "I'll . . . never leave you. . . ."

But she did.

Her eyes closed and she settled against me. Her head lolled forward and she died right there with her cheek pressed against mine. I screamed her name. I screamed and screamed until I tore blood from my own throat.

But all the screams in the world could not bring her back from the infinite sea of darkness in which she now swam. I could actually feel her leave. It was like a whisper against my lips. Her last breath, exhaled as I held her.

I pulled her against my chest and rocked her back and forth as one by one all of the lights that held back my personal darkness flickered and went out.

Chapter One Hundred Thirty-Two

I crouched in the dark. I was bleeding and something inside was broken. Maybe something inside my head, too. Grace lay in my arms and yet she was gone.

I was gone, too.

Slowly, with infinite care and gentleness, I slid from the chair and laid her on the floor. I straightened her arms and legs, and I bent and kissed her forehead and eyes and her lips. For a long moment I knelt there with my head on her chest, praying that I could hear that noble and loving heart beat once more.

But all I heard was silence and the screaming madness that was boiling inside my own head. The door was barred, but the Berserkers were going to get in. I knew that.

I got to my feet. I had Grace's gun. I released the magazine and checked the rounds. I had three bullets left. Three bullets and a knife.

The pounding on the door was like thunder. I knew the door wouldn't hold.

They would get in.

The code had been sent. I pulled the flash drive from the computer and put it in my pocket. Somewhere the Extinction Clock was ticking down. If I was still in this room when it hit zero, more people would die than perished during the Black Death and all of the pandemics put together.

I thought I could stop them. We—me, Church, the DMS . . . Grace—we thought we could stop them.

Now it was down to me or no one. I had to get the flash drive to Bug, and I prayed that he and MindReader could read the codes on the drive and send whatever cancel signal could be sent. It might even be a fool's errand. But Grace had died to get us this far, and with her last breaths she'd given me this task.

If there was any kind of justice in the universe, then a sacrifice so bravely made could not—*should not*—be in vain.

It wasn't our fault we came into this so late. They chased us and messed with our heads and ran us around, and by the time we knew what we were up against the clock had already nearly run its course.

We tried. Over the last week I'd left a trail of bodies behind me from Denver, to Costa Rica, to the Bahamas. And now Grace Courtland was dead.

The pounding was louder. The door was buckling, the crossbar bending. It was only seconds before the lock or the hinges gave out, and then they'd come howling in here. Then it would be them against me.

I was hurt. I was bleeding.

I had three bullets and a knife.

I got to my feet and faced the door, my gun in my left hand, the knife in my right.

I smiled a killer's smile.

Let them come.

Chapter One Hundred Thirty-Three

When the door burst open there were five of them.

I used three bullets and killed three of them. Head shots. I would like to think that some force steadied my hand. I don't know. But I killed the first three through the door.

When the fourth one climbed over the bodies I met him with a knife to the throat. I stabbed him a dozen times. I was screaming. He was screaming, too, trying to back away. I crawled out after him and killed him.

The last of the Berserkers came at me and hit me. I felt my cheekbone break. I felt teeth buckle in their sockets. I don't know what kept me on my feet. I don't know what put the power in my arm to slash him across the throat. Over and over again.

I blacked out for a while, and when I could think again I was covered in blood and the Berserker was . . . ruined.

I staggered across the office to the desk and then shambled around it.

Cyrus Jakoby lay on the floor. He was bleeding from several gunshot wounds. All were serious. None were fatal. That was a shame. For him.

He looked up at me, at my face, into my eyes, and he saw something that tore a scream from him. Maybe it was in that moment that he recognized the implacable, heartless, relentless monster that his victims had always seen in him. Maybe he realized that he was tethered to life by only one slender thread.

He knew the cancel code.

He knew that I would not, could not, kill him as long as he had it.

He thought that he could bargain with that.

He should have looked deeper into my eyes.

I stood over him, covered in blood—some of which was Grace's—and I showed him my knife.

I never had to ask him for the code.

In the end, he gave it willingly.

But not easily.

Epilogue

(1)

Six days later I sat in a wheelchair in a chapel outside of Baltimore. Grace Courtland had no family in England. Mr. Church had appealed to her government to let her rest here near her friends. They argued, but Church got his way.

Everybody came. I don't know how many thousands of people showed up. Grace Courtland was probably the most famous person in the world. The beautiful government agent who saved the world from the Extinction Wave. It was headlines; it was a Hollywood dream story. Books would be written about her; movies would be made. Most of it would be a fiction cooked up by Church's PR people. There are too many villains—the world needs a hero.

My name was left completely out of it, which was only right. Ditto for the DMS. Homeland and a few other agencies were handed the credit while Church erased all traces of our involvement from every database. The key players knew the truth, and that was all that Church needed to keep the DMS in place. No one in government would dare go after us now.

I thought about these things as I sat in the chapel a dozen feet from where Grace lay in state like some warrior queen.

The procession to pass in front of her coffin lasted for hours. The President of the United States sat on my left side. The First Lady sat on my right and held my hand all through it. Most of Congress was there, and ambassadors from over one hundred countries, and the heads of state of those nations that were targeted in the first round of the Extinction Wave. There were Presidents and Chancellors, Queens and Kings. The Air Force did a flyover with the missing-man formation.

Rudy, Bunny, Top, Redman, and the survivors of Alpha Team and as many DMS operatives as could be spared filled the whole section behind us. No press was allowed within a half mile of the chapel. I think Church asked Linden Brierly for that favor and it was done on behalf of "National Security."

Oskar Freund, the son of Church's murdered colleague, came and sat with us. His government had appointed him to lead an international task force to hunt down the remaining members of the Cabal. This fire may have been lit in Germany in the early twentieth century, but modern Germany was having no part in perpetuating it. They went after the Cabal with a ferocity that sometimes shocked the world press. But global public support for the witch hunt was overwhelming.

The coffin was closed at my request. If people knew Grace, they should remember her in their own way, not as some mortician painted her. Her casket was draped with the flags of England and the United States.

*　*　*

I don't remember a lot of what happened after my fight with the Berserkers. Just fragments. A few words and images. . . .

I remember Bunny coming out of the smoke with all of Hardball Team behind him. Bunny was battered and bloody from fighting his way through a pack of Berserkers.

I remember being carried aboard a helicopter. And I remember speaking into a radio, telling Church and Bug about the cancel code. I remember that the trigger device was smeared with blood. Grace's and mine.

I remember looking out of the helicopter window and seeing waves of U.S. troops surge across the island. Someone later told me that the 164 enemy combatants were killed in the action. That included Russian mercenaries, Dragon Factory guards, and the Berserkers. Someone else told me that the SEALs cleaned up a nest of the scorpion-dogs—Stingers, as we later learned they were called. There was no attempt to take any of the transgenic guard dogs alive.

I remember drifting off into a morphine sleep and dreaming that this was all a dream. When I woke up, the hurt was a hundred times worse. Even nightmares are better than some realities.

The line of mourners kept moving and the day dragged on and on. I said almost nothing. I folded into myself. The darkness inside was welcoming.

(2)

The cancel code Cyrus Jakoby had given me was the correct one. By that point he was beyond lying. When our forces raided the Deck they found the Extinction Clock ticking down. It reached zero at noon on September 1, but the release had been aborted. It wasn't a James Bond finish with one second on the clock. By the time Bug hacked the system and inputted the cancel code there was still over seventeen hours left. Seems like a lot of time. But it isn't. They'll probably change it for the movie.

The DMS worked with the State Department, Interpol, and other agencies to identify and locate the operatives worldwide who had been ready to release the tainted water and disease pathogens. There was no way to keep the story out of the press. The bigger the witch hunt became, the more leaks it sprang. When the President of the United States went on TV to make an address everyone everywhere stopped to listen. True to his form since taking office, the President was calm, clear, and candid. He told as much of the story as security would allow: eugenics, transgenics, gene therapy, pathogens made from genetic diseases, clones. Measured against the whole, even the fact that Jakoby and Otto were virtually immortal because of gene therapy was less fantastic than the knowledge that the worldwide AIDS epidemic had been deliberate.

Of course all of this brought out every conspiracy theorist and lunatic-fringe religious nut, and the news shows trotted them out continually. I stopped watching and had the TV in my hospital room disconnected.

(3)

During the raid on the Deck the DMS teams found irrefutable proof that the assassin who had killed Grace was named Conrad Veder and that he was one of four clones of a man named Hans-Ulrich Rudel, the most highly decorated Stuka dive-bomber pilot of World War II. Rudel was a king among professional killers and the only person to be awarded the Nazi Knight's Cross with Golden Oak Leaves, Swords, and Diamonds.

They also found twenty-nine boys who looked exactly like Eighty-two. Rudy spent days interviewing them. Some, he said, were irretrievably psychopathic; others were borderline personalities. All were damaged. The only one who showed any signs of normalcy was Eighty-two.

Nobody calls him that anymore, though. Rudy encouraged him to pick a name, but the boy asked Rudy to pick one. Rudy named him Helmut. It's German for "courageous." The boy picked Deacon as his last name.

Helmut Deacon sat behind me all through that long day in the chapel.

He's asked Rudy to appeal to Church to allow the boy to work with the Red Cross and WHO teams that are caring for the New Men. I think Church will agree.

(4)

The DMS teams on Dogfish Cay found Paris Jakoby when they broke into the Chamber of Myth. He had sustained a heavy blow that fractured his jaw and sprained his neck, and from what the field medics determined, he had still been alive when the transgenic animals in the chamber began feeding on him.

The animals that survived the battle are being kept in a secure facility until someone can decide what to do with them.

A squad of Marines found the underground cavern where the Dragon Factory staff had hidden during the fight. They were low on fresh air, but they had survived. Many of them claimed not to have the slightest clue what Paris and Hecate were doing, and for some polygraphs and psych evaluations bore out their claims. A lot of others had varying levels of knowledge and involvement.

The people at the Deck were a bit more openly involved in Cyrus and Otto's scheme, though few seemed to know what the end goal was. Even so, the "we were just following orders" defense carried no weight at all in the trials that followed.

Those trials are still ongoing. They'll take years.

(5)

I missed most of this. The medivac chopper took me to a hospital in Florida. I was there for eleven days. I sustained a cracked cheekbone, five broken ribs, a torn ligament in my ankle, a hairline fracture of the jaw, and a skull fracture resulting in subdural hematoma. Late the next day the scans showed a dangerous buildup of blood in the inner meningeal layer of the dura, so they wheeled me into surgery and cut a hole in my skull to relieve the pressure. The doctors warned me that I would probably have some memory loss. I wish they'd been right about that, but I remember everything. Maybe one day I'll be happy about that.

Top Sims was in the room next to me and was recovering from surgery to repair the compound fractures. It was uncertain if he would ever be fit enough to return to active fieldwork. Bunny was treated and released, but he stayed at the hospital for almost a week. Rudy, too. Friends from the DMS brought them changes of clothes and hot meals in Styrofoam containers.

They let me out for the day so I could attend the funeral, but I was scheduled for ankle surgery the following day.

After the service, when I was back in my room at the hospital, Rudy sat in one of the two visitors' chairs. Mr. Church came and sat in the other chair.

"How much do you remember?"

"All of it."

"Then you know Cyrus Jakoby is still alive," Church said.

I nodded.

"You didn't kill him."

"No."

"Why?"

"When he heals, after the damage is repaired, I want him to stand trial."

Church nodded. "They will execute him."

"They shouldn't," I said.

"Why not?"

"They should put him on display. In a zoo. In a freak show."

"Will public humiliation redress the harm he's done?"

"I don't know. Go ask a philosopher."

"I'm asking you."

I didn't answer. What could I say?

He stood up. "We'll talk later."

"No," I said. "I'm done. I quit. I can't do this any-more."

He adjusted his tie. "We'll talk later."

When he left I saw that he'd put a pack of cookies on my nightstand. Oreos.

Rudy had been silent through all of this. He said, "Do you really want to quit?"

"I . . . have to," I said. "I'm ruined."

"Your injuries are bad, Joe, but they said you'd make a complete recovery."

I looked away. "I'm ruined."

(6)

On a beautiful morning in mid-September they wheeled me out of the hospital. Rudy was there with a car to take me to the airport. There was no sign of Mr. Church or anyone else from the DMS. Rudy was silent for most of the drive, then, "How are you doing, Cowboy?"

I shook my head.

"The war's over," he said. "The soldiers have come home from the battlefield. It's time to talk."

It took a long time for me to pick the right words. "Why do we do it, Rude?"

"Why do we fight? We fight because someone has to—"

"No," I said. "Why do we hate?"

"I don't know. There are long and short answers to that. Mostly people hate because people are different from them, or because they're the same. It comes down to fear. Our species has always been motivated by fear. We fear what we don't know or understand, we fear differences, and the primitive in our consciousness demonstrates fear through violence. It's what makes us so aggressive. Fear, and greed."

"Is that all? Is that everything that is necessary to explain monsters like Otto Wirths and Cyrus Jakoby?" Despite everything, I still thought of him by that name. As Jakoby he was a worse monster than he'd been as Mengele. "Those men loved what they were doing. They delighted in it. It wasn't fear of other races . . . it was hatred."

"It was evil, Joe. And there is no real definition of what evil is. The best we can do is try and recognize it when we see it, and then try to stop it."

"That isn't good enough, Rude."

"I know," he said.

(7)

While the records recovered from the Dragon Factory were being mined a clear link was made between the Jakobys and the Sunderland family. Harold Sunderland was arrested by police as he stepped off a plane in São Paolo. In light of his connection with the attempted mass genocide, there was no hesitation about extradition.

When FBI agents showed up at the office of J. P. Sunderland to serve a federal warrant, the senator suffered a massive coronary. He was pronounced dead on arrival at Georgetown University Hospital. A clear link was discovered between Sunderland and former deputy information analyst Stephen Preston, the man who had given the false information on which the Vice President acted. However, an exhaustive search of Sunderland's paper and computer records could establish nothing that implicated the Vice President in any wrongdoing.

Vice President Bill Collins dodged the bullet, and nothing about his attempted dismantling of the DMS ever made it to the press. However, CNN was the first to observe that Collins and the President seemed cooler to each other than during their campaign, and Jon Stewart made some jokes about Collins being even more "off the public radar" than Dick Cheney had been.

The Vice President spent a lot of time out of Washington.

On one of his flights to his home state, the Vice President was alone aboard a small military jet. He put in his earbuds, turned on his iPod, and settled back to enjoy the trip. Twenty minutes into the flight someone reached over and turned off the iPod.

The VP woke up and started to demand what the hell was going on. But he never finished the sentence. A man sat across from him. Early sixties, tall and blocky, wearing tinted sunglasses. A slim briefcase lay on the seat next to him.

"What the hell are *you* doing here?"

Mr. Church opened his briefcase and removed a small pack of Nilla wafers. He selected a cookie and set the pack aside. He did not offer one to the Vice President.

"You'd better have a good goddamned explanation for—"

Church said, "Sunderland."

"Bullshit," Collins sneered. "I stand by my—"

"Shhhh," Mr. Church said, placing a finger to his lips. "It would be better for you to listen."

The curtain to the forward cabin opened and Linden Brierly leaned against the door frame. The newly appointed Director of the Secret Service smiled thinly, but his eyes were as cold as ice.

"Mr. Vice President," said Church, "we are going to have a long talk about your future in politics and your general health."

(8)

Weeks later, when I could walk without crutches, I drove to the Warehouse to pack my stuff. Rudy had been taking care of my cat, but I had clothes and a lot of personal belongings in my quarters. I wanted to take it home, to close that chapter of my life.

The guards at the gate waved me through and saluted as I passed. Bunny met me at the staff door, but he could tell I wasn't in the mood to talk, so he just held the door open for me.

I walked through the corridors of the Warehouse, past the labs where Hu and Bug worked. Past Jerry Spencer's forensics lab. Past the office Church used when he was there. Past the conference room and firing range.

Rudy's door was closed and I didn't know if he'd already packed his things. We hadn't talked about whether he was staying on or not.

I found my room and opened it with my key and lingered in the doorway.

I hadn't been there since the morning after the last time Grace and I made love. Someone had straightened the bed, changed the sheets. Replaced the damaged lamp.

Inside I found two things. Against the wall was a stack of empty boxes along with packing tape and labels. Everything I would need to remove all traces of myself from this place. I was done with hunting evil. I was ruined, worn out, damaged beyond fixing. Rudy disagreed, but I was the one who could look inside and see only wreckage and no clear path left to take.

The second item was on the bed. A file folder.

I opened it. Inside was a surveillance photo of a tall man with an austere face. Behind him was a sign advertising a tour of the Riviera dei Fiori. The River of Flowers. A tourist spot on the Italian Riviera. Someone had used a Sharpie to draw a black circle around the man's face. Next to it was written: "Two days ago."

I lifted the picture. Beneath it in the folder were my passport, plane tickets, a credit card with my name on it, and other useful documents.

The man in the picture was Conrad Veder.

I sat down on the edge of the bed. I held the photo in both hands and stared into the face of the man who had murdered Grace Courtland. Then I looked at the stack of empty boxes.

Church had left the decision up to me, though he'd given me everything I needed no matter which path I chose.

Read on for a bonus short story by Jonathan Maberry

Dog Days

From St. Martin's Paperbacks

Dog Days

A Joe Ledger Adventure

by

Jonathan Maberry

Author's note: This story takes place several weeks after the events in *The Dragon Factory*.

Chapter One

When you do what I do, you know death. You understand him, and his consorts, pain and loss.

These things are no longer abstractions. They aren't rarities that intrude into your routine, like when Uncle Bob cashes it in at Sunny Acres on his ninety-third birthday, or when one of your drinking buddies strokes out on the eighth hole, two under par but all the wrong clubs in his bag.

No, when your job is war, when you are a killer, death is a more frequent copilot than God.

Death is around you, he's in you, he's *of* you. Sometimes he's your friend, the best friend you'll ever have—when you're down to the last bullet in your mag and you squeeze the trigger while running and he punches the bad guy's ticket in what you'll always believe was an impossible shot. Not impossible; it's just that death was your wingman that day. Tomorrow he might be going to war under a totally different flag. Death's like that. He's not fickle; he wants everyone on his side.

Every warrior has the same connection. Maybe there are gods and angels up there screwing with the fates of men and Death is the great cosmic bouncer. Maybe there are gods of war and Death is their angel.

Maybe death is more selective than we know, but if so he has an agenda we'll never understand. I know I don't. I've killed bad men, but bad men have killed better men than me.

Who knows why Death favors one man over another on any given day. A lot of guys believe that Death—or someone—listens to prayers and follows rules. These guys wear talismans into battle. Crosses and *hamsa* hands, lucky socks and tattoos of saints drilled into their skin. Sometimes it helps. Sometimes that's the only way we can identify the dead.

Every warrior strives to understand Death. They love him and they hate him in the same breath. In every breath. They try to know him, to know his mind.

Me?

Yeah, I know Death. But I don't worship him and I don't fear him.

He wants me he can have me.

For me, it's a jealousy thing. I envy the cold bastard.

Because he took her.

Her.

My love. Death took the only grace I had left in life.

Death took her and he owns her. She's with him, down in that cold, dark palace in the dirt.

And it hurts so bad.

If I thought that a bullet—from my own gun or one I walked in front of—could buy my passage across the River Styx to her side, if I thought that, I'd ride the bullet all the way down.

But it doesn't work like that.

The priests and the shrinks and your friends all tell you that it doesn't work that way.

Death, you see, is also a jealous son of a bitch. He doesn't share.

So—I keep living.

And I envy Death for the grace he has and the Grace I lost.

Chapter Two

They buried her in September.

By the end of that month I was able to walk without a cane. My hair was growing back, the double vision was gone.

The shakes? Still had those. Nausea, acid stomach? Yeah.

"When was the last time you had a good night's sleep?" asked Rudy Sanchez. Friend, shrink, drinking buddy, fellow mourner. He loved Grace, too. Not in the same way. She was family to him. She was that and more to me. Every single day we could both see the hole in the world where she should be.

"Cowboy?" he prompted.

I shrugged. We were sitting on beach chairs in my dad's backyard. Beers and illegal Cubans. Couple of steaks on a slow grill. Spanish music on the boombox.

"Out loud," said Rudy. "In words."

"I don't know, man. I catch a few hours."

"In a row?"

I shot him the finger, which shut him up long enough for me to finish my beer. He turned the steaks while I got us fresh bottles. Yuengling for me, Anchor Steam for him. He accepted his bottle even though he hadn't finished the one resting on his stomach, and he arched an eyebrow over the opaque lenses of his sunglasses as I twisted the cap off of mine.

"How many is that?"

"Somewhere between not enough and fuck you," I said.

He sighed.

The afternoon was burning its way toward twilight. It was weirdly hot for the first of October. The fourth straight day in the nineties, with humidity to match. If someone left the back door of hell open it would be like this. We smoked our cigars and drank our beer and gazed with thousand-yard stares on the wreckage of our lives.

Well, of my life.

After a while I said, "I went in yesterday."

"To the Warehouse?"

"Yeah. I was hoping Church would be there. I wanted to tell him—you know—face to face."

I could feel Rudy studying me but I didn't look at him.

"Tell him what?" he asked.

"That I was done."

"You've been saying that since Grace died, Joe."

"It's true."

He tapped some ash onto the grass that curled around his flip-flops. "I know. You said that you can't do this anymore, that you were ruined. That's the word you used. Ruined."

I said nothing.

"But you're healing," he said. "The doctors said that you would make a complete recovery—and before you jump all over me *again,* we both know that they were only talking about a physical recovery. They understand that emotional and psychological recovery will take longer."

" 'Take longer'?" I echoed, loading it with the scorn it deserved.

"Yes, Joe. I know you think that this is something you won't or can't get past, but you will. Am I saying that you'll heal completely and without scar tissue? No, and you know that I don't think that. At the same time you should try to address the fact that you seem to feel that you healing is somehow an insult to Grace's memory. That it's a disservice to her sacrifice."

"It is."

"It isn't," he insisted, his tone shifting from best friend to therapist in the way it does when he believes he's right. He usually is right, but this time I couldn't see how.

I sipped more beer and watched the last lonely fireflies burn themselves out above the line of carefully tended hedges. It was a quiet neighborhood. Before Rudy and I joined the Department of Military Sciences back in June, I really liked the quiet order of this place; but now it felt like it belonged to a different world. A better world than mine, no doubt, but definitely not where I belonged. For months now my life had been about weird science, doomsday plots, terrorism, gunplay, and death. While I'd been fighting the good fight, I never noticed that with every battle I fought, every life I took, I was being slowly evicted from the world I knew. Sure, I could come here and drink beer and even smoke a Cuban, but it was window dressing. It was play-acting someone who I wasn't ever going to be again.

Rudy knew it, too.

He'd warned me about it from the start. When Mr. Church had first hijacked me into the DMS, Rudy had warned me about the mark on the soul that violence always left. I hadn't listened closely enough, hadn't heard the full lesson. I'd thought he meant that whenever *I* used violence it would mark me; but that wasn't the whole picture. Any violence around me, any violence I cared about, was going to gouge its gang sign into me, too.

I cared about Grace, first as a friend, then as a lover.

And now I was so badly marked, so thoroughly mauled by everything that had happened, that I knew that I had become a stranger to the people who knew me. It was easiest for my dad to pretend he didn't see it. He was running for mayor and he had the campaign to keep him busy. My brother was still a detective, and when he looked at me I could see the natural cop wariness kick in at high gear. He knew I was different. He saw the bruises on my body, the pink surgical lines, and bitter grief that I could not hide, and without ever saying so in words he told me to keep my horrors away from his family

Did I blame him?

No way.

"Are you listening to anything I'm saying?" asked Rudy, and I realized that he had been talking for a couple of minutes and I hadn't heard a word.

"No," I said.

"Well, at least you didn't sugarcoat that with a lie." He turned to face me. "Anyway, I asked what happened when you went to the Warehouse yesterday."

"The plan was to pack. I wanted to get my shit out of

there and maybe see about resubmitting my application to the FBI."

"Wouldn't that be a big step down? I'm not talking about pay and benefits, but in utilizing your potential as a—"

"Screw that."

"After the DMS, the FBI is likely to be less of a challenge."

"Fine by me."

"Even boring."

"Boring sounds good."

"No," he said, "it doesn't. You think it does because you're still traumatized, but let's be adults here, Joe—you'd never be able to work in something that mundane again."

"The FBI is hardly mundane, Rude. Geez, they're part of Homeland and—"

"—and they don't do what we do. What you do."

I didn't reply to that. Instead I said, "When I got to the Warehouse, Church was out. He's up in Brooklyn. But he left some stuff for me in my quarters. Two things. Two options. Against one wall was a stack of empty boxes so I could pack up my shit and leave."

"And the other thing?"

"There was a file folder on the bed. An intelligence folder. Inside was a surveillance photo of a tall man taken two days ago at the *Riviera dei Fiori*, the Italian Riviera."

"Oh? Who was the man in the photo?"

I drew on the cigar until the coal glowed hot and orange. "Conrad Veder," I said.

Rudy gaped and spilled his beer down the front of his shirt.

"*Dios mio!*" he said and uttered a string of low, vicious curses in gutter Spanish.

"Yeah," I said.

Conrad Veder.

The man who had murdered Grace.

Chapter Three

Later, when the sky was littered with stars and the cooler was filled with empties and melted ice, Rudy and I still sat in the beach chairs. We hadn't spoken in nearly an hour.

Finally Rudy said, "You're going after him."

A statement, not a question.

I nodded.

"When?"

"I don't know. Soon. I talked to our guys in Italy, the ones who obtained the surveillance photos, and Veder has dropped off the radar again. Everyone's looking for him and as soon as he's spotted again they'll get word to me right away."

"Don't bite my head off when I ask this, but what shape are you in to go after that man?"

I shrugged.

"Joe, Veder is one of the most highly skilled and dangerous assassins in the world. Even Mr. Church said that he was in a class by himself. A master of every kind of firearm, skilled in unarmed combat . . ."

"I don't intend to challenge him to a duel, Rudy. I'm going to find him and kill him."

Under most other circumstances Rudy would rise to

the challenge in that kind of statement and we'd wrangle about murder versus self-defense, but not lately. He would never come out and say so, but he wanted Veder dead, too.

"Are you taking the team? Top and Bunny would—"

"No. This is mine."

"Is that wise?"

"I don't care. This is going to be a hunt and it may take a long time. I can't drag around a whole team when I'm sniffing out a trail."

"So—is that why Mr. Church has been talking about your dog?"

"Dog? I don't have a dog."

"Mr. Church told me a couple of days ago that you were going to be training a military dog. Are you doing that to help you hunt this man?"

"Rudy, I don't have a dog and I'm not planning on getting one. You must have misunderstood what Church was saying."

But, as it turns out, I was the one who was wrong.

I did get a dog.

Chapter Four

"I don't want a dog," I said.

We were in the big training room at the Warehouse. The trainer looked from Rudy to Church. "I—"

"You could use a companion," suggested Rudy.

"You need a partner," advised Church.

"I don't want a goddamned—"

"You have a choice," Church cut in. "You train with

the dog and take him with you when we get a fresh lead on Veder, or you don't train with him and I turn the lead over to Interpol and you can read about it in the paper."

I started to tell him what he could do with that idea, but he interrupted me again.

"I'm sorry, Captain, for giving you the misapprehension that this was a debate. Enjoy your training." With that he turned away. Over his shoulder he said, "Bonding is an important part of the training process. I'll leave you to it."

"Hey!" I yelled, but Church was already talking on his cell phone. Or pretending to.

The trainer, Zan Rosin, smiled hopefully up at me. "He's a very nice dog," she said. "He's exceptionally smart and has already passed through standard and advanced training in search and rescue, bomb detection, bark and hold, high-speed disarm, cover and concealment . . ." Her words trickled down and stopped when she saw my expression.

I glowered down at her prodigy of a dog. A white Shepherd. Two hundred and five pounds, with brown eyes that were currently sizing me up the way Rudy sizes up a porterhouse steak.

"He's very friendly," she said.

The dog bared his teeth.

"Look," said Rudy, "he's smiling at you."

The dog began to growl.

"Or not," Rudy amended. "Call me later, Cowboy." He did not actually run, but he walked away very fast.

The trainer and I watched him go, and then she looked up at me with a trembling smile.

"His name is Ghost," she said.

I gave her a withering stare. "I'm a cat person. I don't even like dogs."

Ghost continued to growl. Neither of us was trying to hide our true feelings.

Chapter Five

Conrad Veder dropped off the face of the earth. Interpol and the CIA were looking for him. Church had every resource the DMS could spare looking for him. Barrier, the British counterpart of the DMS, was looking for him. Nobody was able to find him.

I knew that Church wanted to get me back into the fold, to have me take over command of the Warehouse and resume my position as leader of Echo Team. But that wasn't what I wanted.

The only thing Church got was me partnering with the dog.

It was no walk in the park, though. Not for me, and not for the dog. I'm pretty sure the handler, Zan Rosin, began drinking her lunch by the end of the first week.

Training with Ghost was a weird experience for me. I really am a cat person. I have a middle-aged marmalade tabby named Cobbler who disliked dogs as much as I did. When I brought Ghost home for the first time, Cobbler and he failed to bond in a spectacular fashion. Furniture and crockery were destroyed. Neighbors almost called the cops.

Eventually they staked out which sections of my apartment belonged to each of them, and yes, pissing on territorial lines was involved, damn it.

In training sessions, however, Ghost and I began to

find a rhythm. Zan wasn't joking when she said Ghost had been highly trained already. He was top of his class every time, which is why Church acquired him for me, and he was habituated to working with a human partner. Despite our lack of personal warmth, Ghost and I formed a useful two-member pack, with me as alpha and him taking and completing orders with precision.

And by the end of the third week, despite everything both of us could manage, we started to like each other.

Damn it.

At Church's recommendation, I'd created a set of non-standard verbal commands and hand signs. Commands unique to Ghost and me. The more we worked on those, the more Ghost surprised me in that he seemed able to understand and retain a higher than normal number of them. This made Zan Rosin smile every time she visited our sessions.

"I told you he was an exceptional dog," she said with a smug smile.

I debated telling Ghost to bite her on the ass, but restrained myself.

We were working on one set of routines involving oblique-angle gun disarms when Rudy Sanchez came running out of a side door, waving at us. Ghost, who actually *liked* Rudy, suddenly spun and dropped into a fighting crouch between me and Rudy, teeth bared in a very real threat. Rudy skidded to a stop twenty feet away, face going pale, eyes goggling. Protecting the alpha of his pack. Nice.

"Whoa! Whoa, now!"

I said, "Ghost, flat."

It was one of a special vocabulary of code words we'd used every day of the training.

Instantly Ghost's body language changed. He stopped snarling, stood straight, wagged his tail and pretended to be a charming house puppy that would never hurt a fly. Rudy stayed where he was, not buying any of that.

"What is it?" I asked. "I thought you knew better than to come running out here while I'm with the fur-monster."

"Joe," said Rudy urgently. "They found him."

I didn't have to ask who. There was no one else I wanted found.

Veder.

Chapter Six

"What have we got?" I asked Church as I burst into the command center with Ghost and Rudy at my heels.

"CIA sent this five minutes ago," said Church, nodding to the big plasma screen on the wall. There was a picture of a stooped old man buying coffee at a sidewalk café. He looked to be about eighty, with thick glasses and a white frizz of Einstein hair.

I bent close and studied him. A good disguise can turn a rock star into another bland face in the crowd, even to a trained observer.

"That's him," I said.

Church nodded.

"*Dios mio*," murmured Rudy, and he touched his chest at the place where the crucifix rested against his skin under his shirt.

Behind Veder was a menu board printed in two versions of Danish, one I recognized and one I didn't. Church pointed to the second language. "That's Faroese.

It's a Nordic language spoken in the Faroe Islands in the Norwegian Sea. The islands are approximately halfway between Great Britain and Iceland."

"That's where he is?" I asked. "The Faroe Islands?"

"Yes. On Vágar, third largest of the islands."

"When—?" I began, but Church cut me off.

"There's a helo smoking on the deck. You'll take my Learjet straight to Vágar Airport. Langley has a three-man CIA team keeping tabs on Veder. Go!"

Ghost and I ran. Three minutes later we were in the air.

Chapter Seven

The CIA spook who met me at the tiny airport on Vágar looked like he was auditioning for the lead role in *Death of a Salesman*. Jowly face, beat-up old suit, scuffed shoes, and morose brown eyes. Not the kind of guy you'd look at and say: "Now there's an international man of mystery."

He watched me give him the once-over and smiled faintly. "I left my dinner jacket in my Aston Martin. Dick Spurlock."

"Joe Ledger."

We shook hands. He had a rock-hard grip with shooter's calluses. Like mine.

"You're not with the Company," he said, not pitching it as a question.

"No."

"Which alphabet are you with?"

I gave him a bland smile. "An off-the-radar one."

He looked momentarily confused, then smiled. "Ah.

Let me guess, it begins with a 'D', ends with an 'S' and rhymes with 'don't fucking ask'."

"Something like that," I said, laughing despite myself. I liked Spurlock, even if he was a CIA spook.

Spurlock glanced at Ghost, who was discreetly sniffing him with interest more appropriate to a hungry person reading a diner menu.

"Friendly dog?" asked the agent.

"Not so you'd notice."

"Ah."

We walked out of the small terminal building with the amiable pace of old friends. All for show. His car was parked outside, a five-year-old Toyota with plastic over the rear passenger window.

"Part of the act," said Spurlock. "Nobody looks twice at a down-at-the-heels salesman."

"That's your cover?"

"Only recently," he said as he opened the trunk for me to stow my bags. "My team's been tracking shipments of computer technologies. I'm a mid-level salesman brokering old corporate hard drives for resale to smaller companies. We think that's how a lot of bulk data is moving out of this part of the world, as supposedly wiped hard drives in second-hand computer systems. Guess that's not very interesting to someone like you."

I looked at him for a two-count and he glanced away and cleared his throat.

We got into the car and closed the doors. Ghost flopped down on the back seat.

"Okay," I said, getting right to it, "where is he?"

"A hotel, a new one on the far side of the island. Five-story blockhouse style. Ugly but functional. Elevator in the lobby, interior stairs in the back, two exits. I have men front and back."

Spurlock started the car and pulled into the flow of airport traffic. "He's a smart, slippery bastard. One of my team acquired him when he came out of a bank two days ago. We weren't sure it was him at first, but we managed to get a few photos and ran through a facial recognition program." He cut me a hesitant sideways look. "We . . . um, we're afraid that he made us even though we have four guys working him, trading off and keeping very low profile. Throughout the day he changed his clothes and disguise three times, and each time we nearly lost him. Guy's a chameleon. First time he was a French businessman and then he was a tourist with cameras and some makeup so that he looked a little Asian. Then he switched to the old man outfit when he checked into his hotel."

"He still there?"

"I called my team while you were clearing customs. No movement."

"What about room service?"

Spurlock cut me another look, more appraising this time, and he nodded. "Twice. Dinner and breakfast. Two different members of hotel staff each time, and we did full verification before and afterward. Veder didn't knock anyone out and slip out the back in a waiter's outfit."

"Not like in the movies," I said with a grin.

"No," he agreed, "but I'll bet that he won't look like an old man when he does leave his room. Like I said, the guy's a chameleon."

We drove for a few minutes in silence as I digested the information.

Eventually Spurlock spoke. "The woman who was killed. Courtland?"

"Major Grace Courtland," I corrected, and he nodded. "What about her?"

"I never met her. Heard some stuff, of course. She was in all the papers after that whole Mengele thing came out. It was like something out of a Michael Crichton novel. Weird. The media painted her as the hero, the one who saved the day."

I said nothing.

"Is that how it happened?"

"What are you saying?" I asked him, my voice cool.

"Hey, no offense, Joe," he said quickly. "It's just that I know how things work in our world. The person who gets the ink isn't always the one who deserves the praise. I just wondered what her role really was."

He was stopped at a light and I turned very slowly to face him. "Grace Courtland was the best woman, the best person I ever knew and she died in the line of duty. If it wasn't for her, people would be dying in the streets, governments would be blaming each other and there would be missiles in the air. That is not a joke. You and I are alive because of her and anyone who says different is going to fall right off my Christmas card list, you dig? Anyone who speaks one word against her, or diminishes the value of what she did, will have a whole new set of problems to deal with, starting with a dramatic increase in their medical and dental bills. Am I making myself clear?"

Spurlock stared at me so long the light changed and the cars behind him began to honk. Then he nodded and drove on.

After a minute he said, "I wasn't speaking ill of her. I was asking for the inside scoop. Agent to agent."

I said nothing.

"Some of us are so far out of the loop, so far removed from the action, that nothing we do really matters a damn," he continued. "You mostly never hear about an agent going down in the line of duty, and when you do and that person makes the papers you tend to think that there's politics in that. That it's some pencil-neck's idea of spin control from something you'll never be privy to and never understand. And it makes you feel that nothing *you* do matters a wet fart. It's cynical, sure, but there it is."

I said nothing.

"To know that one of *ours*, one of us, did something really big, really important . . . well, hell, that makes everything else okay. All the years spent doing scutwork, all of the reports you write that you think no one ever reads, all the loneliness. I'm not saying this right," he admitted and sighed. "It's just nice to know that we actually *won* one, y'know?"

I took a long breath and let it out slowly.

"Yeah," I said "I know."

"So, no offense, man, okay?"

"None at all."

"Well," he said, "at least we have the bastard cornered. Time for a little bit of payback."

We drove the rest of the way in silence.

The island was green and pretty, but I couldn't care less. Despite the outward show of calm detachment I'd constructed, inside I was going batshit crazy. My head felt like it was full of bees, my gut was sick with greasy sludge. Ghost must have caught some of my nerves and whined quietly. I reached back to pet him and he licked my fingers. It was the first time he'd ever done that and I found it oddly touching.

At the hotel Spurlock pulled around back and the three of us got out. The rear street was little more than an alley with dumpsters, a vagrant speaking in Dutch to the pigeons he was feeding, and a nondescript late-model sedan parked by the exit. As we passed the vagrant, Ghost barked at the pigeons, scaring them into flight. The vagrant cursed him and me even though I growled at Ghost to knock it off.

Luckily I don't speak Faroese, or Dutch for that matter. I'm pretty sure some of his remarks involved me and livestock.

We hurried past him and flanked the car.

Ghost started growling when we were still fifteen feet away, and it had nothing to do with pigeons.

There was no agent behind the wheel.

There was only blood. Ghost sniffed at it and gave a short *whuff.*

Spurlock and I pulled our guns and fanned them up and down the street.

The vagrant suddenly started screaming. Maybe calling for the cops. Maybe calling for God Himself.

"Call your team," I barked, but Spurlock was already speaking into his cuff-mike.

"Henderson! Reed!"

But Henderson and Reed weren't answering, and I knew they never would.

As I approached the exit door I felt Spurlock move up behind me. He had his gun in a two-hand shooter's grip and his face was set and grim. Ghost was right behind him. Spurlock looked from the dog to the car to me to the door.

"You ready?" I asked.

He licked his lips and nodded.

I pulled open the door and stepped back to let him go in first. This was his stakeout and he knew the building. The rear entrance was empty, nothing more than a service door and a short hallway that broke right to the kitchens and left to a set of stairs.

"What floor?" I asked.

"Five." He looked up the stairs. "You go, I'll cover."

I shook my head. "Better if Ghost and I hang back. You know the room; Ghost can watch our backs."

Spurlock hesitated, then nodded. He drew a breath and headed quietly up the stairs. I wondered how scared he was, and how often he'd done this sort of thing. CIA field agents rarely have a James Bond moment; most don't carry guns and even fewer have used them.

Even so, he was well trained, moving on cat feet as he climbed the steps, positioning himself properly to check his corners and turns, keeping his gun up and out the way he should and tracking line-of-sight with the mouth of the barrel. I followed in harmony, watching down the stairs even though Ghost was behind me, and checking the fire doors on each landing.

On the fifth floor, Spurlock covered the door and head-signaled me to go first, but I shook him off. His men knew him by sight, but I was a stranger with a gun. Last thing I needed was to walk into a friendly fire incident.

Spurlock snorted and went first. I don't think my

caution impressed him much. Maybe I wasn't living up to the DMS super-spy image. He ran down the hallway, taking many small steps instead of large loping ones; it was a balancing trick to keep the natural jolts of running from spoiling aim. I was comforted to see that, despite everything, Spurlock remembered all of his training. I'd met a few other CIA spooks that were far less competent.

I came up close behind him, with Ghost right at my heels.

"Which room?" I asked quietly.

"End of the hall."

"Where's your man?"

Spurlock made a face. "I don't know. He should have been in the stairwell where he could watch the hall."

"You have your team on a wire?"

He paused and then met my eyes. "No one's answering."

"Shit," I said, and he nodded.

There was no real cover in the hall, and even the door frames to each of the guest rooms were only a couple of inches deep. So we had to use speed instead of stealth. We put our guns up and ran full-tilt down the hall. I signaled Ghost to stay two paces back and was gratified to see that he was following every one of the commands we'd rehearsed. Yeah, I'll say it. Good dog.

"Kick it," I said. There was no time to explain that I'd had arthroscopic surgery on my knee and ankle after the Jakoby thing. I was weeks away from being able to kick anything. Spurlock shot me another annoyed look, but he kicked the door.

Actually, he kicked the hell out of the door. He used

the impetus of his run to launch into a flat-footed kick that struck the wood right beside the knob and ripped the lock out of the frame with a *bang!* and a spray of splinters. He landed in a tight crouch and pivoted on the balls of his feet, sweeping his pistol across the room; I skidded in behind him.

And froze.

Ghost jolted to a stop in the doorway. He stared into the room.

And gave a single, short bark.

I didn't need him to tell me that all of our haste and caution had been a total waste.

The bodies of the three CIA agents told that story with grim eloquence.

Chapter Eight

"Jesus Christ," breathed Spurlock. His mouth sagged open and the hands holding his gun drooped slowly until the barrel was pointed uselessly at the blood-spattered carpet.

The room was an efficiency. A bedroom with a full-size bed, one overstuffed chair, a television on a chest of drawers, and a tiny bathroom. No wardrobe, nowhere to hide except inside the bathroom and I sent Ghost in to check. He made his whuffing sound and sat in the doorway. All clear.

I stood in the doorway and tried to read the scene. One agent was slumped in a chair, his hands bound with plastic cuffs, a gag tied tightly around his mouth and jaw. There were two black bullet holes above the bridge of his nose. The second agent lay on the floor ten feet inside the room. His hands were not tied and his gun was on the rug a yard from his open fingers. He had one bullet wound above his right eye, and a second in the back of his head. The third agent was right inside the door, bullet holes in his temple and the back of his skull.

In the bathroom doorway, Ghost growled low in his throat, alarmed by the smell of blood and cordite. Spurlock stood in the middle of the room, his pistol down at his side, face slack, eyes moving from one body to the next. He looked like he was a half-step from going into shock.

"Holster your weapon," I said, and Spurlock jumped. When he hesitated I snapped at him. "This party's over and you're not paying attention to your gun."

He looked at his pistol as if he had no idea what it was, then he slid it into the quick-draw shoulder rig he wore under his grubby suit coat. I put mine away, too.

"Check the room," I said. "Check everything. Looks like Veder spotted the man in the hall, lured him here and took him prisoner. Maybe forced him to call the others, maybe kept him alive as a hostage. We'll never know." I moved over to the seated dead man and saw a faint peppering of black powder on the side of the agent's face and clothes. "Yeah," I said, "the shooter crouched down here, behind the chair, and when the second agent came in, he took him with two shots."

"How do you know that?" asked Spurlock.

I pointed to the gunshot residue on the seated dead man and pointed my hand at an angle to approximate the line of fire. Then I crossed the room, clicked my tongue for Ghost to move, and stepped into the bathroom.

"When the third agent entered the room, Veder took him in the temple from here. Then he finished it with one to the back of the head, turned and put two into the guy in the chair. Small entry wounds, no exits. Probably a .22, maybe with a sound suppressor."

"Assassin's gun of choice," observed Spurlock.

"And Veder should know," I said. "He's supposed to be the best of the best."

Spurlock gave me an enigmatic look. "You sound like you're impressed."

I shook my head. "No. Veder's a rat bastard and I want to blow out his lights," I said, "but you have to admit this was a professional job. If we had any doubts that this was Veder, we don't now." I looked at him. "Look . . . I'm sorry about your team. Really. I've lost a lot of people on my teams."

He said nothing and his eyes had a totally dead look to them. As if all traces of life and humanity had drained away.

"Really . . . I'm sorry," I said. "Were you close with these guys?"

Spurlock didn't answer, and I felt like a total jackass.

I cleared my throat. "Okay. Let's toss the room. This all happened between the time you left here to pick me up and now. That's what? Forty minutes? Veder can't have gotten far. Maybe he left in too much of a hurry. Maybe he left something we can use to track him."

Spurlock nodded.

"You start looking," I said, "and I'll call it in."

He lingered there for a moment longer, and then turned away and began searching the room.

I edged toward the door and removed my cell from

my pocket. Church answered on the second ring. I explained what happened.

"That's distressing news, Captain," said Church. "I'll arrange to have the airport closed and have our people do a thorough background check on passengers of all flights departing Vágar in the last hour."

"Boats, too. I think there's a ferry."

"I'll handle all of that, Captain. I've been moving assets into the area since before you left U.S. airspace. If Veder's there, then he's in a bottle and we *will* find him."

"Yes, we damn well will," I said, and I made sure to pitch my voice loud enough for Spurlock to hear. I wanted him to know that his people mattered, too. This wasn't just about my personal vengeance, though in truth—to me, anyway—Grace was all I could think of.

Then I pitched my voice lower. "Look, maybe you should call this in to Langley. Take Spurlock off the hook. He seems like a decent guy, and I'd hate to see him take the heat for a failed mission. It's not his fault that Veder was too much, even for a four-man team."

Church was silent for a moment. "Spurlock's there with you? In earshot?"

"Almost," I said, hoping he'd have the tact not to want to push this conversation any further. Spurlock was probably already wondering to what armpit on the planet his section chief was going to send him. Having an entire team cut out from under you *while* losing your quarry was not exactly a highway to promotion.

"Stay alert, Captain," said Church, and disconnected.

I glanced at Spurlock, who was on his hands and

knees, peering under the bed. Ghost was standing next to him, sniffing at the agent and the bed and the blood that seemed to be everywhere.

Spurlock shot me an irritated look.

"Would you please get your dog away from the crime scene," he said coldly. "He's not helping."

"He's trained for—"

"For what?" snapped Spurlock. "Forensic evidence collection?"

"Well, no, but—"

"Then put him in the bathroom before he screws up any chance we have of finding something useful."

I nearly growled back at him, but I reined myself in. The guy had just lost three people he knew, maybe friends. If he wanted to bitch a little bit, I figured he more than earned the right. So, I clicked my tongue for Ghost. I pointed at the doorway and told him to sit. He did, but he contrived to give me a long-suffering look as if to say that idleness was a vast waste of his considerable talents. Or, I could have been reading a bit too much into a dog's expression. I was beginning to lose perspective on that.

Ghost watched us both with bottomless brown eyes.

"What did Mr. Church say?" asked Spurlock as he continued to fish under the bed.

"Huh?"

"Your boss? What did he say?"

"Oh . . . they're closing the airport, cutting off the ferry. Checking manifests and such. The works. We're putting a net over everything. We'll find him."

"Good." Spurlock had his whole arm under the bed. "Tell me something, Joe."

I began opening drawers in the dresser. The top one

had two pairs of boxers and two pairs of socks. I checked them, but there was nothing.

"The woman Veder killed—Major Courtland—were you friends?"

I opened the second drawer and found a shaving kit. "Joe?"

"Yes," I said softly as I unzipped the kit. "She was a friend."

"A close friend?"

There was no shaving stuff in the kit. Instead I found make-up. Hair dye, several sets of colored contact lenses, false teeth. A high-quality field kit.

"Yes," I said. Very softly.

"I'm sorry."

I nodded and placed the kit on the top of the dresser. In the third drawer I found a dozen passports, a thick wad of currency from five countries, and more make-up. False beards, mustaches, wigs, each in separate plastic bags. There were also two magazines loaded with .22 rounds.

"What'd you say?" I murmured distractedly.

"I said that I was sorry."

I glanced at him.

Spurlock was no longer fishing under the bed. He knelt behind it, and he held a .22 pistol in his hand, the barrel extended by a Trinity sound suppressor.

"Truly sorry," he said.

My mouth went totally dry.

"Veder," I whispered.

"Veder," he agreed.

And fired.

Chapter Nine

Three things happened all at once.

I threw myself sideways and the bullet punched a hole through the air so close that it seared a white-hot line across the outside of my ear.

Veder fired a second round.

And Ghost launched himself across the room. Immensely fast, deadly quiet; moving like a white missile from his spot by the door, crossing the small room in the space between the first and second shot, teeth bared as he leapt.

Veder—Jesus Christ, but Veder was fast.

He pivoted in place and whipped the barrel across Ghost's face with terrible speed and power, catching the dog on the temple and tearing a yelp of pain from him. Ghost hit the floor and slid in the blood, but even as he landed his nails tore at the carpet for purchase. He scrabbled around and came right back at Veder, but again the killer was faster. Veder fired two quick shots even as he threw himself backward away from Ghost's fangs. The first shot punched a hole through the drapes; the second clipped Ghost on the shoulder. With a second yelp, louder and sharper than the first, Ghost collapsed backward, blood splashing all over his white fur.

Veder swung around to take me with the next shot, but now I was in motion, driving toward him, leaping across the corner of the bed. I slammed into him with a flying tackle that knocked him off his knees and drove us both all the way to the far wall. The .22 went flying over my shoulder.

We crunched into the wall and I collapsed down on top of him. I was bigger and heavier and I wanted to snap his bones under me; but Veder was packed with wiry muscles that he'd disguised under the frumpy businessman's suit. He pivoted his hips and drove a two-knuckled punch up under my chin, rocking my head back against the wall. A second punch nearly crushed my windpipe, but I dropped my head, blocking the blow with my chin. Pain detonated along my gum line and I tasted blood in my mouth.

Veder threw himself backward, creating distance between us so he could use his feet. He was good. Really damn good. His first kick caught me on the left shoulder, numbing my arm; the second hit me square in the sternum and that slammed me backward into the wall again and drove a lot of air out of my lungs.

He tried a third kick, but the impact of the last one had shoved him away from me and he didn't have the reach to do more than bruise my chest. I gulped in as much air as I could and kicked out with the point of my toe—not at his body, but at his kicking leg. The reinforced toe of my shoe crunched into his calf, mashing the muscle. I combined off of that, throwing my weight onto my hip and snapped kicks at his ribs, one, two, three, driving a grunt of pain from him.

Veder threw himself away from me and despite the pain he must have been feeling did a neat little backward roll and came out of it on fingers and toes. Then he launched at me. His face did not show a flicker of expression, but instead displayed only a dispassionate—or perhaps disconnected—calm and a professional determination. I'm not even sure I was an enemy so much as I was simply another problem to be solved.

He drove his shoulder into me, catching me mid-thigh and slamming me for a third time into the wall. But I was half-ready for that and as I hit I dropped my upper body weight straight down, using it to put substantial power into a descending elbow smash that caught him between his shoulder blades. The blow flattened him to the floor, but when I bent over to try and seal the deal with a couple of kidney punches, he swept one leg backward and up in a scorpion kick, catching me right on the forehead.

I hit the wall for the fourth time and fireworks exploded inside my head.

Veder rolled onto his side and used his bent arm to sweep my legs out from under me. I crashed sideways to the ground and he scrambled atop me, pinning my arms to my sides with his thighs while he rained punches down on my face.

I could hear Ghost whimpering and snarling only a few feet away, but I couldn't see him.

The only chance I had was to keep his iron-hard fists away from my eyes and nose, otherwise the pain and disorientation would lose me the fight, my life, and any chance I had at avenging Grace's death.

So I buried my chin down and clamped my teeth onto the soft flesh inside his left thigh. I bit down with all of my rage and Conrad Veder screamed.

He also tried to stand up, to get away from my teeth, and I let him, not that I had much choice—his movement nearly tore half the teeth from my mouth. As he rose, I snapped my foot up and kicked him on the ass, and this time he was the one who hit the wall.

With a growl, I rolled sideways, clipping the inside

of his right ankle. Veder toppled over and fell, and even as he was going down, I clawed my way along the inside of his trouser leg until my hip rested on his knee. That gave me the perfect angle and I punched him in the balls as hard as I could.

Veder screamed again, a shriek that rose instantly to the ultrasonic.

Agony gave him power, though, and he hooked his thumb into the corner of my mouth and tried to tear open my cheek. I had to roll with his pull in order to save my face, and that put me right in the path of his other hand. Two punches battered my temple and eye-socket and my left eye went completely dark.

Then Veder squirmed out and kicked me away from him.

I covered my face with my arms, expecting another kick and too disoriented to stop it, but there was no blow. I turned in horror to see him crawling toward his fallen pistol. With a cry, I flung myself at him, but I was too far away and he snatched up the gun, turned, swinging the barrel toward me.

Then something blundered past me, white and red and snarling like a demon from hell.

Conrad Veder screamed yet again as Ghost leapt at him and clamped his jaws around the wrist holding the pistol. There was a muffled bang as the gun fired, but the bullet punched into the wall a foot away from me. Blood exploded from Veder's wrist and he began pounding on Ghost with his left hand.

I staggered to my feet and half-fell across the room. "Ghost!" I snapped. "Off!"

With a growl of mingled rage, pain, and frustration,

Ghost wrenched himself away from Veder, his fur covered with blood and his eyes totally wild. The gun and the gun-hand were still clamped in his jaws.

Blood jetted from Veder's wrist.

I grabbed him by the hair and hauled him to his feet, then kneed him in the groin, head-butted him, and chopped him across the throat so hard that it jolted my whole body.

There was a big, wet crunching sound in his throat, and Veder staggered away from me, his eyes wide with panic, the fingers of his one remaining hand scrabbling at the total red ruin of his throat. He shambled backward and tripped over the body of one of the dead men and almost fell out of the window.

Almost.

I caught him.

I pulled him close and looked deep into his dying eyes. His mouth was trying to form a word. Not 'help.' Not a plea for mercy. His bloody lips formed a word he had said earlier. And, somehow, here in his last moment, maybe he meant it.

"Sorry."

I stared into his eyes, confused by the word. Disgusted by it.

Angered by it.

"Fuck you," I said, and I spit in his face.

Then I shoved him out of the window.

Even with a smashed throat he found a way to scream all the way down.

Chapter Ten

He missed the car by ten feet.

I leaned out of the window and gazed down on the sprawled body. Waiting for the pain in my head to stop. Waiting for my left eye to start working again. Waiting for sirens.

The eye cleared, but there were no sirens.

It was a back alley in a quiet town on a remote island. No one even noticed.

Ghost limped across the floor to me. He still had the hand in his mouth.

I told him to drop it, and I swear there was a look of disgust on his face when he did so. He whimpered softly and leaned against me.

The bullet had torn a furrow along his side, and—I found out later—notched the bone; but he would heal. He was young and strong, and he would heal. I tore up the sheets and bound his wounds.

Together we limped out of the room and down the back stairs to the alley.

Veder was dead.

It felt weird to think that. To know it.

"Grace," I said.

Ghost whimpered.

It took five minutes to load Veder into the trunk of the car. I was in pretty sorry shape. The keys were in the dead man's pocket. Ghost crawled into the back seat; I got behind the wheel.

For a few minutes I did nothing but sit there with my forehead resting on the steering wheel, feeling the pain.

Wondering what I would feel when the pain ended. Veder was dead.

Where was my purpose?

I started the car and we drove out of the town and into the country. I drove aimlessly, unsure of where I was going, unable to read the road signs. The only decisions I made were to steer away from other traffic.

Eventually we found ourselves on a deserted stretch of coastline. Rocky and bare, blasted by the winds and the sun. Bleak.

Perfect.

I dragged Veder's body out of the trunk and kicked it over the edge of the hill. He rolled sixty yards down the slope, halfway to the smashing surf.

There was no shovel in the trunk, just a tire iron. It was enough. I'm not sure I remember digging the hole. I'm not sure why I started. It was probably stupid, pointless, but I did it anyway, working at it with the relentlessness of madness, chopping into the ground, tearing at the soil, throwing away rocks, repeating, repeating. A task assigned in hell and completed with insane dedication.

When the hole was deep enough, I tumbled Veder into it. The gun and the gun-hand, too. Then I covered it over with dirt and rocks and all of the tons of grief that filled my soul.

Maybe I stood over the grave for ten minutes. Maybe it was an hour. I really couldn't say. I remember the sound of Ghost's nails on the rocks as he limped down the slope to join me. We stood there, battered and bloody. He stared at me while I wept.

"Grace," I said.

The wind blew off of the ocean and scoured tears from my cheeks.

Veder was dead.

Every law enforcement agency in the world was looking for him. Church wanted him almost as badly as I had. Church would want to see the body.

I stood over the grave and then looked up and down the coastline. It was exactly the same in both directions. If I drove away I'd never be able to find this place again.

Kind of the point.

I unzipped my pants and pissed on the grave.

Not exactly a marker, but a mark of a kind.

Ghost watched me, his intelligent eyes boring into mine.

I zipped up and turned away. Then I paused at a sound, and I turned to see Ghost pissing a hot stream onto the rocks.

He was a dog, there was no way he could understand why I'd done it. Contempt was not a trait animals could grasp. Right? Besides, he hadn't even known Grace.

Even so, I smiled at him. At the member of my pack.

"Come on, partner," I murmured.

Together, we climbed the long hill back to the car.